Thoughts ◆ of ◆ God

Thoughts ◆ of ◆ God

Michael Kanaly

ACE BOOKS, NEW YORK

THOUGHTS OF GOD

An Ace Book / published by arrangement with
the author

PRINTING HISTORY
Ace trade paperback edition / July 1997

Make sure to check out *PB Plug*, the science fiction/fantasy newsletter,
at http://www.pbplug.com

ISBN: 0-441-00466-0

ACE®
Ace Books are published by The Berkley Publishing Group,
200 Madison Avenue, New York, New York 10016.
ACE and the ''A'' design are trademarks
belonging to Berkley Publishing Corporation.

PRINTED IN THE UNITED STATES OF AMERICA

10 9 8 7 6 5 4 3 2 1

To my wife, Dianne...
She who keeps the candle burning
in the window of reality

God moves in a mysterious way
His wonders to perform;
He plants his footsteps in the sea
And rides upon the storm.

—WILLIAM COOPER

And great is the guilt of those who
oppress their fellow men and conduct
themselves with wickedness and injustice
in the land. These shall be sternly punished.

—THE KORAN

Yes, on the sixth day God created Man,
and then on the seventh day, He rested.
Do you ever get the feeling that, perhaps,
God was in a hurry to get out of the office?

—DISGRUNTLED MINISTER,
INTERVIEWED ON THE EVE
OF THEODORE "TED" BUNDY'S
EXECUTION

Whenever we start thinking too much of
ourselves, of our vaulted achievements here
on this Earth, I believe we should consider
the following: That the Milky Way Galaxy,
of which our own Sun is but a tiny speck,
contains roughly 250 billion stars; and that
within an area of 97.8 billion light years,
which comprises what we humans can currently conceive of as the totality of the universe, there are by conservative estimates
100 billion other galaxies. It is a vastmess
that is truly uncomprehensible.

—ARGUMENT FOR HUMILITY
DONALD SHELBY

prologue

Reflections Out of Time

In a place at the far reaches of the universe, in a place where there are colors no human eye has yet seen, a binary star system explodes. A tremendous flowering explosion, sending light and energy across oceans of time and space. Like a rose, blooming and unfolding, the explosion spreads its tentacles across vast light-years. Slowly, across a span of time too great to be measured, the tentacles of energy fan out, separating themselves into swirling clouds of matter that over eons recondense to form new suns and new planets; which will, perhaps, one day spawn the seeds of life.

Meanwhile, near the center of the explosion, energy radiates and pulses like the beating of a living heart. And at the epicenter of the blast a dense mass of gravity forms. The light and energy particles still spewing forth from the explosion begin to slow. Their outward momentum, their escape into the universe, is stopped and they are drawn back, inward, falling toward the center of the former star system as it collapses in upon itself. Eventually a black hole forms in the depths of space—a deep, unending well, down which all matter, even light, is pulled toward infinity.

In another place, galaxies away, in an entirely unrelated matter, the dinosaurs are dying. Those great beasts who ruled the Earth for a million centuries are suddenly gone.

And the thought is: Creation.

part one

The Hunters

On May 18th, in memory of those who died in the bloody Long Island Massacre, Congress enacted the so-called Vigilante Laws, directing the Bureau of ATF to issue expanded private investigation licenses to qualified individuals. Over the protest of the Prisoner Rights Alliance and other civil libertarians, who termed the legislation as the unconstitutional granting of human hunting licenses, Congress also expanded the Freedom of Information Act to include the release of ongoing criminal investigation records to such licensed individuals. While this legislation does, in fact, concede that justice is for sale in America, at least it is available.

GUN MAGAZINE
THE PUBLIC RELATIONS ARM
OF THE NATIONAL RIFLE ASSOCIATION

one

The stairs were quiet, except for some scramble-brain fuming on fortified grape.

"Park it, floodhead," York growled, and the scramble-brain gulped, slithering back inside his hovel.

Dennison York nodded to his partner, a huge blond body-building freak everyone called the Great Dane, and the two of them continued up the landing. It was dark in the stair-well, the skylights and windows boarded up in a futile effort to keep the Nighthawks out. Unfortunately, there was only one sure way to keep the Nighthawks away, and that was having nothing left worth stealing. York guessed this par-ticular building was safe enough from the midnight looters. Still, he wished he'd brought along some night vision. There was a set of Army-surplus goggles right in the van, and he considered having Ronnie Bates, the team's electronics monitor, run the specs up to him. York hated stumbling around in the dark, especially with a bad guy up ahead somewhere.

"You're getting close," Bates's voice whispered into York's earpiece. "I make the target holed up on the next floor."

"Stationary?" York whispered into the headset. If the perp was that close, maybe they could grope it out a while longer.

"Affirmative," Bates replied. "At least his coat is."

A good point, York conceded. Bates had dusted the target's coat in an uptown diner, and they had been following the magnetic trail for the last couple of hours. Now the perp had gone to ground and it was crunch time, with him and the Dane stumbling around like moles in the middle of Broadway.

"I got a flash," the Dane said, his deep voice sounding like the rumble of thunder in York's ears. "Want me to snap a light?"

"Not with me standing next to you!" York growled. "What if Greeley's waiting for us on the next landing?"

"Then he probably heard us coming up the stairs," the Dane whispered, with all the subtlety of a cannon shot.

"Maybe you're right," York admitted. He was getting too old for this skulking around. That was a sign—when you got too careful tiptoeing through the mind fields, you were sure to get blown up. Of course, if the perp was on the next landing . . .

"Breaking our necks on these fucking stairs is probably as bad as getting shot anyway," the Dane suggested.

"All right, snap the light if you want, but keep it shielded," York whispered.

The light-stick flashed and York saw the Dane's oversize face grinning at him.

"OK, big fellow," York said, returning the grin. "Lead the way. You got the fancy light.

"Take a note," York whispered into the headset as they started up what he hoped would be the last set of stairs. "Remind me to take out a big, short-term life insurance policy on the Dane."

In the earpiece he heard Bates laughing it up in the van.

The stairs creaked under the weight of the Dane's heavy feet, and York followed the big man's shadow up to the next landing. Much to his surprise, nothing terrible happened. It was quiet on the third floor. Dark and quiet, except for the Dane standing in his little island of light. A couple hours yet until dawn, York thought, looking around to get his bearings. Paint was peeling off the walls, papers and empty beer bottles were piled in the corners. There was the faint, unmistakable smell of dried urine hanging in the air. Graffiti was stenciled on some of the doorways, warning the Nighthawks that the interior apartments were guarded by ever-alert, gun-toting residents. Right, York thought, listening to the silence, trying to pick up some telltale sign that this was the right floor. That the man they were following was in fact up here someplace, and, he hoped, not waiting for them to burst in on him. Horace Greeley was the perp's name and he was a righteous outlaw, having toasted more than his share of New York citizenry. Dennison was sincerely hoping Greeley didn't add a couple more notches to his collection before the night was out.

"You're right on top of him," Bates said, his voice strained now as he tried to triangulate the readings from the tracer York was carrying.

"Kill the light," York hissed, and the Dane, sensing danger, twisted the stick closed.

Shadows flew away into the corners like dark birds, and York took a few tentative steps down the empty hallway, moving the tracer around the doorways so Bates could check for a positive reading on the magnetic dust sprinkled on Greeley's jacket.

"There!" Bates whispered. And York made a couple more passes with the tracer so Bates could be sure. "You got him!"

"All right," York whispered back. "Log the time and the apartment number. Plate on the door says 307."

The Dane slipped up close to the door, pulling his favorite break-in weapon, a sawed-off scattergun. York took a sticker mike and hung it on the door.

"Getting anything?" he asked. The Dane was tensed up, ready to crash inside. York reminded himself that he hadn't been joking about the insurance policy.

"A lot of static from the dust," Bates replied. "Hold on, I'm filtering. . . . Yeah! You got interior noise." Over the earpiece York heard Bates chuckling. "A lot of grunting and groaning. Sounds like they're making it, boss."

"There's a surprise," York said, shaking his head. "Outlaws get so much ass. I'd love to know why that is."

York took a pocket torch from his kit bag and was cutting the lock away, trying to be as quiet as possible.

"Let me know if they stop," he whispered into the headset, the torch like a sparkler in his hand.

"You gonna wait 'til they're done?" Bates asked. "That's mighty kind of you. . . ."

"You're an asshole sometimes, Bates!" York whispered. "Next time I'm staying in the van, and you get to put your butt on the line."

"Sorry, boss," Bates said. "There isn't enough money in the whole world . . ."

The door gave an almost audible sigh as the lock separated. The Dane crushed the doorjamb with a massive shoulder and pushed inside with the practiced efficiency of the commando he had once been. There was a strangled shout from the interior, and then the Dane's booming voice telling the occupants not to move a muscle or he would blow their fucking heads off. York rushed in behind him, his own 9mm at ready, but by the time he got to the back bedroom it was over. The Dane had the lights on, and the twin muzzles of the sawed-off were inches from Horace Greeley's head. Greeley, being no fool, took the Dane at his word and was lying across the still squirming girl, not moving a muscle. York pulled the girl away, allowing her to wrap a blanket around herself. Horace Greeley had good taste in women. York couldn't help but notice the girl, who was an Asian with some first-class implants. She was undeniably pretty, even though her eyes were rolling in fear and it looked as if a scream was about to erupt from her open mouth.

"It's all right," York said softly, even though he kept the Nine pointed in her direction. You never knew how women were going to react when you came for their men. "Calm down, nobody's going to get hurt. Horace Greeley, you're being taken into custody."

"You're no fucking cop!" Greeley protested, craning his eyes up at York, looking understandably pissed off. Greeley was a large man, almost as big as the Dane. His hair was cut short, his face ringed with prison tattoos. He looked as if he wanted to leap up off the bed and whomp some ass, which he might have tried to do, if the Dane hadn't yanked his arms behind his back and cuffed his wrists.

"We're secure here," York said into the headset. He then turned and flashed an official-looking badge toward Greeley. The badge itself was quite unofficial, but York found that perps generally calmed down some when he flashed it. "Horace Greeley, you are being apprehended through powers granted to me by the Citizen's Arrest Act, statute number 80465."

"A fucking vigilante!" Greeley hissed as the Dane pulled him to his feet.

"Miss, if you'll help Mr. Greeley get dressed, we'll be on our way," York said to the girl, ignoring Greeley's outburst.

"And if I don't?" The girl looked as if she wanted to spit at him.

"Then we'll just take him like he is." York shrugged. "Makes no difference to me."

He was tired. All this chasing around in the middle of the night was draining his energy levels. He *was* getting too old for this shit. But in the end the girl helped Greeley on with his pants, then York and the Dane took him quietly down the stairs.

"We've got company coming," Bates said through the earpiece as they hit the second landing. "A cruiser's on the way. Somebody in the building must have phoned in an alert."

"You know the drill," York replied. "Feed them our ID number, and tell 'em we'll meet up at the Fifty-fourth Street Station House."

"On it," Bates said quickly.

Downstairs Greeley waited patiently for the Dane to open the sliding door at the back of the van, then stepped up into his seat without help, despite the fact that his hands were cuffed behind him. It was always amazing to York how many of the serious outlaws went quietly. Horace Greeley had burnt at least half a dozen people, yet he walked out of the building and into the van as if he were being taken to the doctor's office. And given his somewhat limited mental

capacities, York recalled from the man's files, that was altogether possible. For whatever reasons, there seemed to be
an inordinate number of mentally deficient people walking
around today. Because of that fact, the courts were reluctant
to hold them responsible for their actions. So it was off to
the hospital to get some help, then back on the street again.
Since Horace Greeley had crossed the invisible line and had
killed a number of folks, it was unlikely he would ever see
the outside again, but there were others like him who would.
York knew that for a fact. He had taken more than his share
of them into custody. Some of them were steady customers,
but that was part of the game. Pick 'em up, then pick 'em
up again in a few years, months, or even days down the
line. York remembered one perp who they popped so many
times, the guy sent them a Christmas card—from Hawaii,
no less. Yeah, life was a funny business.

Now that they'd collared Greeley, York found himself in
a much better mood. He was looking forward to a drink and
a cigar, before sleeping for the next twelve hours or so.
Unfortunately, it took until well after daybreak to get Horace
registered into the Fifty-fourth Street Lockdown Motel. Paperwork, affidavits, proof of service, evidentuary composi-
tions. All drawn out and executed to the exact letter of the
law, because, of course, the police despised York and his
team. After all, he was out doing their job. York supposed
it was some kind of union thing.

So what should have been a quick in-and-out turned into
a marathon paper clip shuffle. Detectives from the Fifty-
fourth, York knew from the police files, had been after Horace Greeley for close to five months. They took their
revenge by conjuring up an endless ream of forms and
sworn depositions that *had* to be filled out: ''So you'll get
proper credit for the bust, General York. We wouldn't want
your check to get held up, now would we?''

No, we wouldn't, York thought, filling out the forms, giving the proper affidavits to three separate officers, all of
whom seemed to have grave difficulties working their computer terminals. A reflection, York kept thinking, of the

same tactics and efficiency they employed in tracking Horace Greeley in the first place.

So it was a couple hours after dawn when everything was properly logged in and York and his team were finally cleared to leave the station. Which meant that the local news crews were waiting outside, braving the late February cold, looking for material to fill their morning TV shows. As York made his way down the steps of the station house, they swarmed around him like a pack of jackals picking over the night's kill.

"How did you find him, Mr. York?"

"Did he put up much of a fight?"

"How was it that you were able to find Horace Greeley, when the entire New York City Police Department couldn't?"

Cameras rolling, electronic flashes popping in his face, microphones shoved practically up his nose. York's head felt like a balloon pumped up with too much helium. The Dane began pushing the newshounds aside so they could make their way to the van.

"How do you deal with hardened criminals like Greeley?"

Once he was near the safety of the van, York turned to give them a chance to take his picture and grab a sound bite. There was, after all, a certain amount of public relations attached to running any profitable operation.

"Mr. Greeley's apprehension was relatively uneventful," York commented. "Once we had him, he came along quietly."

The jackal pack began shouting questions again, their words rolling together like the sound of large storm waves crashing along the shore.

"Horace Greeley killed a number of people!" One reporter shouted the one fact they all knew. "Are you ever afraid dealing with such dangerous criminals?"

"Always," York said tiredly. "But as members of the human race, we're all pretty much criminals, in one context or another."

That prompted another round of shouting, and York took the opportunity to escape into the relatively warm, safe confines of the van. Ronnie Bates drove them away, into the crush of the early morning traffic.

Horace Greeley's mistake, York didn't say as he settled back into the soft cushions of the van, was that he happened to pick the wrong victims. He had robbed and murdered members of a family who had the resources to pay to have him hunted down. Otherwise, he might still be out there, waiting for your wife or girlfriend, or for you when you went out to the car to drive home from work. Because that's what the Horace Greeleys of the world do, and that's why somebody has to go out into the streets and hunt them down. With that thought, Dennison York nodded off into the dark arms of sleep.

In a galaxy uncounted light-years from the Milky Way, the stars float in a dense cloud of primeval gas which allows them to project sound, as well as light. Across the vastness of space these stars sing to one another like humpback whales sounding across leagues of ocean. The whole of this galaxy is filled with a chorus of star voices. And on a planet orbiting a sun near the center of this galaxy, life has spawned. A six-legged creature with multi-faceted eyes lifts its head from a water hole. Its antennae quiver as it hears the sound of the stars singing to one another. The creature tilts its head back and answers the song. Its voice is like a hundred crickets chirping in the night.

God listens, smiling.

 REFLECTIONS ON THE SUBJECTS AS A WHOLE

The Mechanism: A cellular shell, composed primarily of water and carbon. Biped creatures with binocular vision and circular field hearing. Vision limited to the violet and red electromagnetic light bands, hearing limited to the lower range of acceptable predatory survival levels. Sexual reproducing mammals whose young require extensive adolescent care. Hunter/gatherers with enhanced thought processes. Tool users and builders, whose limited technological skills often outstrip their actual scientific knowledge. Emotional beings capable of graphic extremes of love and hate. These emotional swings often create disillusionary and irrational behavior. The hunter/gatherer instinct permeates their social structure, causing hoarding, overproduction, and the need to defend artificial borders.

Purpose of the Mechanism: To provide temporary sanctuary for the spiritual being living within the corporal shell.

Prognosis: The creatures have learned to manipulate their environment to a certain extent, building a variety of agricultural- and technological-based civilizations. To a lesser extent they have learned to manipulate the mechanism, expanding their life cycle and thus, in some cases, have improved the quality of the life cycle. This manipulation of the environment and the mechanism has, unfortunately, come at the expense of the spiritual being within, causing an innate sense of unrest not fully understood by the creatures, given the dichotomy of the perceived improvements in the life cycle of the mechanism. In essence, they have lost sight of the primary objective of the initial experiment: That the mechanism itself was constructed as a vehicle to promote growth in the spiritual being. Further evolutionary changes are hoped for. More guidance and insight on an instinctual level needs to be provided regarding the true nature of the relationship between the mechanism and the spiritual being. Continued observation is clearly indicated before a decision can be reached regarding possible termination of the experiment. Intervention may be called for to prevent possible long-term damage to the spiritual entities residing in many of the mechanisms.

t w o

Dennison York got off the elevator and walked down the hall to his rather shabby two-room office. Jenny was alone at the front desk, fielding phone calls. The Dane and Bates had the day off, after the all-nighter they'd pulled tracking Horace Greeley. She nodded as he entered, flashing him a "good morning" smile, handing him the mail as she cradled the phone against her shoulder. Jenny was in her early thirties, wore her dark hair cut short, and dressed far better than he paid her. In York's mind she was one of the most efficient people he had ever run across. She was constantly dieting, although York thought her pretty and could never understand why. Generally she seemed to be approaching middle age with a dignity he admired. For some reason, which York couldn't understand either, her husband had run off, leaving her with a daughter to raise. That was the problem with the world, from his point of view, anyway—there were too many idiots running around doing exactly what they pleased, without giving any thought to the consequences of their actions. York returned Jenny's smile and went into the inner office to open the mail. Bills mostly.

After a few minutes Jenny came in with a stack of messages, reading them for him as she always did—grinning and commenting whenever the urge moved her.

"Got a thank-you note from the Lake family," she said. "Mr. Lake says he and his wife can finally sleep, now that

Horace Greeley is off the streets. He's wiring the balance of your fee to the Cayman bank.''

"Good," York replied, making a mental note to pay some of the bills. "Anything else interesting?"

"Some network TV interest, and a flurry of magazine offers," Jenny said. "They all want exclusives and the money's not bad. Seems they think you're a hot property, now that Horace Greeley's capture is in the news."

"Tell the TV people thanks, but I'm too busy," York said, knowing from past experience how poorly he came off on that medium. People always expected someone in his line of work to be tall, dark, and handsome, which he most assuredly was not. He would, however, be a fool to pass up the opportunity for a little free publicity, not to mention the inviting prospect of some extra cash. "Pick the best magazine offer and tell 'em I'm interested. But I want the piece to be respectable, and I get final approval on any pictures they use."

"When do you want to do it?" Jenny asked, smiling.

York shrugged. "As soon as they can cut the check."

Jenny laughed, closing the door behind her. York went over to the window, looking down at the dirty snowbanks that lined the streets this time of year. To his disgust, he saw there were garbage bags frozen into the snowbanks, like round, dark stones. Some of the plastic stones had ripped, and trash was spilling out onto the sidewalks. The city was a great place to get away from; this was especially true in winter. He was tired, and suddenly decided he would take some of the magazine money and fly someplace warm. Mobility being the upside to prostitution.

Yvonne Stafford drank her juice and made sure she had her math homework. Her mother was trying to get her little brother, James, to eat his eggs—an all but impossible task. James, Yvonne knew, was like all males. That is, he did only what he felt like doing at the moment. At twelve years of age Yvonne imagined she was becoming something of an expert on the male psyche. At school there were two boys of particular interest—Billy Vaughn, age fourteen, the older man in Yvonne's life, and Tom Haven, who happened to be her own age, and was a constant nuisance. It was incredible to her that someone in the seventh grade could act so immature. Billy Vaughn, however, was a freshman. He played basketball and winked at her in the hallway at school. And when he did that, Yvonne felt her heart race and her legs actually shiver a little. It was an odd feeling, one she hesitated to discuss even with her best friend, Susie Miller, who had been to California and seemed altogether worldly.

"Yvonne, honey, are you all right?" her mother asked. Yvonne broke out of her haze to discover that James had indeed finished his eggs, and even had his coat on.

"Yes, Momma." Yvonne smiled. "I'm fine."

"Well, come on then. Daddy had to go to the office early, so we have to drop James off at school before you, and I don't want to be late."

Her mother was standing in front of the hall mirror, tying her hair with a silk scarf. As always, Yvonne was struck by what a beautiful woman her mother was. Tall and thin, her well-tailored clothes seemed to hug her grown-up body. Her makeup made her face glow and set off her dark eyes in a most alluring manner. It was Yvonne's fervent hope that one day she would look just like her mother, and that she and Billy Vaughn would find true love together. In fact, those hopes and dreams occupied a lot more of her mind these days than she really wanted them to. Sometimes, late at night, she could hear her mother and father in their bedroom. And in those dark, quiet hours, when she hugged her pillow and dreamed about Billy Vaughn, it seemed to be all that she could think of. Billy Vaughn and grown-up love . . . it sometimes seemed like an impossible dream.

Her mother smiled at her and lifted her eyebrows, and suddenly Yvonne felt as if her mother was reading her mind. Yvonne gulped the last of her juice and grabbed her coat.

In his basement apartment off Tremont Avenue in the Bronx, Arnie Watts was thinking about jerking off. Unable to sleep, his head ringing slightly from a half bottle of Nightrain wine and a joint he'd smoked a few hours ago, Arnie

lay naked on his hard cot and touched himself. The early
morning light filtered in through a single dirt-crusted window, illuminating pictures taped to the wall and ceiling
above his bed. Some were from fuck magazines he bought
in the shops over on Forty-second Street, some were pictures
from underground mags he got in the mail, wrapped in
brown paper. As he looked at them, the women and young
girls in the pictures seemed to move. They touched themselves and their mouths opened, forming dark circles. Some
of them seemed to be whispering his name.

—Take me, Arnie. No, me . . . me . . . me.

Their voices became like a hollow bell ringing in his
head. Arnie squeezed his legs together and tried to make his
dick rise, but it wasn't working. His dick sat in his hand,
limp and cold, like a piece of old celery left in the refrigerator for a few weeks. Arnie closed his eyes, the voices
kept talking, but still nothing happened. Finally, in disgust,
he sat up in the bed and cursed softly to himself.

—Impotent motherfucker.

Arnie shook his head, unable to tell if he or one of the
open-legged sluts in the pictures had spoken the words. The
twitch, which he hated, began acting up in his left eye. He
got up and splashed cold water on his face in an attempt to
stop the twitching. There was a mirror over the stained sink,
but Arnie turned away from it quickly, not wanting to see
himself as an Impotent Motherfucker. He wasn't that at all,
and there were plenty of whores over on Forty-second who
could testify to that!

As he turned, his eyes fell on one picture taped up among
the dozens of others. It was a young girl. Very young. Her
breasts like tiny buds on her chest. Her hands just covering
her hairless crotch. She smiled at him, and Arnie Watts
smiled back.

The elevator slipped soundlessly toward the basement garage. Yvonne felt her stomach do a flip, and as they dropped
toward the bottom landing, the outside chill invaded the elevator shaft and Yvonne shivered, reaching down to zip up
her coat. Her mother was watching the lights above the door,

as they blinked blinked blinked toward the bottom. It amused her that all adults watched the floors blink by, as if the elevator might suddenly stop and decide to go sideways. James was rubbing his nose and looked as if he wanted to insert a finger to poke around in there, as he sometimes did. Yvonne stuck an elbow into his shoulder and James glared up at her, dropping his hand to his side. Yvonne glared back, shaking her head in warning.

"What?" James whined, in an attempt to make his high voice sound innocent.

Her mother turned to look at them just as the elevator slid to a stop. Yvonne shook her head to indicate it was nothing to be concerned about. The three of them stepped into the underground cave of the building parking lot. An attendant was drinking coffee in a guard booth. A skinny young man with a thin blond mustache, dressed in a blue worksuit, he smiled in their direction.

"Morning, Mrs. Stafford," he said, his eyes slyly looking up and down her mother's figure.

"Good morning, Tim." Yvonne's mother returned the greeting, actually sounding as though she was glad to see the young man, who had his name stitched into his blue coveralls. "Chilly this morning," she said, congenially.

"Yes, ma'am, it surely is!" Tim said, as though this was the first time he had noticed the cold.

The interplay between adults—and semi-adults like Tim—fascinated Yvonne. It was as if they found the meaningless exchange of obvious information entertaining somehow. Yvonne suspected that Tim's response would have been the same if her mother had said:

"Good morning, Tim. The world seems round today."

"Yes, ma'am, it surely does!" Tim would say, following her mother's body with his eyes as she walked away toward the car. Didn't she see him doing that? Didn't she mind? Adults, boys, even the world itself was often very confusing to Yvonne. There was something about Tim—his eyes, maybe—that Yvonne didn't like at all. She took James's arm and hurried toward the car. A red BMW, with leather seats that were cold in the winter and hot in the summer, before the heat and air-conditioning matched her body temperature. A Beemer, the kids at school called it. Some of them liked the car, others made fun of it. Yvonne tended to avoid the latter. It was, after all, just an automobile. A machine that carried you from place to place. To school, to ballet lessons, to the market. Sometimes to the Cape, although they usually took her father's Land Rover on long trips. The Land Rover was better, in Yvonne's mind. It looked sort of like a Jeep, and hardly anyone made fun of Jeeps.

Once inside, the engine roared to life and they drove out of the parking lot tunnel, into the sunlight. Yvonne passed the time in traffic thinking about Billy Vaughn, and what she might do to get him to talk to her.

Arnie Watts slicked his hair back and smiled at his freshly shaved face in the mirror. No Impotent Motherfucker here. No, sir! Face washed, teeth brushed, hair combed. Arnie Watts looked like your friendly neighborhood bus driver. Or the school janitor, or some guy who works at the plastics factory. He looked like an average nine-to-fiver who stops in at the local tavern for a quick beer after his shift is over, before going home to his wife and kids. That was the first rule in Arnie Watts's game: Blend in. Look like an average schmuck, going about your average life. Smile at the old ladies on the street. Help them with their groceries. Pet their dogs. Ask about their grandchildren.

Really, that was the first lesson Arnie had ever learned. If you're going to be a junkie, never ever look like a junkie. If you're going to be a purse-snatcher, never ever look like a purse-snatcher. All of which Arnie Watts had been at one time or another, with varying degrees of success, during his thirty-five years. Success in any type of criminal endeavor, Arnie knew, began by making damn sure your victims never suspected who, or what, you were. The same principle held true if you were going out on the street to hunt up a little action. And it was in this particular endeavor that Arnie found his greatest success. He was, above all else, a superb hunter. A predator of the first order.

Washed, brushed, and combed, Arnie put on his last pair of clean jeans, a nondescript black T-shirt, his white Nike sneakers, and finally his favorite green army jacket—all of which made him look years younger, and therefore more acceptable to his prey. It had been nearly ten months now since he'd done any serious hunting. The last adventure had taken place almost two thousand miles and several states ago. That was another rule Arnie had learned: Make sure you put considerable time and distance between your crimes. Crimes, he knew from experience, were like seasons and pain to most people—they were quickly forgotten in the grand scheme of things. When spring came, people pushed winter to the back of their minds. When a cut healed, people forgot how much it hurt when the knife sliced open their skin. The human capacity to forget was perhaps mankind's greatest weakness, at least in Arnie Watts's mind. It was this very weakness that helped him succeed in his game, time and time again.

The morning rush hour was passing by his basement window. All the human ants having forgotten how much they hated their jobs, even as they trudged off to go about the day's business. Smiling to himself again in the mirror, Arnie went outside to blend in with the crowd. His van, registered under another name, in another city, was parked several blocks away.

In the farthest corners of the expanding universe, dark-ness washed in like a tide from the eternal night of the abyss. It rolled in great waves, lapping at the edge of cre-ation like a flooding lake. And in that farthest corner of the universe, walls of stars came together to form a dike, which kept the darkness at bay.

There is always darkness pushing in against the light. Constant vigilance is required.

 REFLECTIONS ON THE SUBJECTS AS INDIVIDUALS

It is frustrating that the inner voices of the spiritual beings are almost totally eclipsed by outside stimuli. It is as though, once adapted to the mechanism, the spiritual entity becomes absorbed by the physical trappings around it. Despite extended prebirth conditioning, this phenomenon seems to take place at a very early age in the life cycle of the mechanism, and continues until physical termination, at which point the spiritual entity resumes its normal function. Indeed, the entity itself, in many cases, expresses great surprise at the fact of its own existence once it is released from the physical world. This is true even of those entities who went forth into the mechanism with specific learning goals, which were discussed and planned extensively in the conditioning phase. These goals are largely submerged, however, by the entities' absorption into the mechanisms' physical world. The entities themselves often express consternation at this failure to achieve the desired learning experiences.

It is becoming increasingly obvious that the spiritual beings, once implanted in the mechanisms, become unable, or unwilling, to bring themselves to the forefront and influence the mechanisms' actions. It would seem that the physical side has completely overshadowed the spiritual. This has occurred to such an extreme point, that the spiritual entities residing within the mechanisms have become lost in the vortex of the physical plane. The extent of this absorption has, in fact, caused the individual creatures formed by the grafting of the entity to the mechanism to become unaware of their spiritual nature. The result of this unprecedented event has given rise to extremely chaotic behavior in many of the mechanisms. In addition, it has spawned a series of irrational religious cults and beliefs, which have further undermined the spiritual entities in their quest for knowledge.

Conclusion: The experiment itself has taken on new, often dire, dimensions, in which the spiritual entities themselves could conceivably be at risk.

three

She would get Susie to talk to Billy Vaughn, Yvonne decided. Susie, who was experienced in these matters, would break the ice and smooth the way toward Billy and her getting together. Perhaps next week at the freshman dance . . .

"Yvonne? Would you let your brother out, please?"

Yvonne looked up to see her mother glancing at her rather strangely. Yvonne hurried to open the door, and James got out sullenly to join the other grade-school kids trudging through the open gate into the Harrison Academy, an exclusive private school for K-6 in Manhattan, which both her mother and father insisted was the right place for James; he had the manners of a small ape and would, Yvonne was sure, grow up to believe the Classics were old cartoon shows. So James went to Harassment Academy, as Yvonne and her friends kidded both James and her parents. Yvonne, a product of the New York City Public School System, told herself she didn't feel slighted by the decision to send James to a private school, even though in her heart she knew she did.

"The public schools just aren't the same anymore," her father had explained. "Not like they were when you were in grade school, Yvonne. When James is in junior high, he can go to the public school. Besides, you don't want to leave your friends, do you?"

No, she didn't. The truth was, Yvonne liked P.S. 364,

despite its sometimes unsavory reputation. She liked her friends, and even most of her teachers. It was just that . . . well, it would have been nice to have been given a choice. After all, if the grade schools weren't as good as they were when she was attending them, who was to say the high schools were any better today? Anyway, Yvonne kept her grades up and knew that college was only a few years away. Maybe even Hunter, where her mother had gone.

"Are you really all right, honey?" her mother asked, after they had watched James march inside Harrison with the rest of his uniformed classmates. The Beemer had slipped back into the morning traffic, and they were on their way uptown, to P.S. 364 and her mother's job at the gallery.

"I'm fine." Yvonne smiled, vowing to keep her feet on the ground, and her head in the game—like Coach Willis said to do when they were out on the volleyball court. But what about jumping up to spike? Susie had whispered, prompting a round of muffled laughter. Susie always had something funny to say, which made her an instant hit with most everyone in their clique: The 364th Bomb Squad, they called themselves, after a failed chemistry experiment back in the sixth grade.

"You'd tell me if anything was wrong?" her mother gently pried. Prying, of course, being the eminent domain of adults, parents in particular.

Yvonne gave the standard reply. "Sure, Mom."

"It's a boy, isn't it?" her mother asked, smiling that all-knowing, omniscient smile. Unable to help herself, Yvonne felt the color rising up from the fake rabbit fur of her jacket. "Aw, come on, honey. It's OK." Her mother reached over to pat Yvonne's leg. "We'll talk about it tonight—girl to girl, just the two of us."

Yvonne smiled back, wanting to crawl under the Beemer's seat. Now Susie Miller would have to help with two traumatic problems.

Arnie Watts walked casually up to the rear of his van. The morning traffic was a roar a few blocks over, but here on Union Avenue, people were leaving their high-rises, their

brownstone apartments, heading to their upper-class jobs in
the banks of Wall Street, the insurance offices on Broadway,
the medical clinics that were popping up all over the place
like McDonald's. Some drove, but mostly they took taxis,
buses, the subway, or they walked. On the side streets delivery vans tried to beat the commuter crush. A phone company truck was double-parked, a cable TV van circled the
block, the driver checking numbers against a clipboard
screwed into his dash.

Arnie Watts, looking like a delivery man for a local flo-
rist, approached his van from the opposite side of the street.
He looked things over carefully before crossing to peer into
the driver's-side window. In Arnie's world you could never
be too careful. Some neighborhood kids were on their way
to school. A plump old woman in a crossing-guard uniform
stopped traffic at the corner, directing kids through the
intersection. It was, in most all respects, a normal urban
morning. Normal for everyone, that is, except Arnie Watts.
In Arnie's head the morning air crackled with excitement.
The buzzing from last night's poisons was gone, chased
away by a spectacular adrenaline high. Arnie was fine-tuned,
his senses reaching out, processing each bit of information
the day offered—the chill in the air, voices from passers-
by, the music and talk shows playing inside the passing cars.
Arnie felt himself move into a high state of readiness. Alert.
He was never more alive than when that jarring sense of
danger crawled up his spine and made his brain sing with
the day's possibilities. The hunt—that was what life was all
about.

Arnie circled the van, checking the tires, looking under
the frame to make sure there were no oil leaks, and most
important making damn sure no one had been snooping
around. Something his friend Jerry had once said, when they
had been doing break-ins out in LA: In our business there's
nothing wrong with a little healthy paranoia. That bit of
advice had stayed with Arnie for years and had, he honestly
believed, saved him from doing any serious time. Paranoia
and preparation—they were the key essential elements to
success. He laughed every time he thought about the would-

be robber he read about in upstate New York who got caught popping convenience stores because he had to stop and put gas in his car after pulling a job. And those idiots in South Carolina who had held up a liquor store and came out to find a flat tire on their getaway car. Arnie had actually met a cop in a bar up in Buffalo once who told him, quite seriously, that the dumb criminals were the only ones behind bars. The smart ones were still out on the street and would probably stay there. Arnie had laughed good-naturedly and bought the cop a beer.

"You guys are still doing a hellova job, for my money," Arnie had said. And the cop thanked him.

"We try," the cop had said, acting as though he really meant it. "We sure as hell do our best. . . ."

Arnie, who had just come off a most successful hunting trip in the Midwest, agreed wholeheartedly.

And now the time had come again. The Hour of the Hunt.

Arnie fished the keys from his coat pocket, unlocked the sliding door on the van's side and stepped inside, closing the door after him. He took a few minutes to check his equipment, each movement careful and meticulous. Preparation, that was the key. He checked the tape player. Music was important—both to soothe the prey and mask any unwanted noise. Leather restraints, padded with cotton, screwed into the metal floor of the van, designed to keep the prey secure, yet comfortable. A hood and gag, to be used if necessary. You never knew how the prey would react in the opening moments of the play. And it was a play, carefully acted and scripted. Arnie pulled on the straps that crisscrossed the van's backseat. Satisfied, he moved to the front and started the engine. Full tank of gas, solid oil pressure. In a few minutes the heat gauge rose to its ¼ position, but no further. Careful preparation. Nodding to himself, Arnie put the van in gear.

"Cleared for takeoff," he whispered, grinning, his eyes glinting in the morning sun as he drove up Route 95, across the Harlem River, through the concrete caverns of his hunting ground.

•   •   •

The Beemer slid up to the curb in front of P.S. 364. It was almost eight-thirty and Yvonne knew she would have to hurry to make the homeroom bell.

"Have a good day," her mother said.

Yvonne smiled and stepped out, jumping to avoid a dirty puddle of snow melt.

"I will," she said, closing the Beemer's door, pulling back as her mother waved and sped off, in a hurry to make her nine o'clock meeting at the gallery. And as the car turned the corner, as the other children made their mad dashes for the front door of P.S. 364 before the late bell rang, Yvonne looked down at her empty hands, her stomach dropping away, down toward her knees. Her math homework . . . left on the Beemer's front seat, or back home on the kitchen table. In her confusion Yvonne wasn't sure which. The sinking feeling now involved her brain as well as her stomach. She absolutely could not show up at Mrs. Van Skiver's math class without her homework. She would get detention, or have to stay in and do the work during lunch recess. And that would destroy any chances of the accidental encounter being planned with Billy Vaughn. It would destroy any chance of them ever getting together. All because of her stupid, stupid math homework. It was back on the kitchen table, she was certain of it now. Well, she would just have to go home and get it.

Inside P.S. 364, the last bell for homeroom clanged its dire warning. Stragglers were rushing up the steps, hustling their way inside before the heavy doors to the school's entrance were slammed shut. Anyone entering after those cathedral-like portals were secured would have to report to the principal's office and explain their tardiness.

I'm sorry, Mr. Johnson, my mother's car wouldn't start. . . . We got caught in traffic. . . . I had a dentist's appointment. . . . I felt sick this morning, but I'm better now.

All of which seemed easier to explain than the lame excuse of forgetting your homework on the kitchen table. Besides, it would be a lot easier to face the easygoing Mr. Johnson than that evil witch, Mrs. Van Skiver. The decision made, Yvonne walked quickly up 125th Street, heading to-

ward the bus stop at the end of the block. Having spent all
of her twelve years in the city, Yvonne was well versed in
the bus routes, and even the subways, although both her
mother and father declared the underground rails to be
strictly off-limits. Even so, she and Susie Miller had been
to Coney Island and the uptown movie houses dozens of
times. Yvonne knew she could make it home and back in
an hour or so, give her excuse to old Mr. Johnson, and be
in math class by fourth period. There might be a problem
with a note from home, but that could be dealt with later.

Secure in her plan, Yvonne zipped her coat and pulled
on her gloves as she waited. Of course, she would have to
use her lunch money for bus fare, but that was a small price
to pay. Maybe Billy Vaughn would buy her lunch when he
heard her story. And years from now they would laugh at
the memory of their first meeting. . . .

Arnie Watts turned the radio down as he began cruising.
Howard Stern was making fun of some faggot DJ out on
the Coast, while half-naked women paraded around his stu-
dio. Arnie found this highly amusing, but there was business
to tend to. He was debating about heading out to Forty-
second Street, where there was sure to be some action even
on a cold winter's morning. But it was supposed to snow
later in the day, which would snarl the hell out of the afternoon traffic. That could work to his advantage, he knew,
as the cops would be tied up straightening out the mess and
tending to all the fender-benders. No. No whores today. It
was time to hunt. Time to make his mark on the world. If
he could make his score early, Arnie knew he could have
himself one sweet time riding out the storm. . . .

There! On the corner. Looking up Lenox Avenue, no
doubt waiting for the crosstown bus. Brown hair flowing
over the fur collar of her coat. Young. Twelve or thirteen.
And her face—Jesus, she could pass for the girl in the picture back at his apartment!

—Take me, Arnie! No, take me . . .

The voice clouded his brain for a moment, like a thun-
derstorm rolling across the open ocean. The light turned

green ahead of him. Cars moving. She was alone at the bus
stop. The crossing guard, an old man, walking away from
his station now that school was probably in session. And
here this girl was leaving school. Maybe nobody would
know she was gone for the entire day. A jogger passing. A
guy going into the diner across the street. Everyone, it
seemed, was walking away, their backs turned. Traffic had
moved on. Arnie Watts's senses seemed to expand, taking
in everything. Everything. The people in the window of the
diner, talking among themselves. Laughing, drinking their
coffee, reading their newspapers. In this particular instant,
for this single moment, the street was somehow empty of
cars or buses. The jogger turning the corner, past the neighborhood bakery. The crossing guard almost at the end of
the block, his back turned. The sun, already shining down
into the caverns of the street, illuminating his prey in an
island of light. In a moment of almost perfect clarity, Arnie
Watts saw his window of opportunity. It was one of those
times, one of those special moments when even God's back
was turned on the world. Arnie's nostrils flared like a hunting cat. He slipped the car into gear and rolled forward.

Billy Vaughn had damn well better appreciate all this effort
to meet him, Yvonne thought, stamping her feet against the
cold, looking down at her sneakers, which were getting
soaked. She didn't hear or see the van until it had pulled
into the bus-stop lane.

"Hey, you need a ride?"

The voice seemed to shake her awake. A man had rolled
down the passenger window and was smiling at her from
inside a white van. Yvonne felt a quick moment of unease.
Not panic, because after all, this was the city and one had
to expect a certain amount of hassle. Like Tim the parking-
lot attendant staring at her mother.

"No!" Yvonne said firmly, turning her back, looking
down the street for the bus. And suddenly there was a hand
on her shoulder. The side door of the van was open. She
hadn't heard it slide open. Somehow, there was this man,
still smiling, with his hand on her shoulder. And the world

seemed to slow to a dreamlike crawl. She moved to shrug off the hand. Her feet slipped on the ice as she tried to pull away. Her movements, they seemed so slow . . . and the man was moving faster than it seemed possible . . . an instant of flashing panic. Her mind screaming at her: RUN! RUN! And she tried, but her feet were slipping. Slipping because the man was pulling her. Pulling her into the van!

"Sure you do," he whispered, and Yvonne was suddenly inside. The man was smiling. A cold smile. Like a curved icicle across his face. "It's all right," he said as she pulled against him. "It's all right." Oh, but it wasn't. He was so strong. And there hadn't even been time to scream.

WHAT ARE YOU DOING? Yvonne tried to say, to yell. But his hand was over her mouth. She could hardly breathe! She tried to bite, but her jaws were being held tight. She struggled, she twisted and kicked, but it was like fighting in a dream. She was slow, and the man was fast. She was weak, and the man was strong. In a second, it seemed, her arms were strapped down into the rear seat. Her legs buckled tightly. A piece of cloth stuck in her mouth.

"Don't be afraid," the man whispered, his breath hot in her ear.

DON'T BE AFRAID? her brain screamed.

DON'T BE AFRAID?! Her fear was like ice water in her veins. Yvonne felt her hair standing on end. Her feet, her hands . . . they were cold. Numb. All of her was numb. Tears welled up in her eyes. The gag was choking her. The man put music on. He smiled at her. Like a snake grinning.

"Don't be afraid," he said again. "I'm not going to hurt you. . . ."

No, she whispered to herself. Strapped tightly into the back, as the man moved to the front of the van and drove off. No, no, no, she thought, her brain burning inside her skull.

In the heart of the Andromeda Galaxy, a planet orbits a small, yellow sun—a star that is all but lost in the swath of suns which comprise that galaxy. The planet, itself small and inconsequential in the vast scope of the universe, has long since established a stable orbit in that magical range where the light from the star is strong, but not too strong. The planet's gravitational forces allowed it to evolve through the stages of differentiation, resulting in the formation of continents, oceans, and a delicately balanced atmosphere, rich in oxygen and hydrogen gases. All of which has granted the tiny planet the privilege of supporting life.

It is a green world, blanketed with plant life, yet void of any of the so-called higher animal species. The dominant life forms here are egg-laying bacteria, microscopic in size and extremely prolific. Their life cycle begins in the warm shallows of the inland seas, where they hatch and reach maturity. The young bacteria then float to the surface, where their wing sails open and spread, and the winds sweep them into the lower atmosphere. There, they cluster in huge, sweeping clouds, connected by swirling, ribbonlike bridges of their own kind. The skies above the planet's surface are filled with these clouds of clustering bacteria. Uncounted trillions of them, shimmering and shifting on the winds, defusing the light of their sun into an unending cascade of rainbows, which play across the surface of the planet like gentle lightning. And in the mating season, as the swarms of bacteria swirl high in the air, displaying phosphorescent colors of red, yellow, and blue, egg cases drop down from the clouds like rain, to fall in the shallows of the inland waters. For millennia, through ages of time, this cycle has been repeated.

For millennia, through ages of time . . . then, in an instant, change. A mutation in a single egg case. And for the dominant life forms of this world, there is no escape. A tiny, almost insignificant aberration in a DNA strand causes bacteria to hatch which contain a disease, a virus that eats away the outer walls of the adult bacteria.

As God watches, the skies above the planet darken. The phosphorescent swarms become black as thunderclouds. The shafts of light, the brilliant multicolored rainbows that danced across the planet for millennia, fade and vanish.

And the bacteria, uncounted trillions of them, fall to the planet's surface like dust.

God watches, unable to help. Such are the irrefutable laws of life and death in the universe.

four

Lesia Stafford had stopped screaming by the time her husband made his way home. It was four-thirty in the afternoon, two hours earlier than his usual arrival time, and he had come home to chaos. Two detectives were sitting in the living room with his wife. There was another uniformed cop coming out of his daughter's bedroom down the hall. The cop held a picture of Yvonne. Even though Stafford couldn't see the picture, he knew from the frame it was Yvonne's sixth-grade class photograph. She was wearing a blue wool sweater, he remembered, and a thin gold chain they'd given her for Christmas. Her light brown hair was brushed carefully over her shoulders, and she was smiling. James Stafford loved his daughter's smile. A million-dollar grin, he always said, kidding her. Kidding her, just to see her smile. And now . . . now God only knew when he would see her smiling at him again. God only knew. . . .

Tears fogged his vision, as they had ever since the police had come to the office with the horrifying news that his daughter was missing. The officer with the picture brushed past him, disappearing into the outside hallway, where several of the neighbors had stopped to gawk into the Stafford apartment.

"Oh, Jimmy . . ." Lesia saw him, and his stomach twisted at the pain etched into her face. It was a terrible thing to see. His wife's face—normally so very beautiful—now a strange, almost grotesque mask of fear. A fear so deep he knew it approached madness.

He hurried across the room to hold her.

"Jimmy . . ." she moaned against his shoulder. "I dropped her off right in front of the school. She was standing there, waving goodbye . . . and I just drove off! I was late . . . and . . . oh, my god!"

Her sobs were like convulsions. Like the death throes of a dying person. And as he held her, James Stafford knew his wife was dying inside.

"It's not your fault," he whispered, brushing back her hair, looking over her shoulder at the men in the cheap blue suits. "We'll find her. Don't worry, we'll find her." But even as he said this, Stafford was looking into the detectives' eyes for some glimmer of confirmation. He found none.

"Can you tell us anything more, Mrs. Stafford?" one of the men interrupted. "Has Yvonne ever run away from home before? Even for a few hours?"

"Never," Stafford answered for both of them. "She was the perfect kid. Always on time. Never even stayed out late with her friends."

"Boyfriends?" the other detective asked.

"No." Stafford shook his head. "Just her circle of friends from school."

Lesia had stopped her convulsions and was sobbing quietly, her head buried in his chest.

"Yes, your wife gave us a list," the first detective replied. "We're checking them now, although they all seemed to be in school today."

"And nobody saw Yvonne?" Stafford asked, the reality of the situation closing in around his heart like cold, frozen ropes. Yvonne . . . she was gone. The detective shook his head, pretending to check his notes. "You'll find her, won't you?" Stafford asked.

"We'll do everything we can," the suit answered, and the noncommittal tone of his voice enraged Stafford.

"What the fuck does that mean?" he demanded.

"It means we'll do everything we can," the detective said

again, this time with an edge to his voice. "For starters, we're going to place a tap on your phone, in case anyone calls with a ransom demand. We're checking her friends' houses. We've got a dozen uniforms canvasing the neighborhood here and around the school."

"Where's Jim Junior?" Stafford asked, suddenly realizing he hadn't seen his son since entering the apartment.

"He's with the Thompsons next door," Lesia whispered, pulling herself away, straightening her shoulders, reaching into her husband's breast pocket for his handkerchief.

James Stafford got up from the couch and walked over to the living room window. A light snow was beginning to fall, drifting down from the lead-colored sky to the concrete platform which was the city. Ten stories below, the streets were crawling with people and traffic. To Stafford, the streets suddenly seemed to be dark mazes, filled with skulking strangers, one of whom had taken his daughter. The city, he realized with horror, was a gigantic place.

"You'll find her, won't you?" he asked, deeply afraid that one of the detectives might answer his question truthfully.

On a planet in the cluster of stars known as the Large Megellanic Cloud, some 150,000 light-years from the planet Earth, an aged and infirm female of mammalian descent clung perilously to the shaft of polished rock that was her clan's burial stone. The wind cut sharp edges through the salt canyons, driving bits of sand and dust against her bare skin like a hard rain. Overhead, the orange sun stood tall in the dappled green sky, beating down, burning away all that was not strong enough to stand before it. Thinking this, the female stood up straighter, to her full one meter of height, and turned her horn-covered face into the wind, as if daring it to blow harder. At her feet were the bones of her ancestors—her mother and father, their parents before them, going back uncounted generations, further even than the NameCallers could remember. The bones of her two mates were scattered around the burial stone, as well as several of her children. And now, soon, her own bones would join them, to bleach in the sun until the glorious Final Day, when all the dead around the burial stone would rise up and dance in the glow of God's eternal fire.

She was alone, of course, awaiting that magical moment of her death, as was right and fitting. Death being a solitary experience, reserved for the single heart that stops beating. In anticipation of her death, the others of her clan had held a great feast in her honor, with the NameCallers reciting the long list of her ancestors, her friends standing forth to tell stories of her bravery, her good deeds, and her devotion to clan and family. Then her surviving children had stood beside her, vowing to continue her lineage and revere her name, keeping it alive through their own children. And then she had stood alone in the circle of the firelight, thanking them all for sharing their lives with her, thanking God for her clan and the length of her years. Next, with great ceremony, she had given away each of her prized possessions: the metal knife, handcrafted by her first mate, which never lost its edge; the string of water stones, dipped in the color of the sun, a gift from her second mate; her sewing kit, cooking utensils and pots; even her quilted winter clothing, which, thankfully, she would never again need. And as she basked in the fire's glow for the last time, the clan celebrated her.

In the morning they left her at the burial stone, and had gone down into the valley to hunt the Ixxon, those mighty hoofed beasts who provided the winter meat. She had watched them go, full of pride at the glory of their existence, an existence in which she had played a part, however small. And now the wind was blowing salty grit against her unprotected body, and the sun was beating down, drawing the liquids of life away from her. To these elements she opened her arms in welcome—the sharp wind, the drying sun—for these would complete the weathering process that had begun on the day of her birth, and would prepare her final gift to the clan. When they returned from the hunt, she would be dead. The men would then cut away her skin, already dried and leathery, and it would be used by the medicine women to bind the hunter's wounds, to wrap the gashes made by the Ixxon hoofs, to seal the punctures made by their horns. Thus would her skin become one with the hunters. Thus would she live forever.

 ## REFLECTIONS ON THE SCOPE OF THE EXPERIMENT

In the beginning, when the experiment itself was conceived, it was thought that the physical plane would provide a source of learning that was generally outside the scope of the spiritual entities. Thus, when evolution seemed to provide an agreeable mechanism to achieve this end, the spiritual entities agreed to the implantation. Those dissenting, of course, were allowed to exercise their free will and did not participate. Those who wished to have the experience of the physical plane were conditioned and examined to determine their readiness to take part in the experiment. So it was, in the beginning.

However, as the experiment proceeded, the mechanisms, because of this spiritual infusion, began to make great strides in controlling the physical plane. They achieved a material-based technology, increased food production, and generally made adaptations that allowed for geometric increases in their population. Conversely, as the number of mechanisms increased, so, too, did the need for spiritual entities. It has now become evident that many of the entities currently being implanted have:

1) Not been sufficiently conditioned to deal with the complexities of the physical plane.

2) Not reached a state of spiritual development which allows them to interact with others of their kind at a functioning level.

These problems are manifesting themselves in a number of ways that do not fall within the scope of the experiment.

Many of the entities seem to be increasingly driven by the oftentimes violent instincts of the mechanisms. These instincts, which served the mechanisms well in the early stages of their development, have not been displaced by the presence of the spiritual entities, as was hoped. In truth, in many instances, the mechanisms themselves seem to fight the spiritual influences, often going to deplorable lengths to prove to themselves that the spiritual side of their nature does not exist. The ramifications of this development are many:

There is sadness, where there was meant to be no sadness. There is loneliness, where there was meant to be no loneliness. There is death, where there was meant to be no death.

There are no ceremonial fires being lit, no songs being sung to celebrate the glory of the universe.

five

Dennison York was checking the figures from the Grand Cayman Bank, mentally calculating how much it would cost to buy a decent boat and sail her off into the sunset for the next twenty years. Much more than he had at the moment, he concluded glumly. Maybe in another five or ten years, if he happened to live that long.

Jenny was still at her desk, shuffling papers, glancing out the window at the snow that was starting to fall. York tapped the intercom.

"Why don't you get out of here?" he said. "Get a jump on the traffic."

"Sure you don't need me?" Jenny asked, obviously pleased at his offer. She was, in fact, already reaching for her coat before he could give a cursory reply.

"No, I'll see you tomorrow," he said, watching as she smiled, waved once, and ran for the door.

"Drive carefully," he called after her.

A stupid platitude, he thought to himself as he listened to the sound of the elevator rising up to get her. Really, how many people get in their cars with the idea of wrapping themselves around a bridge abutment? Even though his first wife, Sandy, had done exactly that. So York told everyone to drive carefully, knowing that hardly anyone in New York ever did. Certainly not Ronnie Bates, who had crashed more vans than York could count. And where the hell was Bates, anyway? Caught in traffic, probably.

York got up from his desk and went to the window to watch the snow. It would be an ugly night out on the streets, but with Horace Greeley no longer in circulation, at least they could move on down the list. Probably hunt up a couple of the minor-league bail jumpers the City had contracted for. And then, York promised himself, he was going to take a couple weeks off. Head down to the Keys for a little R&R. His bones longed for the warmth of a tropical sun. He hated the fact that his body ached and snapped in the cold. And it was always cold in New York these days. Whatever happened to global warming, anyway?

Down below, car horns blared their futile honking, sounding like flocks of stranded geese. People stood on the street corners waiting for always-late buses and waved despairingly at full taxicabs. Grinning, York began to sing:

"I left my heart in the Grand Bahamas. . . ." he sang, far off-key, laughing at his own foolishness.

The sad truth was that he had. His second wife had been a beautiful, golden-skinned Latin beauty, a refugee from Cuba. She had married him, of course, because she thought he was a rich American. He almost had been, once, for a while. But a couple of bad land investments had seen to that, and Cellia left him in search of more fertile ground. In the end he hardly blamed her. One thing the years had taught him was the importance women placed on security. Even though he'd never put much stock in it himself, he did understand and even appreciate the perspective. So after the land deals and Cellia's departure, he'd returned to New York, the why of which he was still trying to sort out, some ten years after the fact. He was beginning to suspect there might be some S&M underpinnings in his thought processes.

On his desk the security alarm chimed, and he listened to the clearance numbers being punched in. Good, he thought, breaking away from his window reverie, at least the Dane was on time. Maybe Bates would show up soon, and they could get some work done.

• • •

The two bail jumpers they'd taken down had been fairly cooperative. One of them—a car thief who pushed his luck a little too far—seemed almost glad when they led him out the door of the rundown brick tenement on the Lower East Side. The perp's wife, a gigantic woman of obvious ill temper, cursed the poor bastard mercilessly.

"You fucking asshole!" she screamed, swinging away at the guy, while he was handcuffed, even as the Dane made a halfhearted effort to restrain her. "Look what you've done to us now!" The three-room apartment had been overrun with small children of all ages. "Your stealin' and whorin' have brought the wrath of God down on your head! And now we all got to suffer for your sins! What have you got to say for yourself, asshole?"

The perp had nothing to say, and all but led the charge down the front steps. York, who hardly considered himself to be the wrath of God, promised to send a social worker over in the morning, but it did little to quell the woman's anger at her husband, who York thought had probably been jacking cars just to keep groceries on the table for his wife and their brood. There was, in his mind, room for a certain amount of sympathy for the Robin Hood mentality some out-of-work folks used these days to justify their crimes. There wasn't, from York's point of view, a whole lot of difference between some of the nonviolent break-and-enter perps and the Wall Street stock hustlers who preyed on old ladies and their pension money. Although he had never had a hunting contract on anyone who stole from behind a desk, wearing a suit and tie.

"You all right back there?" York turned and asked the perp, a middle-aged black man with sad, hollow eyes and a tough-guy sneer that carried all the weight of a gum ball.

The perp nodded and went back to glaring out the window.

"You guys should find some respectable work to do," the guy finally mumbled, as if that had been all he was thinking about, staring out at the snowy, dim-lit streets.

The Dane, short-tempered tonight, looked as if he was

about to tell the perp to keep his opinions to himself. But York laughed, nodding his head in appreciation at the remark.

"Sometimes it's respectable," York said.

"Not tonight," the perp replied sullenly.

York was forced to agree. Two minor-league bail jumpers hardly paid expenses. The Dane yawned.

York sighed, thinking about how much he needed a vacation. He didn't give a damn what else happened. He was flying to the Keys in the morning.

Arnie Watts drove around for hours, alternating between talking to the girl and ignoring her. He drove up to Westchester, then round the horn, back over the T.Z. Bridge. There was an element of risk, driving around with her in the back. Especially since it had started to snow a couple hours ago. You never knew when some clown was suddenly going to decide to crunch your fender, or if you were going to miss a stop sign at an unfamiliar intersection. The cops were always around, lurking, but there was a panel he could close behind the driver's seat. Besides, the adrenaline fix, the danger element, was an exciting part of the game. Not the best part of the game—that was still to come—but the fact that you could get caught surely did heighten your senses.

Arnie's stomach grumbled, and he knew the girl, who had been strapped down in back of the van all day, would also be mighty hungry by now. That was one of the reasons for all the driving around in the early hours after a hunt. You had to wait until the prey's hunger overcame their fear. It also gave them time to get used to the way things were. That was important, too. Give them time to fight the restraints, to cry and curse you, which they always did in the beginning. Then you could park some place quiet and go back to talk with them in a reasonable manner. Sometimes you could even make friends with them, which always made things easier. The truth was, kids were a lot better than adults in that regard. They adjusted to reality quicker, were quicker to trust, and quicker to give into the inevitable. Arnie liked that about kids—it was easy for them to learn the rules of the game. And he always made it a point to make things easier for those who learned the rules of the game.

"You hungry?" he asked, pulling over after what he determined was a reasonable amount of time. They were off on a back road in the lower Catskills. It was still snowing, and if anybody stopped to ask, Arnie had a can of antifreeze ready to top off the radiator. Everyone believed in car trouble. The girl looked up at him and nodded, even as she tried to sink back into the confines of the chair. Arnie took that as a good sign.

"You like McDonald's?" he asked, being sure to smile. Again she nodded. "OK, then, why don't we stop and get something to eat. Would you like that?" No nod this time, so he repeated the question more firmly. "*Would you like that?*"

Tears leaked out of the corners of her eyes, but she nodded this time.

"Good girl," Arnie said, patting her head kindly. Of course she tried to squirm away, but that didn't stop him from marveling at the silky softness of her hair. And the way the tears made her dark eyes glow. Yes, this was a good one, he thought.

"You don't have to be afraid," he said softly. "I won't hurt you. . . ."

It was a lie which neither of them believed, but a lie which was important for the girl to pretend to believe. He looked down at her and made his voice sound sad, yet convincing.

"As God is my witness, I don't want to hurt you. And I won't, if you do exactly as I say."

She stared up at him, the shock of being taken leaping from her eyes. He could almost see it, like lightning flashing in her brain. Sometimes at this point in the game they fainted, or began struggling so hard they hurt themselves. But this one seemed strong. That was good, too. The strong ones were always the best.

"I want you to listen to me carefully," Arnie said, sitting down across from the girl, sounding serious and authoritative. It was, after all, a matter of extreme importance for them to know who was in charge. "I want to take the gag off your mouth. . . ."

Her eyes were suddenly alert, not dull and glazed like some. That was very good. She was paying attention. A most excellent sign.

"I want to take off the gag so you can eat," Arnie continued. "But if you scream, if you make any sound, I'll have to put it back on. And I'll have to make it tighter than it is now. I don't want to, but I will. Do you understand?" A nod, the eyes not moving from his face. Very good. "OK, I'm going to take it off now, and you're not going to make a sound. Understand?"

He reached behind her and gently untied the strip of cloth, folding it up in front of her, stuffing it into the pocket of his jacket. Out of sight, out of mind. The game being played according to precise rules.

"Is that better?" he asked. And she nodded again, swallowing, but not making a single sound. Yes, this was indeed a good one. She had passed the first test with flying colors. "How about a drink of water? You must be thirsty. You can talk if you want."

"Yes," she croaked, her voice dry and raspy. "I'm very thirsty."

That was, of course, another part of the game. Even if she tried to scream, her voice would have been a muted, dried-out whisper. But this one learned the rules quickly. He rewarded her with a long drink from his water bottle, squeezing the water into her mouth until it ran down the front of her coat. Arnie then made a gracious show of wiping the excess away, being careful not to press too hard. This was the time of trust-building. A critical part of their developing relationship. But, as Arnie knew well, trust is always a function of trial and error.

"All right, we're in the McDonald's parking lot right now, and I'm going to drive up to the window and order us some food. But you have to be very quiet. Bad things will happen to you if you're not real quiet." He studied her closely to see if she understood, and to try and judge if she would behave. "OK, I'll be back in a couple minutes with some burgers and sodas, and we'll have a little picnic. Would you like that?''

The girl bobbed her head and Arnie smiled, moving to the front of the van, closing the hatchway behind him. They were, of course, nowhere near a McDonald's, or any other place where the girl could be heard if she decided to break the rules and scream for help. They were at the far end of a deserted mall parking lot, the stores empty and bankrupt, the lot filling with snow. But the girl didn't know that.

—Warning! Warning! This is a test of the early-warning system. In the event of a disaster . . .

Of course, the girl didn't know it was a test, either. And she surely didn't suspect how much she had riding on the outcome. Arnie put the van in gear and drove it in a circle around the empty lot. He stopped and loudly ordered food into the empty air. The girl didn't make a sound. Arnie grinned at his luck. He could really pick the good ones! He almost bet that he could get away without gagging her again when they found a real burger joint. But that was a senseless gamble. So, despite the fact that she jerked her head around real good, he got the gag back on and drove around looking for the Golden Arches. After he'd gotten their food, Arnie laced the girl's quarter pounder with a ground-up tab of Demerol, and she gobbled it down in seconds, never noticing the sleep-inducing seasoning. Another reason for the long drive—if they were really hungry, his prey never did notice the spiked food. Arnie had even tried one himself, just to make sure nobody was going to get sick from the Dem because of some hidden, secret ingredient the Micky D people slipped into their fat patties.

It would be pretty stupid, Arnie thought, to go through all the trouble and danger of the hunt just to poison your prey in the back of the van.

He parked the van outside his building, then went into the back, where the girl was sleeping, strapped into the seat. She would sleep for a couple more hours, then be groggy for another hour or so after. Plenty of time to get situated in the apartment and move the van a few blocks away. But there wasn't a lot of time to waste. He got the big army duffel bag out of its storage compartment. It was four and a half feet long, and deep enough to hold the girl comfortably. He'd re-inforced the bottom of the bag with a thin sheet of laminated plastic, thick enough to support a body inside the duffle with-out having it sag in the middle, yet thin enough not to add much extra weight. The girl went seventy-five to eighty pounds, he guessed, lifting her dead weight out of the van's seat, laying her in the canvas bag, then zipping it up. It was the size of a large laundry sack, and Arnie had made a point to haul his dirty clothes to the coin laundry in it, so anyone who might be watching had seen him carrying the bag before. He'd even spilled his clothes once, when the people upstairs had been sitting out on the stoop, enjoying a warm fall eve-ning. They'd laughed at him, of course, but he took their kid-ding good-naturedly and had even brought a few beers out to them afterward, to show there were no hard feelings. It was all part of the game—fitting in, creating the necessary illu-sions and diversions.

So now, as he carried the duffel out of the van and into the building, anyone looking out their windows on this snowy night would think he was just doing his laundry, even though it was a shitty night for it, snow piling up and the wind blowing stiffly through the canyons of the city.

As he knew it would, the storm worked to his advantage, keeping the other residents along the street inside their rat-hole apartments, no doubt sitting numbly beside the glow of their television sets, pretending their lives weren't dull and miserable and devoid of almost all excitement. But that was the way of things—they were part of the herd, while he was a hunter.

Once inside, he double-locked the door, made sure the shades were drawn, and unzipped the duffel bag, carefully lifting the girl out, laying her on the bed. Damn, but she was pretty, he marveled. Young and unspoiled. Her eyes closed softly in sleep. He would probably be back long be-fore she woke, but again there was no sense taking any chances. He got the other set of leather straps from the dresser and tied her, spreadeagled, securely to the bed posts.

He thought for a moment about starting the next phase of the game right away, but knew it would be an unnecessary indulgence. There was plenty of time . . . plenty of time.

He opened her mouth and tied the gag around the back of her head. Then, before leaving, he turned the radio on, just loud enough to drown out any noise, in case she somehow managed to spit the gag out. That had never happened in all his hunting excursions, but Arnie Watts was careful to follow all the rules. It was especially important now as he looked at the girl lying on the bed and his heart started to beat like a drum in his chest, and the first, faint stirring of arousal moved below his belt. Looking down at the girl, so young, so vulnerable, he knew he could jerk off now . . . but that was also an unnecessary indulgence. Patience, that was the key. He checked the girl's restraints and went out into the cold to move the van.

On the way back, trudging through the snow, he stopped to pick up a pizza from Sal's, along with a six-pack of beer and a couple of sodas for the girl. She was probably too young to have developed a taste for beer, and he wanted her to be happy. It was snowing hard now, the radio saying how the storm was deepening. Arnie knew they would be spending a lot of time together over the next few days. Yes, he liked the girl already. And he wanted her to be happy.

A couple of hours later Yvonne stirred. She moaned softly, coming awake, pulling at the restraints that tied her to the bed, as her eyes fluttered opened. Arnie Watts sat across from her, watching for one of his favorite times—that telltale moment when the prey realized all this was not some sort of terrible dream. And yes! There it was! Oh, and it was a good one! That instant of fear, of cold, sharp terror as she looked wildly around the room. As her eyes fell on him. As the realization of what had happened caused her small body to shake like a wet dog.

"Hello, Yvonne," Arnie said quietly, having gotten her name from the school ID in her purse. "Did you have a nice sleep?"

The cat stretched to its full eight-foot length and felt the muscles ripple along its flank. The cave smelled of marking urine and carrion; familiar, warm scents to the beast, causing it to rattle its vocal cords in a growling purr. Outside the cave, dusk was settling across the valley below. Shadows creeping out from under the rocks and the thick trunks of conifer trees. The river shimmered with black light in the twilight. Soon the triple moons would rise and animals would come to the water to drink. He would take one of the soft-bellied deer tonight, he knew. It was the time of their rut, the scent of the does' heat riding the air currents in dripping waves. When this season came, the deer were less wary, their nostrils filled with the call to mate. And in this season the cat took a deer almost every night.

The smell of their musk brought the taste of blood into the cat's mouth. He licked the saliva off his lips with a rough, red tongue, stretching his jaw muscles with a twist of his powerful head. His teeth, two inches long and serrated, were offset in his mouth, forming a bristling array of sharp knives, which held the prey securely, no matter how much it struggled. The claws in each of his eight toes could extend half a foot, to disembowel whatever animal happened to cross his path. The cat was also equipped with night vision in its two sets of eyes, as well as sonar capability originating in the fatty bubble in front of his brain. He could smell blood for miles and hear branches breaking from across the valley. At close to three hundred pounds the cat was, by far, the dominant predator on this particular world, which rotated slowly around an unnamed red sun in the shadow of the Crab Nebula.

Twilight drifted into darkness, giving the cat a further advantage. His black-and-gray coloring matched the shadowy world of the triple moons, allowing him to approach his prey virtually unseen. As he watched from the entrance of the cave, the moons rose. One after another, like flowers opening their round faces in the star-strewn sky. Carefully, with the inbred instincts of a natural hunter, the cat emerged from his lair.

The wind brought a myriad of smells. The rutting musk of the deer, the earthy scent of nocturnal rodents scattering before him, the fishlike smell of water birds roosting along the cliffs above the river. And the smoky, fiery stench of the bipeds, camped at the far end of the valley. The bipeds, who also took the soft-bellied deer during the rutting season. The cat twisted his head, sending out clicking sonar waves, listening as they returned, giving him the lay of the land and the placement of all nearby creatures. The bipeds, who tasted of fish and smoke when he took them as prey, were not in the area. The cat gave them a wide birth, unless he was truly hungry. They had no claws, were not particularly fast, and their teeth were dull. But they had sharpened sticks that could pierce his hide, and they carried fire that could disrupt his senses. He did not fear them, and if they invaded his hunting territory he would stalk them. But they ran in packs generally and could be a nuisance.

The cat prayed to his god, the first of the triple moons, to curse them. He also kept a pile of their skulls by an altar in his cave. The bipeds were, he thought, inordinately evil creatures. They worshipped the sun and rutted with their females even when they were not in season. They also killed more of the deer than they could eat, hoarding the meat against others of their kind. And their fires often blew out of control, blackening huge areas of earth. He wondered, sometimes, at the wisdom of the gods, that such a creature should be created. They were, he thought, as useless as flies.

s i x

The phone rang and York stabbed at it angrily, furious at the incessant ringing that interrupted his dreamless sleep. It wasn't often he enjoyed the luxury of dreamless sleep, and it pissed him off to no end when some fool interrupted it. Particularly when he was on vacation.

"Yes?" he snapped into the receiver, prepared to royally ream out the desk clerk, who had obviously rung up the wrong room with a wake-up call. The clock near the phone announced that it was 8:30 A.M. An ungodly hour to be jerked awake when one was on vacation, as he planned to tell the desk clerk in no uncertain terms. He was quite surprised to hear Jenny's voice on the other end of the line.

"Dennison?" she asked, the phone crackling with bad connection vibes.

"Yeah, it's me," he said loudly, shaking himself awake, swinging his legs over the edge of the bed. "Speak up, we've got a bad connection."

It was a continual source of annoyance to him that some government bureaucrats had decided to allow the breakup of the best phone service in the world in order to appease the Gods of Commerce.

"I just got a call I thought you should know about," Jenny said, her voice sounding apologetic, even through the static.

"Jesus, Jenny, can't the Dane and Ronnie take it?" York

heard himself complaining. He hated to whine, but three days away from the madness of his office was not nearly enough. "It's only Wednesday," he complained, even though he knew Jenny wouldn't bother him unless it was something out of the ordinary.

"It's kind of important, I think," she said, confirming his suspicions.

"OK, that's all right. You know how I am in the morning," he apologized, scrambling around the tiny nightstand for something to write on.

"Have you heard about the Stafford kidnapping?" Jenny asked. "It broke here yesterday morning. I just got off the phone with her parents a couple minutes ago."

"Kidnapping?" York was trying to clear his head. "No, I pulled the plug on any news when my plane took off. How bad is it? Give me the details. . . ."

Then he found himself on the 2:30 flight back to New York, watching regretfully as the jet banked over an array of sand beaches on which other people, who led normal lives, lay in the sun and splashed in the blue-green waves. Unable to help himself, York envied their lives of quiet illusion. Normal people, he knew, have no idea about the kind of world they live in.

Dennison York, however, knew all too well. As the plane climbed and leveled out, the seat belt light went off, and the flight attendant came by offering headsets for the movie, beverages and food. York ordered a scotch and some ice cubes. He looked out the window at the clouds and the sky, knowing the kind of situation he was flying home to, and he couldn't help but think about how he had come to be in the vigilante business in the first place. It was, in fact, the reason behind the breakup of his first marriage, and the reason behind Sandy's descent into a mental state that caused her to wrap herself in a metal coffin around a bridge abutment. It was also, he knew bitterly, the one time in his life he had failed, utterly and completely. Failed as a man, as a husband and father—and even as a human being. And in the years after, he had failed again, unable to protect Sandy from the demons that ate away at her, until there was nothing left of her, except an empty husk out of which all the emotion, all the life, had been drained. He had failed, even, to protect the thing most important to them in all the world—their son.

Billy York had been nine years old when it happened. Dennison himself had been thirty-two, working crazy hours as a homicide detective in the LA Police Department. Sandy had gone back to school, to be a lawyer, no less. A vocation York considered both disreputable and vile. Lawyers have ruined the country, he argued. Sandy, smiling, agreed whole-heartedly. And, of course, in the end she had made him see her point—that the profession could use some honesty and integrity. What better way to change the system than to work inside it? As usual her argument was convincing and rational. She would, he suspected, make an extraordinary lawyer. In a way, it was a logical progression.

They'd been radicals together in the late eighties. Sandy at the forefront of the antinuclear movement. Really, how stupid was it to build reactors along one of the world's major fault lines? She'd been involved in abortion and civil rights, even as he'd slipped away to the edges of conformity, graduating from UCLA, joining the police force, holding down a job, making a living. Growing up, his father had told him, facing up to the realities of family and responsibility. That he had followed in his old man's footsteps helped to mend some of the fences between them. Then Billy came along, and Sandy turned her energies to the PTA and the school board. A few years later, when they'd become somewhat settled, she made the decision to continue her own interrupted education. York supported her, of course, never truly believing that she was the type of person to sit at home and bake cookies. They'd hired a person to watch Billy when he came home from school, to straighten up the house a little and cook supper; an older Latino woman, who'd raised a passel of kids of her own, and who made the best chili York ever tasted. Maxine was her name, and she and Billy had bonded almost instantly. Maxine took him to the zoo and to the park after school, and even had one of her nephews teach Billy the finer points of soccer.

And then one day . . . one day the whole world changed. It was as simple as that. One day the sun came up like it had done every day previously. Only it didn't set on the same world, and it never again rose for Dennison York in the same way. Even now, looking at it from the expanse of a decade and more, looking at the white clouds holding up the plane like some strange ocean waves, with the taste of J&B sharp against the back of his mouth, with a bad cop movie playing silently on the screen in front of him—with all those little grab-bag pieces of reality he used to distract himself. Even now, the thought of what had happened that warm spring day in LA, the merest touch of it brushing his mind, hit his chest with all the force of an eighteen-wheeler plowing into him. The memory of it, burning his eyes, forcing his mouth open in an audible gasp . . .

"You all right, fellow?" the guy next to him asked, looking up from his laptop, clearly afraid that York was going to lose his lunch all over the computer.

"Yeah, I'm fine," York mumbled, the memory of That Day, and the days that followed, washing over him like an acid bath . . .

"You all right?" the cop had asked, reaching for York's arm as they stood behind the glass cage at the city morgue. That time York had been unable to reply.

The attendant behind the glass had just covered Billy's face with a sheet. His son, pale and unmoving, wrapped in white sheets, eyes closed as though he were sleeping. His son, in the wrong place at the wrong time. Dead. Caught in the middle of a gang shooting. Struck by a stray bullet. Killed instantly. Dead. Dead.

And even though he had seen countless other bodies in his line of work, York's legs had somehow forgotten what it was they were supposed to do. He stumbled and the cop caught his arm and sat him down in a nearby chair as the attendant closed the curtain. York heard the gurney being rolled away, wheels squeaking.

"I'm really sorry," the cop said, sounding as though he really meant it, as though this wasn't something he said every time he was forced to escort a relative to identify

another victim of the senseless violence that had emerged
like a terrible plague on the city's streets.

"My god," York whispered, holding his head, unable to
stop the tears.

Then the cop was gone, and detectives from his squad
led him back upstairs. Only he wasn't one of them this
time—he was from the other side, a victim. A tragedy, they
said, trying to comfort him. A real fucking tragedy. But they
had the guys who did it. We got 'em, York, they said, and
they're taking a long fall. Maxine, they assured him, could
identify the gunmen. York nodded, the numbness fading
into a cold rage that burned his heart like frozen pokers
stuck through his ribs.

"They killed my boy," he said miserably. "They killed
my boy. . . ."

And nothing could change that. Nothing, forever and
ever, until the end of time. Naturally, they wouldn't let him
see the suspects, and it was strongly suggested that he take
some time off. So he left the station house, a cruiser giving
him a ride to the hospital, where their family doctor had
placed Sandy when she couldn't stop screaming after York
had told her what had happened. He went up to her room
and cried alone, holding his wife's sedated body.

That should have been the worst of it, but it wasn't. Sandy
ate sedatives like they were candy, alternating between
deadened sleep and bouts of uncontrolled crying. She could
not even attend the funeral, in which his boy was put into
the ground like so much trash in a landfill. Buried, York
thought, soon to be forgotten amid the unending pile of
names taken by this plague that visited itself upon America.

And so York sat next to his housekeeper Maxine at the
service. Maxine, who kept apologizing—apologizing for
something that was not her fault, but which also ate away
at her own heart. He could see it in her eyes—the scene
replaying again and again in her mind. This poor, devastated
woman, whose only fault was that she had taken Billy to
the park so he could play with his friends. This memory,
this abomination, York knew, would haunt them all, for all
the days of their lives. And it was, as he comforted Maxine,

that he came to the conclusion he would not let this act go unpunished. The rage in his heart turned from ice to fire, and back to ice again. Revenge. He would have revenge for this outrage, if it was the last thing he ever did. In the end, it almost was.

The killers were both fifteen years old. Too young to be tried as adults, yet somehow old enough to be carrying semi-automatic weapons around on the streets near a park where children played. He had been there at the arraignment, to look into their eyes, to see their faces. And he saw that their eyes were cold, their faces set in gang-banger sneers.

And York, who had seen it all before, knew the drill.

"They'll be tried as juveniles," the DA had said, tiredly, when York went to him, demanding justice. "As you know, Detective York, once convicted, they'll be sent to JV detention until they're twenty-one."

"And then?" York growled, already knowing the answer.

"And then they'll be turned over to the probation department," the DA replied, shaking his head as if he played no part in this injustice. "It's the law, Detective. You know it as well as I do."

"The law is useless," York said, feeling the cold burning in his stomach. "My boy is dead."

"I know," the DA said, as if he didn't know that at all.

York had gotten terribly drunk that night, hoping to erase the demons now running rampant in his mind. Pictures of his son, lying cold and lifeless under the dark earth. Pictures of the man Billy might have been, except for the animals who had taken his life as easily as one might step on an ant. It was at the beginning of his second bottle, with his wife filled with chemicals in the upstairs bedroom, that York devised the plan that led to his final failure as a man, as a husband, and as a human being. It was a thing that shamed him during all the years to follow, but a thing, he had long since decided, that he would do again . . . and again and again.

So he had gone to Maxine a week before the trial was to begin. Maxine, who was to sit in the courtroom and identify the killers, so they might spend a few, brief years in some dormitory cage. Maxine, whose grief weighed upon her thin shoulders like Christ's cross. Maxine, whose fear of testifying against the gang members was only slightly less than her sense of duty to her murdered charge. And he convinced her not to do it. To change her testimony and say that she couldn't actually be sure those were the two monsters who had entered the park that afternoon, firing so indiscriminately, so senselessly, that they had taken the life of someone they had never met, someone they had no idea even existed. Now, because of what they had done, that person truly did not exist. Except in York's tormented mind.

She had stared at him across the short expanse of her kitchen table. An old woman, made even older by the weight of this unfair burden, her kitchen walls covered with pictures of Jesus and the Virgin Mary, her fingers clutching a tiny silver cross. She looked into York's eyes, and something inside him sensed that she knew his plan. That she knew the extent of his own inhumanity. But the demons were loose in York's mind. The cold fires of revenge burned in his heart, and he prevailed. Maxine, in her fear and confusion, agreed not to testify against the killers.

"God forgive me," she said, crying, even as York left her alone with her grief.

Of course, the detectives working the case were outraged, as well as the DA, when their principal witness suddenly couldn't remember what she had seen. Their instincts led them to York. But proving his manipulation was another matter.

Yes, Maxine told them. Mr. York had been to visit, but she couldn't remember what they talked about. And she was sorry, but she just wasn't sure who was in the park that day.

It was the first time, but not the last, that law enforcement officials vented their anger and frustration at him. The worst offense, in their minds, was that he was one of them.

"She's just not sure," he'd said, coldly, when they confronted him. "You wouldn't want to convict innocent people, would you?"

"You can't take the law into your own hands," they had

droned on and on and on. But in the end York had the last word.

"There is no law," he said, turning in his badge and his gun. "And there is no justice. Not here, not now."

So the gang-bangers had been set free, with all the TV cameras in LA covering their release. There was talk of injustice, but York knew better. He took a job in a real estate office and waited, as weeks and months passed. The killing of his son was forgotten, pushed aside by other, more recent violent deaths. Forgotten, except by York and his wife. He watched, with increasing horror, as she slipped away from him, falling into a terrible abyss of grief from which he knew she would find no escape. Then one day, months later, on a business trip out West, he purchased a twelve-gauge pump at a gun show under an assumed name, with a driver's license bought on the same streets the gang-bangers owned in LA. He'd taken the gun home in the trunk of his car, carried it wrapped in plastic garbage bags into the basement. There he sawed down the barrel and stock, until he could hide it under his jacket—and then he had gone hunting for the first time.

He was careful, having studied the pictures of his son's killers as he worked in the basement, cutting down the gun. And he remembered with almost perfect clarity the night he'd found them, sitting on a porch stoop, drinking beer from a paper bag. Laughing and smoking cigarettes. He remembered thinking: They were laughing while the body of his son was buried under a pile of cold, damp earth. The gun had exploded in his hands, even as their bodies exploded. They had been, at the time, sixteen years old, and he left them, tattered husks that had once been human beings, their blood splattered against the porch steps.

The gun, thrown off a bridge out in the canyons, along with the gloves and coat he had been wearing. The basement, long since cleared of any incriminating evidence. He drove home to shower and await the police. It was two days before anyone made the connection, and when they came to arrest him, he went quietly, not saying a word. There had been a trial, but with a lawyer hired with the last of his savings, and without any solid evidence, eventually he was freed. His name, of course, had been dragged through the papers, but surprisingly, when the stories ran, he had become something of a media hero, and so in the wake of the groundbreaking Vigilante Laws being passed, his new career was launched. Sandy had long since left him, and having nowhere better to go, he made his way to New York, where his particular talents were in constant demand. Within a year of his departure from LA, Sandy drove her car into the bridge pilings. He told himself it would have happened anyway, whether he was there or not.

"You sure you're all right?" the man next to him asked again.

York nodded. Eventually the seat belt light flashed overhead, and the plane banked on its descent into JFK.

The blue sun was setting behind a bank of bright red clouds, like a swath of blood spilled across the sky. A lone figure, a scale-plated male of reptilian ancestry, looked down into the valley at the twisted remains of his ship. It had been, at one time, a cargo vessel. Its function had been to shuttle ore from the outer planets to the Home World. The Home World, he decided, was the bright star that rose in the western sky between the twin moons of this uncharted planet on which he was now marooned. Translucent lids dropped over his flat eyes, filtering the sunlight. His long tongue slipped out between his lips in an instinctive reflex action, testing the air for unfamiliar sounds or scents. There was never much of either on this bleak world.

The mistake had been made, he concluded, when the former cargo vessel was converted to a ship of war. The procedure itself had involved fitting the vessel with a jury-rigged innerstellar drive and mounting laser weapons in the fore and aft cargo sections. The job had been done, as was now obvious, in a rather haphazard manner by government engineers at the beginning of the hostilities between the Home World and the filament beings of the yellow star, Annulias, some dozen light-years from the

Candle Stream. It had been a foolish war right from the beginning, as most were. The filament beings were so different from his own species that the two races had virtually nothing in common. They did not compete for resources or for planets. Indeed, they could not breathe the same air or eat the same foods, and could only communicate using digital translators programmed to configure a widely varying numerical system, which computers from both sides seemed to understand.

The war itself, he now understood, was an economic ploy by the Home World government—a misguided, deranged effort to bolster support for a space-based defense system. The war had begun after a long, involved media campaign by the military, playing on the public's innate fear of the filament creatures. It was unquestionably a campaign of racial hatred directed at what the military perceived as a "soft target." This was a tactic the military commanders of his nation had used many times among his own people with great success. The use of contrived war had, in fact, propelled his country into dominance on the Home World. It was inevitable, he supposed, that the military planners would use these same tactics on alien races when they were encountered, and predictably they had done so. He now saw that the campaign had begun almost as soon as first contact had been made with the filament creatures, following a faithful meeting of star vessels in the Candle Stream. It was a subtle thing at first, focusing on the filament creatures' nonreptilian appearance, specifically the fact that they resembled larger versions of the jellyfish found in the primeval seas of M-3. The media also never failed to mention the creatures' odd sexual practices, and the fact that they seemed only vaguely interested in the Glorious Empire of the Home World.

Surely contact with another sediment race must have been as surprising for them as it was for us, he mused, looking down at the wide furrow his ship had made in the tangled vegetation of this deserted world. Sediment races were a rarity—like gold or fossilized mammal eggs—and so should be treated with the respect accorded to precious things. The gods, he knew well, do not appreciate the destruction of precious things.

He came every evening to sit on this outcrop of rock, to stare down into the valley, where the remnants of his ship rusted into the earth, and the bodies of his crewmates, buried under tons of twisted wreckage, gave up their flesh to the pale slugs which burrowed in the dark soil and seemed to be the only form of life here. His rations long since exhausted, he now spent most of his long days digging in the damp ground, gathering piles of the slugs, on which he now subsisted. It was, to say the least, a meager existence. The fact of his continued existence was one of the things he had the most difficulty coming to terms with. Why? he asked himself a hundred times a day, a thousand times a month, ten thousand times a year—why had he survived, when all the others had died? All the others. Each and every one of his species . . . all dead. With only him left alive, on this godforsaken place, at the edge of nowhere. It was a thing he could never understand, not in all the long years he had spent marooned here. Not in all the lonely nights, staring sleepless up at the stars. Not in all the empty days, digging in the ground for the miserable food that kept him alive. His shipmates, they had been the lucky ones, crushed to death on that long ago day when the ship had shrieked through the atmosphere, slamming into the earth, digging its own grave in the empty valley below.

Yes, the media campaign had been subtle at first, but it had quickly gained momentum, feeding on fear, until everyone on the Home World hated the aliens, and had become convinced that an attack by them was both inevitable and imminent. Of course, as events unfolded, it became obvious that this was a complete, fabricated lie. But somehow the people had been convinced. Even he himself had been convinced. He now wondered if running subversive media campaigns had been taught at the highest levels of military command school. It was a question that would forever remain unanswered, for the simple reason that there was no one left to whom he could present the question.

The war itself had been an unmitigated disaster right from the start. It quickly became obvious that the filament beings were not a "soft target." In truth, they could have destroyed the Home World whenever they wished to do so, as they possessed technology the military commanders had never even imagined. Their response to being attacked by the pitiful ships of the Home World had been simple and devastating. They had merely sent shielded drone vessels into the sun around which his planet orbited, disrupting it to an extent that it had gone nova in a matter of days. Exploding in a massive outpouring of energy that had turned the Home World and all the outer planets into clouds of incandescent gas. The filament creatures had then hunted down each and every star vessel that had managed to escape the destruction. And they had done so as easily as one might pick up a slug, roll it onto a stick, and cook it over a fire. It had been that simple. That quick. That efficient.

So now he came every night to sit on the stone ledge, to stare into the valley, and to ask his questions to the stars. There was never any response. When he cried, which was often, his sobs were heard by no other living creature in all the universe.

⟨◈⟩ REFLECTIONS ON THE SECONDARY ASPECTS OF THE EXPERIMENT

As was previously noted, the technological advances gained by the implantation of the spiritual entities caused a dramatic increase in the population of the mechanisms. The scarcity of entities to be implanted resulted in an unforeseen problem—that the vast numbers of mechanisms surpassed the availability of desirable entities. Thus it became necessary to allow a number of mechanisms to be released into the population without spiritual entities. It was assumed that these mechanisms would merely serve as a control population, and that being at such a severe disadvantage without an implanted spiritual entity, they would simply live out abbreviated lives within the general populace.

For the most part, this proved to be the case. However, there are a certain small percentage of these mechanisms who seem to be operating and adapting on an instinctual level to the society created by the implanted mechanisms. These mechanisms, unfortunately, seem to be functioning on a predatory level, which was common to the developing species prior to the implantation experiment. They are not, as was expected, easily identifiable within the general population. The instinctual cunning and violent nature of these individuals, coming as it does from the species' primitive past, is exhibiting itself in a number of disturbing ways. It was thought that these individuals would fall under the control of the more sophisticated members of the society, namely the implanted mechanisms. This, unfortunately, does not always appear to be the case. In certain scenarios, it is possible for the unimplanted mechanisms to achieve control and domination over their implanted brethren. The reasons behind this aberration are not entirely clear at the present time. The assumption must be that a certain low percentage of the unimplanted mechanisms are inheriting, possibly through genetic transfer, cogent intelligence which allows them to function at a high level of ability despite the fact that they have no spiritual entity implanted. The results of this malfunction fall into three distinct categories:

1) The unimplanted mechanisms function within the society with no restraints or morality.

2) They are operating at high levels of intelligence, yet without the accompanying rational and emotional mental facilities gained by the implantation of the spiritual entities.

3) A number of undeveloped mechanisms, even those with implanted entities, are falling victim to these predatory individuals, who are living within the pe-

rimeters of the structured society, yet are free to act with impunity on the instinctual commands generated by violent primeval memories.

Observation: All power in the physical plane, whether it is of the flesh or of the mind, is illusionary. The transitory nature of the physical plane, the very fact of birth and death, make this an irrefutable fact. It is curious, therefore, that the mechanisms seem to expend so much of their energy grasping for that which is illusionary. It is, perhaps, a function of the termination factor—the seemingly imminent destruction of the physical body—which causes them to react in such an irrational manner. The perceived lack of control over their own life spans seems to drive many of their activities, in some cases actually causing their own early termination, or worse, the early termination of others. Control over other mechanisms appears to allow them to ignore, for short periods anyway, their own mortality. This thought process may well be a sign of basic malfunctions within the mechanisms themselves. It is certainly a malfunction among those who are driven to harm, or even terminate, other mechanisms.

Question: Is the knowledge of physical death such a corrupting agent that rational thought is impossible on the physical plane?

seven

The Dane met York at the airport. They collected his bags and made their way outside, where Bates was involved in an argument with a taxi driver over who was blocking what lane. Bates, of course, was well aware that he was in the wrong, but was playing the argument for time until the Dane reappeared with York. They sped off, just as the outraged cabdriver was going under his front seat for a tire iron, completely unaware that those he was planning to attack were, in fact, armed to the teeth. Not that Bates, who considered himself a conscientious objector in his boss's private criminal war, would ever resort to actual violence.

"Violence," Bates often proclaimed, "is the last bastion of the weak."

York tended to agree, knowing himself to be an inordinately weak man, living in an even weaker world.

"Anything new on the Stafford kid?" York asked, pouring coffee from a thermos Bates somehow always managed to keep full.

"Nothing," Bates replied, weaving the van through the airport traffic. "Jenny's monitoring the police bands, and she's jacked into their computer system, but so far, zip."

York nodded. The Dane was in the back of the van, checking the loads on his weapons, for probably the fiftieth time today, York suspected. Paramilitary training being a most effective form of mind control. But the big man seemed always ready for whatever life or the bad guys might throw at him. Over the years York had become a big fan of the training techniques that drove the Dane to his state of always-readiness.

"What's the time frame?" York asked, directing his question to the backseat. Bates was pretty much useless when it came to things like time frames.

"Girl got snagged sometime early Monday morning," the Dane replied. "Figure between eight-fifteen and eight-forty-five A.M., just after her mother dropped her off at school. So we're about fifty-eight hours in."

"You want to go home or to the office first?" Bates asked. He already knew the answer—in fact, he had drawn out the route to the Stafford apartment in his mind. But he figured it wasn't his place to make the call. Besides, one could never tell how Dennison York's mind worked. Figuring the old boy out was sort of like doing the *New York Times* crossword puzzle blindfolded. Theoretically it was possible, given a few billion tries, but the odds were definitely against it.

"No, let's swing by the station house on Fifty-fourth and pay our detective friends a visit. Maybe they've got something they're not putting over the wire," York said, picking up the van's phone, punching in the office number.

Bates laid on the horn and switched lanes to catch the expressway. In the back the Dane clicked his weapon shut.

"Jenny, you got the prelim paperwork done on this Stafford mess?" York asked, grimacing as Bates nearly caused a multicar pileup. "Good, it's signed? All right, I want you to fax a copy to the duty captain at the Fifty-fourth. Make sure you highlight the info release section, so the bastards will be sure and see it. I'm going to swing by to see if they're keeping anything under wraps. OK, then call the Staffords and tell them I'll be there in an hour or so. Thanks, kid. Talk to you soon."

York lit his first cigarette of the day and in deference to Bates, cracked the side window.

"Fifty-eight hours," he said, mostly to himself. "The asshole could have her anyplace by now."

• • •

Arnie Watts was tired. He hadn't gotten much sleep in the last couple days, and it was starting to catch up with him. It had finally stopped snowing, sometime yesterday, he thought, but time was running strange for him. The game was almost over, and he was starting to feel the letdown that always came after it was finished. The girl was on the cot, curled up in a small ball. Her skinny legs pulled up to her chest, the bones in her spine sticking out like tiny fists. She was not at all appealing. Not at all like the young girls in the magazines. She certainly hadn't turned into the prize catch he'd hoped for in the beginning. He'd been forced to keep her doped up most of the time to keep her from biting and scratching. Plus, she cried all the damn time. The truth was, he'd be glad to get rid of her.

On the bed, Yvonne Stafford moaned. Arnie got up and popped a couple aspirin to clear his head as he tried to plan out the end game.

"So, they brought in the hired guns, did they?" The duty captain scowled as York officially presented his credentials and his written request for the investigation files under the Freedom of Information Act. The captain was in his late fifties, York guessed, his hair graying, although it seemed he kept himself in reasonably good shape. Still, York knew Thomas Cassady was of the old school, as was nearly everyone in the higher echelons of the NYC Police Department. York was well aware of the obvious—Cassady deeply resented this intrusion on his home turf. So, of course, he was going to play games, York saw right away, even though the two of them had been down this road before.

"Just give me what you've got on the Stafford girl," York said tiredly. "We'll be on our way and out of your hair."

"All you're gonna do is fuck up our investigation," the man growled, trying to make his voice sound dangerous.

"Are you close to this guy?" York demanded. "If you got an arrest ticket on him, just say the word and I'll go away. You know the rules as well as I do."

"Yeah, I know the fucking rules!" Cassady snapped, slamming his hand on the desk. Blustering and puffing up, York thought, like a bird protecting its nest. So York knew right away there was no arrest ticket. In all probability he was wasting his time here, because the investigators had turned up nothing.

"I'm just trying to do my job," York said, making a conscious effort to soften his tone, even though he knew the clock was ticking and with each hour that passed the chances of finding the girl diminished. At least the chances of finding her alive. "I'm doing what I'm paid to do, just like you are. We could work together on this, you know."

"The New York City Police Force does not work with hired guns!" Cassady glared. "You have no authority—"

"Goddamnit!" York yelled, losing his composure. Outside in the hallway he saw the Dane get up from his chair and stare into the room. "That girl's been gone over fifty hours now. You know as well as I do what her situation is! And you're sure as hell familiar with my authority! Now, get me a copy of the fucking detective reports, or so help me God, you'll have every lawyer in the city crawling up your ass. And they'll be following my trail. Do we understand each other, Captain?"

"We understand each other!" Cassady spat, watching as the Dane reacted to their shouting by moving toward the door. "Now get out of my office and take your fucking goon with you!"

"As soon as I get the report," York said again, lowering his voice.

Cassady, his face a brilliant apple-red, reached into a desk drawer and threw a folder across the table.

"If you interfere with my people, I'll personally see your license revoked!" Cassady growled.

York picked up the packet and slammed the door on his way out, rattling the glass. It would not have been the first one he'd broken, and the bastards always charged him an arm and a leg when he did. The law was a strange thing, when the people supposedly in charge of it fought the very rules they were protecting. Still, he had sympathy for them—not for assholes like Thomas Cassady, but for the men and women on the street, who were doing the actual dirty work. They had to conform to a mind-boggling mountain of rules and regulations, which in many instances actually kept them from doing their jobs with any degree of efficiency. That was why the Vigilante Laws had been enacted in the first place. The public had gotten so fed up with the violence and crime that permeated their lives, the politicians had actually been forced to do something about it. And in typical fashion, instead of dealing with the real problem—the extended legal bureaucracy and the mountains of rules and regulations—they had gone outside the loop and passed laws issuing hunting licenses to men like Dennison York. It was, perhaps, not the most optimal solution, but at least it was something. In the end it seemed to work. The public was given a bone, an outlet for their anger and frustration, and the politicians were all elected back into their various offices. Meanwhile, York and others like him were free to act in their clients' behalf. Bounty hunters, the media called them. Hired guns, to others. The names meaning nothing to York. To him, it was simply a job, one for which he seemed to have a particular innate talent. It was a job, in most cases. Except in instances like this. Then it became a vocation.

The file was thin, as York suspected it would be. He leafed through it as Bates raced the van toward the Staffords' Park Avenue address. No witnesses, no leads. The girl simply vanished into the air. One of hundreds across the country every year. As if the earth opened up and swallowed her. In the back of his mind, York hoped that hadn't actually happened.

On a world in one of the 100 billion known galaxies in the universe, a blind worm burrows deep in the dry, sandy soil. The worm nudges aside granular bits of arid clay, dirt that has not known the sweet touch of water since the time the first crustaceans crawled along the swampy plains of the planet Earth. The worm feels its way along beneath the surface, probing with microscopic hairs, hoping to find some bit of food on which to feed, or another of its kind with which to mate. The worm has not eaten during the span of time its small brain can contain memory. In fact, it cannot recall the feel of sustenance coursing through its body, or remember the momentary spasm of the mate. But up ahead in the sand it senses movement—an almost infinitesimal vibration, signaling the existence of another living creature. The worm pushes forward, instinct driving it, the sharp, probing hairs expanding in the search. The vibrations become steadier, more localized, and the worm thrusts its segmented body through the sand, breaking finally into the nesting chamber of a fat, colorless grub. The grub, also blind, does not realize the worm is upon it, until it has already been encircled and the digestive acids carried in sacks along the worm's underbelly have been splashed across the grub's body. After a time the flesh of the grub is broken down into a soupy pool of nutrients, and the worm feeds.

Several hundred feet above this life-and-death struggle, unknown to both worm and grub, a tiny point of light rises in the eastern sky, cold and dim upon the frozen surface of the planet. In the purple twilight that passes for day on this world, nothing moves, except for shadows. The shadows, which are themselves only barely definable images in the weak light of the sun, pass through the rusted curves of metal arches, through rubble and broken buildings that once, eons ago, were cities. Cities that were once thriving, lit with the technology of a race of beings whose name and image are now only a forgotten memory—a memory lost in the depths of time. Their civilization, which once spread to the other planets in this solar system, faded and died thousands of centuries before the first Earthling ever looked upon the stars. These worlds, now empty ruins, will never again know the touch of a living creature upon their surface.

It is a place in the universe where even God does not visit. It is a place where the experiment failed.

REFLECTIONS ON THE TERMINATION FACTOR

Other than the desire to reproduce their species, nothing influences the thoughts and actions of the mechanisms as much as the knowledge of their own physical termination. The death of beings on the physical plane is, of course, predetermined by the laws of evolutionary genetics. It is quite impossible for evolution to create a high-level, functioning mechanism from microscopic beginnings without extensive mutation, which in itself necessitates generational procreation. In this way, death is one of the principal building blocks of life on the physical plane. Also, as is increasingly obvious, ecosystems can only support a finite number of organisms, whether they are insect, fish, reptilian, mammal, or any combination thereof. Thus, the passing of generations to make way for evolutionary changes is as desirable as it is necessary. Further, it has been observed that creatures of unusual longevity tend to create static, closed societies, in which the opportunities for learning outside the so-called norm are severely restricted. Conversely, societies in which longevity is at the lower end of the dominant scale, tend to be chaotic and unstable, which also negatively effects the learning experience. And since learning is the principal reason behind any series of life experiments, its advancement must be encouraged.

Even as termination on the physical plane is both desirable and necessary, the mechanisms' obsession and fear of this eventuality, even among those who are implanted with spiritual entities, has become problematic. In many cases the subjects have developed the irrational belief that physical death is, in fact, the end of their existence. This has given rise to a number of religious cults that prey on the subjects' fear, even to the point of promising eternal life to those who follow the specific rules of a particular cult.

This misguided attempt at control of the mechanisms' lives has been entrenched in the developing societies since the time of the first implantations, often with cataclysmic consequences. It would seem, therefore, that the implantations themselves have had a direct causal effect on the rise of these various cults, and that the cults in turn fueled the obsession and fear associated with physical termination. It was thought that the introduction of the spiritual entities into the mechanisms would have had the opposite effect, given the supposed increase in awareness of life beyond the physical plane. This, however, has not been the case. While the increased awareness did cause the mechanisms to contemplate the fact of their existence, the appearance of the religious cults actually inhibited awareness of the spiritual plane.

This has caused innumerable problems, not the least of which is the submersion of the spiritual entities into the physical plane to such an extent that awareness of their true nature has, in many cases, been lost completely. It is another sign of the difficulties the entities have existing within the structure of the physical plane. In fact, it is only after the termination of their physical mechanisms that the entities once again realize the fact of their own immortality.

Conclusion: It now appears almost certain that there is a malfunction in the physical makeup of the mechanisms. They are somehow able to construct a barrier between the physical and spiritual worlds. This barrier prevents the implanted entities from realizing the true nature of their transitory connection to the physical plane. This barrier, reenforced by the cult religions, severely limits the entities in their learning experiences, and thereby hinders the growth process. It is hoped that further evolutionary changes, combined with more intensive training at the preimplantation stage, will eventually overcome this malfunction and lead the entities to a deeper understanding of their true nature as immortal beings, even as they live out their lives on the physical plane. Until that time it seems likely the obsession and fear of death, with the accompanying delusionary behavior this lack of awareness precipitates, will continue.

eight

Lesia Stafford was sick and tired of the Valium the doctor had prescribed to keep her quiet. She was also sick and tired of sleeping, which she had done sixteen of the last twenty-four hours. She was through with being kept in a groggy, half-thinking state, like some wild animal caged up and heading for the zoo. She was determined to wake up and remember, no matter how painful those memories might be. If she could do that, Lesia believed, she might be able to recall some critical detail, some tiny, cast-off bit of information that might help unlock this terrible puzzle of her daughter's disappearance. Even though, in the rational part of her mind, Lesia knew she had been over that morning's events a hundred times and there was nothing—no clue, no hint as to what had happened, much less *why* it had happened.

Along with the drugs, Lesia was sick and tired of feeling miserable and helpless. It was dark outside. She could see the city lights coming in through the slits of the blinds as she curled up, hugging the pillow on her bed, wondering if she had the will to actually get up and do something about the frustrating, powerless sense of oppression that seemed to have taken over her life. Tears came as she realized it was night, and that Yvonne was out there someplace, lost in the dark maze of the city. Oddly enough, she found herself with the strong urge to clean the bathroom and cook something. And perhaps make love to Jim. God, how could she think that way, with Yvonne gone? But all this was a normal reaction, she recalled reading. In times of tragedy, human beings want to revert back to the standard, everyday events in their lives. Normalization, Cosmo called it. And hell, you can't argue with the Bible, Lesia thought, pushing herself out from under the covers, heading for the shower to soak her aching head. Then maybe she'd make up a big pot of spaghetti.

Jim was in the living room when she emerged from the bedroom with a towel wrapped around her head. A familiar-looking detective sat on the couch, leafing through a magazine. Both he and Jim trying not to stare at the telephone on the table in front of them. Jim, clenching his fists, as if he could will the phone to ring. A call from Yvonne, telling them she was all right. Even a ransom demand—then at least they'd have something to work with. This horrible silence, this gray state of not knowing, was stretching everyone's nerves to the breaking point.

"Lesh, honey." Jim finally looked up after she was several steps into the room. He got up and hugged her, a gesture she appreciated. "You holding up?"

"I guess." She nodded, taking his arm as though it were a crutch. "No word?"

"Nothing." Jim shook his head. Of course, she knew that already. If there had been anything, the slightest rumor, he would have told her. "Listen, hon, we've got to talk," he said quietly, leading her over to the couch.

The detective smiled at her. He was a creepy guy, in Lesia's estimation. Young, brush-cut hair, cheap blue suit— the strong, silent type, apparently. She never trusted the strong, silent types. Usually they were that way because they couldn't think of anything bright to say. Like: Hello.

So she sat on the far end of the couch, away from the silent detective. At the moment there were only the three of them in the apartment. Little Jimmy had been shipped up-state to stay with his grandparents. Despite their offers to come down to the city, James had convinced them that the best thing they could do was take Jim Junior into a familiar, calm environment. That surely made sense to Lesia, who longed for such a sanctuary herself. Jim had taken both her hands and was staring at her. Oddly, it was the same look he'd used when he told her how he'd invested all their savings in a surefire stock venture. When had that been? Fifteen years ago? Two thousand dollars they'd gambled, and lost, of course. Today, the tires on their two cars cost almost as much. But Jim was talking to her, and she wasn't paying any attention. Her mind, usually focused and disciplined, seemed to have developed this propensity toward wandering.

"What?" she asked as Jim frowned at her.

"I said, I've hired someone to help us," Jim repeated. "Someone who might be able to find Yvonne. . . ."

Someone who might be able to find Yvonne? That caused her brain to snap awake.

"Who?" she asked, as if that somehow made any difference.

"His name is Dennison York," Jim said, for some reason casting a sideways glance at the detective, who was scowling into his magazine. "He's a professional hunter."

"A hunter?" Lesia was uncertain, wondering if she had heard correctly. "Why do we want a hunter?"

"Les, this man hunts criminals," Jim said quietly.

"Oh," she replied simply, as if this explanation suddenly made perfect sense. Then she went into the kitchen to start her spaghetti sauce.

Ronnie Bates pulled the van into a delivery zone and, unashamed, put a medical emergency sign on the dashboard. York was already out the passenger side and pretended not to notice. Bates stepped up to the sidewalk beside his boss, looking back at the van, as if he suspected something terrible was going to happen to the vehicle in his absence. It was usually his job to wait in the van, monitoring communications, serving as a lookout while York and the Dane went about their clandestine activities. Even though he was only going up to the victim's apartment to check the electronic surveillance the cops had supposedly put in place, this movement represented a change in precedent decidedly counter to the way things usually ran. It was a precedent that, in Bates's mind, moved him one step closer to the firing line. Like dusting Horace Greeley's jacket with magnetic powder while making a coffee run. He'd been careful to complain long and loud about that one, yet here he was, out of the van once again, inching closer to the front line.

"Hope nothing happens to the van," Bates said. They'd left the Dane back in the vicinity of the school, where the girl had disappeared. It was not a particularly good neighborhood, especially at night, but York thought it might be useful to have the Dane poke around, just to see what sort of slugs were squirming about. The Dane had nodded, without comment, seemingly unmindful of the neighborhood's dangerous reputation. And, in truth, Bates thought the Dane considered the danger to be fairly inconsequential. So the Dane was walking a tough inner-city neighborhood, asking prying questions, while he, Bates, was worried about leaving his van and walking into a secured building with a guard at the front desk. Well, Bates reminded himself, like his boss said, a man should know his limitations. And he knew he had more than his share, while other men like the Dane and York seemed to have none. Shaking his head, Ronnie Bates hurried up the steps after his boss.

It was strangely quiet in the Stafford apartment. The mother, Lesia, came out to meet them, but then after a couple of minutes had disappeared back into the kitchen. The detective barely nodded in their direction, which was to be expected, as they were clearly invading his turf. York and the father of the missing girl talked quietly in the corner, while Bates looked over the wiretap on the family phone. It was an efficient system, although fairly low tech. It was always amazing to Bates that one of the largest police forces in the country didn't keep up with the latest technology.

"What's it look like?" York came over to see how the inspection was going, while the girl's father went and got some pieces of recently worn clothing, and other personal effects, from his daughter's room. A downtown lab would later use the clothing to get some skin samples and, along with hair from the girl's brush, work up a scan program using her DNA. York was always preparing for a worse-case scenario.

"It's OK." Bates shrugged, aware that the detective was watching them closely. "Standard stuff. They can trace numbers, of course, and they're feeding into a tape relay to match voice prints and isolate background noise. They'll have to keep the caller on the line for fifteen or twenty seconds to make the trace, though."

York nodded. The cop was up now, standing over them as they inspected the phone.

"I suppose you could do better?" he asked.

"There's always better," Bates said, shrugging his shoulders. The cop gave a short laugh as Jim Stafford returned with the articles York had requested. Stafford heard the conversation and looked concerned.

"Are you saying they're not going to be able to trace the call?" he asked, directing his question toward York.

"No," York said. "Their equipment will do the job. Besides, you're not going to get any ransom calls. Not legitimate ones, anyway."

"What makes you say that?" Stafford asked, suddenly glad Lesia wasn't in the room. Bates noticed the man was staring rather pointedly at the detective, as if such a call had been all but promised.

"It's been too long," York replied, using his best matter-of-fact tone.

"You don't know that!" the cop said, sounding hostile. York ignored him and collected the articles Stafford had brought, zipping it all into an airtight plastic bag.

"But it's still possible, isn't it?" Stafford asked.

"You're damn right it is!" the cop interjected.

"Anything's possible, Mr. Stafford, but I try to deal with probability," York said, shaking his head. "Almost all ransom cases have some kind of contact within the first thirty-six hours. The man who has your daughter, in my opinion, isn't interested in money. I'm sorry."

Jim Stafford sank down into a nearby chair, looking as though someone had just punched him in the stomach.

Meanwhile, the detective looked as though he, too, wanted to punch someone. Namely, Dennison York.

"I can't tell Lesia that," he said miserably.

"And you shouldn't," York said. "Don't upset her any more than she already is."

"And you're sure it's a man?" Stafford asked, realizing even as he said it that he was grasping at straws.

"That's pretty much a certainty," York replied, glancing at the detective. "The police think so, also. They've been running their dumb file since the abduction was reported."

"Their dumb file?" Stafford asked, sounding confused, which he was, and had been since this whole thing had exploded on him, over two days ago now.

"What's a dumb file?" he asked again.

"That's when the police run the names of known perpetrators of a particular crime," York explained, trying to put the best spin on it. In a case like this, there was a fine line between informing a client and destroying all their hope. He thought he was getting close to that line with Stafford, but the man had a right to know what was going on. "In this case, known abductors and sexual offenders, people who have been caught doing this sort of crime. That's why it's called the dumb file. The dumb criminals get caught; most of the time the smart ones don't."

Stafford looked up at them from his chair. His hands were shaking, his eyes were filled with a horrible sadness, and with fear. Ronnie Bates had to look away.

"It's standard procedure for them to do that, Mr. Stafford," York said quickly. "It works, sometimes. There's always the possibility they'll find your daughter by tracing these men."

"And if they don't?" Stafford asked.

"That's why you've contacted us," York said softly. "You've done the right thing, done all you can at the moment. Let the police do their job, and let us do ours. Now, I assume the detectives already asked, but did your daughter keep a diary? Something where she wrote down her day-to-day thoughts? Sometimes those are helpful."

Jim Stafford shook his head. "Just some school papers,

a letter Yvonne started to her grandmother. Her math homework . . . She must have forgotten it that morning. We found it on the kitchen table.''

"Her math homework?" York asked. "I'm sorry to ask, but was this an unusual occurrence? Was she having any trouble in school?"

"None at all," Stafford replied. "She was an exceptional student—straight A's from the third grade. Why in God's name did this happen to her?"

Stafford looked both stunned and bewildered. York had no answer for him. York nodded at Bates, and they picked up their coats.

"We'll be in touch in the morning, unless we have something before then, but I wouldn't count on that," York said, putting his hand on Stafford's shoulder and nodding at the detective, who seemed to grimace at the two of them. "We'll let ourselves out," York said, deciding not to bother Lesia Stafford with any social pleasantries.

Out in the hall York paused by the elevator and took several deep breaths: Bates looked at his boss, suddenly concerned York was having some kind of attack.

"I hate these fucking cases," York whispered after a moment. Every time he dealt with the death of a child, it brought back the memory of his son, lying on a cold slab in the hospital basement. And, in truth, York held out little hope that they would find Yvonne Stafford alive. If they found her at all. But he would still damn well try.

The elevator was rising up through the middle of the building as York stood up and straightened his shoulders.

"Come on, let's go find the Dane," he said. "Maybe he stumbled on something."

In the van York punched in the office number. Jenny, working late, reported no new information. York sent her home to get some sleep, after first asking her to make a note to check with building security at the Stafford apartment building, to make absolutely sure there was no way the little girl could have come home that morning. Perhaps backtracking to pick up her homework? York wondered. Anyway, it was after nine and there was nothing to be gained now by overextending his team. Later, if they got close, they might all be working round-the-clock shifts.

The Dane was waiting for them near the school. He'd circled the surrounding blocks, dropped some seed money on the neighborhood bandits, but had come up empty.

"We'll all go home and get some rest," York concluded, even though it troubled him that he was unable to come up with any alternatives. But it was too soon to go cruising the sleazy bars and nightclubs, where whispers of an abduction might be circulating through the underground community. All of which would happen later, after the perp had dumped the girl. He hoped to God that it didn't come to that.

"Maybe the cops'll catch a break running the dumb list," York said. Bates and the Dane nodded in agreement, although none of them believed it would happen. "I want us all at the school at eight-fifteen tomorrow morning to do a walk-through."

The bathroom door creaked open, throwing a panel of bright light on the stained, ragged carpet. The radio was playing, as it always was, to drown out any unwanted noise. In the darkness of the inner room the bed squeaked.

"Yvonne? Yvonne, honey, are you awake?" Arnie Watts whispered, closing the bathroom door, crawling onto the cot beside her. He was glad she was still warm to his touch.

 REFLECTIONS ON THE DEATH OF INNOCENTS

Throughout the entire course of the experiment, from the very first of the implantations, it was realized that not every implanted entity would have the opportunity to reach physical maturity within its mechanism. Evolutionary factors, in many cases, dictate the premature termination of a mechanism. Genetic errors within the mechanism may cause early termination. Outside factors in the unstable environment of the physical plane may unexpectedly cause the death of an individual mechanism. In the event of these unforeseen circumstances the implanted spiritual entity is retrieved, usually unharmed, sometimes wiser for the experience, sometimes not. In the grand scheme of evolution the termination of a single mechanism is a relatively minor inconvenience. And as no harm comes to the spiritual entity itself, the incident is passed over as an evolutionary misstep.

The territorial nature of the mechanisms, however, often causes the eruption of widespread, wanton violence. This uncontrolled violence, by its very nature, results in the unwanted termination of large numbers of mechanisms before their allotted period of longevity has been reached. These events, while unfortunate and unnecessary, are a result of the deep-seated predatory instincts of the mechanisms themselves. When the experiment was conceived, one of the primary goals was the usurption of these undesirable traits in the makeup of the mechanisms. While this goal is far from being realized, some strides have been made in that direction. The entities themselves, when agreeing to the implantation, are aware of the unstable nature of the developing societies. While the termination of mechanisms under these circumstances is both vile and abhorrent, it is not totally unexpected. As previously noted, the harm to the spiritual entity is negligible, and the trauma of the event is usually felt more grievously by those entities left behind in the physical plane. (Of course, if they were able to come to an awareness about the nature of the relationship between the physical and spiritual planes, there would be little need for the traumatized outpouring of emotion that always accompanies these unfortunate circumstances.)

There is, however, a most disturbing development in the behavior patterns of certain mechanisms. There seems to be a propensity of violent, almost animalistic disregard for the basic instincts of right and wrong in some of the mechanisms. They appear to be perpetrating unspeakable violence upon other members of their society, and not because of the usual territorial or self-preservation instincts prevalent to the species, but merely because of some deep-seated desire to visit harm on other mechanisms. The savagery of these incidents cannot be disregarded, as they have the potential not only to disrupt the integrity of the experiment, but also, by the vicious nature of the attacks, to traumatize the spiritual entity residing in the victimized mechanism. The emergence of this behavioral pattern, which is primarily engaged in by those mechanisms who are not implanted by spiritual entities, has the potential for dire consequences.

Question: Is there indeed a malfunction in the mechanisms, or is some other force at work within the context of the experiment? Are these unimplanted mechanisms somehow being guided to harm vulnerable spiritual entities? The magnitude of this possibility is staggering.

nine

Promptly at eight-fifteen the next morning Ronnie Bates pulled the van up to the front of P.S. 364. Kids were on their way into the school. The majority of them escorted by frightened parents, who knew all too well it was simply a matter of chance that their own children were with them today. They herded together in tiny, close-knit groups. York and the Dane got out, while Bates replayed recordings of the police radio reports of the previous night. Jenny was already in the office, tapping into the cops' computer system to see if anything had come up on the dumb files. A security guard came out from the school to move the van along, but left them alone after the Dane produced their hunting license. The man did, however, extract a promise they wouldn't bother any of the children. York had read the police interviews of Yvonne's classmates, concluding, as the cops had also, there wasn't anything to be learned by upsetting them further. Yvonne Stafford, by all the reports, had been a first-class student and a good friend. Everyone wanted to help, but no one had seen her Monday morning. It was, York reflected, an odd twist of fate that this sort of thing always seemed to happen to the good ones. He, personally, could not remember a case where the school bully or a marginal student got snatched. That was a curious thing, one he hoped some smart crime statistician might look into some day.

But for now there was this kid, and the fact that she had disappeared from the face of the earth. York forced everything else from his mind and concentrated. It was the Dane's job to keep the world at bay while York walked around and surveyed the situation, at times mumbling incoherently to himself. Meanwhile, Bates was recording everything York said, so they could go over it later on the chance that some rambling thought might provide a key.

"We know she was here," York said, standing in the spot where Yvonne Stafford had exited her mother's car, now three days ago. "Her mother drove off. The girl waved. She turned toward the school. ...."

York stopped talking and turned a circle, looking off in each direction. Through the window of the van, Bates swore he saw his boss's eyes glaze. The Dane turned a group of curious onlookers away.

"The security guard at the school door is positive she didn't come inside," York said. "But the perp didn't take her here. Too close to the front door. The sun's hitting the glass. He couldn't tell if anyone might be watching. She moved away from here, and away from the entrance. Why?"

Bates saw that York was looking down at his hands, which were empty.

"Her homework!" York said suddenly, remembering what James Stafford had told him. "She didn't have her homework. She forgot it at home. Straight-A student, she didn't want to go to class without it. So she has to go back. But her mother's already gone. So ... so she walks up to the bus stop!" Even as he was mumbling to himself, York was walking up the block, oblivious to everything else around him. "Three, maybe four minutes have passed since her mother left. Bus stop's at the end of the block. Ronnie, check the crosstown schedules from eight-twenty."

Bates scrambled to comply, punching in the transit number on the cell phone. The Dane was standing by York, looking up and down the street, as if he might actually spot the girl.

"Light at the corner," York continued, studying the traffic flow. "One-way street heading north, away from the bus stop. And one-way here, where she was waiting. So either direction he came, he had to go through the light and pull up here. And he could only go in one direction after he stopped at the curb. Right here, where she was waiting for the bus."

"Crosstown bus comes through here at eight twenty-eight," Bates said, relaying the information through York's earpiece.

"So, maybe a six- or seven-minute window," York whispered. "Coffee shop on the far corner. Maybe a jogger, or somebody out walking their dog . . ." York turned, and at the end of the block saw the school crossing guard walking away, shuffling, carrying his STOP sign under his arms.

"There!" York shouted. "The crossing guard! Dane, grab him. Ronnie, check the police interview file on the crossing guard."

The Dane began his long, distance-eating stride down the block and caught up with the old man in his bright orange vest before he'd taken a half-dozen of his shuffling steps.

"Crossing guard went off duty at eight-fifteen," Bates said from the van. "The cops talked to him, but he never saw the girl."

"No, he didn't," York said, following the Dane, who was now talking to the crossing guard. "But I bet the perp drove right past him! Ronnie, grab a tape recorder and get us a table at the coffee shop. We'll have to interview whoever was in there, too."

Evert Hart was a retired factory worker who lived up on Union Avenue and worked as a crossing guard mostly for something to do, after his wife of forty years passed away two years ago. He dunked a doughnut into his black coffee and seemed rather confused at the questions and the tape recorder.

"I talked to the police, twice," he explained, sounding apologetic. "Told 'em I never saw that poor girl. They ought to shoot the son of a bitch who'd do something like that."

York nodded in agreement. Bates and the Dane left them alone and were talking to the patrons and waitresses, flashing a picture of Yvonne Stafford, even though York was aware the cops had already covered that ground.

"I'd like to help," Evert Hart said, shaking his head. "But I just plain didn't see her."

"I know you didn't," York said slowly. "But I believe that whoever took the little girl drove right past you while you were walking home."

"You don't say?" Hart looked up, pushing his glasses back on his nose.

"How's your memory, Mr. Hart?" York asked carefully.

"Sharp as a goddamned tack!" the old man bristled. "Just because the body gets a few years on it, don't mean the brain turns to Jell-O, you know."

"No insult intended." York forced a grin. This was precisely the response he'd hoped for. "Now, I'd like you to think back. See if you can recall any of the vehicles that passed by that morning after you left the corner."

"Damn." Hart crinkled his brow. "Didn't pay much attention, you know. . . ."

Then, to York's surprise, the man began to reel off the names of delivery trucks, the model and color of several cars.

"And just before the bus went by, there was a van, I recall. Plain white van . . . no delivery signs or anything."

Before Evert Hart could blink, York was on his feet, motioning for Bates and the Dane.

Unfortunately, no one else in the coffee shop could confirm the van's sighting, although one waitress thought she remembered something like it. York called Jenny and asked her to make an appointment for Hart to visit a hypnotist over on Eighth Avenue, in the long-shot hope that the crossing guard might have the license plate number locked in some forgotten corner of his brain.

"Anything I can do to help," Hart had said, agreeing to York's suggestion.

York also told Jenny to call the duty captain at the station house, to share the information. The more eyes looking for the van, the better their chances of finding it. Assuming the perp was still in the city. And there were thousands of unmarked white vans in New York. But it was their first lead, and York clung to it like a drowning man clutching a life jacket.

Arnie Watts's eyes fluttered open. He lay quiet for a few moments, waiting for his mind to clear. He hadn't meant to sleep so long. Light crept into the room through the bottom of the shade, filtering into the basement room like fog rolling off a river. The girl was still curled up, asleep beside him. He reached over and touched her, and even in the depths of her drugged sleep, she moaned and tried to move away from him. She was tied by her wrists to the bedpost, so she was only able to twist a little, pressing herself against the peeling paint of the wall.

"No . . ." she said, pulling briefly at her restraints, but Arnie lay quietly, and after a moment she was still.

Outside there were the sounds of traffic and footsteps crunching on the snow. The room was hot and stuffy, and it smelled worse than usual. Like standing, putrid water and moldy towels. Like stale beer and unwashed bodies. Arnie's nose wrinkled at the smell. He stank, and the girl stank even worse. If the game didn't end today, he'd have to stick her in the shower. Plus, the girl hadn't been eating, and she had developed a most annoying cough. He was growing tired of her. Yes, he decided, the game would definitely have to end soon.

A plan began to take shape in Arnie's mind, and he smiled, mulling over the various possibilities. The fact that it was winter offered a greater challenge than usual. The ground in this part of the country was frozen solid, the rivers were iced over, except the Hudson and East Rivers, where they emptied into the Atlantic and the saltwater tides kept the water open. Usually, anyway. This had been an incredibly cold winter, and he wasn't sure if there was ice on the Hudson or the East River. There sure was a hellova lot of snow. . . .

Snow! The thought of it made him sit bolt upright. The

girl groaned and tried to press herself deeper into the wall. Watts ignored her, as there was suddenly more urgent business. Cursing, Arnie pulled himself out of bed and fumbled around for his clothes. The fucking snow! He was supposed to move the van so the plows could clean the street. Snow emergency, the late news had said. Then he'd fallen asleep. And now it was day and the assholes from the city's Public Works Department were probably out towing vehicles— towing his fucking van! Sweet Jesus, that would really screw things up! He pulled on his clothes, grabbed his coat, and made for the door.

He hurried down the 200 block, moving as fast as he dared, without attracting undue attention. Another block down, two over to 203rd Street, and in a minute he'd be in the clear. As he rounded the corner and saw the back end of the van, Arnie smiled, slowing his pace.

Thank you, God, he whispered to himself, his breath rushing from his mouth like he was some strange, overtaxed steam engine. But then, as he was walking calmly toward the van, the damn van moved! Arnie stopped for a second, staring in disbelief, hardly believing his eyes. The van seemed to jerk forward, first an inch—then a foot! A guy in a dirty blue snowmobile suit came around the driver's side and waved his hand.

"You got it!" the guy shouted.

"Hey, wait!" he shouted. The guy in the greasy snowmobile suit looked up to see Arnie running toward him through the snow.

"That's my van!" Arnie shouted.

"Sorry, pal, it's already up on the rack!" the man shouted back, waving to his companion in the truck. The van jerked forward again. Arnie ran up and pounded on the van's side.

"Come on." Arnie tried to flash his best salesman's smile, even as the panic gripped his stomach and squeezed it up into his throat. Even as the guy in the snowmobile suit was shaking his head.

"Once it's up on the rack, it goes," he said, sounding sorry, but not looking it. In fact, he had a downright surly grin on his lips, Arnie saw.

"Listen, I have to have the van to go to work," Arnie pleaded.

"I got work to do too, pal," the guy said. "You can pay the fine and pick it up at the impound lot on Baychester."

"I'll give you a hundred bucks to leave it," Arnie said, trying to keep the desperation out of his voice. "I'll move it over to the other side of the street—it'll be out of the way, and you'll have the hundred."

The guy stuck his hands in the pockets of the dirty snow-suit, looking up and down the street. A police cruiser was at the far end of the block, tagging cars to be towed.

"You got the hundred?" the guy asked.

"Cash money." Arnie grinned, the panic settling back down into his stomach. "No receipt or nothing. Just between you, me, and Mr. Franklin."

Arnie fumbled in his pockets, and the panic returned with an almost audible thump into his chest. His bankroll . . . it was back in the apartment, tied up with a rubber band, stuck inside his Nikes.

"Jesus, man, I left my money back at the house," Arnie said, half-smiling, the fear locking the muscles of his face, except for the twitch above his eye, which had suddenly returned. The tow-truck guy was turning away, shaking his head. Unable to help himself, Arnie grabbed the man's shoulder. The man turned, shrugging away Arnie's hand, his eyes menacing. "Listen, give me fifteen minutes. That's all. Come on, what's fifteen minutes? No shit, I got the hundred."

The guy hesitated, still shaking his head.

"A hundred for you, and a hundred for your partner," Arnie said quickly.

"Fifteen minutes!" the guy snapped. "After that, you pick it up at the impound lot."

"You got it! Thanks for the break!" Arnie had already turned, running back up 203rd Street.

"Yeah, yeah," the guy mumbled, watching as Arnie ran like somebody was chasing him with a gun. What the hell, it was time for a coffee break anyway.

•   •   •

Yvonne Stafford groaned, tears blurring her eyes. She hurt. Every part of her hurt. Confusion swept across her mind like a cold wind, freezing her thoughts. She could feel her brain, twisting in her head, as she tried to remember what had happened, then just as quickly tried to forget. Her stomach rose up and she felt like she was going to be sick again. Yvonne rolled over on the bed, the sheet under her gritty and smelly. Through the fog of her nightmare, she realized suddenly that she was alone. The man was gone somewhere, and even though the mere thought of him made her want to scream, she swallowed her fear. He was gone! She was alone! If she could get to the door, she could get away! Escape . . . Oh, God . . . She could escape!

Frantically Yvonne began pulling at the leather straps that held her to the bed. The straps, which had once gripped her in a viselike grasp, were loose now. She had not eaten in days, it seemed, so her wrists were thinner. Escape—dazed, and with the pain shooting through her body like hot needles, that one word burned in her mind and filled her with a frenzied energy. She pulled and yanked and bit at the straps, her body flailing on the bed, just as it had when the man had done those things to her . . . and godohgod, she felt her hands squeezing through the straps! One had pulled loose and she stood on the bed, twisting the other hand free. Free . . . She was free! Panting, she leaped off the bed, looking wildly around, realizing she was naked and her clothes were nowhere in sight. No matter, her brain told her—no time! The door was there! She ran to it, fumbling with the lock, crying, her fingers like wooden sticks. And as she clawed at the lock, there was suddenly a sound on the other side of the door. Footsteps, then the rattling of a key in the door. A key turning the lock! The man—HE was back! On the other side of the door! Pushing it open . . . Yvonne threw her weight against the door, fighting to slip the dead-bolt chain on its metal slot. Fighting, she knew, for her very life.

But even as she pushed, the door pushed back. The chain slipped and the door was rammed open, throwing her onto the floor. And HE stepped quickly inside the tiny apartment, staring at her on the floor. His eyes burning like fire. Her brain screamed—oh god oh god oh god—and she tried to make her throat scream, even as her brain was doing, but only a hoarse, cracking sound came out. A sound that died on her lips as HE slammed the door shut. She tried to crawl away, to escape. To run. Somewhere. Anywhere. But there was no place to go. Finally a scream worked its way out of her mouth, but the man was already jerking her to her feet, covering her mouth.

"You shouldn't have done that," he whispered, his face close to hers, the image of it blurred by her tears. "You shouldn't have done that," he said softly, his breath hot on her face, scalding her cheeks.

"Please don't . . ." she tried to say, but his hand was grinding her lips against her teeth. She tasted blood and the room seemed to twist and turn like a roller-coaster ride. The music was suddenly turned on, louder than before.

"You shouldn't have done that!" he said again through clenched teeth, locking her arms behind her.

And it seemed like forever before darkness came from someplace deep inside her head, rescuing her from the pain.

On a planet in the fourth arm of a spiral galaxy called the Milky Way, the Soul Catchers gather. Linking together, they form a bridge between the physical and spiritual planes. Their work is often harsh and demanding, as death visits this place in sudden and unexpected ways. Their task is further complicated by the nature of the physical plane. The mechanisms here have a tendency to cling to life with a tenacity that defies logic.

In the murky half-light between the physical and spiritual planes, in a place that is not a part of any world or space, the Soul Catchers gather, cloaked in their foglike forms. Their whispers riding the night winds. Their breath often seen by the living in half-remembered spectrums of vision, or in dreams. Sometimes they are glimpsed passing, ghostlike, riding the light of stars. The Soul Catchers gather in the ether between worlds. Waiting. Vigilant. Knowing that each entity, in its turn, will one day reach for their warm, dark hands. . . .

t e n

Y ork stood at the window of his office, watching the midmorning traffic as it jammed up near Manhattan College. Word had just come in on Evert Hart's hypnosis session, and the crossing guard hadn't seen the license plate, although it was confirmed that a white, unmarked van had passed Hart that morning as he started for home. The Dane was waiting in the outer office, listening to the police scanner, his feet propped up on a desk. Ronnie Bates was going over the cops' internal files, and Jenny was reviewing the computer net, on the odd chance that the dumb file had produced more than a fleeting suspect.

"We double-checked the hospitals and morgues?" York asked, wanting to be absolutely certain they'd covered all the bases.

"Us and the cops both," Bates answered.

"The shelters and that woman over on Forty-second who runs the abuse hostel?" York knew he was fishing, but at the moment it was all he had.

"Done and done," Jenny responded, her eyes locked on the computer screen. Of course they had and York knew it, too. But she was used to him asking. It was part of his thought process, almost as though he was thinking out loud.

"Where's your car parked?" York asked suddenly, staring down at the street below.

"Mine?" Jenny asked, looking up now. That was an odd question. "In the garage downstairs. Why?"

"Snow emergency," York replied, nodding at the street. "They're towing for the plows."

It was quiet for a moment. Bates shuffling papers, Jenny tapping keys, the Dane fiddling with the scanner.

"Just for the hell of it, let's check the impounds," York said. Hey, fishing was fishing.

"The impounds?" Bates asked, cocking his head like a dog that just heard a strange sound. "You think this guy let his van get towed? That'd be kind of stupid. Thought you said this perp was a sharp one."

"He is," York replied. Jenny was already on the phone, punching up the numbers. "That's why we'd better hope he makes a mistake, or we'll never find him. Maybe he's not used to snow emergencies. I know they got me the first time I was here in winter."

"Worth a shot, I guess." Bates shrugged, trying to remember which side of the street he'd parked their own van on.

"I got one . . . no, three white vans," Jenny said, her hand on the receiver. "They're checking to see if there's any more."

York picked up the lot addresses Jenny scribbled down as Bates grabbed his coat and rousted the Dane.

"I guess a wild-goose chase is better than no chase at all," Bates mumbled.

"That's the spirit," York said, following them out to the elevator. "Your optimism is an inspiration to us all."

Bates grumbled something about York's mother, but York ignored it. On their way over to the first lot, Jenny called with two more possibles. It was in the first of this group on a used-car lot off Baychester Avenue in the North Bronx that they crossed Arnie Watts's trail.

"You know, these are private vehicles," the lot attendant said as York slipped a thin metal rod into the edge of the doorjamb—the universal locksmith, as the tool was called in the car-jacking trade. The door swung open, and York popped his head inside. The Dane, standing between the lot attendant and the van, did his imitation of a brick wall. The attendant was clearly upset, not so much at the fact that York was breaking into the van, but that he was standing here witnessing the whole thing. Jeffrey Rolley, two years past fifty and forty pounds past healthy, knew he'd be a damn sight more comfortable if they just let him return to the shack.

"Mister, I got to ask you not to take anything," Rolley said, sounding miserable, realizing he was quite helpless against the oversize white baboon, who seemed to be the little guy's bodyguard.

"I promise you, we won't," York answered, disappearing into the van's interior. To Rolley's relief, the guy called York reemerged only a couple of moments later, and without any stereo equipment. His eyes, however, scared the living bejesus out of old Jeffrey, who had the sudden impression that this little man, climbing out of the van like a clumsy monkey, was very dangerous indeed. His eyes burned like some monster in a late-night cable movie. Rolley crossed himself against the Evil Eye.

"I think we've got it!" York said, his voice low, almost sounding like a growl.

"Got what?" Rolley asked, but York didn't seem to hear him.

"Go back to the van and get Ronnie. There's a seat in the back with straps. Tell him to get a hair sample, if there's any around. And tell him to be damn careful not to disturb anything. I just want the hair sample. The police lab team can do the rest. Have him call Jenny. Tell her to inform the duty officer at the Fifty-fourth that we've found a probable on the perp's van."

The Dane was off in an instant, loping like a long-legged deer.

"Who brought this vehicle in?" York asked, his dark eyes seeming to crack like a whip in Jeffrey Rolley's mind.

"Why, I believe it was Billy Case, but I'd have to check the book," the attendant replied, wondering if this man expected him to run off, too.

"Do it . . . quickly, please," York snapped. "Where's Billy Case now?"

Apparently, he expected just that.

"He's out on a call, I guess," Rolley said, wondering whether or not he was supposed to be giving out this sort of information.

"Find out where," York ordered.

And Jeffrey Rolley, who hadn't run anyplace since the Army some thirty years ago, was surprised to find himself running back toward his shack, even though he had no idea why.

"Like I told the cops, I can probably ID him," Billy Case said nervously. "He offered me and Al a hundred bucks not to tow his van. But that's against the rules, you know."

York nodded. They'd caught up with Billy Case and his tow truck over in the South Bronx. The detectives had already taken Billy's statement, and even grilled him for a couple hours over at the Manhattan station house. His partner, Al, had called it a day after all that bullshit, Billy said. But Al had never actually talked to the guy.

"I know it's against the rules," York said, smiling, as if he truly believed that Billy Case, upstanding citizen, would really turn down a long yard just to slip somebody's van down off the rack.

"Look, I already told the cops all I know. I even helped 'em draw a sketch of the guy. That's it, I don't know nothing more." Case swallowed, not liking this second interrogation one bit. Who the fuck did this jerk think he was, anyway? Pulling him over like he was some kind of criminal. Everybody seemed to be treating him like he was some kind of criminal.

York already had a copy of the police artist's sketch, and even had a printout of Billy Case's interview at the station house. Unfortunately, the sketch resembled any of a thousand different people, and Case's interview had been less than stellar. The police team had dusted the van for prints, but there was nothing on the FBI wire. On the plus side, they had a positive match on the hair sample, so there was no question that this was the van used to kidnap Yvonne Stafford. The cops were doing a door-to-door search around the neighborhood where the van had been towed, so York decided to track down Billy Case and have a little chat. It had not gone well.

"Can I go now?" Case asked, but the little guy with the big head seemed not to be listening.

"So this man, he came down the street, offered you a hundred not to take the van, but you towed it away anyway?" York asked for what was probably the tenth time.

"That's right." Case sighed. Shit, the cops had only asked twice. It was lucky, Case thought, that he and Al had had time to get their story straight.

"Mr. Case," York said slowly, his face uncomfortably close to Billy's in the cab of the truck. "Do not fuck with me!"

Billy Case squirmed, feeling suddenly like he was a bug about to be impaled in some kid's cigar box. He tried to move away, but York reached out and grabbed him by the collar.

"Hey! You can't . . ." Billy squealed. But the man's hands were surprisingly strong, and Billy couldn't pull away.

"I said, don't fuck with me," York whispered. The guy's partner, big as a goddamn house, stared into the driver's-side window. Billy Case was reminded of the time the mob had visited him, saying that his truck was now going to come under their protection. Billy went limp and nodded.

"This man, he offered you a hundred dollars," York continued. "And then what happened?"

"He didn't have the cash with him," Billy Case stammered. "He said to wait fifteen minutes and he'd be back with the money. Then he ran off. Me and Al, we waited, but he never showed. So we took the van in. That's all, I swear. He ran off and we never saw him again."

"And he ran back down 203rd Street?" York asked, letting go of the man's collar, feeling sorry now at his outburst, as he always did after he lost his temper.

"Yeah, like I just told you," Billy said, moving away,

wondering if the danger was over. "Look, the cops—"

"I'm sure they'll want to talk to you again," York said, his eyes flashing as he stepped out of the truck's cab.

"Shit . . ." Billy Case mumbled, cursing softly to himself. It was getting so a guy couldn't hardly make a living anymore.

When his eyes finally cleared, Arnie Watts's head was pounding. There was still a red haze outlining his vision, as though he were looking at the world through a bloody fog. His clothes were scattered around the apartment, and there were long scratches on his arms and chest. They burned, like somebody had lit matches on his skin. He sat back, leaning against the corner of the bed, trying to catch his breath. The girl lay in the middle of the room, her arms and legs stretched out, as though she was still trying to crawl away across the stained rug. Only she wasn't moving. She looked like a white scatter rug someone had thrown carelessly on the floor. Her dark hair covered her face, which was turned away from him. He kicked at her leg with his bare foot. She was cold to the touch, like a slab of beef from a meat locker. This part of the hunt was over, he knew.

A chill shook him, the wind blowing in from the taped-up bathroom window. The game had taken a sudden, sour turn. Arnie knew he had no one to blame but himself. Well, himself and the girl. But she had paid for her mistake. Paid in full. Now he was going to have to hustle if he didn't want to pay, too. Arnie knew he had a serious problem and it was going to take some first-class planning to make things right. Only he was tired and his brain was still hazed from dealing with the girl. He shivered again and forced himself to get up and find his clothes. As he pulled on his socks, he reached down and felt the back of the girl's neck for a pulse. There wasn't any, and she was as cold as ice. This one had been trouble right from the beginning, he thought bitterly. It could have been so good, but now it had all gone to hell.

"Bitch . . ." he mumbled, going into the closet for the duffel bag. He'd have to stash the body, then come back for it once he got his vehicle problems straightened out. There was always some kind of fucking problem. He rolled the girl over, folding her limp legs so she'd fit into the army bag. Experience had taught him that it was extremely important to get these things taken care of quickly, before the body locked up. Once, he remembered, out in the Midwest, there had been this corpse that had frozen up like a fucking marble statue. . . .

"Shit!" Arnie cursed softly.

There was blood on the rug under the girl. Leaking from a gash in her neck—where, he guessed, he had bitten her. He didn't remember everything, exactly, but he would later. Later, when the hunt was officially over, he would replay each moment in his mind, and the memory would stay with him for months and months, he knew. Then it would fade, as they all did, and he would have to go hunting again. But for now, he had to concentrate. He had to clean up this mess.

Blood was the worst damn thing. Blood and bodies, that was how people got caught. Arnie got a Hefty garbage bag from the kitchenette and tugged it over the girl's head, yanking it down until it covered her feet. He didn't particularly like touching dead bodies, but it was a necessary evil. Another Hefty from the feet up, and he rolled the body into the canvas bag, zipping it closed, hauling it back into the closet.

At least that part was over, he thought. He took a container of bleach from under the sink and scrubbed at the blood stain on the rug. He jerked the sheets off the bed. They went into another garbage bag, along with the girl's clothes and the towels used to blot the blood out of the rug. Arnie shook his head as he stood at the sink, washing his hands. Cleaning up was always the worst part.

In the shadowy realm between the spiritual and physical planes, the Soul Catchers went about their work, collecting entities from mechanisms that had ceased to function. Like a soft, invisible rain, the Soul Catchers moved in the gray area between life and death where the spiritual entities waited. Some entities were confused, others in a state approaching ecstasy. Some stood near their mechanisms, shocked and frightened at their sudden release. Others found their own way into the shadows between worlds. Some thrived on the experience, some did not yet fully understand what had taken place. All were collected and comforted, then swept away into the spiritual plane, like leaves on the autumn wind.

There were, however, exceptions.

The entity of the young girl, still retaining the form of her mechanism, had left the prison of her flesh. She hovered in the murky area between life and death, unseen by the other mechanism in the room, who was still immersed in the physical plane. There the Soul Catchers came to her, whispering words as soft as summer breezes. They touched her gently. They brushed away the tangled thoughts that danced like sparks in her shimmering, fog-like form. Then, when the sparks were gone, when the form itself was smooth and glowing like moonlight, the Soul Catchers led her back to her body.

For this entity it was not yet time to leave the physical world.

As the other mechanism left the room, there was a barely audible gasp from the dark confines of the closet. Fingers clutching at plastic. Scratching noises, like the sound of small creatures caught in traps.

eleven

Jenny was ringing in on the van's phone, and Ronnie Bates switched it to the speaker as he, the Dane, and York were all studying a map of the area around 203rd Street in the Bronx.

"The evidence team is going over the vehicle in the tow lot, and they've got units doing a house-to-house in the surrounding neighborhoods down by you," Jenny reported. "They've got a composite sketch on the wire. I think yours is better, Ronnie, by the way."

"Of course," Bates said softly, as if there had been any doubt.

"Did you offer ours?" York asked.

"I did, but it was refused," Jenny's voice crackled. In the background York could hear the scanner channels she was monitoring. "They're really mad this time, Dennison. Cassady said he's going to have your hunting license this time—for, and I quote, 'fucking with evidence and witnesses.' "

"Remind him that we found the evidence and the witnesses," York said, sounding vaguely disinterested. "Put in the log that we did not disturb any of the evidence in the van, other than taking a hair sample, which is within our rights. Also, that the interview with Billy Case took place after the police spoke to him, and that we shared the new information as soon as we had it."

"Already did," Jenny replied. "I offered our hair sample, too, but they said they had their own. Cassady called and said he was filing a court order to get you to cease and desist. I passed him off to Mitchell, who read him the riot act."

"Good." York found himself grinning, in spite of the circumstances. Harvey Mitchell was the firm's mouthpiece, and a real tiger when anyone messed with York or his team. York had once pulled Mitchell's brother-in-law off the street and into a rehab clinic, one step ahead of the narcotics unit. Most of the time Mitchell didn't even bill him, particularly if the job entailed harassing bureaucrats, which Thomas Cassady was, even if the precinct captain himself didn't think so.

"Seven minutes or so from this corner," York said, turning back to the business at hand, looking around in all three directions the perp could have gone. "At a dead run, that's what . . . four or five blocks?"

"The station house is assembling units to expand the search," Jenny reported.

"Tell 'em they'll need everybody they can get," York said, looking both at the map and his surroundings, a forest of apartment houses stretching as far as the eye could see. "Christ, there's a thousand places where this asshole could be holed up! OK—Dane will take the west, around Tremont. Ronnie, you take a turn in the van around the whole four or five blocks, then start flashing the sketch. I'll go east, up the 200 block and do the same. Somebody around here has to have seen this guy. Check the stores first. The delis, the bars, the fast-food joints. We'll meet at the corner, right here, in an hour. Let's hope we get lucky."

The Dane slipped out of the van like a ghost. York stepped out behind him. Then, to York's utter astonishment, two police cruisers swept down the street, lights flashing, sirens blaring.

"Sweet Jesus!" York whispered, reaching back inside the van, grabbing the phone. "Jenny! Call the station house. Tell Cassady to kill the bells and whistles, for Christ's sake! They're gonna spook this asshole!"

• • •

So far, so good. The messiest part of the job was behind him. Arnie walked quickly away from a Dumpster behind an Italian restaurant on Union. The plastic bag he'd tossed in contained the girl's clothes, the sheets and towels used to clean the apartment. Even the bedframe had been washed down with bleach. All traces of the girl had been erased. Except, of course, for her actual body. But he was going to get to that shortly. Watts grinned at his reflection in the restaurant window. Clean Dockers, a nice sweater from Macy's, quilted ski jacket. With his hair combed and his teeth brushed, Arnie figured he looked damn near human again.

Now, to get the van back, and get the hell out of here. He had already decided to drive south and maybe get rid of the body in some backwater river in the Carolinas. He'd fill the duffel bag with stones or concrete blocks and toss it off a bridge someplace. Then maybe he'd take a trip out to the West Coast. It'd been a while since he'd seen LA.

Arnie knew he'd have to lose the deposit on the apartment, but money wasn't a problem, at least not at the moment. He still had a couple grand in his bankroll, some of which he'd have to use to get state ID out on the Coast. Three or four sets, so he could tap the welfare system for some ready cash, then maybe make a run down into Mexico and Greyhound some dope up north. Money was hardly ever a problem for Arnie Watts, or to anyone else who knew how to milk the system. Hell, he'd even work a little, if it came to that. But right now, he had to get the van from impound.

He tried to pick up a cab on East Tremont. Of course, with all the snow and cold, there weren't any around. The fucking cabbies, they were all uptown picking up the big-money fares. Arnie caught a bus, then walked up toward the station house on 238th Street. Somehow, going in to find out the lot where they'd towed his van didn't seem like a real solid plan. So Arnie found a pay phone and ragged on the desk officer for a couple minutes about how they'd towed all the cars off the 200 block.

"Look, pal, just pay the fine and pick it up at Thacker's

Garage on Baychester!'' the officer had finally grumbled.

More bullshit, walking through the ice and snow of half-shoveled sidewalks. Arnie was still a block away when he saw the cop cars swarming around the impound lot. Four cruisers parked at odd angles, a swarm of suits and uniforms. Alarm bells started ringing inside his head. Serious alarms. Watts turned quickly and began walking back the way he'd come. The adrenaline pumping, feeling like popcorn going off in his head. OK, he thought, they had the van. They had the fucking van! What had he left inside? A flashlight, a shovel, gloves for the end game. Not much else. Except for the straps still tied to the backseat. The fucking straps . . . and he hadn't washed out the back, so they'd probably be able to find hair or fiber samples from the girl's clothing. With those, he knew, they would be able to link him to the girl. Even in the cold air, Arnie felt himself start to sweat.

He walked, trying not to hurry, trying to look casual. They had the van, but they didn't have him. The registration was under a false name, listing a phony address up in White Plains. They'd get his prints, too, but he had been careful to keep his record clean. A traffic ticket here and there, but nothing traceable. So what to do? Go Greyhound. Go Go Go. That was the fucking ticket! The plan formulated itself as he walked. OK, he had the clothes on his back, his wallet, and some cash. Could he make it with that? No, the thought came back. He had a perfectly good gun taped to the back of the dresser in the apartment. And another set of ID tucked away in his closet. Some credit card numbers he was saving for an emergency, and the rest of his bankroll. He'd need all that stuff to get over wherever he landed. Walking up the 230 block, he passed another used-car lot. A guy with no gloves and a worn overcoat was brushing snow off windshields. Maybe he should spend some of the two grand and buy an old junker to get him out of town. Hell, why not hook a car, load the girl in the trunk, and make tracks? No, that was stupid. The last thing he could afford to be was stupid. Shaking himself, he caught a cab in front of the

Dunkin' Donuts, got out at the 200 block, and walked down toward his apartment building.

Smiling, nodding at the Korean shoveling snow outside his grocery store. Bet that fucker has a nice car holed up someplace, Watts thought bitterly. No, no, no. Get back to the apartment, grab the gun and the rest of the stuff and bus it on out. Lock the body in the closet. That was the logical course of action. Fuck it, he could even get out now, then come back in a couple weeks and collect the body when he had some wheels. Maybe the used car wasn't such a bad idea . . . No good. No fucking good! There'd be no time to clear the registration or get insurance.

Walking past 201st Street. Smiling at the old ladies cleaning snow off their stoops. His building up ahead. Jogging up the steps, slipping inside. Inside, safe. Maybe. Sure, he could just hole up here for a couple days. Arnie sat down on the bed, trying to clear his head. Think, goddamn it! Think! And the thought hit him, folding his stomach like he had been hit with a baseball bat. How had they found the van? It had been locked up tight. Unless some asshole broke into it. He should've pulled the straps from the backseat. Damn it all to hell! Or . . . or somebody had seen the van when he snatched the girl.

Maybe somebody saw him? No way to tell. Not for sure, anyway. So, it was settled. He had to get the fuck away.

Outside, a police car went screaming by, as if to confirm his worst fears. The fuckers—they were dragging the streets for him! He could feel it. That sixth sense he always had. The voice whispering in the back of his head. It had saved him many times in the past. Now Arnie Watts listened to it closely. And the voice told him to run. To run as quickly, as far as he could! Because they were here—right on his street, and they were closing.

The decision made, Arnie acted quickly. The gun, a solid Nine, taken from in back of the dresser, loaded up and stuffed into his jacket pocket. The cash and credit card numbers. There was no time to be thinking about that. There was only time to run. Clothes? No, he'd look suspicious walking down the street with the suitcase or his knapsack.

He took off his boots and traded them for the Nikes, and was out the door, pulling his wool hat low, wrapping a scarf around his chin.

From under the closet door, the barest whisper of breath. The sharp scent of fear. Yvonne Stafford, weak from her failed effort to escape, was forced to bite her tongue to keep from screaming. HE was on the other side of the door. She could hear him moving, shuffling furniture. Then the door slammed again. Fearful of a trick, she waited in the dark- ness, listening to the sound of her own heartbeat. Feeling the tears trace warm lines down her cheeks. Her skin burn- ing, then frozen, in alternating waves. Remembering. For- getting. The dark closet, she decided, was not such a bad place to be.

Outside, the street which had once been so familiar was now a strange, dangerous world. People seemed to stare at him over their shoulders. The fear of getting caught, like a shadow hounding his footsteps. Another cop car cruised by, slowly, with no lights or sirens. Arnie walked, keeping his head down. Where to go? Uptown. Across the river. Away from here. Then he'd catch the first bus or train out of the Port Authority. The first fucking one, heading anyplace.

And then, out of the corner of his eye, he saw a stranger—a big white fucker—talking to the Korean grocer. Showing the slant-eye a flyer of some kind. Arnie Watts wanted to run, but made himself walk. Quickly, but calmly. A van drove up beside him. The guy inside glanced in his direction. Just a quick look, then the guy turned away. But the look was too quick, too casual. The alarm bells were ringing like chimes in Arnie's head. The vanman was an- other white guy. Young, bare-headed. The van stopped at the light on the corner. Arnie slowed down, watching care- fully. Yeah, the fucker was scoping him. Trying to be real cool about it. Sideways glances out the side mirror. Another cop car slid through the intersection. They were gonna snag him! Jesus, they were gonna snag him! The sixth sense kick- ing in strong now, stronger than ever before. Like an alarm clock singing in his head. They're gonna get you, a voice said from someplace deep inside him. You got nothing to lose!

The light was about to change. The vanman trying to look at him, but not look at the same time. Arnie was even with the van now, walking along the side of the street, ducking in and out of the parked cars. The vanman was looking away, watching for the light to change. Arnie put his hand inside his coat pocket, clutching the Nine. Walking quickly over to the rear fender of the van, sliding up the side. A deep breath, the fear of getting caught reenforcing his nerves. It was now! The chance to get away was now! He ran up and jerked the driver's door. And it opened! Unlocked. Sweet Jesus, it was unlocked. . . .

"Move over, or I'll blow your fucking head off!" Arnie said, flashing the Nine, keeping it low against his body. The vanman's eyes popped open, wide as mushrooms, and Arnie was inside, pushing the asshole away from the wheel. The light changing, the van rolling forward as the asshole's foot came off the brake. And as easy as hopping a freight train, Arnie Watts was in the driver's seat.

He wanted to punch the fucking gas, to bug-ass out at a hundred miles an hour. Adrenaline causing his legs to shake. One hand gripping the wheel, the other keeping the Nine pointed below the dash, at the vanman's midsection.

"Put your hands on your fucking knees and don't look anyplace except out the front window!" Arnie hissed, forcing himself to put the blinker light on to make the turn up the 200 block. "Touch the door handle and I'll put a hole in your belly the size of a fucking half dollar! Understand?"

The dimwit guy nodded, the color draining nicely from his face as he stared out the window. Arnie Watts felt his heart hammering, the adrenaline pumping. This was the best hunt yet.

"We're gonna take a ride," Arnie said carefully, almost cheerfully, even flashing the asshole a smile. "If you don't do anything stupid, you'll be all right. No need to panic, we're just gonna take a little ride to Jersey. Then I'll be on my way and you can go home and fuck your old lady. Right?''

Ronnie Bates nodded again, hardly remembering he had no such person at home, hoping he wouldn't throw up or mess his pants. The whole thing had happened so quickly it had a surreal feeling to it. Bates felt dizzy and his vision seemed blurred. Almost like he was about to have some sort of out-of-body experience. Like the kind of thing he'd read about people having just before they died. Ronnie Bates was quite certain he was about to die. This was the guy, all right. The one they'd been hunting. And now the perp was driving the van up toward the Expressway, away from the Dane and York, who wouldn't even know he was gone until he failed to make their pickup. How long? Bates found that his brain seemed to be stuck, like a truck in mud, the wheels spinning, but going no place. Maybe an hour before they missed him. Sweet Jesus, how could he have been so stupid as to leave the door unlocked? He should've hit the gas. He should've . . .

Ronnie Bates came to the slow realization that none of that mattered. What mattered was that he stayed alive until York and the Dane came for him, as he was certain they would. Right now, he had to pay attention, wait for the right moment, and escape. He was alive. He wasn't hurt. Not yet, anyway. That was what mattered.

A police cruiser passed them, and the perp didn't even blink an eye. He was an icy bastard, that was for sure. And he didn't hurry, but drove carefully, down Tremont, catching the Cross Bronx Expressway. Heading, no doubt, for the George Washington Bridge.

''What the hell you got in here?'' Arnie asked, nodding at the electronic equipment. ''A whole fucking Radio Shack?''

Bates didn't know if he was supposed to answer, so he didn't. The police scanner was on, the dispatcher directing units to the area around the 200 block, from where the perp was now calmly driving away.

''You were looking for me, weren't you?'' the guy asked.

Bates saw the perp was watching him out of the corner

of his eye, obviously waiting for a reply. So Bates nodded and the guy grinned, slowing down for a light at University Avenue.

"Looks like you found me, huh?" he said, letting out a loose laugh, which sounded to Ronnie Bates like the rattling of bones.

The small feathers on the back of his head stood up on their quills, pricking his skin like needles. There were screams coming from the dark caverns beneath the fortress walls. Terrible, high-pitched screams. The type reserved for the most intolerable agonies. He shuttered, thinking about the atrocities that were now—this very minute—taking place behind the stone walls of the Viceroy's enclave. And, shamefully, he gave thanks to the Heavens that it was not him or his family twisting on the hot metal slabs of the Viceroy's torturers. Quickly he gathered his goods from the wooden stall in the marketplace and fled, following the maze of streets to his burrow.

He was, he knew clearly, an insignificant individual, trapped for some inexplicable reason between the powerful forces fighting for supremacy on this equally insignificant world. They had come here two decades ago, in the time of his father. Landing in all their fire and fury, searching for metals and gasses to power their huge machines. They had seemed, in the beginning, to be gods. Riding the dark spaces between stars, working their will upon the universe. And upon the people of Ullius. Only now, with the screams piercing the night air, he and everyone else knew them not to be gods, but devils. Evil beings who seduced with magical technology, and then took payment by stripping the feathers and skin of those who had fallen under their spell. All in their relentless search for metals and gasses . . . and traitors to their unimaginable cause.

He walked down the steps to his burrow, suppressing the urge to run—who knew what spies might be lurking in the dark? He did, however, close the door quickly behind him, throwing the iron bar across the latch. Pretending to himself that the lock somehow meant that he was safe and secure. His mate came to him in the hallway, drying her hands on a frayed towel.

"Are you all right?" she asked, her voice sounding like the swaying of flowers on a spring day. "I was afraid . . ."

"Yes, yes, I'm fine." He sighed, hanging his pots and flutes and carving utensils on their pegs inside the door of his workshop. "There was a protest in the paddock. Growers demanding payment for their impounded sectors. The leaders were caught . . . the fools!"

She came to him, slipping her arms around his neck. Soft feathers ringing her face in white down. He brushed them flat with the back of his hand. She was so very beautiful, he thought, his breath catching as he pulled her to him. Through the locked door, the screams that had been so loud in the marketplace were little more than muted whispers. He walked with her into the kitchen, where supper waited on the table he had made on their wedding day. She lit candles and he rolled a sheet of their favorite music into the machine above the fireplace. The sound of stringed instruments blocked out the terrifying whispers that rode the night winds.

After they ate, he held her as they sat together, preening in the firelight. Silently he gave thanks that it was not their turn to be visited by the darkness. Not yet. Not today.

 ## Reflections on Dark Spirits

Musings: Light/Dark. Life/Death. Good/Evil. For every action there is an equal and opposite reaction. For each day there is a night. The laws of the physical plane are exacting in their simplicity.

Fact: The actions of certain mechanisms are clearly outside the boundaries of morality and decency. The question then becomes the motivation behind these actions. Violent behavior can be attributed to inherent primeval forces only when this behavior is based on an underlying need to protect territory or possessions. However, when carnage and wanton violence are directed toward members of the society who pose no threat to territory or possessions, other motivating factors must be considered.

One of the initial goals of the implantation experiment was to introduce spiritual entities into the society as a means of directing the mechanisms in their search for a more developed social structure. However, as was previously noted, the proliferation of mechanisms caused a number of mechanisms to be introduced into the society without implanted entities. For every action there is an equal and opposite reaction. It is possible, and perhaps even probable, that outside forces have intruded into the void created by the introduction of unimplanted mechanisms, thus injecting an alien presence into the heart of the experiment.

Conclusion: It would seem that another, previously unknown spiritual force is at work, guiding the unimplanted mechanisms. It must be remembered that all mechanisms are endowed, to a certain extent, with the capacity for Free Will. This inclusion was deemed necessary for the development of the emerging society, both from a technical and internal standpoint. Free Will, of course, carries with it the responsibilities of choice. It seems clear at this point that a select few of the mechanisms are choosing darkness over light, evil over good, death over life. It is imperative at this juncture to discover the nature of this outside force, and to counteract it by whatever means are determined necessary. The society itself is on the verge of advancements that will take the mechanisms into the realm of other worlds and other civilizations in which similar experiments are active. If darkness is the predominant choice within the context of this experiment, then the society must not be allowed to impose its choice upon others.

Question: Is Evil truly a viable force in the physical plane? If so, should life experiments in this arena be continued?

<u>twelve</u>

Y ork and the Dane met up at the corner of 202nd and Tremont. They were close, York could feel it. Several people had identified the sketch, although none could supply a name.

"Yeah, I seen the guy around," a bartender at one of the local taverns had said. "Stops in once in a while. Lives around here someplace, I guess. Quiet guy, drinks a couple beers by himself, watches the ballgame, and leaves. Never any trouble."

The Dane also reported a positive ID from the Korean grocer over on the 200 block. Same story—no name, no address. Just an average guy, buying bread and oranges.

They stood together on the corner for a few minutes, looking up and down the street. It was getting cold, the afternoon fading, a sharp wind kicking up, scattering the few people who were braving the outdoors. Once these people were locked inside their apartments, York knew, any information they might provide would be locked away, too.

"Where the hell is Bates?" York asked, stamping his feet. A police cruiser went by. Other units were going building-to-building. "Have you seen the van lately?"

"No," the Dane replied, looking irritated. "Maybe he's caught in traffic."

"Not much traffic this time of day," York observed. "He

passed me awhile ago, up on Union. He should be some-where around here.''

The Dane nodded in agreement.

"Only he isn't,'' the big man commented.

York grumbled under his breath and unfolded the cell phone, punching in the van's number. It beeped, but there was no response. Angry now at being left hanging in the cold, York called Jenny at the office.

"Jenny, you heard from Ronnie lately? Neither have we. See if you can raise him. Yeah, we've got a line on the perp. No, don't call the Staffords yet. We don't need the father down here. Just see if you can find Bates and the van.''

"Don't touch it!'' Arnie Watts snapped.

The beeping was getting on his nerves, but eventually it stopped. They were on their way across the George Wash-ington Bridge, heading into New Jersey. Far below, the Hudson River was a dark, angry-looking ribbon of water. Arnie had no real plan formulated for when he got out of the city. He supposed he'd just keep on driving. He knew he would have to give some serious thought to the asshole in the passenger seat. There were, he realized, a lot of pos-itive aspects to having a hostage. But there were also a lot of negatives, too. . . .

The waves of panic had stopped sliding up and down Ronnie Bates's body, and for that he was grateful. His feet were cold, but he was hesitant to ask if he could turn up the heat. He felt as though the wall of silence he had erected between him and the perp somehow shielded him from any immediate disaster. And the phone ringing was a good sign. It surely meant that York had missed him and was trying to find out where the hell he was. Help would arrive soon, although Bates had no idea what might happen when it did. So he sat in the passenger seat, quiet and shivering. Curi-ously, even though he hadn't done so in years, Ronnie Bates found himself praying.

•   •   •

"Nothing?" York said, his anger now turning into mild concern. "Check the phone company to see if there's some sort of problem with the channel. You already did? Well, we're not going to wait outside for him much longer."

"Maybe he had another accident," the Dane suggested.

"He better have had," York snapped, shaking his head even as the words came out of his mouth. "I'll have his butt if he just left us here!"

"Ronnie wouldn't do that," the Dane pointed out.

"I know," York admitted, his concern deepening.

Police cruisers glided up and down the streets like hungry sharks; foot units canvassed the neighborhoods. They had more than enough manpower, at least for the moment, York thought. Besides, his feet were damn near frozen and his stomach was growling like an angry dog. The Dane, who seemed impervious to such things as cold and hunger, was waiting to resume the search. York, however, decided it might be a good idea to let the cops do their job.

"Come on," he said to the Dane. "Let's get something to eat. Jenny'll ring us if they find the perp."

"You're the boss." The Dane shrugged, following York into a nearby diner.

For a man who gave no indication he had been hungry, York noted, the Dane ate as though he suspected this might be the last time he ever saw food. They were sitting at a corner table, so York could watch the street on the chance that Ronnie Bates might drive by looking for them. York sipped his coffee, dividing his attention between the passing traffic and the Dane, who had just inhaled his third burger.

"Something happened to Bates," York said, more to himself than the Dane, who at times also seemed impervious to conversation. "Where the fuck is he?"

"Maybe he ran across the perp," the Dane said, looking up at York, his eyes cold, like topaz stones.

"He would've called—wouldn't he?" York asked.

The Dane only shrugged his shoulders. The cell phone beeped on the table and York snatched at it.

"Yeah? OK, we're on it!" He was already pushing himself up from the table, even as the Dane was stuffing the last of his food into his mouth. "It was Jenny. They found the guy's apartment!"

"The girl?" the Dane asked.

"Don't know," York replied, throwing money on the counter, running for the door.

They had been close all along, York realized. Just a block down and over toward 203rd Street. There were cruisers outside, uniforms roping off the building. York pushed his way through the gathering crowd, flashing his license, and with the Dane following him, made his way inside.

"Sweet Jesus," he whispered, shouldering past the uniforms guarding the door, stopping inside the doorway as though he had run into a wall.

Yvonne Stafford's body was laid out on the floor, covered with a blanket. At first, York thought she was dead. Her eyes were closed, her skin the color of new snow. Several officers were leaning over her, pumping her chest, forcing air into her lungs. Still, she looked to be dead. York felt sick. It wasn't right, he thought. . . . Then one of the girl's hands twitched, and an officer bent down with his ear to her face.

There was something terrible, horrible, awful wrong. Something so wrong . . . that she couldn't even think about it. It was this place she was in. Dark and choking. She had tried her hardest to get out. But couldn't. It was this place . . . No. It was HIM. HE had done things to her . . . only she couldn't remember what. Exactly. She wanted to scream. But couldn't. It was so dark. She wanted to go someplace . . . someplace where she didn't hurt anymore. But she couldn't get out. Of here. Of her body. It was much easier to do nothing. To lay here. In this dark place. Where she could sleep. Maybe forever. That was what she wanted, she decided. To sleep. Forever. But then there was light again. Hands on her. Again. HIM. Again. She wanted to scream. But couldn't. It was much better just to sleep. And wait for forever to come. . . .

"She's breathing," the officer said, and the others redoubled their efforts.

More sirens screaming outside. An ambulance crew rushing into the apartment, practically running York and the Dane over. In another minute Yvonne Stafford was carried out. York watched her being rolled away, the bile rising in his stomach. She was like a dog he had seen once—starved and abused to the point of death. Even though it had survived, the animal had never been the same.

Teams of detectives were combing the apartment. Other officers were pounding up and down the stairs in the hall, searching the floors above. A search, York knew instantly, that would prove futile. Whoever was responsible for this had already fled. And the thought came suddenly: What had happened to Ronnie Bates?

—No, a right here, the voice said, and Arnie Watts listened, jerking the van into a side street. A left, the voice said. Wait. Now go!

Arnie Watts listened and did what he was told, keeping his cool, trusting the sixth sense he seemed to have developed over the years. Trusting it totally, without question. But it was strange, he thought, pulling the van back into traffic. Mighty fucking strange.

It was the same voice that told him the exact moment to yank the door open, when the van's driver had been waiting at the stoplight. The same voice that told him when it was clear to grab the girl. The voice that whispered what to say when some cop pulled him over, and explained to him what to do with the bodies. He had stopped wondering about the voice long ago, merely accepting it now as a part of him. It was, he knew, the same voice that crept into his consciousness before a hunt, telling him what to do and where the prey might be found. It was, he knew also, a dark voice. Some might call it a demon, but Arnie Watts chose not to. It was just a voice to him, coming from someplace deep in his head, where his eyes couldn't see. Like a tunnel, miles long, inside his mind. A well, a black hole, from which whispered instructions floated up into his thoughts. He could hear it now, more clearly than ever. And he knew that if he listened, the voice would save him. . . .

Once across the GW Bridge they followed 95 until it turned into the Jersey Turnpike. Bates was watching carefully now, looking for a chance to bail out. Maybe when they slowed for traffic, or stopped at a light. But as soon as they slowed, the muzzle of the gun was pointed at his rib cage. The perp drove carefully, but not so carefully as to attract attention. They even passed a couple of New Jersey police cars, but the guy didn't even glance at them. The cell phone had stopped beeping, at least for the moment, and the scanner, locked into the cop bands, gave no indication that road-blocks were being set up.

Surely York missed him by now and was on their trail, Bates thought. Somebody must have seen the jacking. York would be quick to put out a bulletin on the van. Yeah, and then what happens? Bates wondered. A shoot-out, probably. And there was little doubt in Bates's mind about who was going to be first on the firing line. He was in a world of trouble and didn't have the slightest idea what to do about it. His brain felt like it was caught in a loop, spitting out the same thought, again and again.

Think, goddamn it! Bates found himself casting sideways glances at his abductor. The guy didn't look all that tough. The Dane would make hamburger out of him in a second. Except for the gun, of course. The muzzle of it, pointed as always in his direction, looked about as big as a man's fist to Bates. Not even the Dane would fight a gun, he decided. No, he had to use his head. Had to think . . . Talk to the guy, maybe. Humanize himself, make it harder for the perp to drop the hammer. He'd read that someplace, although Bates had his doubts about it working with this guy. The perp probably thought as much about killing a human being as other people did about eating a steak. Cows were put on this earth for people to eat, or so the argument went. So what happens if you ask the question on a different level? Why were human beings put on the world? Bates had the sinking feeling that this particular maniac had already wrestled with that moral dilemma. And that he had used the Jeffrey Dahmer solution to the problem.

"Where are we going?" Bates asked, deciding to at least try and save himself. Watts looked over at him and grinned, as if he had read the same article as Bates.

"Don't know," Arnie said casually, as if they were out for a leisurely drive around the countryside. "Anywhere in particular you'd like to go?"

"How about home?" Bates quipped, his stomach tightening as the facade he was trying to project crumbled around his shoulders like a tinfoil umbrella.

"How about Hell?" Watts asked, still smiling, pulling out to pass a slow-moving garbage truck. Arnie Watts did not like smartasses, but he also realized that this was entirely new territory. He had never ended up with a hostage before. Certainly not a full-grown adult. New territory had never been particularly appealing to Arnie.

Bates could think of no reply, so he sat quietly again, the strategy forgotten, concentrating on keeping his stomach where it was supposed to be. After a few minutes, however, he noticed the perp glancing over at him.

"So, you gonna tell me who the fuck you are, and why you're driving around New York in a rolling electronics store?" The questions were asked in an offhanded manner, but Bates knew that was not at all the intention. "You a cop?" the perp asked finally as Bates was still pondering the first set of questions.

"No." Bates shook his head, fishing around inside his brain for a suitable lie. He found none. He was suddenly amazed to hear his mouth ask the question that for some reason seemed foremost in his mind. "Where's the girl, anyway?"

Watts looked over, his eyes narrowing. There was a long pause. As if, Bates thought, the guy was actually considering the question.

"If I wasn't a real trusting sort of person, I'd say that was a cop question," Arnie said, his voice low and cold, like the sound of sleet hitting a windshield. Ronnie Bates wished now that he had kept his mouth shut. They were flashing along the interstate, passing signs for Newark and Bayonne. Finally the perp turned to him, ignoring the road altogether. "How about you dig out your wallet, hotshot," he snarled. "Seems like we need to get to know each other a little better."

The detectives were still turning the apartment while evidence units dusted the place for prints. Yvonne Stafford had been rushed to the North Central Medical Center and a unit dispatched to the Stafford apartment to inform the parents their daughter had been found. That had been several hours ago. The Staffords, York knew, were already at the hospital. Jenny was tapped in, giving him updates. The little girl was critical. The doctors refused to comment on her chances.

York had been at the scene for almost four hours. He'd sent the Dane out into the street to canvass for Bates and the missing van, but there was still no sign of either. Jenny called the precinct and an APB had been issued. The police had set up roadblocks and every street unit had the perp's composite, but so far the net remained empty.

It was getting dark outside, a light snow falling. York stepped out into the hallway for a smoke when the Dane came through the crowd around the cop's paper fence with a guy in tow. He was young, in his early twenties, wore a short leather coat, and looked as though he wanted nothing to do with any of this. But the Dane, York knew, could be very persuasive.

"Think I got something, boss," the Dane said, all but pushing the guy into the hall.

York took a long pull off his cigarette, waiting while the guy shuffled his feet and glanced nervously at the cops still working the perp's apartment.

"He saw the van," the Dane prompted.

"Saw it where?" York asked, his eyes pinning the guy to the floor like a bug he was about to squash. Not an altogether fair tactic, York admitted to himself, but the guy seemed hesitant and what he knew might be critical.

"Parked at the light at the end of the block," he said

quickly. "Like I told your buddy here, there was two guys in it. That's all I seen. . . ."

It was night now, and the perp seemed content to keep driving. They were rolling full tilt down 95, having left New Jersey behind some hours ago. Bates thought they might be in Maryland by now, but wasn't exactly sure. They'd passed signs for Wilmington hours ago. The perp seemed to know the road and blended in with the truck traffic. Bates was hungry and he had to make a pit stop before he peed his pants. Jesus, didn't this guy ever have to stop? Bates was beginning to wonder if the perp at the wheel was human. Somehow, he found the thought chilling.

"I got to go," Bates said as things approached critical mass.

"So go," Watts said. Bates stared glumly at the road as the white lines passed by like dashes in some obscure Morse Code message.

Finally, a half hour past Baltimore, Bates felt the van jerk off the side of the road, swinging into a quiet, deserted rest stop. There were eighteen-wheelers parked in a lot out back, the drivers who had run out of road hours sleeping off the foggy haze of too much travel. He had been dozing, too, Bates realized, snapping himself awake. The van pulled up to a fenced-in picnic area.

"OK, here's what we're gonna do," Arnie Watts said, sounding grim and businesslike. "We're walking over to that bathroom. We're going inside. You got one minute, exactly, to do what you got to do—then we're back in the van. No talking, no eye contact with anybody, or you're dead on the spot. No discussion, no warnings. You're dead, and whoever you talk to is dead, too. You got it?"

Watts had never actually talked to an adult like this before, although he had played out such scenes in his mind. It was far different from convincing children you were going to hurt them. Adults, he now knew, were already half-afraid to begin with. Arnie grinned. This new territory thing was turning out to be very exciting.

"You got it?" he repeated, feeling mean. This was how real killers felt, he realized.

"I got it," Bates said, grabbing the door handle. He made it inside, barely.

The warning turned out to be unnecessary, as there was no one else around at this late hour—three A.M. by Bates's watch. The perp stopped at the soda machine outside, fishing around in his pockets for change.

"You got any quarters?" he asked, and for some reason the question struck Bates as funny, and he laughed out loud. Here he was being kidnapped by a child murderer, and the guy was looking to bum a quarter off him.

"I got a single," Bates replied, his response sounding ever more absurd. Like they were friends coming back from a ballgame, making a pit stop on the way home.

Incredibly to Bates, the perp punched out two Cokes and handed one to him. Bates took it without comment. He tried to remember if he had ever heard of such a thing occurring during the course of a crime. He decided he hadn't, but it must happen, he rationalized. Whatever else, the human body still makes its demands for food, drink, excretion, and sleep.

Back in the van, Bates nursed his Coke and tried to fight off the last of the body's requests. He was exhausted and found himself nodding off, hypnotized by the hidden message in the road's cryptic stripes.

"Where are we going?" he asked again, hardly able to keep his eyes open. They had been driving for hours, the thought coming to him that the perp must be equally exhausted. Bates found himself increasingly haunted with the idea that the guy would fall asleep at the wheel. That they would both die in a fiery crash.

"South," Watts snapped. The voice was tense, but he did not tell him to shut up, Bates realized. So maybe the perp wanted a little conversation to keep him awake?

"Want me to drive for a while?" Bates heard himself offer. This whole experience, he decided, was making him crazy.

"Are you retarded or something?" Arnie asked, laughing a short, sharp laugh.

Sort of like a hyena, Bates thought, his exhaustion replacing his earlier feelings of utter terror. Sure, he was still afraid, but he was also still alive. It seemed reasonable that if the perp wanted to kill him, he would have already pulled the trigger.

"No," Bates answered, sounding hurt. He had a lot of faults, he knew, but had never before been accused of having a defective brain. "I just thought you must be tired, and I didn't want to get into an accident."

"You're already in an accident," Watts replied, and Bates was struck by the truth of the remark. York had been right, this guy was no fool. Perhaps, then, he might listen to some form of reason.

Are you going to kill me? Ronnie Bates wanted to ask, but didn't.

"How far south?" he asked instead. The perp ignored the question, so Bates decided on another tack. "They've probably got an all points out on the van," Bates said, trying to sound casual. Actually, he found that he was surprising himself by taking all this so calmly. It was the kind of situation in which he always believed terror would overwhelm him. But so far, it hadn't. Here he was, sipping a soda, conversing with a man who was, in all probability, a serial killer. At least that had been York's profile of the perp, and Bates had been associated with York far too long to doubt one of his assessments.

"Yeah, they probably have," Watts agreed, reaching over to snap on the police scanner.

"So it's only a matter of time before somebody spots us," Bates continued. Getting things out into the open— things that they both already knew—seemed like a good idea to Bates. It would work on the humanizing aspect, which he felt was critical to achieve, and might provide some insight into what this guy planned to do. The perp glanced over at him.

"Well, I guess you better hope that doesn't happen,"

Arnie Watts said. " 'Cause if it does, I don't plan on going out alone."

"You're probably going to kill me, anyway," Bates said softly, surprised that the words had actually come out of his mouth.

"Probably," Watts agreed again, which was obviously not the response Ronnie Bates had been hoping for. The terror rose up in his stomach again, turning the soda into the taste of warm metal in his mouth. The moon had risen out of the northern mountains. The Appalachian Mountains, Bates thought. So he watched the moon for a while, trying to block out the almost offhanded way the perp had answered him.

The years played across the old woman's body, in much the same manner as the songs her grandmother used to sing. Grandmother's voice, she remembered, was cracked and broken, yet her songs had been filled with strength and spirit. Grandmother, dead these many centuries, she thought sadly. And now, incredibly to her, *she* was the Ancient One, dispensing whatever wisdom she could muster, to whoever would listen. A winged vehicle roared above the leaves of her wooden house, splitting the very air with its thunder. She shook her head and her fist at its passing, her almond-shaped eyes, bright red and glowing in anger. She had seen much in her four hundred plus years, and lately none of it had been good.

Gathering herself, she walked outside to her porch, overlooking the Southern Sea. The waters were calm, as they usually were this time of year. Clouds of airborne algae drifted on the far horizon, shimmering in the light of the Double Suns. The cats, who hunted for her in the surrounding woods, came out of their dens at the end of the porch and rubbed themselves against her legs, licking salt from the pores of her scales. The old woman's flat, pug nose twitched in the middle of her deeply wrinkled features. The air smelled fresh, with the scent of kelp and salt rising from the beaches below. The water itself reflected the deep blue of the sky. But even though on the surface everything seemed to be well with the world, she knew that it was not. The large, sea-going mammals who once filled the bay with their feeding and mating frenzies, came here nc longer. Birds were now an unusual sight along the shoreline, except for the scavenging Whitetips who combed the sand for the fish and turtles that floated in regularly with the tide, dead and stinking. And above her house, infernal machines droned past in ever-increasing frequency. No, things were clearly not right with the world: From the view of her long years, she could see the changes that the shorter-lived members of her species could not, or did not wish to see. She hoped someone might come to this place, to seek her wisdom, but there had been no visitors for years and years. Now, she feared, there never would be.

She reached down to pet the cats, and the house swayed gently beneath her, demanding attention also. She patted the long, flat branch of her porch, in sympathy to its unheard cry. The earth and Her creatures knew the plight of their world, if others did not, she thought. Her house, which was made in the old style, out of living wood shaped and grown by master gardeners—artisans who were themselves now extinct—responded in its silent, stoic manner. She smiled briefly, running her hand over the smooth surface of the wood, her lips parting to reveal the nubs of long canine teeth, worn down through centuries of use. She feared, also, that she was the last of her lineage who would inhabit this sacred place.

The changes had begun during her mother's last century of life, some two hundred years ago now. They had been small, almost imperceptible at first. But her mother, endowed with the Third Sight, had felt them. In those days people still made the pilgrimage to this place, and her mother warned them about the changes she felt. Her warnings, obviously, went unheeded. And perhaps, her daughter often thought, the dire nature of the prophecies had been the reason people stopped coming to hear the words of the Ancient One. As if not hearing the words could somehow make them untrue. That had not been the case, either, and now centuries later the damage had been done. The sea mammals and water birds, driven to oblivion. The turtles and fish, now fit food only for the scavengers. The continents, she knew, teemed with people and machines. The people barely fed, the machines fed constantly. It was a thing, she thought, that was already beyond repair, at least as long as her species existed in the manner it now did. But that, too, she thought, was about to change. Whether or not there would be anyone left after the change took place was now the question.

For years she had been considering the problem, trying to see it in a different light, other than her own shaded view. She, of course, thought that people should live following the rules of the old ways. That they should grow their dwellings out of living wood and take from the earth only those things that they needed to survive. A simple, thoughtful, uncomplicated existence. She knew, also, how impractical that was, and how easy it was for her, living as she did for many times the normal span of years, to preach this wisdom. That was, if there had been anyone around to preach to.

But it was not progress, even with its many false faces and promises, that she railed against. There was always progress, in one form or another. Had not her grandmother spoken of the long-ago time of her own mother, when people dressed in hides and rode beasts to the marketplace? When famine and disease walked the land, hand-in-hand with kings and their armies? And how was that different from today? she wondered. The kings had other, less threatening names. The diseases were now primarily those of old age and excess. Hunger was confined to those whose ill luck or laziness had taken the food from their mouths, at least such was the view of those with full bellies. Indeed, she wondered, was there truly such a thing as progress, other than the beasts people rode to the marketplace and the dwellings in which they lived?

No, it was not progress, or its illusion, which now drove the engine of the world's destruction, she knew. It was something deeper, darker, which seemed to live in the hearts and minds of people. It was, almost, as if something sinister and brooding had come to be born inside them. Something that caused them, inexplicably, to seek their own destruction. Her mother had known it, and now she herself felt touched by its thorny grasp. It was a vile thing, embedded in the very marrow of the world.

The algae clouds on the far horizon began to darken as the Double Suns set behind them. The suns would rise and set for a million, million more times, she knew. But for how long would there be people here to watch them? Overhead, a winged vehicle, miles up in the air, caught the last light of day. The old woman sighed and, gathering herself, went back inside her fortress home. These days she did not like the coming of the night.

 ## REFLECTIONS ON THE EMERGING DARKNESS

Fact: It has now been confirmed that an outside agent is indeed at work within the context of the experiment.

In the very beginning, when Light was introduced into the universe, Darkness fled into the depths of the abyss where it found shelter and sanctuary. It lives there still in that place beyond the expanding galaxies, in the realms of the infinite. Further, it must be admitted that Darkness will eventually conquer the Light. Stars will fade and die. Galaxies will collapse in upon one another. Finally, in some far distant epoch, evolution itself will cease. The Light will have expanded its energies and Darkness will once again become the dominant force. So it has happened in the past, so it will happen again in the future. No experiment dealing with expendable energies can hope to last for an infinite duration.

The curious thing about Darkness, however, is its overall strategy for survival. In the beginning, as it retreated into the depths of the abyss, Darkness also managed to hide parts of itself in smaller, unseen places. Like a tree sowing seeds on the wind, so did Darkness plant seeds of itself in fertile ground, where it grew virtually undetected. Darkness, as it has now been discovered, has managed to conceal itself on a subatomic level, attaching itself to the smallest particles, which are themselves the building blocks of life. In this manner Darkness has found a means to exert a definable force on certain mechanisms in the physical plane. This fact seems irrefutable, particularly when one examines the events that continually disrupt the evolutionary plan set forth in the beginning of the experiment.

The dark forces, it is now obvious, have implanted themselves in the cellular makeup of the mechanisms. In this manner Darkness has become an undeniable factor in the evolutionary concept itself. It has discovered a way to entwine itself in the physical characteristics of the mechanisms, and in some cases is able to exert significant changes in the behavior of certain mechanisms. It now seems probable that all mechanisms on the physical plane are polluted to some extent with the propensity toward damaging behavior, either to themselves or to other mechanisms in their habitat. This seems to be especially prevalent in the ongoing experiment. The odd thing is that all mechanisms do not act on this inclination. At least not on the surface.

Question: To what extent do the actions of the few impact on the fate of all involved in the experiment?

thirteen

Dawn broke across the New York skyline, cold and weak, as though the sun had become as tired as Dennison York felt. He watched the light creep into the sky, a pale light, hardly able to displace the dark. It was dark in the office, too. York had sent Jenny and the Dane home sometime after midnight, to get some sleep. York had caught a few hours on the couch in his office. And now, looking out at the dawn, with the smothering taste of too many cigarettes and too much coffee in his mouth, he found himself looking out at a day he wished he could avoid.

He taped a picture against the windowpane—a composite of the perp provided by the building superintendent, which was better than the description given by Billy Case, and the super had given the police a name, William Ryder. It was undoubtedly a phony, but it was something. The Staffords had spent the night at North Central, of course. Things there were not going well. York had stopped by the hospital around midnight. He found it almost impossible to look at the girl, lost as she was in a cavern of pain. And her parents. Lesia Stafford, sitting in a chair by the bed, holding her daughter's hand, tranquilized, York could tell, by the glaze in her eyes. The girl's father, standing helpless at his wife's side, looked as if he wanted to be. York had stood by, powerless and ineffective in the face of their horrible grief. Later, in private, he had offered his resignation to James

Stafford, who was torn not only by the trauma of his daughter, but also by his own inability to comfort his wife. York, standing on the outside looking in, tried to understand their feelings. He did, to some extent. It had been horrible when his son died. He did understand grief. This situation was not unlike his own, except for the finality. Not surprisingly, Stafford's response had been much like his own.

"No," he said, refusing York's offer, his eyes filled with the hollow light of pain. "I want you to stay on the case. Please . . . find this son of a bitch! Find him for me . . . for us."

The man's tears had been shed without shame or embarrassment, but Stafford's rage seemed to catch him unaware. As if he had not realized the extent of the anger that had suddenly been born inside him. York understood. He understood it all.

"I don't think I can live, knowing that monster is out there," Stafford whispered, the very words choking him. "Knowing what he did to Yvonne . . ."

York merely nodded and then he'd left, just as a priest came to give Yvonne Stafford absolution for whatever sins she might have committed. York knew there were no words of comfort he could offer, no ceremonies, no litanies. The only thing he could do was his job, and hope that was enough.

And now, dawn had come. The monster was out there somewhere, and Ronnie Bates was with him. Or dead. Either way, there was a job to be done.

Jenny and the Dane came in at eight. York had a pot of coffee on. He had stripped down in the office bathroom, splashed cold water all over himself, and changed into a clean set of clothes he kept in the office closet. All of which made him feel only slightly better. In truth, he felt like he was hung over, his head buzzing from lack of sleep. But that would dissipate, he knew, as the morning progressed. It always did. There were a lot of people stronger and tougher than he was—the Dane being one of them—but York's strength lay in his tenacity, in his ability to keep going while others fell by the wayside. It was, he often reflected, his one saving grace. So he popped a couple of aspirin, gulped another cup of coffee, and got to work.

Morning pleasantries were largely absent, and there was an understandable air of urgency as each member of the team settled into their workstations. Jenny tapped the police computer, looking for any leads that might have developed during the night. The Dane played back scanner recordings, while York filtered through all the updated file information, looking for something that would tell them what happened to the perp and Ronnie Bates.

Unfortunately, they turned up exactly nothing. The Dane had checked Bates's apartment on his way in, following York's orders. The perp was smart, York knew, and it was not out of the question that he might be desperate enough to hole up in an obvious place, like his hostage's own apartment. But there had been no sign of Bates or the van, and he hadn't contacted his parents, either. York had promised to call them with the first bit of information he had on their son. It didn't look as if he would be making the call anytime soon.

"The guy ran," York concluded after they'd determined the police roadblocks had turned up no sightings of the van. The Dane looked up, questioning. The running part was pretty obvious. "No, I mean he really ran," York explained. "He's out of the city, probably out of the state."

"And he took Ronnie with him?" Jenny asked hesitantly, as if she were afraid of the answer.

"That's what I think," York said, staring out the window, sipping coffee, trying to put yesterday's events together in his mind. "Mr. Ryder, or whatever his name is, thought the girl was dead and was getting ready to dispose of the body, but things fell apart for him. We were close, and he knew it. So he was trapped and hijacked the van, with Ronnie in it. Bates was probably checking him against the sketch when it happened. Damn it, I wish I'd had the headset on. I would have known right away."

"You couldn't exactly cruise the streets wired," the Dane pointed out. "You'd have been too easy for him to spot."

"Yeah, like Ronnie was," York said, unable to shed the

responsibility he felt for Bates's abduction. "I should've stayed with him. He's inexperienced."

"Bates is a big boy," the Dane said, looking at York from under his eyebrows. It was uncharacteristic for York to blame himself for another's mistake. Bates had obviously screwed up. And whenever you screwed up, you paid the price.

"So this Ryder grabbed the van," York said, forcing himself back to the business at hand. "And he knew we were on top of him, so he had no time to get rid of his passenger. He had to get the hell out."

"The police were ringing off the area," Jenny pointed out. "He must've known that, from the scanner in the van."

"Right." York nodded. "He was only a step ahead of them, and that probably saved Ronnie, at least in the beginning." York had moved over to a map of the city, spread out like a poster on the wall behind his desk. "And he realized he had to get out of the city, so he ran for the nearest state line." York touched the map. "He crossed the GW Bridge, into New Jersey."

"Your friends at the Fifty-fourth agree," Jenny said, pulling the information from the computer bank. "They informed the FBI late last night that they had an interstate felon. They made the call just after midnight. A composite of Ryder and a photo of Ronnie went out over the hotline at the same time. The Jersey State Patrol picked up the APB then, and the rest of the police forces in the country, too."

"Fifteen hours is a long time," York said, shaking his head. "You can drive a long way in fifteen hours."

"So what do we do?" the Dane asked. Jenny's grim look mirrored the big man's question, and also gave the answer they all knew.

"We have to wait for something to turn up," York said. Either the van, or Ronnie's body, he didn't say. Bates, he knew, was excess baggage and would be discarded at the first opportunity.

Arnie Watts, in fact, was thinking along those very same lines. They were holed up in a tiny motel, well off the beaten path, outside of Durham, North Carolina. Bates was asleep, presumably in the bathtub, locked into the windowless bathroom, handcuffed securely to a pipe under the sink. Arnie had made an interesting discovery rummaging around in the van's equipment—two sets of first-rate metal bracelets, one with the standard short chain, and another set with a longer chain, obviously to be used as leg irons. It helped solve the immediate problem of hostage security. Once he had seen the cuffs, Bates pretty much resigned himself to the situation. He had gone in the bathroom quietly, exhausted, as Arnie himself was, also, and seemed grateful for any place to sleep. That was a funny thing about the lack of sleep, Arnie thought. It would make the strongest man weak and docile, and Arnie knew instinctively that Bates already had enough of those two qualities. So with Bates locked up tight, Watts moved the bed to block the bathroom doorway, and got some much needed shut-eye himself.

But now, with the first light of day creeping into the curtained room, Arnie was awake, considering his options. In truth, the problems were becoming complicated. The van, hot as molten lead, was parked out back. There had been no opportunity to ditch the vehicle, just as there had been no chance to get rid of his unwanted hostage. At least not without dramatically increasing his chances of getting caught. A dead body left by the side of the road, or in a roach-infested motel room, would be as good as a neon sign to those who were now hunting him, Arnie knew. But the van was smoking hot. A vehicle change was definitely the first order of business. But then again, maybe the first thing to do was unload this Ronnie Bates person. Arnie's hunting experiences had been, to this point anyway, limited entirely to the younger members of the human race. He had no qualms about killing Bates—it was, he realized, a virtual necessity if he hoped to get out of this mess. But if he had learned one thing during his hunting career, it was the difficulty posed in getting rid of the evidence. In this case a hundred-and-sixty-pound man.

Those mafia guys had it good, Arnie thought, lying on the bed, working the action on the Nine. They had access to vats of acid, or they could bury their bodies in concrete pilings, or dump them in the ocean weighted down with chains. But for anyone else, bodies were always the sticking point. Everybody who got caught at this game went down because of bodies. Thinking this, Arnie Watts remembered Yvonne Stafford, zipped into a duffel bag in the closet of his apartment. A cold shiver dimpled his skin, causing Arnie to wrap himself up in the bed's single blanket. Bodies, they were everyone's downfall. And now he had both a potential body and a van to deal with. It was enough to give a man a headache.

But it wasn't the van, exactly, that the cops were looking for, Arnie reasoned. It was a *blue* van, with New York plates. Lying on the bed, Arnie Watts grinned. One problem down, one to go.

"Up and at 'em, Master Bates." Watts pushed the bathroom door open, grinning at Ronnie Bates, who was awake and sitting on the edge of the bathtub. "Master Bates," Arnie repeated, liking the joke, fishing the cuff keys out of his pocket.

Bates, suddenly forced to remember the trauma of junior high, when that particular joke had been the rage, looked up and glared. He had not slept much during the night, chained to the bathroom fixture, trying to construct a viable escape plan, which always seemed to avoid his tired brain. The situation, he realized, was critical. The perp had now had time to sort through his various options, and it was obvious to Bates that his presence was certainly a problem. One that was easily resolved. Bates knew that, in all probability, he was going to die soon. That thought, somehow, made it even more difficult to think clearly.

"Let's go," Watts said, gesturing with the always-present gun. "We've got some miles to do this morning."

Miles, it turned out, were not the morning's primary objective, however. The perp kept Bates in the back of the van, the leg bracelets slipped through a ring in the floor, which Dennison York had installed for exactly the purpose for which it was now being used. Meanwhile, the perp made a series of early morning recons to neighboring motels. To

Bates's surprise, Watts returned with three sets of license plates. Two from North Carolina, and one from Virginia, all commercial tags. On one of the country roads outside Durham, he pulled over and put one of the Carolina plates on the van, stashing the rest under some radio equipment in the back. He offered no explanation, but Bates quickly realized that by stealing three sets of plates, from three different motels, the perp had probably taken a large step toward throwing off pursuit. They stopped for gas in Raleigh, with Bates still locked in the back.

"Don't make a sound," Watts warned. "Or I'll kill you and anybody who hears. Understand?"

Bates nodded that he did, and he believed the threat to be valid. Sitting in the back, hearing Watts joke with the attendant, Bates was struck by the coldness of his captor. That the man could laugh and make small talk about the weather, just as easily as he would shoot everyone in the vicinity, should Bates decide to call out for help or start banging on the door demanding to be set free.

Even though it was still early morning, it was hot in the van. Bates sat in the rear seat and sweated, trying to figure out what he should do. York or the Dane would have had a plan in place, he thought, miserable at his own incompetence. At the fear he felt, constricting his throat, wrapping itself like a snake around his chest. The truth was, he felt like crying, and that made him feel more miserable, more incompetent. Plus he needed coffee. The lack of caffeine was making his head pound. Which was really fucking ridiculous. Bates cursed himself and his situation. He was going to be killed and all he could think about was how much he needed a cup of coffee. As if that would somehow make everything all right. He might as well try and wrestle the gun away from this asshole and save himself. What did he have to lose, anyway? Your life, his brain whispered. Your life . . .

So Ronnie Bates sat in the back of the van, staring at the disconnected radio equipment, pulling from time to time on the steel bands wrapped around his ankles, and waited for the perp to follow through with whatever plan he had devised. Ronnie Bates, floating along on the River of Time, hardly making a ripple. Bates was now also convinced that the guy might just be smart enough to pull it off, to escape what appeared to be certain capture. York always said that the most dangerous criminals were those who combined basic intelligence with a high degree of luck. There was no substitute for good luck, York said, whenever the discussion turned to the criminal element. And this perp seemed to have more luck than anyone Bates had ever encountered.

Bates heard the driver's side door open, then the van's engine turned over. The road began thumping under him and the front panel slid open.

"Want some breakfast?" the perp asked, handing back a cup of coffee and two powdered donuts. To his disgust, Bates found himself grateful for the offering, taking the coffee with shaking hands. Before the panel slid back, Bates saw a case of black spray paint and a box of heavy duty plastic garbage bags on the front seat. The coffee, however, chased his curiosity away.

There was Light suddenly. Bright and infuriating. Light that burned her eyes and kept her from sleeping. Sleeping and waiting for forever. The two things she wanted most. The Light brought her awake. Reminded her of the pain her body felt. Her body . . . once able to move so freely. To run and jump without hurting. Her body . . . now felt as though someone had removed all her bones and replaced them with heavy stones. And she was imprisoned here, in this heavy bag of stones. Her body . . . good only for sleeping in now. But the Light. Tried to keep her awake. She didn't move, but in her mind, she cried. The tears looked to her like golden raindrops falling into a silver lake of mercury.

On a world in a circular galaxy, so far from the Planet Earth that no human being had yet seen the light of the galaxy's youngest suns, a river was about to explode. The priests had spent the last several days in conference on the Holy Mount, measuring the proximity of the Five Moons to one another, observing the cycle of the stars as they turned in the night sky. Word filtered through the villages. The people, humanoids, gathered along the shoreline for this once-in-a-lifetime event. The Elders, those few who had been small children when the river last exploded, spoke in excited whispers, telling stories of the wonder the clan was about to witness. Even as the novice priests visited the campfires, reminding people of their duty to God and to their clan.

The sun rose, pink and sharp, lifting off the summit of the Holy Mount. The priests, weary from their work, trudged down the mountainside to announce that this was indeed the day when God would make Himself known. The people gathered together to receive their blessing, so those who might die this day would find their way swiftly to the campfires of the dead. Thick ropes, made from the fibrous bark of thorn trees, entwined with the hair of past martyrs, were brought forth and tied to the mighty column-trees lining the river. Men prayed, children looked on in wonder at the waters of the river, which for the moment seemed calm and peaceful. The women cooked ceremonial foods of strength and courage to feed their husbands, fathers, brothers, and lovers.

The sun slipped through the first half of the sky. Multi-winged birds called to one another across the orange grasses. The wool-makers huddled together on the rocky slopes above the river. The hooved meat herds stamped and grunted along the far plain. The entire world, it seemed, was waiting for what was about to happen. And the people waited, whispering to one another. Men tested the ropes, swinging out from the riverbank like tethered birds, swooping back to the rock ledges along the bank. The priests studied the sky, worrying about the accuracy of their measuring instruments.

Then, the ground rumbled. Softly at first, like the sound of distant drumming. The grass began swaying. Flocks of birds took to the air, startled. The wool-makers howled, the meat herds stampeded, and finally even the column-trees began swaying. The earth itself heaved, and the people cried out as the river began to boil and hiss like a steaming cauldron. From the depths of the smoldering water, great boulders of white rock shot to the surface, bobbing, floating like ice chunks in winter. The priests moved among the men, filling them with the blessings of strength and bravery, urging them on. First one, then another swung out over the water, landing on the great slabs of rock, tying their heavy ropes to jagged nodes along the rocks' surfaces. And when the ropes were secure, those along the shore heaved and pulled, drawing the sacred stones toward shore. Many of the men who swung out over the bubbling water were crushed as more and more of the white stones shot to the surface. Many slipped from the wet, slick stones and were swept away by the river's sudden surge. Hands and arms, feet and legs became caught in the crush of stone. The water churned red, and the stones themselves became stained with the blood of martyrs. Those along the shoreline screamed, as loved ones disappeared in the turbulent storm of boiling water and sharp stone.

But by day's end a dozen or more of the sacred stones had been dragged to shore and lifted from the surging waters. As the sun slipped below the grassy plain, the earth ceased its rumbling. The river flowed calmly once more. The priests inspected the stones, whose white, inner light glowed in the darkness, and they gave thanks to God and to those who had given their lives to enrich the clan with these treasures. Fires were lit, the survivors toasted with spring wine. Songs were sung, testifying to their bravery.

In the morning the stones were pulled farther from the riverbank, lest they be lost to the winter floods. Then the stone cutters began chipping away at the white surfaces. Slabs were cut out to honor those who had sacrificed their lives retrieving the precious stones. The priests were given small, rounded pieces of the bright rock, which they wore set in leather collars around their necks. Those few of the people who cried out about the loss of a husband, father, brother, or lover were quickly silenced. There were, after all, monuments to be built.

fourteen

James Stafford sat by his daughter's bed, watching as she fought against demons he could only imagine. He had just tucked her feet back under the covers, remembering when she was born and how he had marveled at her tiny toes, smaller than the nail on his little finger. The doctors, he knew, had told him about his daughter's injuries only in the most vague terms. And for that, he was grateful. Lesia sat with Yvonne most of the night and was now asleep in the bed by the door. Stafford wondered if his daughter would ever come back to them, and if she did, would she ever be the same? In the back of his mind he thought about the monster out there, somewhere. A monster of such magnitude that it had done this to his little girl. He shivered and, leaning down, began whispering in Yvonne's ear.

The worst part about waking up was that they wanted to talk to her. Wanted to make her say things. To listen. To remember. But she preferred to lie in the bed, even though she knew it was not her bed. But it was a place where she could wait, quietly, to sleep again. A part of her wanted to ask where she was, and how she came to be here. But that part was quiet, too. Every so often, she opened her eyes and watched the tubes attached to her arm. Wondering if they were putting things in, or taking things out.

York stood outside the girl's room in intensive care, marveling at all the technology the hospital used, and still they couldn't reach inside the girl's mind to fix the most broken part of her. James Stafford was in the room, so he didn't want to disturb them. No, that wasn't it at all, he admitted to himself. He had no idea what to say, or what to do. So, generally, he visited Yvonne Stafford from the hall. Somehow, he didn't think it mattered much. Every day Jenny said the same thing:

"She hasn't said a word. Not a single word. The doctors still won't allow her to see the perp's sketch. The trauma's simply too near the surface, they say. Poor girl."

Both York and Jenny shaking their heads. Both of them, in their hearts, thinking of Jenny's young daughter. What was the saying? There but for the grace of God go I. There but for the grace of God go any of us, York thought. Every day they went through the missing-person reports. Hardly a day went by when some kid didn't show up on the sheets. Even when you factored runaways and parental squabbles, there was still an unbelievable number of children disappearing all across America. No one in the office said it, but York could tell they were all thinking the same thing: How many monsters are out there preying on kids? A lot, York concluded. Was it dozens? Was it hundreds? He didn't know. Nobody knew, he was discovering.

Ronnie Bates's head cleared some after the infusion of caffeine. And the donuts, stale as they were, tasted as good as a big, thick steak from the Butcher Block. Bates brushed the powder off his shirt and began to reconsider his situation. York and the Dane, he realized, would think his response up to now to be downright pitiful. They would have done *something*. Yeah, and they'd probably be dead, he rationalized. He was still alive and that was something. He still had a chance to survive this, and maybe even capture the perp in the process. Wouldn't that be something? he thought. Even the Dane would have to give him some respect then. Thinking that, Bates shook his head, realizing the absurdity of it.

A couple more hours passed as Bates sat fitfully in the backseat, his brain slamming into brick walls every time he tried to think up some plan of escape. It was much worse stuck in the back of the van, unable to watch where they were going. But at ten-fifteen by Bates's watch—even though he wasn't sure of the time zone anymore—he felt the van pull over and stop. Another license plate run? Or maybe the police spotted the van! Bates felt his heart hammering at the possibility, but then he realized he would have heard the sirens. There wasn't much time to consider any of the hundred other possibilities that popped into his mind, because the side door popped open and the perp was standing there with the gun pointed in Bates's general direction. He tossed the bracelet keys in, and they rattled across the floor.

"OK, out." The perp waved the weapon and Bates rubbed his ankles before climbing out into the bright sunshine, blinking, wondering if his sunglasses were still in the glove compartment.

They were parked, Bates saw, on a deserted road, over which a gravel truck had made a tentative pass, probably some years ago. Brush was thick along the side of the road, thin poplar trees lining both sides of what might be a two-lane road, provided that any two vehicles who happened to come upon each other both hugged the dirt shoulders. There were no houses, not even any electric lines overhead. The only things that suggested human habitation were the thin ribbon of road and a stretch of old barbed wire, long since overgrown with weeds.

"There's spray paint in the front seat," the perp said. "Get it and start painting the van."

"You want me to paint the van?" Bates asked, wondering if his ears were working correctly.

"Yeah, paint the fucking van!" Arnie Watts repeated, his voice cold and angry. "Are you deaf?"

"No," Bates said, moving around to the front door of the van. The perp, he noticed, stepped away when he came close, as if he was expecting Bates to try something. Paint the van? Bates shook his head. So maybe the guy was going to just drive off into the sunset, right past the cops, with a spray-painted van and Carolina license plates? It was an absurd plan, in Bates's mind. But one which, unfortunately, might work.

"Just hurry it up, for Christ's sake! And don't paint over the fucking headlights!" Watts growled, flashing the gun, drinking coffee from a giant 7-Eleven cup, as Bates worked the plastic top off one of the cans and began covering the blue surface with the dull, black paint.

The paint dripped and streaked as sweat dripped and streaked across Bates's face. The sun was overhead now, as one side of the van was finished. A monumentally shitty job, Bates saw, with blue swatches poking through in any number of places. It was slow going, too. The nozzles on the cans kept blocking up and sticking, no matter how much he shook them. The perp came by every once in a while, jabbing a finger onto the black surface to see how fast it was drying. Even though it was a terrible paint job, Bates now began to see that it might just work. At least it would be good enough to fool a cop cruiser passing on the highway. It was at this point that Bates realized the true extent of the danger he was in. There was the real possibility now that the perp might actually escape. And even though things were very confused in Bates's mind, he was aware that it was reasonably certain he would be expendable. In point of fact, Bates thought, he was expendable as soon as the van was painted.

"Better splash some more of that stuff over here," the perp said, pointing to an area Bates had only lightly dusted, figuring that if he could let enough of the blue show through, he might still have a chance. Providing, of course, he was still in the van. And still alive. His hands turning black from the four spray cans he'd already used, Bates moved over to redo the area on the side panel. The perp slid away, his finger never leaving the Nine's trigger.

As the day stretched into afternoon, Bates took his shirt off, soaked it in water from a jug in the backseat, and tied it around his head. It was eighty degrees or better, hot for this time of year. Funny, Bates thought, how it could be blistering hot in one place, and still be only a couple days' drive away from snow. Bates, who had never lived anywhere except New York, always found this interesting. Even though friends spoke about Arizona or California, where a person was only a couple of hours away from such extremes in temperature. Still, it was amazing to Bates that you could drive just a little while, and it was as if you were in an entirely different country. He occupied his mind with these thoughts, preferring them to the reality of his situation.

Half the van was painted now, or at least streaked with black lacquer. That was pretty much the best that could be said for it. Bates's fear was that it might be good enough.

Clouds crept across the sun during the early afternoon, and for a while it looked as though it might rain. Bates grinned to himself, thinking about rain washing the black paint off the van, making long, dark streaks in the road. As though a tar truck had sprung a leak. Hardly inconspicuous. The perp, also realizing what might happen should it rain, watched the sky nervously.

"Hurry it up!" he snapped at Bates. Arnie Watts liked the tough-guy sound to his voice. Much to his surprise, he found it worked just as effectively on adults as kids, provided, of course, that you had a gun.

The sun was well along its afternoon trek. A flock of crows called to one another in the trees. A squirrel ventured across the tarmac bridge between woods, stopping to stare at them—invaders into the world of rodents. Then it ran to other, more important matters. The van was well over half done, with only another side panel to be painted. Bates stopped for a moment, wiping the sweat from his eyes.

HE'S GOING TO KILL YOU!

The thought struck him like a blow to the side of his head, and Ronnie Bates staggered under its impact.

HE'S GOING TO KILL YOU!

The truth of it was unavoidable. Bates controlled the urge to run and forced his mind to work. It was now or never, he thought frantically. He had to try and save himself, or he was actually going to die.

The perp was looking up at the sun as it drifted in and

out of the clouds, shielding his eyes, tapping the barrel of the gun against his leg. Bates got a fresh can of spray paint and moved to the remaining blue panel, working his way around, spraying the black lacquer in wide, sweeping arcs. He stopped and looked down at the wheel well. From the corner of his eye, Bates saw the perp's attention shift from the sun to the wheel.

"What's this in the tire?" Bates asked, running his hand over the tread.

"What?" Arnie Watts asked, suspicious.

"Looks like a nail," Bates said. "A big fucking nail!"

"Shit . . ." Watts said, bending down to look.

Bates turned and sprayed him full in the face with the black paint. Watts yelled and jumped back, wiping at his eyes, staggering. And Bates ran, heading for the line of trees. Watts shouted again and behind Bates the gun cracked. Two, three, four times. Bates jumped the sagging barbed-wire fence. The gun roared again and this time Bates felt his legs go out from under him, even as he fell into the brush. His left leg burned, like someone had stuck a blow torch against his skin. His pant leg was wet. Blood, he realized numbly. But he was crawling now on all fours, pushing himself up into a half-crouch. Running again, shuffling sideways like a crab, the brush scraping against his face and arms. The gun cracked again, snapping branches around him. All of which made Bates run faster, or so it seemed to him. The fire in his leg ran down like lava into his ankle and then leaped straight up into his hip. He was staggering, but still kept going, spurred on by the sound of footsteps along the road, by brush breaking behind him as the perp followed him into the thick woods. Bates ran until his leg finally betrayed him and began flopping around at his side like a broken tree branch blowing in a heavy wind. Bates stumbled, falling face first into a patch of soft moss. His fingers clenching the ground as he tried to make himself rise. Gasping, his breath burning like his leg. And then a shadow came to stand over him. The clicking of a gun being cocked. Bates tried not to think about the fear that gripped his throat like choking hands. A second later there was a loud roar, and Bates stopped thinking altogether.

Dennison York snapped upright in his chair, his eyes wide. Jenny looked up from her computer. The Dane stopped his pacing.

"You all right?" Jenny asked.

"Yeah, I guess," York said, unable to shake the feeling that he had just been jarred awake from a very disturbing dream.

"You look like you just saw a ghost," the Dane commented. York laughed a little too quickly and went back to studying the file on his desk. It was the latest FBI reports on stolen vehicles along the southern interstates. There was, York decided, nothing useful in it. Jenny came in and put a hand on his shoulder. For some reason, it felt very comforting. He smiled up at her, his mind replaying the same question, over and over: Where the hell was Ronnie Bates?

Arnie Watts was sweating like a pig, and he hated to sweat. He finally had the body wrapped up in garbage bags, tied with clothesline and stashed in the back of the van. The paint job was done, and Arnie was waiting for it to dry. He'd brushed the blood off the side of the road with branches and tossed the bloody leaves in the brush on the other side of the broken fence. Bodies were such a pain in the ass, and Arnie knew he had to ditch this one as soon as possible. It was hot, and even with the air-conditioning on in the van, this corpse wouldn't keep long.

As soon as the paint was tacky he got in and drove back to Durham. He picked up Interstate 95 and drove until dusk. He stopped off in Lumberton, bought some cinder blocks, a good length of chain, and some master locks. He then drove down 95 until after midnight. With the moon rising on the swampy lowlands of Lake Marion in South Carolina, Arnie found a bridge off Route 301, outside Santee. There he wrapped the body in chains, weighted it down with the cinder blocks, and locked everything up tight with the master locks. He drove across the bridge twice, making sure nobody was fishing the shoreline. He parked in the middle of the bridge, killed the lights, and swung the body over the railing. It landed with a loud splash. Then Arnie drove for another few hours, before finding a cheap motel in Yemassee. He slept for the next few days, before deciding to take a trip out to California. San Diego was nice this time of year.

On a world in the fourth arm of the spiral galaxy called the Milky Way, a child lay on a bed of nails. At least it seemed that way to her. From someplace far away, someone was calling her name. It was a soft voice, warm and comforting. And she wanted to answer. Wanted to open her eyes and tell him that he shouldn't worry. That she was all right. Only she wasn't.

It was strange. She didn't hurt anymore. In fact, she didn't feel anything. It was as though her mind existed as a completely separate thing from her body. Like a movie she had seen once—late, late at night, while staying at a friend's house. A really bad movie in which a person's brain had been removed from his body and existed in a vat of some smoky liquid. Oddly, that was how she felt now. As though her brain had been removed and she existed now in some sort of vacuum. Alone and separate from the outside world. The outside world . . . it hardly seemed real to her anymore. As if the entire universe were only this dark, yet somehow safe place. And she wanted to stay here, hiding in the darkness. Where voices came to her, whispering comforting words. She felt safe here. Safe, as though nothing could hurt her. Ever again. Only lately the voices had been telling her that she needed to return to the outside world. To her body and her life. But the truth was, she didn't want to leave the sanctuary of this dark place.

She smiled to herself, thinking again about the brain in that awful movie. Living alone within its glass bubble, filled with warm liquid. They had made it seem like such a bad thing—to exist without a body, to live only in your thoughts. She and the other girls had laughed, she remembered. Laughed to cover their fear. She and the other girls

. . . Whose house had it been? The girl had once been her best friend, she thought. Only the name and the face were both lost. As though they belonged to another life. The life she had Before. She had trouble remembering that other life. There were holes in her memory. As if her mind was an apple through which worms burrowed, leaving behind long, empty trails. . . .

"Yvonne, honey, open your eyes." The voice floated to her through the darkness. Her father's voice, she knew suddenly. "Talk to me, baby. Come on, Yvonne. Come back to us. . . ."

And she wanted to. But it wasn't as easy as that. Because she also wanted to stay here, where it was dark and safe. Like pulling the blankets over your head on a cold winter's morning. Caught, with only your thoughts for company, in that peaceful world between sleeping and waking. It was, she realized, much easier to sleep than to wake. Because when you woke up, you remembered. And she didn't want to remember. She wanted only to sleep. So she did. For just a while longer, she promised the voices.

Light, soft as the full moon behind a bank of thin clouds. Light, which seemed to whisper from the depths of the darkness around her. Shadows visiting in the dark. Holding her, rocking her, as if she were an infant in her mother's arms. For some reason, she could remember that long-ago time with the greatest clarity. The smell, the warmth of her mother's body. The safe feeling. She clung to that feeling, as though it were the only thing in all the world that could make her feel safe. If she woke, she would be afraid again. She would hurt again. She would remember. No, she whispered to the shadows. I don't want to remember. . . .

Light, soft as a full moon behind a bank of thin clouds.

"Yvonne, honey, come back to us. . . ."

Safe. She only wanted to feel safe. That was all. It seemed like such a simple thing.

The Light, brighter. Like the first rays of the sun at dawn.

Light, creeping into her vision. Dim reds and yellows. The bright blue of a lake under the afternoon sky.

"Please," she whispered. "I only want to feel safe."

Crying. The Light even brighter. The sun rising, playing across the shadowy valleys of her mind. The soft darkness retreating. She wanted the darkness back. Wanted to lay in its comforting arms. To hide there. Forever.

"I'll keep you safe, Yvonne. I promise."

Her father's words, as bright and sharp now as the Light. Crying. Someone was crying. It was her father, she realized. And he was crying because she had reached out with her arms and was hugging him.

Crying. The outside world, she thought, was a place of tears.

 ## REFLECTIONS ON THE EFFECTS OF TECHNOLOGY

It has been argued that technological advancements achieved by mechanisms in emerging societies have a negative effect on the evolutionary cycle within any life experiment. The general statement is that technology allows certain damaged mechanisms, namely those with undesirable genetic traits, to achieve a longevity that under normal circumstances would be impossible. It is further argued that these mechanisms pollute the gene pool through procreation, thereby producing an extended lineage susceptible to a variety of diseases, mental imbalances, and other malfunctions that would be expunged from the gene pool during the course of normal evolution. Thus, the theory is that technology weakens the species as a whole by eliminating the principal evolutionary law, that being Survival of the Fittest.

In fact, the reverse is true. The goal of evolution is, first and foremost, to produce a strong, functioning mechanism capable of survival in the hostile environment of the physical plane. This goal is usually achieved during the first stages of development. It is during the early stages of a successful experiment that the survival law is followed with all of its harsh, exacting components. However, once the survival requirements are met, the function of evolution changes. The challenge for the evolutionary forces then shifts from the physical to the mental state of the mechanisms. This realignment of goals, and its successful implementation, is critical to the continued survival of any dominant species. Given the proper evolutionary conditions it is a fairly uncomplicated process to produce a dominant species. The successful experiment will, however, go beyond that elementary goal. For a dominant species to move further up the evolutionary scale, it is essential for them to discard the instinctual mind-set which allowed them to rise to domination in the first place.

The challenges here should not be underestimated. The survival instincts are deeply encoded and are therefore not easily dismissed. This is particularly true in the case of territorial hunter\gatherers for whom the survival law has been paramount to their continued existence. The inability to discard this early genetic encoding is the principal reason behind the failure of many of these experiments.

Thus, the introduction of technology affords the implanted mechanisms the opportunity to restructure their developing societies away from a material-based, hoarding mentality, and allows the development of a society based on the secondary evolutionary goals. Namely, the creation of a compassionate society in which the individual is cherished not for the goods or services they provide, but simply for being a living entity.

This emotional development is critical on several fronts. First, by learning to care for the individual as an entity, the implanted mechanisms will develop the emotional stability necessary for long-term survival as a dominant species in the physical plane. Second, by developing the technology required to care for disabled, underdeveloped, or damaged mechanisms, the society as a whole will benefit as they learn to eliminate the effects of genetic malfunctions and other accidental occurrences which are common in the physical plane. They will, in effect, be able to contribute to their own evolution in this manner, and will eventually strengthen the genetic pool through the use of technology.

The dangers here are apparent and unavoidable. For the experiment to achieve success, the mechanisms themselves must achieve a balance between the technological and emotional growth. Technological advancement without the required emotional stability will, in most cases, lead to an abrupt discontinuance of the experiment. Conversely, the restructuring of a society away from the hunter/gatherer mentality is usually not possible without technological advancement.

Conclusion: This particular life experiment is now reaching such a crossroad. Observations indicate that either advancement to the next stage of development or failure of the experiment is imminent. The intriguing part of this experiment lies in the fact that a society has developed in which the individual mechanisms perceive themselves to be a part of a communal whole. This communal mind-set, common in territorial agriculturists (which itself is only a variation of the hunter/gatherer society), seems to give its members the perception that the society itself is greater than each individual member. The confusion caused by this misconception allows the members to believe that society is so tightly structured that individual mechanisms cannot effect change. In fact, for better or worse, the individual is the society, with each member having a direct causal effect on the outcome of the experiment.

The Damselfly

The damselfly: A predatory insect which uses overpowering strength and size to capture its prey. The prey, usually the common housefly, is immobilized and held securely by the damsel's strong sets of arms. Once its prey has been grasped, the damselfly inserts a feeding tube into the victim's body and consumes the living insect in much the same manner as a spider. The damselfly is one of the insect world's most formidable predators.

fifteen

The ice cubes rattled around in the bottom of York's glass. Dry, like the sound of old people coughing. There was a football game on television—the Giants and the Eagles. Back in the old days he would've been riveted to the screen, but on this cold, damp Sunday afternoon it barely held his attention. A commercial came on. One of hundreds, it seemed. He got up from his chair and walked over to the window. The rain looked as if it might turn to snow anytime. Cars slogged by, wipers flashing. Summer was a distant memory, fallen by the wayside like the leaves on the trees. The whole world had that bare, brown, prewinter look to it.

It had been eight months now. Eight months since Yvonne Stafford had been pulled from the perp's apartment, more dead than alive. Eight months to the day since Ronnie Bates rode away in the van—off the face of the earth, it seemed. Eight months and not a single worthwhile clue. York's apartment smelled stale, like leftover beer, and he knew he should have taken Jenny up on her invitation to Sunday dinner. But he wanted to be alone today, for some reason he didn't quite understand. Making pleasant conversation, even with Jenny and her daughter, did not seem appealing.

Eight months . . . and still he was haunted by what had happened. Maybe the Staffords had the right idea, he thought. After Yvonne had finally been released from the hospital, they had packed up and fled the city, moving out of state to the Connecticut suburbs. He hoped, as did Lesia and James Stafford, that by leaving they could put it all behind them. That, somehow, they could return their lives, Yvonne's especially, to some semblance of normalcy. Surely not forgetting, but perhaps starting over. Hardly a day went by when York didn't toss the very same idea around in his head. It had been a bitter thing. It still was. Like a flood or an earthquake—something that passed in time, but was never truly far from the minds of the survivors.

Surviving, York knew, was not always the easy path.

The phone rang and he let the answering machine pick it up.

"Dennison, it's Jenny. The invitation's still open. We won't be eating until around five, if you want to come over. Or later on. I'll be here. Talk to you later."

Jenny. He felt guilty about not talking to her. York knew he should call her back. They could sit on the couch in her living room; he would look at her and listen to the sound of her voice. They would comfort each other. It was strange how their relationship had come about. It seemed to be a thing born of their mutual grief. When Ronnie Bates did not walk, grinning, through the front door, the team's three survivors had seemed at first to have been pulled apart. The Dane spent more and more time at the gym. York immersed himself in the task of finding clues. Jenny, it seemed, was left with everything else. It wasn't fair. York knew that, but pushed the thought from his mind. If he could look long enough and deep enough, he felt, he could solve the puzzle. But he hadn't, of course. And sometime after the first month Jenny had come to him as he stood by the window in his office, brooding.

"You can't be responsible for everything," she'd said.

Somehow that had been the start of it. He'd reached over and touched her arm. And something had passed between them. Something almost intangible, yet undeniably significant. Both had leaped back from it at first. Like a person touching a hot stove, York had thought. But gradually over the following weeks, they went to dinner, to movies . . . and the rest had happened naturally.

Eight months . . . and he'd chased down every lead, no matter now trivial. Chased them all across the country. He knew all too well that the business had gone to hell because of his obsession. The Cayman bank account depleted. The money from the magazine interview as well. There had been no additional offers after the story broke. York had gone from hero to goat in the span of a thunderclap, gored by twin prongs of failure. He failed to find Yvonne Stafford before a beast that hid itself in the guise of a human being had preyed upon her. He had failed again to protect one of his own from falling victim to the beast. The fact that the police had also failed in each of these endeavors was not relevant. He had, by the very nature of his business, set himself above the workings of the bureaucracy. In a sense, they were expected to fail. But he was not. And the press played it for all it was worth, tarnishing his image further. Failure, York knew, was the ultimate public relations disaster.

The office phone had turned suddenly and ominously quiet. Even the city contracts had dried up over the ensuing months. Instead of checks in the mail, he was now receiving dunning notices. But all of that, he kept telling himself, had nothing to do with his obsessive behavior toward finding the perp. He wasn't looking to resurrect his business, or even save his admittedly poor reputation. No, it was a question of revenge. He knew that as surely as he knew his name.

Revenge. He wanted it, could taste it sometimes, like a corroded penny in his mouth. Just like that long-ago time in LA. York knew how terrible revenge was. Knew all too well what it had done to him the last time. Knew, even, that it would do nothing to absolve him of his guilt. No, it might not absolve his guilt, but it would sure go a long way toward squaring his accountability. Because there was no question, in his mind anyway, about his responsibility. Perhaps not entirely for the Stafford girl, but he sure as hell bore the brunt of the blame for what had befallen Ronnie Bates. Damn it! He should've kept the fucking headset on. He should've stayed in the van with Bates. He should've . . .

The drink tasted like dust. York grabbed his coat and went out to walk in the cold rain, leaving the television on in the living room.

The bus left Port Arthur, Texas, in a roar of diesel fumes and gritty dust. Arnie Watts watched from one of the window seats. Oil rigs, power lines, one-story shacks, old men rocking on slanted porches, tire swings and laundry hanging in the yards, trucks in a great hurry to go no place. For it seemed as though there was no place to go in the wide, flat Texas countryside. Clouds draped the horizon like badly hung curtains, weatherbeaten men in tractors drove past hulks of rusted farm machinery. Everyone and everything trailing a fog of dust wherever they went. Which was no place.

Arnie Watts sure felt as if he was leaving nowhere, heading nowhere. He'd spent a forgettable couple of months in Texas and was damn sick of the place. Too hot, too many wetbacks, too much shit-kicking music, not a breath of air that didn't have dust hanging in it. And besides that, a deplorable lack of opportunity, economic or otherwise. Texas, clearly, was not the promised land. It was amazing to him that so many Mexicans still thought it was, as they poured across the border like ants, clogging up the welfare system with their American-born children, making a natural-born white man stick out like a sore thumb.

Arnie had ended his Texas adventure without even enough gas money to escape the state. He'd been forced to sell the van, which he'd driven down from Montana, to some cutthroat used-car dealer just to get bus money out. Montana—that had been another bust. He'd fenced the electronics equipment in Butte, stripped the van bare to pay for a real paint job and new tires, then took the road south through Colorado. After which he had gotten trapped in the sinkhole they called Port Arthur.

Despite his dislike for Mexicans, Watts had taken up with a brown-skinned woman from south of the border, who had a taste for cheap wine and wild weed. But who also had a tin-roof shack and didn't seem to mind fucking him on occasion. But, Jesus, she was mean when she got drunk, and he'd made the mistake of slapping her around a little. More than a little that last time, Watts admitted to himself. Her relatives had gotten it into their heads to extract some payback, so Arnie bugged out before her brothers actually carried out their threat to cut his nuts off. Not that it would've happened the way they'd planned, Watts thought, grinning to himself. He probably would have had to plant at least one of the bastards before they realized they were messing with the wrong dude. The Nine would've made quick work out of any who didn't get the message. But then there would have been the Law to deal with. No, it was better to get the hell out. Oh, but wait till they found out what he'd done to their fucking whore of a sister before he'd split. Arnie smiled, looking out the window. At miles and miles of nothing.

It was getting so the Dane, whose real name was Vir Ekendland, hated coming to work. Indeed, if one could call it work. For the most part he just sat around the office, playing errand boy while Jenny scanned computer records and York read clippings from the Express service. Occasionally York would have him order up the details on a particular story that looked promising, but that and coffee were about the extent of his responsibilities these days.

Sitting around had about as much appeal to the Dane as root canal. As was his custom, he began his day with a brutal workout at Gold's as soon as the doors were open in the morning. That was, if they hadn't been out all night chasing bad guys, which he and York hardly ever did anymore. And nothing bothered the Dane so much as inactivity. One of the joys in his life was lifting the gym's iron weights until his muscles seemed to cry out and his body released its poisons through his sweat. It was a glorious feeling. And, too, there was more than a little vanity involved, the Dane admitted to himself. An avid skier, he knew he looked like a Viking raider sweeping down the mountainside, set to plunder the ski lodges, which he had done with wild success in his younger days. That, in fact, had been one of the principal causes behind his divorce from Inga back in Stockholm.

The Dane, strapped into a weight chair at Gold's, counting his reps as he looked at himself in the faceted mirrors along the walls, couldn't help remembering her. The thought made him push his muscles harder, contorted his face with effort. Remembering. Blond hair sweeping over her strong shoulders. Her skin tinted with a light red hue, like the clouds at sunrise. And she had loved him. He was sure of it. It was one of the few things in life, outside of himself, he was completely sure of. That, and the fact he had been a fool to push her away.

But there were in life certain inevitabilities, he knew. Inga's loss was one. The fact that he had been fated to leave his native Sweden was another. He knew these things, knew them as well as he knew how much weight his arms and legs could lift on a given day. That was another reason why he loved the iron so much. It gave his mind clarity. Most men, he knew, live their lives with cluttered minds. They have no clarity, no sense of center. This was particularly true in America, and especially in these times when physical labor has been replaced by desks and computers. In these times, the Dane thought, men work solely with their minds, forgetting the body in which the mind was encased. The sweat poured off him now and he smiled, although those around him might have considered it a grimace.

Inga. He had decided to go home and find her.

The iron fell back with a clang, and he unstrapped himself, standing, suppressing the urge to roar. The Dane dressed in the nearly vacant locker room and walked out into the street, the fresh chill of the November air sinking deep into his lungs. But soon the cars and buses would clog the air with their fuming stench, making it all but unbreathable. People hurried past him as he walked the six blocks to the downtown office. Most of them, he knew, were incredibly weak and had no idea about the secrets the iron held. America, he thought, had become a land of overweight lawyers. A land of greed and weakness. A place ruled by inept bureaucracies, where criminals preyed almost at will upon the weak. During the years he had spent in New York, he had watched the city change. Watched it become a dirty Third World hovel. The envy of the world. He suspected it would not remain so too much longer. He thought it would be good to leave here before things got worse, as they were sure to do.

A young woman in a soft leather coat smiled at him as he entered the office building. He smiled back, having seen her before. She was not Inga. Not even close. He punched the security code for the top floors and rode the elevator up to the sparse offices for which York, he suspected, paid far too much rent. Jenny was at her desk.

She smiled. "Good morning."

The Dane smiled back, acknowledging her greeting. Something about her manner always made him smile, no matter what dark thoughts were intruding on his mind. She would make a good Swede, he decided. But even Jenny was not Inga.

Dennison York was in his office, pouring coffee and reviewing a stack of clippings from around the country. How would York react when he found out about the plan to return to Sweden? Should he even tell York about his decision? Probably not. York would shake his head and try to talk him out of it.

York looked up and saw him pacing. The Dane cringed. The man would now know everything before the morning was out.

"Everything all right?" York asked from the half-open doorway.

"Fine." The Dane waved, moving over to his work area in the outer office. There would be plenty of time to explain later, maybe over lunch.

The Dane's workstation consisted of a desk, a chair, a computer he hardly ever used, and several books, including a dictionary. Although in all his time here the Dane couldn't remember writing a single word. His morning task these days consisted mostly of reviewing the major East Coast papers. The *Times,* the *Globe,* the D.C. yellow sheets. There was, the Dane concluded, such a thing as too much news. But this was what York wanted him to do—to look for leads, anything that might connect to Bates's killer. So like any good soldier the Dane followed orders.

In his office York drank coffee and worked his way through clippings. Out front, Jenny took care of the mail, scanned the police files on the Stafford/Bates case, and answered the phone on those rare occasions when it would ring. Typically, the Dane sat for a while reading his papers, then around ten went outside on the pretext of an errand, if there were not actual errands to be run. Today he went out to get a *Boston Herald.*

The panhandlers were on the streets in force, no doubt hoping to get move-along money to catch the bus south. Like flocks of migrating birds. The dirty-sweatered swallow. The wine-sipping sapsucker. The rheumy-eyed jay. The Dane shivered, and it was not from the cold. He would be leaving soon, too. There was no question about it now. Aside from a few trips up and down the Atlantic coast to check out leads, he and York had done nothing all summer and fall. It was as if York had completely lost his focus. York, usually one of the most centered men the Dane knew, was now off on a wild, illogical tangent. It was, in the Dane's mind, a sign of weakness. And the Dane had a rule about being around weak people. The weak are, by nature, dangerous and were to be avoided. The weak cannot face the truth—either about themselves or the world. The truth was that Ronnie Bates was long dead, and his killer long gone. There was nothing York could do to change that fact, so it was necessary for him to move on. But somehow York had become transfixed by the past events. Trapped by them, unable to escape the almost bewitching hold they seemed to exert. The Dane sensed trouble. While his heart told him to stay and fight, his instincts whispered to him that he should flee. That he should run back to Sweden, find Inga, and together they would raise fine Viking raiders.

The sun was nearing its noonday height. The lunch crowd was coming out of the secure floors, as the Dane returned with the *Herald.* The young woman in the leather coat and sunglasses smiled at him again. The Dane smiled back, knowing that the universe was filled with unsuspected traps.

The Greyhound, bumping along Route 10 across the Florida Panhandle. Past Tallahassee, over to old Lake City, then up Route 75 into Georgia. Valdosta, Macon. Changing buses, for some reason, heading toward Savannah and the coast, riding tires filled with night air. Been to Georgia before, Arnie thought, watching the lights of small towns pass like embers against the wall of the night. No need to linger here, he thought. No, sir, got enough Georgia peaches. And the image of the boy came to him—the one he'd taken off the streets of Roswell, three or four years ago. Maybe even five or six. Time was a strange thing to Arnie Watts. It went fast, then slow, then not at all. But the boy . . . his round face, corn-colored hair, and wild blue eyes. Eyes rolling in his head like marbles twisting. The boy's face, suddenly appearing in the dark mirror of the window, staring back at him. Arnie Watts, unafraid of ghosts, stared back, unmoved, unfeeling. Even when the little girl from LA joined the picture. Then the one from Akron and Bedford. And how many from New York? Was it three? Yes, he could see them all, winking in and out of the light, like stars blinking. He carried each of them around in his head, wherever he went. Like old photographs some people kept in their wallets. Only Arnie kept his memories in his mind, where he could take them out in dark, quiet moments. Remembering their faces. Remembering their pain . . . so he could make it his own.

And as it did every time, the picture reflecting in the window of his mind changed. The faces became places. The smiles became screams . . . his screams.

"Arnie! You little bastard! Where the fuck are you?"

The man yelling, stumbling down the rickety steps on the back porch. Arnie, small and young, like the ones he himself had taken. Running, hiding. The heavy footsteps clomping behind him.

"Arnie! You better get yourself back here!"

The voice booming. His father coming for him. As he ran

and tried to hide. Falling, always falling in his mind. The footsteps behind him. The shadow looming over him.

"There you are, you little shit. . . ."

Laughter. The shadow over him. And Arnie, lying face-down in the grass. Watching things crawl along the ground. Ants, beetles, tiny unnamed insects. And a larger creature. A heavy, multiwinged, dark-eyed insect. A damselfly, with its thick, tubelike body, and long, strong limbs. It had caught something, its prey. The prey, a common housefly, struggled briefly in the unyielding arms of the damselfly. Being eaten alive, the juices sucked from its body. Its eyes flat as it struggled, uselessly, against the damselfly's power. The damselfly's eyes also flat, almost lifeless, uncaring as it de-voured its prey. . . . Arnie, caught in the unyielding grasp of his own predator. Being devoured, alive. His own eyes, flat and uncaring. Struggle, useless and futile. But in the picture inside his head, the image changed. Arnie became the dam-selfly. And beneath him, the faces and bodies of his prey, wrapped tightly in his grasp. Struggling, useless, with futile effort. Finally giving in to the inevitable, just as he had been forced to do, all those long years ago. Eyes flat and lifeless. The life and death struggle of the damselfly and its prey.

The Greyhound stopped off in Jeffersonville. Arnie Watts stayed on the bus, staring out the window. Seeing nothing.

The sickness was in the water, she was certain of it. Some microscopic thing they simply could not isolate. She walked through the darkened healing ward, past lines of sand beds filled with patients. All of them in various stages of dying. And she was struck again by the terrible feelings of helplessness and frustration. Despite her long years of training, there seemed to be nothing she could do. The suction cups on the bottom of her bare feet gripped the smooth stone floor as she stopped before one of the beds. She took a moment to change the color of her skin from the mottled red of anger, to the soft yellow of compassion. If she could not cure, at least she could offer that.

The child looked up at her, lying in the warm sand of its deathbed. Its eyes, the fiery blue of fever, angry black

welts crossing its face and body like shadows. She took
the child's hand in her own, biting the webbing softly in
the universal sign of understanding. The child seemed tc
smile, but she couldn't be sure. Anesthetic worms, sensing pain, emerged from the sand and covered the child's
arm, injecting their painkilling venom. The child, so young,
not yet having undergone its sexual metamorphosis,
drifted back to sleep. Later, when the child was dead, the
worms would feed on its body, rejuvenating their anesthetic powers. But for now, the child was at peace. That
was the most that could be hoped for, at present.

She left the bed, feeling her color change involuntarily
back to one of anger. It was so unfair. The entire healing
ward filled with children. This terrible plague, taking the
young and defenseless. It was a thing so horrible it was
completely beyond her understanding. The bile in her
stomachs rolled and she fled the ward, needing air. In the
hallway, which was empty this time of night, she stepped
into a vacuum tube and rode to the roof of the healing unit.
There she stood at the railing and drew the thick fog of the
night air deep into her breathing chamber. Below her, por-
tions of the city still burned. The fires, thankfully, were
distant. She could see blimps hanging above the flames,
dropping lakes of water on the burning buildings.

The world, she thought bitterly, was filled with madness, with chaos. The heavy machinery of the army lined
the streets, cordoning off large sections of the city in which
the males had been quarantined. The Red Core of the Female Guard were now charged with protecting the city, as
they seemed, for the most part, immune to the plague. The
Plague of Madness, it was called. This terrifying disease
which drove the males of her species to commit unspeakable acts of violence, even upon their own children. The
males were infected, she knew, but all were victims of the
plague. Victims piled upon victims, filling the wards of her
healing unit. Some said the madness was genetic, affect-
ing the males in some unknown manner. Others said it
was the Devil, visiting His evil upon the world. But the sickness was in the water, she believed. And they would find

the cause, eventually. For if they did not, she feared that the end of the world was at hand.

Below her, flames danced in the night sky, like beacons.

 REFLECTIONS ON THE CAUSE OF MADNESS

Perhaps the most disturbing aspect of observation in the physical plane is the propensity of certain mechanisms to commit acts of violence for which no rational motivation can be ascertained. The injection of Dark Spirits into the experiment is undoubtedly the force behind these acts, but the acts themselves remain unexplained.

If the theory is true that all mechanisms on the physical plane are polluted to some extent with this as yet undefined dark force, then it seems logical to assume that all mechanisms will, at some point, commit such acts. This, however, is not born out by observation. The fact remains that the vast majority of mechanisms, even those damaged by the wanton violence of others, do not develop this abhorrent behavioral pattern. It is, therefore, imperative to discover the motivating factors behind this behavior.

Fact: The cycle of violence is self-perpetuating. Victims become perpetrators, and their victims—those whose mechanisms do not become terminally damaged—then have a greater statistical chance to become perpetrators themselves. This, as has been noted, does not hold true in all cases. And there within lies the real question. Why do a select few of the damaged mechanisms seek to perpetuate the cycle? Further, as in any behavioral cycle, this particular behavior must, by definition, be rooted in some specific event in the past. But again, observation indicates that not every perpetrator is a victim. A small percentage of those involved have no previous historical reference point on which to base the motivations for their actions. It appears that in some manner they are able to completely override the moral values of the society. It should also be pointed out that these moral values are not simply restrictive rules installed by the present society, but are rooted deeply in the instinctual survival patterns of the mechanisms' ancestral past. Protection of the young is a paramount structure in the tribal organizations on which the emerging society is based. The instinct of the hunter/gatherer is to produce succeeding generations. This, of course, is not possible if predatory behavior is practiced on or directed toward those who will produce the succeeding generations.

The quandary here is obvious. Those mechanisms who have survived to a point where their physical strength and accumulated knowledge are an asset to the society should, by nature, strive to protect those who have not yet achieved that level. Logic dictates that for the society to have reached this admittedly early stage of development, this must indeed be the case. The observed behavior, therefore, defies all logical explanation.

Fact: Cyclical, perpetuating behavior operates on a base of ever-increasing frequency. Thus, the incidence of victim-based violence must also increase.

Question: Do the outside forces within the experiment have a more expanded goal? Can it be the aim of these forces to actually dismantle the fabric of the emerging society? Toward what end? Is Evil simply a goal unto itself?

sixteen

"I'm thinking about leaving the States ... maybe going back home to Sweden," the Dane said, trying to sound casual, even though major life decisions were agonizing to him.

York nodded, hardly looking up from his Chinese food. It was Wednesday and York always had lunch in a little hole-in-the-wall Chinese restaurant across the street from their office.

"Don't blame you," York said, twisting noodles around his chopsticks. "If I had someplace to go, I'd probably leave, too."

"You can go anyplace you want," the Dane said, after a few moments of consideration.

"Yeah, I know," York replied. "But it'll be the same wherever I go. I tried running away once. Didn't work worth a damn. Some things you just can't get away from."

"I'm not running," the Dane said, obviously miffed. "Just leaving."

York nodded again, pulling the stuffing out of his last egg roll, sipping his sake. The Dane was not the type of man who could sit on the sidelines for long, York knew. And there surely hadn't been much action lately. York quite rightly blamed himself for that. In truth, he blamed himself for most everything. Another despicable middle-age trait.

"You think you'll be OK, going back, I mean?" he asked.

The Dane had not left his native land under the most desirable circumstances, York knew, although the details were vague. There had been an incident back in Stockholm. A barroom fight and a man had been hurt. Hurt bad, York gathered, as the Dane had confessed during their job interview, like a parishioner spilling his sins to the village priest. Of course, this was exactly the kind of man York was looking for, and he had hired him on the spot. Much to the Dane's surprise, it seemed. And now the wheel of life was turning, the Dane exiting like some forlorn Shakespearian character. It seemed to York as though the wheel of life had been spinning wildly out of control for some time now.

"I guess it'll be all right," the Dane said. "The guy must be out of the hospital by now."

York laughed—too loudly. The cook in the back looked out, eyeing him suspiciously, even though York had been coming here every Wednesday for years.

"When are you leaving?" York asked.

"Before Christmas, maybe?" the Dane replied, remembering how beautiful Christmas was in Stockholm, keeping the secret of finding Inga to himself.

"Fair enough." York nodded, feeling the wheel shift beneath him. Jenny, however, was about to throw it completely off track.

"You're not going to believe this," she said when they got back to the office. She was pointing at the computer screen, her eyes flashing with excitement. "The van, our van, was sold to a used-car dealer in Texas, not more than two weeks ago. It turned up on an FBI tracer."

York and the Dane were on the next plane to Houston International.

Money was becoming a problem for Arnie Watts. He had bused out to Myrtle Beach, South Carolina, his last few C-notes folded up inside his Nikes. Enough to rent a room at one of the downtown bed-and-breakfasts. Enough to keep him going for a few more weeks, but that was it, he thought miserably, throwing his backpack on the bed in a tiny room off Peachtree Avenue.

It was time to take the path of last resort—to get a job. The very thought of it was abhorrent, but the option of living on the street was even less appealing.

Arnie stuffed his socks and underwear in the top drawer of the dresser, tucking the Nine safely away under his BVDs. The air conditioner was off, and Arnie opened the window for some fresh air. The breeze rolling in from the nearby ocean. Gulls screeching to one another, people strolling through the nearby shops. The air smelled like salt and hot dogs. Like sand and seaweed. Closer at hand, the sound of kids playing. Their cries sounding to Arnie Watts like the strains of some dark, unwritten opera. They were in the park across the street, swinging, playing ball, climbing on monkey bars. From his second-story window, Arnie watched, standing behind the curtains. He watched for a long time. His chest tightened until he could barely breathe. It was, he knew, almost time to go hunting again.

In the Houston office of the FBI, Dennison York flashed his credentials and asked to see an investigator. There was the customary delay, the usual hemming and hawing, as phone calls were made from a back room and his license verified. Finally a blue suit came into the waiting room where York and the Dane had been waiting. The suit was thin and trim, with close-cropped hair cut so short the man seemed almost bald. York stood and offered his hand, which was ignored. The Dane merely stood. The whole scene was uncomfortable, damn near hostile—the last thing York wanted.

"Agent Hostings," the man introduced himself curtly. "What is it, exactly, that we can do for you?"

"I believe my office called ahead," York replied, hating the fact that he had somehow been put on the defensive. "We're looking for information on a stolen van which was recovered from a used-car dealer in the Port Arthur area. . . ."

"There's a lot of stolen vans in Texas," Agent Hostings

said, sounding as if his lunch had been interrupted.

York felt the blood rising into his head. He took a deep breath to calm himself.

"This van was involved in an abduction and a possible homicide in New York," York said through clenched teeth. "I'm assuming you people took prints. I'd like to formally request that information under the Freedom of Information Act, if it's not too much trouble. I believe your office has photocopies of my authorization."

"Come with me." Hostings nodded, turning on his heel in practiced military fashion. "You'll have to fill out the request forms."

Request forms in triplicate, York discovered. Along with confidentiality statements, notices of intent, three separate identification checks . . . all notarized and signed off on by two separate offices.

"And the government wants to take over health care," York whispered to the Dane. That earned them another wait in the cool-your-heels room when the paperwork was finally in order. Agents strolling by, glancing in at them. The word *vigilante* bantered about in the hallway. Then, just when York was about to explode, Agent Hostings came back with a thin folder which he ceremoniously handed to York, as if it were a flag at a VIP funeral.

"Sorry about the wait," he said, smiling to show he wasn't sorry at all.

"We really appreciate your help." York smiled back. Hostings glared and left. Another agent in the same blue suit, silent and stoic, escorted them out.

"That's another reason I'm going back to Sweden," the Dane said as they walked back to their rented car. "The bureaucrats, the lawyers, the government police, they run everything. America's turning into a Third World dictatorship."

York nodded, thumbing through the file. There was no sense arguing, York knew. Besides, there was a strong possibility the Dane was right.

"They matched the prints," York said. The Dane was driving them back to the hotel. The match came as no surprise to either of them. "The only name they have is William Ryder—the one our guy gave to the apartment manager in New York. Nothing more in the computer. No work record, no credit history."

The Dane nodded. They had what they had before—exactly nothing.

"They also lifted Ronnie Bates's prints from the back," York continued reading. "And some woman from Port Arthur. They interviewed her. Listen to this quote: 'The guy was a fucking asshole. Called himself Burt Reynolds, you know, like the movie star.' Apparently our guy beat the hell out of her before he left town. The woman says her brothers will kill him if he ever shows his face around Port Arthur again."

"Well, now we know where not to look," the Dane said, trying to make a joke. York ignored it. "Can we get the van back?" he asked.

"Nope, impounded," York replied. "We can look at it, if we want. But for some reason it's stored down in Galveston."

York considered it for a moment, but decided against it. Galveston was quite a haul, and the report said the van had been stripped to the walls. A long ride, just to visit Ronnie Bates's ghost, York thought.

"We could swing by Port Arthur and talk to this woman," he suggested. "Delores Sanchos. Maybe there was something she forgot to tell the I-Men."

Port Arthur, Texas, was a gloomy, depressing oil town, which looked to have gone bust a decade or so ago. The Dane and York drove down a thin, dirty ribbon of road, pulling into what appeared to be an old squatter's shack, perched on a patch of ground suitable for growing stones and scrub brush. Delores Sanchos eyed them suspiciously from behind a broken screen door.

"He was a fucking asshole." She repeated her testimonial about the man who called himself Burt Reynolds, showing York faded bruises along her arms and legs. "I knew it was a phony name," Delores said, laughing bitterly, lighting a cigarette. York, who had quit again during the summer at Jenny's insistence, looked on enviously. "The bastard beat me and was rotten in the sack to boot!" she snapped, waving off the memory, as if this was simply one of many such encounters. "If my brothers ever catch up with him . . ."

"You don't have any pictures of him, do you?" York asked, fishing. "Maybe one you forgot about when you talked to the authorities?"

The Dane was leaning on the fender of the rental car out in the driveway, watching the dust blow in the distance. Delores, York saw, was glancing at him through the cloud of her cigarette smoke.

"Big one, ain't he?" she said, laughing again. Trying to change the subject, York thought.

"This man we're looking for, he's very bad, Delores," York said carefully. "Did the FBI tell you what he did?"

"Killed somebody, they thought," Delores said, shrugging, as if this was an everyday occurrence and not something to be overly concerned about.

"He kills children," York whispered. "And he treats them real bad before he does. I'd really like to catch him, Delores, but we don't have any pictures of him."

Delores, dragging on her cigarette, staring out at the Dane in the yard. Hesitating.

"Delores . . ." York said softly. "Can you help me?"

"Well, he didn't like it . . . to have his picture took," Delores said, smiling weakly. "But this one time, right after we first started up . . . when I thought he was a fun guy, you know?"

York nodded, folding his hands to keep them calm. Christ, what he wouldn't do for a cigarette.

"Well, one night my friend Linda, from down the road, came over. We had some drinks, scorched some weed, you know? And the three of us sort of started in. Linda, she loves to have her picture took. . . ."

"So you took a photo of Linda and this Reynolds man, together?" York asked, playing down his excitement.

"Well . . . yeah." Delores laughed, sounding embarrassed

about the whole thing. York hardly believed that to be possible.

"I need that picture, Delores," York said. Delores, playing coy, hiding behind a veil of tobacco smoke, smiled at him.

Finally, after some coaxing in the form of twenty-dollar bills, York left with a blurry Polaroid of Arnie Watts, aka Burt Reynolds, doing the doggy walk with a rather large woman named Linda. The woman appeared to be laughing in the picture. The man had a sneer painted across his face. Aside from the circumstances revealed in the picture, he was, York thought, a very average-looking man. It would be impossible to pick him out of a crowd, assuming his pants were on. Out in the yard York handed the picture to the Dane.

"That's him!" York said, hurrying into the car.

The Dane, staring at the figures, shook his head and handed the photo back to York, as if it burned his fingers.

"Scummy bastard," the Dane mumbled, jerking the car into gear, throwing up gravel as he pulled away.

York nodded in agreement, the perp's face etched into his brain. It would be there for a long time, he knew. Back in town he hunted up a tobacco shop and bought a pack of Dunhills.

"I would like us all to welcome Ronnie Stafford to the Golden Chicken family," the kid said, introducing Arnie Watts, who was dressed in ball cap and apron, to the rest of the night shift. A bunch of pimply-faced high school students, with a sprinkling of dropouts and other assorted losers, Watts thought. Arnie, smiling, like the proverbial cat who ate the canary. Or in this case, a greasy old fried chicken. A printed name tag on the breast of Arnie's new white shirt announced: Ronnie, Assistant Night Manager.

"I'd like you all to help Ronnie learn the ropes here," the kid continued, nodding at each of the half dozen members of the Golden Chicken night shift. The kid was in his early twenties, and in Arnie Watts's mind, filled to capacity with the false authority of someone in charge of something as meaningless as a fried-chicken joint. "I'm sure Ronnie will make a fine addition to our team."

Right, Arnie thought. A fine addition to the team. Arnie, smiling on the outside, thunderclouds crashing his brain on the inside. A fine addition to the asshole brigade. The meeting broke up, and Arnie, low man on the totem pole, got to work the fryer. Dumping wire baskets of frozen chicken parts and french fries into a vat of bubbling grease, sucking smoke fumes, sweating like a pig. But one eye, always, on the cash register, watching carefully as the night-deposit bag was zipped up and dropped in a poor excuse of a safe.

A fine addition to the team, Arnie laughed to himself as he walked back to the rented room on Peachtree Avenue after the Golden Chicken closed at midnight. They'd see what kind of addition he was soon enough. They'd see just who and what they were fucking with. But patience, Arnie knew, was the key to every enterprise. So he spent the next week working the much-hated fry machine. He made jokes with the waitresses and counter help. Just a regular guy, putting in his hours. That was the game, of course: Fit in, work your way inside, find out when the heaviest night was, when the most money was zipped into the deposit bag.

Watts spent the nights doing his time in the windowless kitchen of the chicken joint, going home to a few bottles of beer and some light weed scored from one of the dropouts at the restaurant. And spent the days walking along the beach or sitting in his room, planning his escape, listening to the sounds of children playing in the park across the street. A week, then two. Then on Friday, Arnie went to a car lot on Court Street, where he bought an old Chevy for three hundred dollars. Got an insurance card and plates with the last of his ready cash. Late that night, after his daily encounter with frozen dead poultry, Arnie had himself a couple extra beers to celebrate his impending departure from Myrtle Beach.

Saturday night, on his way to work, he swiped a set of new plates from an old Chrysler that had been parked down the block on a side street ever since he had blown into town. He filled the Chevy's tank, checked the fluids and tires, and, for the first time in weeks, went happily off to work.

The Saturday night night shift. Busy time. College kids in town. Military personnel from the bases across the bay. Good times, cold beer, and fried chicken all around. Finally, two A.M. crawling around on the kitchen clock. The door locked, as the last customer is pushed out of it. The outside lights turned off, so as not to attract any more mothlike patrons. The final cleanup of the day beginning. Chairs piled on tables. The inside lights dimmed, to hide the place from the attention of any unsavory, late-night roamers. Too late, thought Arnie, pretending to swamp down the fry machine, waiting as the official night manager cashes out the registers, stuffing all the loot into the deposit bag. Arnie watching, as the kid moved away from the alarm button under the counter.

Arnie, ripping the Nine from his duffel bag, kept under the fryer. Leaping around the counter, gun at the head of the pimple-faced night manager.

"Move and I'll blow your fucking head off!" Arnie whispered. The kid, a twenty-something wanna-be, stares down the barrel of the Nine, unbelieving. Looks ready to shit his pants, Arnie thought, as the kid gives up the money bag easily, wisely.

"Listen up, people!" Arnie called out to the waitresses and counter help, busy splashing with their cleaning rags and mop buckets. "Everybody in the back, quick and quiet. Do it now and nobody gets hurt!"

Momentary panic, the herd filled with the instinct to flee. But the door's locked and the gun's pointed in their direction. The dropout losers thinking it's a joke. At first. After all, this is Ronnie. A good guy. Smoked weed with the boys on break. Joked with the girls. He's gotta be screwing around. . . .

But the gun is too real. Ronnie's face twisted into a scowl. His voice a low, angry growl.

"Move it, you assholes, or you're dead!"

So they moved, pushing and crowding together. Nobody wanting to be out front, or caught in the back. The herd instinct, in its most pure sense. Stumbling along as Arnie pushed them into the walk-in cooler and slammed the door shut as they huddled together, still hardly believing. Betrayed by one of their own.

With everyone inside, Arnie took a bicycle chain and lock from the duffel bag and wrapped the handle of the cooler up tight. Then, stowing the Nine in with the cash from the deposit bag and changing his greasy work clothes, Arnie turned off the lights. On the way out he grabbed a bucket of leftover chicken and locked the door behind him. The Chevy parked out back, ready to roll, and Arnie was away, with at least a few hours of lead time before anybody checked for their missing kids.

Arnie, smiling to himself, munching chicken as he drove north on Interstate 95, a cool three grand tucked away in the trunk. Yes, it was a chance, he knew. And he was not a man who ordinarily took those kinds of chances. But that's the way it goes sometimes, he understood. Money talks, and you got to do what you got to do. As he crossed over the state line into North Carolina, headlights probing the dark, Arnie Watts began to think seriously about his next hunting expedition.

The white dwarf star held her planets securely. She kept them in slightly oscillating orbits and filled them with the radiance of her life force. She had been fortunate. During the long span of her six billion years of existence, several of the planets had, at one time or another, developed advanced life forms. Many of the forms had flourished, achieving the higher levels of evolution. One group of beings in particular had been extremely successful. They rose to dominance on their own world and had even ventured out into the solar system, exploring the other worlds the white dwarf star had spawned. These creatures, which she had felt privileged to nurture, had learned many of the secrets of evolution and were able to genetically engineer transport mechanisms, which they had used to travel within the solar system. She had enjoyed observing these industrious beings and was saddened when their time in the universe had ended. For a few million years—

such a brief time in the history of the Cosmos—they fed off her energy, building a series of civilizations that had flourished progressively in a most extemporary and honorable fashion. But they were gone now, and the star was alone with her planets. She was aware that her energies were fading and held out little hope that another such race would have the time to advance to the higher levels of evolution before she herself died. Still, the white dwarf star watched the passing of time, as she had for the last six billion years, ever hopeful that the Gods she worshiped might grant yet another miracle.

In the cold darkness between her planets, the white bones of great, space-traveling animals floated in the dim starlight. Long abandoned by their creators, the animals' bones were now pitted and stripped of their armored flesh by small particles of dust that floated in the night with them. These extraordinary beasts, who had once flown between planets, carrying within their bodies the civilization that had spawned them, were now only relics. The white dwarf star often looked upon these bones as they circled in her gravitational field and felt, always, a mixture of awe and reverence for their creators.

Time passed, marked now in empty eons. And it seemed to the white dwarf star that time passed all too quickly.

 ## REFLECTIONS ON TIME AS A MITIGATING FACTOR WITHIN THE CONTEXT OF THE EXPERIMENT

Observation of the emerging civilization and the evolution of the mechanisms themselves must also, of necessity, include a study of time itself. The measurement of time, as defined by the passing of Light, always becomes an integral part of the mechanisms' thought processes once cognitive reasoning is achieved. This, of course, is due to the mortality factor, which is so much a part of life on the physical plane.

Once this factor is introduced, it becomes, unavoidably, a strong force within the experiment.

The short lifespan of the mechanisms, which itself is a necessary function of generational procreation and the efficient use of natural resources, provides a strong motivating factor in the advancement of the civilization. Proper use of their allotted lifespan drives the mechanisms toward achievement in their selected fields, as their limited perspective denotes that results are necessary within the lifetime of the individual mechanism. Oftentimes, of course, this is not the case, as many significant projects begun by individuals do not reach fruition until the succeeding generations. This time constraint is one of the principal factors that binds the mechanisms into a cohesive group and allows the civilization to flourish. The seeds of this behavior pattern are planted in the early stages of a dominant species' development, when the mortality factor is introduced by cognitive reasoning. The ability to pass knowledge to the succeeding generation is, in fact, the first step to a progressive society.

The mechanisms in this particular experiment achieved this ability at a very early stage in their development, which is a contributing factor in the rapid growth of their civilization. However, it must be noted that the mere passing of information to succeeding generations does not, in itself, guarantee continued advancement. There is, within the context of this experiment, a fundamental lack of knowledge among the general populace regarding the true nature of the technological advancements implemented by a select few of the mechanisms. In order for advancement to continue at its present rate, it is necessary for *all* members of the society to understand the technology upon which their civilization is based.

This is a fundamental problem in life experiments where advancement in the technological fields outpaces a society's ability to make the technology understood by all its members. Past experiments have shown that the results of this type of rapid advancement, combined with the inability to promote true understanding across the spectrum of society, always produces detrimental—and even disastrous—results.

First and foremost in these instances, an underclass of mechanisms is created who have no input into the technological advances, other than its use. Generational procreation then dictates that each succeeding generation of this underclass will become further removed from a true understanding of the emerging technology. These generations, and those which follow, will eventually become a statistical majority, forming a vast subculture of underdeveloped mechanisms. This massive underclass, having no way to contribute to the technological-based society, will then become a drain on the resources of the society. As past experiments indicate, an underclass that is closed off from the technological knowledge of the society will eventually, out of necessity, destroy the emerging civilization, either through violence or by the sheer weight of their numbers. This is particularly true of a civilization that is rooted in a hunter/gatherer tradition, and most certainly true in this specific experiment, where the instinctual behavior patterns of the hunter/gatherer society are so closely related to the present civilization.

Further, studies have shown that even if violent overthrow can be avoided and if the resources of the society remained undepleted, advancement of the civilization will be severely restricted, and perhaps even derailed, by a secondary statistical phenomena, known to the mechanisms as a Shrinking Database. Eventually the creators of the technology will not have a large enough generational pool to assimilate the knowledge that must be passed on to the succeeding generations. The technology itself will then wither and die, along with the society it supported.

Thus, the limited lifespans of mechanisms in an emerging technological society forces all those within the society to participate equally in the advancement of the civilization. Technology without understanding is one of the principal downfalls of emerging societies, and it must be said that this particular experiment seems headed in that direction.

The solutions are obvious, but unfortunately not easily implemented. Here, again, the short lifespans and the close proximity of the mechanisms' historical past play a critical role. Just as an underclass is created by a lack of knowledge concerning the fundamentals of the technology, so, too, is an upper class evolved encompassing those individuals who possess an understanding of the workings of technology. In a material-based society, the natural inclination is for those individuals enjoying the benefits of an upper-class status, to pass these benefits to their offspring. One of the simplest methods of maintaining a generational-based power structure is to restrict the flow of information outside that structure. By limiting educational access to one's own descendants, the succeeding generation's place in the power structure is assured, as is the place of the underclass. The lack of knowledge regarding the technology employed by the society then becomes self-perpetuating and the fall of the civilization assured.

It is imperative, therefore, that the members of the society develop the ability to see beyond the limits of their own mortality and introduce understanding of the technology to all members. The hoarding mentality, so basic to the hunter/gatherer mind-set, must be expunged if the civilization is to survive. Knowledge and understanding, like sustenance, must be open to all mechanisms in the society. It is hoped that the continued introduction of spiritual entities will achieve this goal.

Time here is critical.

seventeen

"**M**essage for you, sir," the desk clerk said, handing York a folded note. Neat and professional.

"Thanks," York replied, trying to remember if you were supposed to tip in these kinds of situations. He took the folded paper, smiled, and turned away. No tip, he decided. Not for a phone call, anyway. Phone calls were hardly ever good news.

"Jenny wants us to call," he said to the Dane, once they were in the elevator. The Dane hadn't asked, but York figured it was out of politeness. "Says it's important."

The Dane nodded. They were going nowhere fast, he thought. Sweden looked better and better. He was now thinking about leaving before Christmas. They could be back in New York, doing something productive. Instead, York seemed to have become even more obsessed since the van's discovery. Still, they had a picture of this guy now, even if there was no name to put with it. Actually, there were too many names. For all the electronic intrusion into people's lives these days, finding one person out of millions was not an easy task. Particularly if the person operated outside society and outside the law. That was the flaw in the plan, of course. Society kept records on just about everyone—credit reports, Social Security numbers, even fingerprints. On everybody, that is, except for a few criminals who were smart enough to avoid all of society's invisible traps.

And this perp, whoever he was, seemed adept at avoiding these traps. But still, York's obsession with finding him seemed undiminished. His boss, the Dane knew, was nothing if not persistent.

In the room the Dane sipped a diet soda from the portable fridge, while York put the call in to New York.

"Yeah, Jenny, it's me," York said, cradling the phone, lighting a cigarette. He pulled deeply on the tobacco and smiled. It tasted so damn good, even if it was just smoke. To hell with what the do-gooders on the television and in the papers said. He loved his Dunhills, and in some part of his brain he looked forward to croaking at the age of eighty, clutching one tightly between his fingers. "You get the picture we faxed?"

The first thing they had done upon leaving Delores Sanchos's house was to visit a photolab in town. The picture Delores had given them was cropped and blown up to show the perp's face. Then York had zapped the photo to Jenny, with instructions to feed it to the Fifty-fourth Street Station House, in exchange for Cassady calling off the licensing board, which had been dogging their trail for months.

"You matched it up with the sketches then? Yeah, I thought so, too. And you matched it where?" York's voice rose up like a foghorn, the cigarette dangling forgotten at the end of his hand, dangerously close to the rumpled bedding.

In the New York office Jenny perused the East Coast papers. The morning had only been interrupted by the ringing of the incoming fax bell. As soon as the picture appeared, Jenny contacted the Fifty-fourth, with the suggestion that they call off the licensing hounds. Particularly as several months had now passed and it seemed unlikely that York's hunting permit would be pulled, no matter how well deserved the police department thought the punishment might be.

"Dennison has a picture he wants to share," Jenny said, staring at the grainy fax reproduction.

"A picture of who?" Cassady asked, in disbelief. Jenny

sent the photo and a short time later the phone rang again. "Tell him I'll consider letting him keep his license," Cassady said. Which was as close to an agreement as they were likely to get, Jenny knew. So the deal was struck and the perp's face put on the interstate wire.

That had been two days ago, and since then Jenny found herself unable to focus on anything except the photograph. The picture, York was certain, of the man who kidnapped Ronnie Bates. She still couldn't bring herself to think of Ronnie as dead, even though Dennison told her repeatedly that she should not hold out any false hope. And he was right, she knew. He was right about lots of things. She smiled to herself, thinking about York—the way he quickly averted his eyes when she saw him looking at her; the way he touched her hand, seemingly by accident; the way he found time to be with her and Gena. He was, she decided, a good man in a world where there was a severe shortage of that particular commodity. In this line of business, you find out just how bad the shortage is, she thought.

The picture was set on top of a folder, pushed away into a corner of her desk. Almost as if she wanted to push it away onto the floor. It sent shivers up her spine just to look at it. The face was a mask, she knew. Behind that mask a monster was hiding—a monster who had done those awful things to the Stafford girl. And to many others, according to Dennison. So it was perfectly understandable, she decided, that such a face would haunt her. But Jenny was unable to shake the feeling that there was something else. She had seen that face before. Somewhere, someplace. In one of the papers? she wondered.

And so she went back through the East Coast papers. Combing the *Times,* the *Herald,* the *Post,* the *Jersey Sentinel,* the *Cape Codder.* Finally, in the *Raleigh-Durham Express*—in a small story on the second page, there was a story about a robbery down in Myrtle Beach. A fast-food place that was stuck up last Saturday night. That in itself was hardly unusual, but the story contained a police sketch of the man they thought might be responsible. She held the grainy photo on the corner of her desk up to the newspaper article, and immediately put the call into York.

"It's the same guy," Jenny said, sensing York's excitement on the other end of the line. "He robbed a chicken joint in South Carolina. The article quotes the local cops as saying they thought it was an inside job. So he must have been working there."

"We'll be up there in the morning," York said, checking his watch. "I'll let you know where we're staying."

From his chair near the window, the Dane sighed. More wild-goose chasing across the country. And it was a very big country.

Hershey, Pennsylvania, smelled like chocolate. The smell was there, hanging in the air like the smell of rain before a storm. Only the smell never went away. Not when it rained or snowed, not even when the wind blew in from the north off Lake Erie. The chocolate smell permeated the earth itself in Hershey and was now a permanent fixture of the town.

Not that the inhabitants seemed to mind, Arnie Watts noted on several occasions, when the odor was particularly strong. No, they laughed and nodded good morning and went about their business, filled with the knowledge that the chocolate stench was the smell of security for their town and all its residents. Chocolate was like gold or silver to the folks of Hershey, Pennsylvania. Like an old western boomtown, only here the mine would never run dry. Not with all the fat people in America stuffing themselves like pigs, Arnie Watts thought as he sipped a cup of coffee in a diner off Route 22. Not with kids all over the country eating Hershey bars and Hershey kisses.

The thought of kids sitting in parks, eating Hershey bars in Hershey, Pennsylvania, amused Watts. He himself was partial to the ones with almonds, but doubted he would eat one for a while. Not after spending an entire week with the smell of chocolate hanging in the air like some kind of sulfuric fog. The smell was, he thought, even in his clothes and in the upholstery of his new van.

The old Chevy had been traded in for a Volkswagen van, which was sitting in the diner's parking lot, registered under the name of Paul Reynolds of Pittsburgh. The Chevy and a grand of the holdup money having been left in a car lot in Wilkinsburg. Along with another hundred dollar bill for a new ID purchased from a friend of the same sleazy car dealer where he'd bought the van. Living in a motel in Hershey for the last week had cost Arnie some more bucks, but there was still plenty left from the chicken heist. He'd gotten slightly over three grand, although the insurance company had probably been popped for five g's. That was the way of the world—everybody stealing from everybody else. And just about everybody getting away with it, if they were smart. Still, he didn't like doing robberies. Stupid people did robberies, because they couldn't think of any other way to hustle money, and they usually got caught. Getting caught, Arnie knew, was largely a matter of poor planning and bad luck. It was, he realized, entirely possible that the authorities might match his prints from the New York apartment with the chicken joint, if anybody bothered to check. That made both New York and South Carolina off-limits, at least for the foreseeable future. Not that it was any big deal. It was, after all, a mighty big country.

"I think I'll have a tuna sandwich, Anna," Arnie said, smiling at the waitress as she passed. He had come to this roadside diner every day for lunch the past week. He knew the girls on this shift pretty well by now. "How're the kids? Betsy get over her cold?" he asked.

"She's fine, Mr. Reynolds." Anna smiled back, wiping down the table on the other side of the aisle, slipping a dollar's worth of quarters into her apron pocket. "Thanks for asking. . . ."

"That Mr. Reynolds is a nice man," he heard her remark to one of the other waitresses. Both of them nodding politely in his direction. Everyone smiling. The sun shining on chocolate-filled streets. Arnie Watts winking at Anna Burrows and her co-worker, Mary Jo, enjoying his tuna sandwich.

•   •   •

Memories are a funny thing, she thought, sitting in the chair, which smelled like new shoes and furniture polish. The room had plants and pictures and raised, printed wallpaper. It wasn't a bad room, really, even though it had an underlying feeling of secrets. Secrets told, secrets kept inside. There was a reason for this, of course. This was the room where they wanted her to tell her secrets. In fact, it was just another place in a long series of rooms in which Yvonne Stafford found herself these last few months. And the people in these rooms, even though they smiled and talked softly to her, were upset that she wouldn't tell her secrets. She could tell that, even though the people tried to hide it from her.

A woman doctor sat across from her at a long desk which seemed much too big for the room. It had been the woman who made the statement about memories, and was now waiting for Yvonne to respond.

"I guess they are," Yvonne said finally, when it seemed that agreement was called for. Adults, she knew, generally made such statements and then waited for people to agree with them. But really, who knew if memories were a funny thing or not?

The woman doctor smiled. Yvonne tried to smile back. But lately she found it hard to smile. It just didn't seem as though her face worked like that anymore. Yvonne even tried smiling at herself in the mirror when she brushed her teeth. When she did, she thought her face looked like some kind of Halloween fright mask.

"What I mean," the woman said, "is that memories hide from us sometimes. They disappear into locked doors in our minds. Like when something bad happens to us. When bad things happen, our bodies get better, but the memories can stay hidden and sometimes they can prevent us from healing ourselves. Do you know what I'm saying, Yvonne?"

Yvonne nodded, noticing suddenly that her sneaker was untied.

"So we have to talk about these memories," the woman said. "We have to talk about them, so they don't make us sick."

Yvonne nodded again, wanting to reach down and tie the laces, but knowing that it would be a mistake to do so. It would look like she wasn't paying attention. Even though she was.

"I don't remember," she said instead, and the laces blurred as tears came to her eyes. She blinked, not wanting the tears. They were stupid. Just like sitting here was stupid. Why couldn't they just leave her alone? That was all she wanted—to be left alone. It didn't seem like too much to ask.

"That's all right," the woman said gently, even though Yvonne could tell it wasn't. "We can talk about something else. How do you like your new school?"

"It's OK," Yvonne said, shrugging, looking out the window behind the woman and her long desk. It was late afternoon and already getting dark. The trees, empty of leaves, seemed sad as they waited for the night.

"I think I want to go home now," Yvonne said, and the woman nodded.

The drive home, to the new house, was long and quiet. Her mother, it seemed, had finally tired of asking the same questions, over and over.

—Would you like to talk . . . about anything?

—Sometimes things happen to us and they're not our fault. You know that, don't you, honey?

—You can tell me anything. Anything at all. You know that, don't you, Yvonne?

Sometimes it seemed like a kind of desperation crept into her mother's voice, then Yvonne would nod and smile her Halloween smile, knowing how awful it looked. Knowing that what had happened to her had, in some way, happened to all of them. And that nothing anyone could say or do would make things like they were before. It was, Yvonne sometimes thought, as if a giant hand had reached down from the sky and had pulled all the happiness out of their lives. Like a dentist taking out a tooth, leaving behind a great, gaping hole. A wound that would be with them always, no matter how hard they tried to forget about it.

Memories were indeed funny things, she decided, watching as the car passed houses filled with light. As other vehicles went by them in the night. In any of the houses, she now knew, monsters might be living. In any of the cars, trucks, or vans . . . HE might be waiting. It was a thing she knew, but refused to say out loud. Saying it, she thought, might make it real. Might make any of it real. It was possible, she hoped, to hide behind a wall of silence. Memories might be funny things to some people, but to Yvonne Stafford memories were nightmares.

Did you have a nice sleep, Yvonne?

The words were echoes, like thunder drumming across distant clouds. In the dream she was standing on the street corner, waiting for the bus that never came. The voice whispered from behind her, and she wanted to run. Tried to run. But her feet seemed tied with heavy stones. She tried to kick the stones away, to make herself run. But she was slow, as if time itself was frozen, and she was caught in its shadowy, icy grip. And the cold crept up through her legs, tightening its hold, until she knew it was impossible to run. Impossible to escape.

Did you have a nice sleep, Yvonne?

The words were like tentacles, wrapping themselves around her. The world was filled with a gray fog, and in the fog, shadows moved. Terrifying, nameless, shapeless shadows. And then the eyes came, dropping out of the sky like stones. Bright and glowing. Eyes that gleamed at her with a deep, gnawing hunger.

No . . . please, no . . . she whispered, caught in the web of the nightmare, struggling to wake, to force her head up from the pillow, to pull her own eyes open. To escape.

But there was no escape. Hands reached out from the shadows and touched her. Horrifying in their soft caress. No escape. Because she knew what would happen next. What always happened next in the dream. She would die. Every time. She wanted to scream, but the hands were over her mouth. HIS hands! And she knew, suddenly, as she always did, that it was not a dream. That it was real. That she was going to die. That HE was going to do terrible things to her, and she was going to die. That she had already died, deep inside. And she knew, suddenly, as she always did, that she should've run away. But didn't. And knew, in her heart, that was the final secret . . . the thing she could never tell. She should've run away. But didn't.

He stumbled on the female late in the afternoon, just as the sun was touching the snowy peaks of the Far Mountains. The woods were filled with shadows and at first he thought the female was simply another ghost, one of many he had encountered in his headlong flight. His brain was filled with the stench of death, his body numb with exhaustion. The burning towns and villages of his people were as vivid to him as the deep forest and lonely valleys through which he now traveled. He had been running, it seemed, for days. Running from the carnage the Outsiders were inflicting upon his race. They had come out of The Void, the great stretch of water that flowed to the end of the world. Their ships powered by the wind, which seemed to answer their every command. Even though his people had tried to resist, how can you fight those who command the wind, the thunder, and the lightning? The answer, sadly, is that you do not. You bow down before them, or you perish. His people had perished. Even here, deep in the forest, the smell of smoke rose on the wind like an unseen, suffocating cloud. The fear, which had driven him these last days, squeezed his chest as though he had fallen victim to a spider constrictor. The beast inside telling him to: Run! Run! Run!

But the sight of the female made him slow and stop. She was sitting in a clearing, staring at a group of bodies laid out on the grass before her. An older male and three yearlings. Her mate and three children, he thought, watching her from the tree line. The female was so absorbed in the death before her that she did not even sense his approach. Her brain, like his own, had been dulled by shock. The female's own death, he knew, was not far away. She would die either from grief or fall victim to one of the many predators that roamed this wild place. Or the Outsiders would find her in one of their sweeping patrols.

He had seen and felt more than enough death, so he stopped running and came to her, slowly, allowing his scent to rise until it permeated even the depths of her sorrow. When she turned finally to look at him, his heart welled up in pity. For some reason, the sight of her sitting beside the bodies of her family eclipsed all the horror he had witnessed these past days, and tears filled his eyes, falling in great drops down the thick hairs of his breathing tubes. He sat beside her, wondering what comfort he might offer, what solace he could provide. In the end, he decided there was none, so he dug a large hole in the soft ground, and with her help placed the bodies in the earth and covered them. Then he took her forearm and led her away, deeper into the gathering darkness. Not a word, not a sign, not a thought had been exchanged. Their mouths and minds closed, they simply walked until the darkness overtook them.

He made a small fire for them in the shelter of a rock ledge. He then took his hunting knife and cut a vein in his arm, filling a cup with blood, which he gave her to drink. He pushed the cup on her and finally she took it, sending him a thought of gratitude. As the night settled in over them, the stars like bits of white stone in the sky, she began licking his many wounds, running her rough tongue over the matted fur of his pelt. He, in turn, preened her back and ears, his hands and teeth passing over the scars the female had accumulated during her lifetime. As the Sleeping Moon rose behind the Far Mountains, he slipped the light filters over his eyes and prepared to rest. The female, however, reached into a totem sack around her neck and brought forth an icon of the True God, placing it by the fire, to keep watch for them during the night. He looked at the icon, at its soft, yet stern features. At its pelt, meticulously combed, the hairs of its breathing tubes braided in the manner denoting nobility. He thought of the Outsiders, and what they had done to his people. The blood spilled, the lives ended so cruelly. The whole of his civilization destroyed. And he kicked the icon into the fire, despite the mind-screams of the female. He darkened his light filters and turned away to sleep, knowing with certainty that there was no such thing as the True God.

eighteen

Everyone knew the Last Stop Motel and Boardinghouse should have been closed down years ago. John Hammond, an old retiree from Lancaster, who paid the weekly rate for the last five years, knew it. Nomad, the town drunk, who was an occasional boarder courtesy of the county welfare office, knew it. Old Mrs. Dish surely knew it—being sole proprietor and housekeeper at the Last Stop for the past decade, since her husband, Murphy, had up and died, his heart exploding like a ruptured tire at the tender age of sixty-two. Even Smokey knew it, Mrs. Dish suspected, and it was almost impossible to be sure what a dog was thinking unless you were feeding it. Which was, she realized, a lot like her late husband, Murphy.

And now Arnie Watts knew the Last Stop Motel was a rundown, ramshackle collection of clapboard huts, quaintly called cabins, built on an acre or so of played-out farmland. The last vestige of which, the old farmhouse itself, was home to Mrs. Dish and a select few "permanent" boarders. The farmhouse was built back in the early days of the twentieth century, when this area of Pennsylvania was still sanctuary to an independent breed of dirt farmers and dairymen. For years now it looked as though the next winter was surely going to be the last the old house would see. The roof sagged in the middle like an old couch. Bricks from the twin chimneys, heavy from the January ice and jarred loose

by heavy trucks pounding by on Route 422, had a discon-
certing tendency to drop down from the eaves like frozen
pigeons. Not that Arnie himself had ever had the pleasure
of sitting out a January ice storm in the hinterlands. And
after hearing the tales from John Hammond in the front parlor, he certainly had no intention of hanging around long
enough for the experience. No, it was cold enough now,
with the early November winds shaking wet leaves out of
the trees, where they fell to the ground like used bars of
colored soap.

Watts could hear the rain now, battering the roof of his
rented cabin. The electric heater glowed red, contrasting
with the dim light of the tiny black-and-white TV. Arnie
wrapped himself in a wool blanket that stank of mothballs
and lay on the rock-hard bed, watching the snowy screen as
it projected barely visible outlines of game-show contestants
answering questions no human being had any right knowing.
If they were so damn smart, Arnie wondered, why did they
all sound like such pitiful losers when the host stopped the
show to interview them? It all confirmed his theory that
people spend large chunks of their lives learning things that
were absolutely useless when it came to actually living. That
people, even the supposedly smart ones, had no idea why
they were here, and knew even less about what it was they
were supposed to be doing. Really, who gave a shit that
Edward the Second was the King of England in 1310?
Wouldn't you be a lot better off knowing how cars work,
or how to make electricity from windmills? The whole fucking world, Arnie decided, made about as much sense as a
jigsaw puzzle with half the pieces missing.

Angry, he got up and flipped the TV off. The screen faded
slowly from white to gray, but seemed to take forever to
actually turn itself off. He stared at the screen, at the movement that seemed almost visible in the shadows. As though
the machine were somehow receiving a transmission from
some hidden dimension. Dots of light, like a code. A message that someone, or something, was trying to project. He
turned the set on, then off again. Watching. Finally, it turned
into a dull, black window. A closed window on an empty

world. No message, no nothing. That, he knew, was the real message.

Outside, trucks thundered by in the darkness. Inches from the front door of the cabin, it seemed. Rattling windows, sending earthquake vibrations through the wooden floor. He looked beyond the thin curtains, at the truck lights, stabbing spotlights, ripping through the rain and fog. Like spaceship lasers, the light dripping with road spray. Clouds settling in on the treetops, wrapping the half-bare branches in a smoky haze. The cabin, he realized, stank like mothballs and rotted onions.

Arnie Watts went back to sit on the bed, wrapped in the old wool blanket. He stared at the floor, then stared at nothing. This wasn't where he was supposed to be, he thought. At least he hoped it wasn't.

—Did you have a nice sleep, Yvonne?

The words twisted up out of the black well in back of his brain. As though someone, or something was throwing tiny pebbles against the window of his mind. Telling him to wake up, to get moving.

—Did you have a nice sleep, Yvonne?

The moment, the instant of her fear replaying inside his head, like a favorite movie one never tires of watching. Her eyes opening, blinking, realizing that it was all not some terrible dream. Arnie Watts, sitting in the darkness, the red glow of the electric heater like a primitive campfire. While outside, the world went about its nighttime business. Unknowing, unsuspecting. People living their brief, empty lives.

—Did you have a nice sleep . . . ?

Arnie Watts smiled, remembering.

It wasn't that Yvonne Stafford didn't like the new house. She did. It was surely a lot better than their old apartment. The new house had an upstairs, her room was bigger, and there was even a family room in the basement. There was a yard and trees, and a garage attached to the house, so they could walk right out to the car when it was cold or raining. It was beautiful, actually. Except that . . . except that, she didn't feel comfortable. It wasn't just the new house. It was everything. She didn't feel comfortable anywhere. Not in her room or at school or at the mall. Nowhere. No place. It was as if she didn't belong anymore. Belonged nowhere. No place.

Certainly not here, where the people next door came over and welcomed them to the neighborhood. In this place where everyone seemed friendly. They smiled and waved, and even stopped to talk when they passed you on the sidewalk. She surely did not belong here, where the night was quiet and peaceful. She and her family—Lesia and James and James Junior—cooked out on the back patio. There was serious talk about putting in a pool next summer. And Jimmy had friends who came over and played video games, all of which made her brother decidedly less obnoxious these days. But still, she didn't belong here, in this place where her father caught the train to work every morning, and her mother had a new job at a real estate office, which allowed her to spend a lot more time at home. It was, everyone agreed, a wonderful place to live. Much better than their old life in New York.

"We should've done this years ago," Lesia Stafford said, at least once a week.

"That's the truth," her father always replied. "Isn't it, Yvonne?"

She nodded, smiling. Like thin, high clouds spreading a veil over the sun. She didn't belong here, she knew, because she was supposed to be dead.

Summer had faded away and they raked leaves together. They washed the cars on Saturdays and ordered pizza and didn't worry every minute about locking the doors . . . except for Yvonne, who always, always locked the door to her bedroom. And made sure the window was shut tight and the curtains closed. And lay awake anyway, watching the shadows on her ceiling, listening to cars passing in the street. Wondering. Wondering, if one of them was HIM. If she would wake up in the middle of the night—some night, any night—and find HIM standing at the foot of her bed. Lying awake, she prayed . . . prayed that someday she would stop being afraid. And sometimes late, late at night, she cried. Holding her pillow as waves of terror jolted her body like electric shocks. Crying, softly, she thought. But always her mother would hear and knock quietly on her door.

"Yvonne . . . Yvonne, honey. Open the door, baby. Let me in, honey. . . ."

And sometimes she would allow her mother into the room, where they would lie together on the bed, surrounded by posters and stuffed animals, and shadows. Her mother would hold her, whispering as the night pressed in on the room like a dark, smothering cloud.

"It's all right, Yvonne," Lesia would say, holding her daughter, rocking her as though she was a small child again. "It's going to be all right. . . ."

But it wasn't, Yvonne knew. It would never be all right. Because sometimes when she closed her eyes, HE was there. Standing over her, or even lying in the bed next to her.

—Did you have a nice sleep, Yvonne?

His words, like knives pressed against her skin. Sharp and cutting. And even though she never said it out loud, there were times when she wished with all her heart that she had not returned to be among the living. That she could sleep in peace and wait for forever to end. It was a terrible thing to wish, she knew. It was, in fact, one of the worst sins. Even worse than what HE had done to her. It was a terrible thing to wish you were dead, even to hope for it sometimes.

It wouldn't be all right. Not ever. Because she wasn't her anymore. She wasn't Yvonne Stafford, charter member of the P.S. 364 Bomb Squad. The truth was, she knew, that person had really and truly died. She wasn't herself anymore, and never would be again. She was someone else now. Someone for whom fear was a constant companion—a shadow that never really left her. And she cried because she wanted to be herself again. She wanted to be Yvonne Stafford. But she never would be—not ever, not ever. . . .

"I want to be me again," she said to the woman behind the long desk. Sometimes, these days, her mother sat in the chair next to hers. Sometimes Yvonne was in the room alone with the woman doctor.

Every Saturday at noon she and Lesia drove together to New Haven, where Yvonne would sit in the office, which smelled like new shoes and furniture polish. The woman doctor, who knew somehow that she was keeping awful secrets locked away inside, would try to get her to tell the secrets. But she wouldn't, couldn't tell.

"But you are you." The woman smiled gently.

"No, I'm not," she would say. Sometimes she would cry, sitting in the chair, and the woman would come around from her desk and hold her shoulder.

"I just want to be me again," Yvonne would say.

And after, she would sit outside the room while Lesia talked quietly to the woman doctor. Sometimes her mother would cry.

"It will be all right, Mrs. Stafford," the doctor would say. "Time is the greatest healer."

But the woman was wrong, Yvonne knew. It would not be all right. Not ever.

"What do I do?" she asked in the soft quiet of the night, after the tears and the fear had passed, and her mother left, thinking her to be asleep. "What do I do?"

The shadows, moving and shifting on her ceiling. The curtains shimmering, as if a breeze had somehow passed through the closed window. The shadows, drifting down to touch her forehead. Warm, like the summer sun, and she would sleep.

The diner closed at ten o'clock. By ten-fifteen Anna Burrows was running out to her car with a newspaper held over her head. The rain was cold, chilling her shoulders and legs. The other waitress, Mary Jo, locked the door to the diner and sprinted to her own rusted-out Toyota truck.

"See you tomorrow!" they yelled to each other, both fumbling for their keys, each hoping the old heap would turn over in the cold and damp. As always, both waited until the other's engine roared to life. Snapping on the headlights, they grinned and waved, then splashed on home, squinting as the wiper blades struggled with the rain.

Anna yawned, reaching for a cigarette in her coat pocket. She wiggled her sore toes, trapped in the confines of her sneakers all day. Betsy would be getting ready for bed. Fortunately, David was working the day shift at the plant this week, so they wouldn't have to pay a baby-sitter. The extra money could pay the phone bill, with the rest getting stashed away for Christmas presents. This was good, Anna thought, smiling. Plus she'd be home in time to tuck Betsy into bed. And maybe David, too.

Rain dripped around the corners of the windshield in tiny rivers. The wipers barely keeping up. She drove past the Last Stop Motel and Boardinghouse without a glance.

Rain drenched the entire Eastern Seaboard, falling in cold sheets along the northern states, driving the homeless into shelters, reminding everyone that snow and ice were on the way. Jenny did not like being alone in the office on rainy afternoons, particularly when it got dark so damn early. York had called at three o'clock, asking for any updates. Of which there were none. He and the Dane were in Myrtle Beach, and the airport was socked in.

"You know the Dane," York said, sighing into the phone. "Refuses to step on an airplane if the sun isn't shining."

"I don't blame him," Jenny replied, staring out the office window, the rain like tiny hammers against the glass.

"There's not a hellovalot more we can do here," York said. "It was our guy who took off the chicken place. All the workers identified him. You did real good."

"Thanks," Jenny said. "But he's long gone, right?"

"That's what they think down here. I tend to agree." York sounded tired, she thought. And more than a little frustrated. But then he had been that way for months. "We'll be back in New York tomorrow afternoon. Even if I have to drag the Dane onto the goddamn plane!"

Laughter along the phone lines. A hesitant silence. Reach

out and touch someone, the ads said. Not hardly, Jenny thought.

"I miss you," she said. More hesitation.

"Me, too," York said back. As if he could have said anything else, Jenny thought, kicking herself for boxing him in like that. What was it about men, she wondered, that they found it so difficult to communicate on anything remotely close to an emotional level? The G.I. Joe mentality, she had read someplace. While she was stuck with the Barbie doll/romance novel view of life's relationships. One was just as bad as the other, she decided.

"Well, then, I'll see you tomorrow," York said finally.

"I'll be here," she replied, holding on to the phone for a few seconds to be sure he had actually hung up, hating that part of her that made her cling.

After the call she checked the police computer again and ran through the clippings so they'd be ready for Dennison, in case he and the Dane caught an early flight. Unfortunately, there were a large number of clippings. Kidnappings, like those of Yvonne Stafford, reported from all around the country. Kansas City, Duluth, Rochester, Albany, Los Angeles, Denver, Boston. And, of course, New York. All the majors, and reports from tiny places no one had ever heard of before. Keene, Shawkee, Brattleboro, Essex Junction. So many news stories. All more or less the same. Young children disappearing, dropping off the face of the earth. Some never to be found. Others discovered as skeletal remains months, or even years, after their abductions. The cases going, for the large part, unsolved. What in the world was going on? she wondered.

"Did you ever stop and ask how many twisted, sick people are out there doing this kind of thing?" she'd asked York one day after they had gone through an entire notebook of their clippings. The look in his eyes told her immediately that she had asked the wrong question. Of course he thought about it, she realized. They had all been thinking of little else these past months.

"Every day," he replied, his teeth grinding as his hand reached for the cigarette package that wasn't there. "I think about it, then I try to put it out of my mind. Really, it's hideous to consider.''

"I wonder how many of these are our guy?'' the Dane asked, uncharacteristically adding to the conversation.

York had nodded. They all wondered that, too, Jenny realized. And even though the subject had never come up between her and York, both knew that Jenny had been keeping a more careful eye on Gena's comings and goings. Although you can't live in fear, Jenny kept reminding herself. It was simply not a rational way to live. Besides, it was quite impossible to watch a teenager every minute of the day. Or even a younger child, for that matter. There were moments when your kids would be on their own, however brief those moments might be. The alternative was to live locked up in your house or apartment. And that was not really an alternative. America—land of the free, home of the brave—Jenny thought.

Still, after York called, she picked up the phone and punched in the neighbor's number, where Gena stayed for a couple hours in the afternoon when there were no after-school activities. Activities that were becoming more and more frequent. Softball practice, soccer, club meetings, trips to the mall with friends. Human beings, especially young human beings, were highly social creatures, as Jenny herself well remembered. And would you have it any other way? she asked herself. No, you had to be pleased that your children were going out into the world. Pleased and paranoid both at the same time. An odd combination, she thought. The phone rang half a dozen times, fueling the sense of unease that seemed to follow Jenny around like a shadow these days. Did her own mother feel this way? she wondered. She'd have to ask next time they talked. And she would call her mom this weekend, Jenny vowed. A promise made on a dreary November afternoon. It had a fifty-fifty chance of being kept, she realized.

"Cindy? Hi, it's Gena's mom. Is she there? Good, can I talk to her for a second?''

Reaching out to touch someone. Guess those ad people aren't entirely stupid, she thought.

• • •

"Guess I'll have a burger and some fries," Arnie Watts said. "No rush, when you get time."

Anna Burrows smiled. Arnie winked at her. Anna found herself wondering what this Mr. Reynolds did for a living, that he was in the diner at all hours of the day and night.

In the old farmhouse, converted to boardinghouse and motel by her late husband, Marjorie Dish plopped herself at the kitchen table for her afternoon tea and toast. The rainy weather bothered her joints, plagued these last few years by the rheumatism that had bent her own mother in the last years of her life. Marjorie Dish, who besides being an innkeeper, had at one time been a schoolteacher, as well as wife and mother to four sons, often found it incredible that she had now grown old. At least that her body had grown old. In her mind, she was still thirty years old, or thereabouts. True, she had a tendency to fall asleep reading a book or watching television after ten o'clock at night. But aside from that peculiarity, she hardly ever thought of herself as being old. She wondered if it was that way for everyone who lived for three-quarters of a century.

She had few regrets, except that Murphy had died so young. She should have kept him away from the bacon and eggs. And maybe the fact that her boys had moved so far away. But that was a family trait. She herself had done the very same thing, leaving the family farm to go to teacher's college. And that was before the war, when women just didn't do that sort of thing. Certainly not good southern girls. No, they stayed in the communities where they were born, married local boys, planted gardens, and sang in the church choir. But not Marjorie Dish, who took off from South Carolina to see the world and ended up in an old farmhouse in Hershey, Pennsylvania. A farmhouse that looked curiously like her daddy's back in Conway. It was curious, also, that one of her sons, Little Evan, had settled back in the very country she had left so many years ago. Of course, Evan wasn't little anymore. But in her thirty-year-old mind, he still was. And once a month, like clockwork, he sent her the weekly paper from her old hometown. It was a silly thing, she thought sometimes, that she read the paper from a place she hadn't lived in for more than fifty years. But she did, perusing the obituaries, the editorials, the crank letters about the school board. Sometimes she thought she saw a name that looked familiar. Mostly in the obits these days, she admitted.

The sun came out, throwing splashes of light across the kitchen table. John Hammond was rocking in the front parlor, Smokey's tail an inch away from the creaking chair. She'd bring John some tea in a few minutes, she thought, stretching her legs under the table, hoping she could avoid taking any medicine for her aching joints until after supper. Turning the pages of the *Conway Examiner*. Remembering high school, barn dances, bonfires, hayrides, and Charlie Eggard's clumsy advances. She had been wrong to encourage him so, when she knew there was never going to be anything serious between them. Charlie Eggard, who ended up owning the hardware store on Main Street. Who had he married? She thought she used to know, but the name and the face escaped her. But one face in the paper jumped out at her. It was just a drawing, the story itself taken from the Myrtle Beach Times. But there was no mistaking who it was. The man in the number three cabin, Mr. Reynolds! That narrow chin and those close-set eyes. That was him, she was sure of it. And robbed a chicken place in Mrytle Beach! My God!

"Mr. Hammond, come look at this!" she called.

Betsy Burrows and her friend, Carol Ann Huxley, wanted to be singers. Their fantasy, however, did not involve standing in front of a band, belting out songs. Being girls of modest dreams, they wanted to be backup singers. To stand in the shadows, maybe bang on a tambourine, and sing rhythm. They spent hours together in Betsy's room, listening to CDs, practicing for their big break.

"Do-wa. Do-wa-diddy," they'd sing, swaying to the music, clapping hands, making up dance steps.

They also pretended they were sisters, dressing alike whenever possible, even weaving their hair into the same, pulled-back style. Both were the only children in their respective working-class families, a situation they regarded as a grave injustice. As well as being famous backup singers, Betsy and Carol Ann both planned to have large families. And, of course, to live next door to each other. If they could somehow manage to marry twins, they thought, their children would even look alike. Looking in the mirror, the pretend game that they were sisters could have been a reality. Both had long, sandy-brown hair and dark eyes. They were both thin and lanky. (The perfect figures for backup singers, they thought.) Both played field hockey and sang in the school chorus. The fact that this description fit more than half the girls in their seventh grade class went, apparently, unnoticed.

On weekend nights when they slept over at each other's houses, they talked until the morning hours, planning their lives down to the smallest details.

Three children each, but not until they were older. Twenty-three, at least. Two girls and a boy. Christene, Carol Ann, and David. Dorothy, Betsy, and James. Their husbands probably wouldn't be in show business, but could manage their careers and watch the kids when the band was traveling.

No church weddings. They were both going to be married in a field of flowers. Together, on the same day, if that could be arranged. But then how could they be each other's bridesmaids? Never mind, figure that out later.

And wouldn't it be cool if we could plan it so the kids would have the same birthdays?

You can't plan that!

Sure you can. You count on the calendar and do it on the same night.

Do *it* on the same night?

Laughter. First muffled giggles. Then uncontrolled, full-blown roaring.

"Hey! You two want to hold it down in there? Some people are trying to sleep, you know!"

Heads buried in pillows. Eyes closed, tears of laughter running down the slopes of soft, warm cheeks. The warmth,

drawing them together, until more often than not, they fell
asleep holding hands under the covers. Sisters to the end.

"Do-wa. Do-wa-diddy . . ."

When he returned to the Last Stop that afternoon, Arnie
Watts thought he saw Old Lady Dish staring out the back
window at him. When he turned to look, he was sure he
saw her hiding behind the curtains. You couldn't hide a
sparrow behind those flimsy curtains, he thought, much less
a hundred-and-sixty-pound grandmother. She was certainly
odd, even for an old, backwater woman, but he had never
seen her spy on people. Arnie Watts's radar began singing
in his head, like the air-raid bell on the firehouse when he
was a kid. What the fuck was going on here? He kicked the
mud off his shoes and went inside the cabin. Periodic
glances out the tiny window confirmed his suspicions. She
was definitely checking him out. But why?

"It's him," Mrs. Dish whispered, even though she and
John Hammond were the only ones in the kitchen, indeed
in the whole house. The Nomad was out somewhere on one
of his many drunken excursions.

"I'm not sure," Hammond said, shaking his head. The
truth was, he had not been sure of anything his eyes told
him for the last ten years. A fact that hadn't escaped Mrs.
Dish's attention.

"You couldn't see a moose across the road," Mrs. Dish
admonished.

Hammond said nothing. There was no defense against the
truth.

"Should we call the police?" Mrs. Dish asked, unable to
keep her eyes away from the window.

"I'm not calling the police," Hammond said. "You go
ahead if you want to. Then that guy can sue the hell out of
you when it turns out you're wrong."

Now it was Mrs. Dish's turn to be quiet. Watching the
news these days, she knew Hammond's comment was a real
possibility.

"We've got to get a closer look at him," she suggested.

"Maybe you do, I don't!" Hammond said. Then Mrs.

Dish gave him such a scathing look he all but wilted. "All right, all right. I'll see if I can get him to have a beer in the parlor this afternoon. Then you can spy on him up close."

"If it's him, I'm calling the police," Mrs. Dish said firmly. "I won't have thieves around here."

John Hammond was about to mention the Nomad, who had seen the inside of the county jail more times than he had seen a roof over his head. But instead, he wandered back to his rocking chair to look out the window and watch the puddles in the front yard dry up. Poking your nose where it didn't belong, he thought, was a good way to get it bit off. Smokey, he noted, hadn't moved at all, despite the excitement.

In his cabin Arnie Watts was pacing. Glancing out the window, he was sure he saw the old lady peering through the curtains. He was uneasy, and he didn't like being uneasy. He considered packing up and leaving, but somehow sensed there wasn't any real danger. Not yet, anyway. But it was close, real close.

"How do you know what will happen?" she asked, her voice trembling along the higher range of audible sound, thus denoting both urgency and concern.

"I don't, not exactly, not for certain," he admitted, projecting authority, if not confidence. He was, after all, Senior Facilitator in this laboratory, set along the planet's Third Volcanic Rim.

"Then do you think it wise to continue?" she asked, clearly invoking the Second Principle of Experimentation.

It was, as they both knew, a foolish and outdated Principle. Really, what was the point of experimentation if one was allowed to proceed only if the outcome was known in advance?

"There is a certain necessity, wouldn't you say?" he countered.

Her silence was augmented with frequency vibrations, which suggested agreement, but advised caution. He nodded. There was a need for caution, but there was a deeper need for answers. His experiment, while radical, would not damage the ecosystem any further than it already was, and might, in the long-term, provide information on the results of the Restoration.

The issue settled between them, he combined the chemicals and prepared to inject the mixture into the fissure at the base of the cliff. His superiors, of course, would denounce him and perhaps revoke his license if they did not care for the results of his experiment. They would most certainly terminate the laboratory's funding, and could, if they pleased, terminate him as well. But that was a chance he was willing to take.

After the experiment had been set in motion, before the first results came back to the tracking monitors, the two of them went outside to watch the sunset, which was quite spectacular, especially out here along the Volcanic Rim. The sun seemed to explode when it rose and set through the red haze of the cloud cover. This was, in fact, the reason behind the collapse of the ecosystem, and the desperation behind the Restoration Program. As they stood together at the edge of the cliff on which the stone laboratory sat, both marveled at the reds and purples that danced in the sky, as though the tentacles of God were waving at them. This twice daily explosion of color struck fear in the hearts of many, he knew, enjoying this quiet moment of contemplation. But for him and his mate, the sun's continuing spectacle was something they had witnessed since birth, and they never tired of its brilliance. Not even when their subsequent education and training revealed the dust clouds to be portents of disaster. Which, undoubtedly, they were.

It had begun in the years just after their egg cluster hatched, when the bonds between them, ancient, yet well defined, had already been established. As the Scriptures said: "Those who are born to the same cluster shall be connected by marriage and property until the end of their days." And so it was, despite the fact that the two of them did not put much stock in the Old Ways. It was curious, he thought many times, to be so bound by a thing which one did not truly believe. Still, he and his mate seemed to have found love together, as well as a certain camaraderie in their work. Even if the work, lately, had become a divisive issue between them. No, it was not the work, he decided. Rather the results, which they both suspected and feared. He reached over and wrapped her in the webbing beneath his arms. She responded with frequencies of caring.

It had begun decades ago, when they were hatchlings together, both young and unaware. The increased volcanic eruptions threw vast clouds of dust and gases into the atmosphere, causing an immediate and protracted disruption of the ecosystem. Insect harvests along the grasslands dropped dramatically, causing food shortages and eventually famine among the clans. The scientists of the Extended Clan proposed a series of solutions, each one spectacular in their failure. Harvest weights continued to fall as the eruptions increased both in number and intensity. The economy, tied so closely with food production, began a long downhill slide, from which there seemed to be no recovery. Rumors circulated that the volcanic activity was caused by government programs designed to tap thermal energy from the planet's core and to extract dwindling fuel reserves from deep beneath the continental plates. The rumors, while never proved, caused an upheaval in the already volatile political landscape. Thus, even as the need for scientific knowledge became paramount, the resources and political will to fund experimental projects vanished. Then, when fundamentalists came to power, the ancient Principles designed to control scientific discovery were revived from the Scriptures. And so the situation worsened, feeding on itself, even as the clans starved. Finally, with the world teetering on the brink of disaster, the scientific community banded together and the Restoration Project was established, with each new cluster programmed and educated in the Sciences, in the hope that a solution might be found.

Yet how foolish it was, he often thought, to produce generations of scientists, while shackling them with the hopelessly outdated Principles. It was, he knew, a concept born of fear, superstition, and political necessity. As the volcanic eruptions continued to grow, the fundamentalists seemed to exert more and more sway over the Elders of the Extended Clan. In order to save ourselves from this scourge, they argued, we must adhere to the Scriptures, for are they not the Word of God? The prophets and doomsayers seeding the ground, bringing to reality the very destruction they feared.

He shook himself from this reverie as the sun drifted down behind the mountains and the grim, starless dark took over the world. His mate pulled away from his webbing.

"We should check the readings," she said, looking up at the cloud-filled sky, barely suppressing a shiver that was deeper than the sudden chill of the night.

He followed her inside, almost reluctant to confirm what he already suspected. In the end, he feared, the fundamentalists and progressives like himself were conducting an empty argument. In the end, nature would have her way, no matter what the Scriptures did or did not say.

Inside the stone walls of the laboratory he found his mate staring at the monitors and printed readouts, her look confirming his worst fears.

"Can this be right?" she asked in disbelief.

Standing next to her, watching the numbers as they flew by on the screen, he found he could say nothing. Numbers, he knew, were one of the few things in the world that did not lie. The eruptions, he saw, would continue to increase on a geometric scale. The Restoration was doomed to fail. He reached out and wrapped her in his webbing. This time her frequencies were those of fear.

Many cycles of time later, when they had passed through the stages of life and death, and were hatchlings together again, the world had undergone its metamorphosis. Shrouded under a canopy of clouds, they wandered the grasslands with the few remaining members of their clan. In the dim twilight of the day, they picked insects from the stunted stalks of grass and ate them as they foraged. At night around the campfires, the Elders read from Scripture and sang chants to the glory of God. And he found himself haunted by strange memories of another life.

◆ REFLECTIONS ON THE SEARCH FOR FAITH IN THE PHYSICAL PLANE

Within the context of any life experiment, at that point when evolution pushes a dominant species' thought processes into the early stages of higher awareness, it is natural for the mechanisms to begin questioning their place in the universe. This exploration of self can be traced to the predomination period in the mechanisms' history, and usually reaches its apex with the insertion of implanted entities and the accompanying strides toward a technological-based society.

Observation has shown that in most instances, the developing technology finds itself at odds with the older, entrenched beliefs of the previously dominant religious community. The resulting conflicts between these two seeming diametrically opposed factions, often causes both internal and external upheavals within the emerging society. In many instances, in which one faction is able to successfully undermine the efforts of the other, failure of the experiment becomes unavoidable. As previously noted, the development of technology in the absence of a deeper understanding regarding the true dynamics of the universe, always produces disastrous results. Conversely, the inability of the religious community to accept technological advancement, even to the point of adjusting their time-honored doctrine, yields the same unfortunate results. The successful experiment will incorporate an expanded view, utilizing to the fullest extent that which can be seen and measured, yet balancing this new knowledge with the undeniable fact that there is another world, the spiritual plane, which cannot be seen or measured, but which exerts a definable force upon the physical plane.

In the early stages of an experiment, if the mechanisms are able to overcome the initial conflicts of this restructuring, and the use of force has been discarded by both competing factions, there is usually a period of calm and reflection. During this period, which may last for a protracted time, the technology of the society pushes forward with its experimentation and discovery, while the religious community seeks to come to terms with what it perceives to be its reduced role in the civilization's advancement. It is during this period of adjustment that the individual mechanisms themselves experience the internal upheaval of this conflict. It is at this point that the mechanisms' true search for the enlightenment of self begins.

Also, it is at this critical juncture in the development of the society that the individual mechanisms are at the greatest risk. As observations have revealed, it is at this turning point, when the foundations of primitive beliefs are being replaced, when the economic base of the hunter/gatherer civilization is being transformed by the technological revolution, that the world may be seen by the individual to be retreating into chaos. When this viewpoint manifests itself in the minds of the mechanisms, they become susceptible to violent and irrational behavior. As the individual is, in fact, the society, it is possible for the civilization itself to unravel, causing an abrupt failure of the experiment.

Equally important, this manifestation may be considered as one of the prime motivating factors in the wanton violence certain mechanisms exhibit toward others of their species.

There are several forces driving the mechanisms in this, and in other life experiments. The external forces are obvious: the short lifespan of the individual mechanism has been discussed; the evolutionary factors, specifically the early states of the mechanisms' development and the close historical proximity of their primitive past; the technological upheaval, with its accompanying economic and belief restructuring. But another, even more powerful force is at work here, namely the implanted entities.

It is, of course, the entities themselves which are the principal components fueling the drive toward a technological society. The development of an advanced civilization, with its increased learning opportunities, remains the central focal point of the experiment. This goal, however, is directly impacted by secondary aspects, such as the mechanisms' search for self. The implanted entities play a primary role in this internal struggle, as the mechanisms attempt to define their place in the universe.

Faith, in the end, is no more than the knowledge of self. However, as has been noted, the implanted entities often find themselves overwhelmed when immersed in the complexities of the physical world. The search for faith then becomes the entities' search for what they once were, and will be again, in the spiritual plane. The confusion of the physical plane, the continuing and unabated infusion of sensory data, particularly in primitive mechanisms which have not developed filtering and data organizational brain patterns, often causes even the most experienced entities to flounder, helplessly adrift in the physical realm. The anxiety resulting from this sensory overload is, in fact, the disrupting influence behind many failed learning experiences. Further, as the anxiety levels increase, as the entity is unable to center itself in the physical world, the individual mechanism then becomes at risk. It is possible at this point for the entity to lose control over its mechanism. The mechanism will then, of necessity, revert back to its primitive instinctual programming.

Conclusion: If there is indeed a flaw in the experiment, it manifests itself at this juncture. The flaw may be defined as a loss, or an absence, of faith. It is unfortunate that necessity dictates the implantation of entities into primitive mechanisms, but the logistics of the experiment are such that waiting for evolutionary factors to prevail simply is not feasible, given the time constraints of solar and planetary development. Add to that the learning experiences required by the entities within their respective mechanisms, and it becomes readily apparent that the window of opportunity remains limited. The opportunities for the entities to excel, however, are clearly enhanced by this approach.

Question: Is it possible that the definition of Evil is, simply: Confusion?

nineteen

"Just coffee, please," Arnie Watts said, sliding into a seat at the counter. It was early evening, the sun having recently set on the syrupy Hershey streets. Anna Burrows looked over at him, wondering if something was wrong. It was suppertime and Mr. Reynolds usually stopped by to eat something around suppertime. Plus, he looked kind of agitated.

"Everything OK?" she asked politely. A good waitress, like a good bartender, always had a word or two for the regular customers. Her mother, who had worked at the Elk's Club for years, had given her that advice.

"Fine, thanks," Arnie said, his voice sharper than he meant. He smiled, trying to compensate. "Had some bad news about my father, is all."

"Oh, I hope he's all right," Anna remarked, sounding to Watts as though she actually meant it. She did, in fact, having lost her own father only two years before.

"It's not that serious," Arnie said. "Thanks for asking, though. I appreciate it."

Smiles all around. The coffee appearing like magic. Arnie Watts gave himself a couple of bonus points for quick thinking. There could be no bad news about his old man, who had been in the grave for the better part of a decade. And it wasn't even bad news back then. For Arnie Watts, and for his sister, their father's death had been a decided relief.

Arnie himself had been plotting to help the old bastard along into the next life for years. Truth was, he felt sort of cheated when heart disease did the job before he could.

No, tonight he was bothered by events a bit closer at hand. A couple hours ago that old fuck, John Hammond, had set him up for an ID. Watts was pretty sure about when it had happened. They were in the parlor together, he and Hammond. Four o'clock or so, the sun warm against the peeling paint of the windowpanes. Outside, leaves from the oak trees, falling late, rode the soft afternoon breeze. He and Hammond tipping back a couple of Rolling Rocks.

"Brewed right in Pennsylvania," Hammond said, sounding like one of those contestants on the game show. Know-it-all bastards. "Yes sir, they can have that Milwaukee shit. They brew their beer right out of that poison lake, you know."

Watts nodded. From the corner of his eye, he saw that nosy Mrs. Dish peering out of the kitchen at him. The sixth sense kicking in like a laser shot to the brain, like he was standing by the front window, posing for a police lineup. He drained the bottle and left, the alarm bells blowing like a strong wind in his ears. It was time to get the fuck away from here, he felt, although he couldn't say exactly why. He rolled the van out of the boardinghouse parking lot, watching as the old woman and Hammond cackled together like a couple of hens who had discovered a weasel hole in their chicken coop. He drove around town for a while, trying to sort out just what the sixth sense was telling him. Then he stopped in at the diner. It was, he knew, Anna Burrows's early night off. That's what the sixth sense was telling him, he decided. It was time to get down to business.

The plane was late getting into JFK. It had been a bumpy flight and the Dane's nerves were decidedly on edge. He had been more sullen and withdrawn than usual during the flight, York noted, if that was possible. And now as they waited for their baggage to appear on the carousel, the Dane seemed downright perturbed. York thought this was probably due to the big man's inability to control his fear at being hopelessly trapped in a thin metal tube, traveling at an insane speed thirty thousand feet in the air. York himself had wanted to get down on the tarmac and kiss the ground. He suspected a lot of people did, after being jostled around in the clouds. Decorum, however, prevented it. Still, for a former soldier, the Dane showed a curious lack of faith in the Gods of Fate, York thought.

Their bags showed up a couple of minutes before Jenny, and the Dane did a half-turn away when Jenny hugged York, as though she, too, had some terrible premonition about their trip home. York, equally embarrassed by the public display of emotion, endured it for a second or two, then grabbed for his own bags, as if he could somehow hide behind his luggage. Jenny, ever alert to these types of maneuvers, stepped away and smiled at them.

"It's good to have the two of you back," she said, raising her own protective walls.

The Dane grunted a response and led the charge out of the airport, Jenny and York following at a more leisurely pace.

"I missed you," she said softly.

"Missed you, too," York said, trying to put more feeling than was possible into the few words. Fortunately, Jenny seemed to get his message and took his arm briefly as they walked toward the parking lot. Women were pretty sharp at reading between the syllables, York decided. Which was a good thing, he thought, because relationships between the sexes would never amount to anything if they didn't. The truth was, he felt comfortable when he and Jenny were together. And when they were apart, it seemed lately that he found himself fighting constantly with a strange lack of concentration. As if part of his brain kept wondering where she was, what she was doing, if she was all right. When she was here in front of him, his mind could answer all those abstract questions.

There was a dichotomy here, he was aware. One part of him was like the Dane—leery of any loss of control and certainly resenting the resulting lack of concentration. But the rest of him was perfectly content to wallow in abstract thought when she was away from him, and to watch her almost constantly when she was near. It was, he realized, a dangerous preoccupation. Between Jenny and the guy they were tracking, it seemed to York that he had no room in his brain for anything else. Perhaps, he thought as they loaded the luggage and started for home, this was the reason behind the Dane's sullen mood. What to do about it, however, seemed too perplexing to consider. York realized he had the feeling these days that he was running a race with blinders on, like an old trotting horse on its last legs. Thinking more about the pasture than the business at hand.

"Anything new on the home front?" he asked in an attempt to bring himself back into focus. But it took Jenny a moment or two to realize he meant the investigation.

"Just what I told you on the phone," Jenny answered. For some reason, she had taken over Ronnie Bates's taxi responsibilities. She was swinging her small Subaru into the traffic flow. It looked icy and the Dane sat uncomfortably in the back, watching the road with much the same look he had on the airplane. An odd mixture of detachment and subtle fear written on his face. He seemed glad to be let out at his apartment building in upper Manhattan.

"Why don't we take tomorrow off and pick up again on Wednesday?" York suggested, helping the Dane pull his bags out of the trunk.

"You're the boss," the Dane said, as if he had already resigned himself to writing off another day.

Back in the car, York chuckled to himself, shaking his head.

"What?" Jenny asked.

"Nothing," York said. "I just never knew anyone who didn't like a day off."

"Well, I do," Jenny said, reaching over to pat York's leg. "Got any ideas how we can spend the free time?"

York laughed, deciding the blinders fit him nicely.

"Do you ever think about fate?" Jenny asked. They were lying together in her bedroom, the night spread softly like the blankets around them. Actually, this was the first time he had spent the entire night with her. And the truth was, he was exhausted. A randy detective told him once that was the true joy of a younger woman. He hadn't believed it at the time.

"Fate?" he asked, in an obvious attempt to stall for time until his brain caught up with his body. Their night together, he now realized, had been carefully planned and orchestrated, with Gena playing a major role, he suspected. She was sleeping overnight at a friend's house, as she had reminded both of them at least three times during dinner. While grinning into her milk, York thought.

Jenny was looking at him, her hair soft across her shoulders. She was indeed beautiful, York thought, pulling her closer. It seemed to him that for the first time in a long while, he was thinking about how inordinately lucky he was.

"Yes, I think about it a lot," he admitted. She was looking at him again. To see if he was serious, York thought. "I think we're given certain choices," he said. "That we're put in situations. And if we choose correctly, then Fate rewards us. If not, well . . ."

"We get punished?" Jenny asked.

"Seems that way, doesn't it?" York said, even though his reply sent him deeper into an odd state of confusion.

In the diner Arnie Watts finished his coffee and dropped a dollar on the counter.

"I'll see you girls later," he said to Anna and her co-worker, Mary Jo. "Save me a piece of that apple pie."

Smiles all around. It was six-thirty and dark as midnight outside. You can thank old Ben Franklin for that, Arnie thought, remembering one of the answers from the know-it-all game show. The cloud cover hung low in the sky like an old quilt. It would undoubtedly rain again before the night was over. Anna Burrows's shift was up at eight, he knew. Watts planned to drive around a little and make his return to the diner around seven-thirty. His van was parked by Anna's old Chevy in the lot, and as he made a show of dropping his keys, he slipped into the Chevy from the passenger side, so the roof light wouldn't come on. In a heartbeat he located the ignition wires under the dash and jerked one of them loose. He was back, jiggling with the lock on his van in seconds. As he crawled into the driver's seat, Watts looked carefully around to be certain his movements had gone unnoticed. Trucks rumbled by on Route 422, throwing their lights up against the low clouds. There was no one in the windows of the diner and only a couple other vehicles parked by the entrance. It was a clean hit, he decided, his face an emotionless mask as he cranked the van out of the lot and headed down the road into Hershey to kill the next hour. By then, it would be time to get down to business. He could feel the excitement building. The adrenaline pumping, his senses seeming to leap out into the night. He saw the faces of truck drivers lit up by their dash lights. The television sets glowing in the houses he passed. Women at their kitchen sinks, doing the supper dishes. Small night animals scurrying along the side of the road, playing life and death games with huge, roaring machines, making decisions for which evolution never prepared them.

Arnie Watts loved it when the hunt was about to begin. His mind felt as if it were full of strobe lights.

Betsy Burrows was putting away the supper dishes. That was the deal. When her father cooked, she did the dishes. When she cooked, he did them. It was simply part of the routine. Her mother had been working at suppertime for as long as Betsy could remember, except on weekends, when her mom made them eat together "like a real family." It was a drag sometimes, but there was a nice feeling about it, too.

"Dishes are done!" she called into the living room, where her father was watching the news. Another nighttime ritual. Adults, Betsy noted, were far too preoccupied with the news. Personally, she found the news depressing and usually repetitive. The same stories on night after night, except for some occasional big event, which almost always turned out to be not that big a deal at all. Like that football guy and his slow, slow, slow police chase. Her parents had watched that for hours. She and Carol Ann had looked at it for all of five minutes. Thank God for cable, she thought.

"I'm going to call Carol Ann," she said. "She's coming over to study."

"Just make sure you two get your homework done," her father called back.

Didn't I say we were going to study? she almost said, but then thought better about it. Her father was nice, but didn't appreciate the finer points of sarcasm, especially when the news was on. She thought maybe it was something that happened to you when you got older. Perhaps it was connected to the first gray hairs, about which her father didn't like to be teased either. Adults were too sensitive about their appearance, she decided, punching in Carol Ann's number on the speed dial.

"Can you come over?" she asked. "Good . . . oh, and bring your history book."

"I'm telling you, that was him!" Mrs. Dish said, scraping the last of the potatoes and gravy into Smokey's bowl. The dog, who got his name from sleeping too close to the fireplace as a pup, seemed to be paying more attention to her than Hammond.

"Maybe, maybe not." John Hammond sighed, loosening his belt. He and Mrs. Dish were the only two at the long dinner table. The Nomad was still out on a toot someplace, and the cabin renter didn't seem interested in paying the extra money for meals. He was a fool, Hammond thought, pulling his shirt out over his belly. Old Mrs. Dish was some cook, better even than his wife had been—God rest her soul. But like his wife, the woman also had a tendency to beat a subject to death. Like that Reynolds fellow. What were the chances that some guy who robbed a restaurant all the way down in South Carolina would end up on their doorstep? He'd made that very point, not five minutes ago.

"Well, I guess he's got to show up someplace, wouldn't you say, Mr. Hammond?" Mrs. Dish had replied.

John Hammond, who had learned early on in life to pick his fights carefully, shut his mouth. Mrs. Dish was convinced and there was obviously nothing he could do about it. What she wanted, he knew, was for him to join in on this foolishness with her. That, he could do something about.

"I really feel like I should call the police," Mrs. Dish was saying, for what Hammond thought was probably the tenth time.

"My advice is to lock up your purse, collect your rent in advance, and wait for him to leave," Hammond said. "I think he'll be gone pretty quick. He seemed mighty itchy in the parlor this afternoon."

The apple pie was tasty, Arnie Watts admitted to himself. He said so to Anna, who took the compliment as if she herself had personally baked it.

"Why, thank you, Mr. Reynolds," she said, smiling, wiping up his coffee ring with her ever-present cloth.

Her curiosity was getting the better of her, Watts noted. There were few other customers in the diner, now that the supper hour was over, and she seemed to be spending too much time checking his coffee cup. Waitresses were usually outgoing people by nature, Watts knew. Talkative and curious about their regular customers. She would ask something about him soon, he knew. She was getting up her nerve now. He watched her, like a playful cat toying with a mouse.

"I hope you don't mind me asking. . . ." she said, and Arnie Watts grinned. That was one of the best things about the opening rounds of the game, when he could tell with precision how people would act. "But what brings you to Hershey, anyway?"

In other words: What are you doing in our town, on our turf? How do you make your living? How much money do you have, that you can eat out every day of the week? She was used to dealing with truck drivers and town people, he knew. People she could categorize and slip into prescribed niches, like the coffee cups and plates behind the counter.

"No . . . I don't mind at all," he said casually, running through his list of prepared answers, picking one that would seem the most plausible. "I'm in sales, computers actually.

Been talking to the folks over at the plant, to see if I can get them to upgrade their equipment.''

"Isn't that interesting," Anna Burrows replied. Watts knew it wasn't at all interesting, but it provided a niche into which she could place him. Truck drivers, plant workers, salespeople. He had been officially categorized, and therefore made into an acknowledged person. A person wasn't really just a name, Arnie knew; they were an occupation as well. And now he was Mr. Reynolds, computer salesman. She felt as though she knew him better, he could tell. So she could trust him, a little at least. And a little trust was all Arnie Watts needed.

"Actually, I'm just about finished here," he said. "I'll be heading on home to Hartford in a day or two. Wife's birthday is Saturday," he said, twisting the silver wedding band he always wore during any extended stay in a small town.

"Can't miss a woman's birthday," Anna replied.

"No, ma'am," Watts said, chuckling. "Well, I better hit the road," he said, checking his watch. Eight o'clock on the dot. "Got a lot to do tomorrow."

"That's it for me, too," Anna Burrows said, wiping her hands on the towel, untying her apron.

"Oh, you're out early tonight?" Watts asked politely. "Come on, I'll walk you to the parking lot."

Good night's all around. The other waitress starting the late-night cleanup. The cook, scraping down his grill. Arnie Watts, the perfect gentleman, holding the door open for Anna Burrows. Outside, it was cold and damp, with a mixture of rain and ice pellets spitting out of the dark, rolling sky. In other words, a typical late fall evening in good old Pennsylvania, Arnie Watts thought.

"Have a good night, Mr. Reynolds," Anna Burrows called, opening the heavy door of the old Chevrolet.

"You, too," Arnie said, opening up the van, watching as Anna tried to start the Chevy. After a minute he walked over to where her car sat, like a metal boulder placed there by a passing glacier, unmovable until the next ice age.

"Won't start?" he asked the obvious question. "Pop the

hood, I'll take a look." Watts studied the engine for a few moments, hunching his shoulders against the icy rain. "It's no good!" he yelled over the rising wind. "I don't see anything wrong!"

"Goddamn car!" Anna cursed, coming out to stand by Arnie in the dim light of the diner, anger and frustration drawing deep, shadowy lines on her face. "I'll have to call David. . . ."

"Nonsense," Arnie Watts said, flipping the collar of his coat up around his neck, clapping his hands to warm them. "There's no reason for him to come out on a night like this. I'll be glad to give you a lift."

"I don't know. . . ." Anna replied, obviously hesitant. "I don't want to put you out. . . ." Offering him and herself a face-saving avenue of escape. Arnie Watts felt his body coil like a snake. The hunt was on. The prey had no chance of escape.

"It's nothing, really," he said. "Listen, there's no sense in us standing out in the weather. Why don't you go back in the diner and tell Mary Jo and Ed that your car's on the fritz and I'm giving you a ride home. Give David a ring and tell him you're on the way. You can get a mechanic to look the car over in the morning. It's probably nothing, a loose wire or something."

He could see her mulling over the plan he'd outlined. It made sense to her, he knew, because it covered all the bases. David wouldn't have to come out in the bad weather and pick her up. Mr. Reynolds, he was a regular customer, sort of. A salesman talking to the plant people. A nice enough guy. She trusted him, really. Mary Jo and Ed would know why she left her own car. David would know she was on her way home. It wasn't that far, after all.

Don't get in the car with strangers, she heard her mother saying, across two decades of time.

But Mr. Reynolds wasn't exactly a stranger. And if he wasn't a stand-up guy, he surely wouldn't have suggested she call David. And he did want her to tell Mary Jo and Ed that she was riding home with him. If he had something else in mind, he'd never do that. . . .

Arnie Watts watched her walking toward the diner and knew what was running through her mind. He knew, also, that she would be back to accept his offer, probably over her husband's objections. It was her decision, after all, and couldn't she be trusted to make up her own mind . . . ?

"This is very nice of you," Anna Burrows said, climbing into the front seat of the van.

"Hey, my pleasure." Arnie smiled, turning over the motor. "Don't think anything of it."

Headlights reaching out, pushing aside the dark. She sat very far away from him, of course. Her hand near the door handle, without making it obvious. Arnie Watts was careful to keep both hands on the wheel, so as not to spook her. Still, there was an undefinable tension in the air, almost sexual with its undercurrent of fear.

Should I have done this? he knew she was thinking.

What if . . . what if? Mr. Reynolds was looking at her, she noticed, his eyebrows lifted up on his forehead. She stared back at him, questioning his look.

"I guess I need directions," Arnie Watts said, smiling.

"Oh, right," Anna Burrows said, laughing at her own foolishness. How could he drive her home if he didn't know where she lived? "You go down to the light and take a right on Thirty-nine. It's a couple miles up the hill, on Holland Drive."

"Got it," he said, reaching over to turn up the heat.

He took the right at the light and Anna began to relax. He was, in fact, taking her home. Wasn't that what she expected? And if not, why in the world would she ever get in the vehicle with him?

"We're the third house from the corner," she said. "Ducks on the mailbox."

"Ducks, huh?" Arnie grinned, swinging into the driveway. It was a long gravel drive, with an old two-story white house waiting at the end. A neat looking place, he noted, set off in a grove of pines, lit up like a lighthouse. "Nice house," he commented, parking near the front door.

"Thanks, we put a lot of work into it." Anna accepted the compliment, wondering now why she had had that odd moment of fear. It had been foolish, really. "And thanks a million for the ride."

"My pleasure," Arnie Watts said, smiling.

"Can I offer you a beer or something?" she asked, almost as an afterthought as she got ready to close the van door. "I'm sure David would like to thank you for saving him the trip."

"Well, I don't know," Arnie said, shaking his head. "Hey, maybe one beer."

It surprised her, Arnie knew, that he accepted her invitation. Asking had been the polite thing to do; she just hadn't expected him to take her up on it. In the back of her mind he saw her wondering if there was really any beer in the fridge.

"Good." She smiled, swinging the door of the van closed as Arnie Watts killed the engine and followed her up the steps. David met them at the front door, his normal mistrust of strangers disarmed quickly by Arnie Watts's salesman smile.

"David, this is Mr. Reynolds. He gave me a ride home and I offered him a beer," she explained as she introduced the two men. "I hope we have some. . . ."

"I think we can manage," David said, surprising her by sounding pleasant. Exchanging pleasantries with new people was not usually his strong point. "Good to meet you, Mr. Reynolds."

"No, please." Arnie Watts grinned. "That's my father. Call me Ron."

Handshakes, a quick tour of the kitchen and living room, a cold beer for the taxi driver. Arnie Watts commenting most favorably on the decor. Which was, he thought, Early American Middle Class, barely. A little shop talk. How computers will make American business more competitive on the world market.

"As long as they don't cost jobs," David said warily.

"You don't have to worry about that." Arnie Watts smiled. "It always takes a human hand to run the machines. It's all a question of training."

Sage nods. The television talking in the background. A

TV news magazine rattling on about plants closing and jobs being lost to foreign market places where the weekly wage would buy a loaf of bread and a candy bar in an American supermarket. All of which the conversation politely ignored. Then from upstairs, footsteps. Two girls came down the stairs, looking casually at the stranger in the living room.

"We have company?" one of them asked.

"Ron Reynolds, this is our daughter, Betsy, and her friend, Carol Ann Huxley," David said. "Mr. Reynolds was kind enough to give your mother a ride home from the diner."

"Your car broke down again?" Betsy asked. "You really should get rid of that old thing."

"Pleased to meet you," Arnie Watts said, smiling warmly, but not too warmly.

The two girls nodded in his direction, then retreated into the kitchen to raid the refrigerator. Arnie Watts felt the snakes coiling around in his stomach. The hunt was on. The prey had no chance of escape.

"Well, I'd better be on my way," he said, finishing the beer in his glass. "Got lots to do tomorrow."

"Thanks again," Anna said as they saw him to the door. Waves and smiles all around.

Arnie Watts drove back to the Last Stop, adrenaline racing through his body like the floodwaters of a broken dam. At the door to his cabin he stopped and took a deep breath of the cold night air. Sounds came to him, sharp and crystal clear. Trucks rolling by on the highway, a cat poking around in the shadows of Mrs. Dish's front porch. Trees creaking in the wind, the sound of icy drizzle leaking from the sky, hitting the fallen leaves. There were dim lights from inside the boardinghouse, the flicker of the television. Members of the herd huddled around their electronic fireplace, their minds numb and unknowing. Senses dulled by the infusion of meaningless information. Arnie Watts pulled the night air deep into his lungs. It was good . . . good to be alive.

And a few miles away, the prey waited. Completely unaware that the hunt was on.

In a galaxy so filled with stars and bright, gaseous nebula that it is known to some of its inhabitants as God's
Breath, a planet orbits a small yellow sun, both nearly mirror images of the Earth and its star:

The Hive buzzed, singing its morning prayer to the Sun,
now lifting off the horizon. The creatures within crawled
through mud-and-wattle chambers, exchanging scents
and chemical molecules. They moved, in carefully preor-
dained order, to the opening of the Hive and made their
way out into the early morning light. On the tree branch
that the Hive encircled, they fanned their long wings,
warming themselves, preparing for the day's tasks. One
by one, they lifted off into the air, their droning sound reflecting off the canopy of leaves, and in their passing
caused a scurry of activity on the ground below, as other
insects and small animals hurried to hide themselves from
the swarm.

One of the creatures lifted its thick body from the tree
branch, already knowing its destination. Its wings, when
folded back along the eight-inch length of its body, formed
a high, tentlike structure, which kept out water and re-
tained warmth. In flight, however, the wings beat so rapidly they seemed to encircle the insect's body in a halo of
reflected light, as the sun's spectrum passed through the
wings' multilayered membranes. Indeed, the very fact of
its flight seemed strangely contradictory to the creature's
size and bulk. It appeared as nothing less than an artillery
shell passing through the morning air. An artillery shell that
could stop and hover, and change direction in the blink of
an eye. As its hive-mates fanned out, each moving toward
a favored feeding ground, the lone insect followed its own
flight plan, certain that the morning meal awaited.

The girl woke and yawned, peering out the window at
the new day. From downstairs she heard the familiar
sounds of morning. Her father, finishing his breakfast,
leaving for the fields. The spring rains were now over and
plowing had begun in earnest. Her mother called to her to
hurry, so the girl might complete her chores before it be-

came time to catch the transit bus for school, its steam engine even now billowing on the horizon as it bounced along the bumpy dirt roads. Outside, the sun was drying the morning dew. The spiny birds, named for their quill-like feathers, had come out of their coop and were pecking the ground, waiting to be fed. The soft-pelted Longears were hopping around their cage, drinking from long, glass tubes hung along the side of their enclosure. As she watched, her father walked across the yard, heading for the high earthen walls of the barn.

The girl shook herself from the covers and dressed quickly, running downstairs, out into the cool damp of morning. She grabbed a bucket of grain from inside the cavelike entrance of the barn and spread the pellets across the yard for the spiny birds to eat. Then she rolled the heavy milk containers down to the road, for the factory truck to pick up. Next, she went to the Longears' hutch and put two measured cups of bark and dried flowers into their feeding trough. She stopped then and picked up one of the smaller soft-pelted animals, born only this past spring. The animal nestled into her hand and she stroked the tiny Long-ear for a moment, before taking it up a short ladder to the top of the hutch. There, she dropped the Longear into a small, open-topped cage, set on a wooden pole above the hutch. Then the girl ran back inside to eat her breakfast as the smoke from the school bus's exhaust rose ever closer.

The insect flew in a halo of light, passing over fields of grass and small streams, which wound their way through the valley, past stands of newly leaved trees. Its large, multifaceted eyes caught signs of movement below—rodents feeding in the thick brush, birds guarding their nests in the meadows, flies and beetles collecting on the carcass of a dead animal along the tree line. The insect flew onward, however, certain of easier prey. Suddenly below, there was a flurry of activity, as large warm-bloods ripped up the earth with their beasts and their machines. The insect slowed its flight, sensing the destination was near. Its infrared vision showed waves of warmth drifting up into the air. The movement of another group of warm-bloods, many of them. The insect banked against the rising air currents, its long, heavy body falling like a bullet toward the ground. . . .

In its cage at the top of the hutch the young Longear heard the low droning and began circling the small cage in panic. It looked for a place to hide, but finding none, it curled itself into a ball in a corner of the cage. . . .

The insect dropped out of the sky like a heavy piece of hot metal. Its long arms unfolded and it slammed into the prey, wrapping the appendages around the soft, yielding body. The animal struggled for a moment, kicking and jerking, but the insect unfolded its long, thin feeding tube and drove it into the back of the animal, inserting at a point below the rib cage, where the vital organs waited. As it began to feed, drawing the juices of the living animal into its own body, the prey ceased to struggle, giving itself up to the inevitable, quivering slightly as its life force was drained. Until finally the victim's eyes became as flat and dead as those of the huge fly that preyed upon it.

The girl yelped as the insect fell out of the sky and attached itself to the back of the young Longear. She watched from the kitchen window, peering out with a mixture of curiosity and dread, drinking her milk as the insect fed.

"Did you feed your pet?" her mother asked, washing up the breakfast dishes.

"Yes, Mother," the girl said, still staring out of the window, fascinated. "Its wings are truly beautiful, don't you think?"

 ### REFLECTIONS ON THE USE OF DARKNESS WITHIN THE EXPERIMENT

Consider the experiment as a work of art. In all successful creative endeavors, the shading between light and dark is the critical factor. Within this context, darkness may then be considered as a useful tool in achieving the desired result—that being the creation of an enlightened, technological society, one which is not only able to perpetuate itself, but is also able to give meaning to the lives of those within the society, and thus provide expanded learning experiences for the entities who have been implanted into this cycle of the experiment. Consider further, in the most abstract terms, that light and dark bear the same relationship to each other as good and evil. Within this limited context, it then becomes possible to see the mechanisms' struggle in the physical plane as one of injecting light onto the canvas of the experiment.

The question has been raised: Does the appearance of darkness within the experiment denote an attempt by outside forces to derail the developing society, to tear down what is being built? The answer must be that this is, in fact, the case. That the goal of these counteracting forces, while unanticipated, nonetheless serves a viable function within the confines of the experiment. Further, it must be admitted that the purpose of these outside forces—to destroy any civilization or group of mechanisms who elect through their own Free Will to embrace choices which are detrimental to their own development, is both desirable and necessary.

The physical laws in this particular life cycle have been constructed in such a manner that all vacuums strive to be filled. These axioms allow the expansion of light into the dark void, the birth of suns, planets, and galaxies, the movement of these systems in conjunction to one another, and the attraction of atoms and molecules, all of which are the very building blocks of life within the universe. As has been previously stated, the Laws of the physical plane are exacting in their simplicity. The forces which attract or repel celestial or subatomic particles are the same forces which rush to fill other vacuums. The Laws are such that all equations are continually in balance.

So, in this context, must the so-called dark forces be considered. When there is an absence of morality, immorality will rush to fill the void. When knowledge is not pushed to the forefront, ignorance must be the result. When life is not cherished, it will not be preserved. When there are no songs, silence will ensue. In the end, the Laws of the physical plane will prevail, simple and exacting in their content. Thus, it is for the mechanisms themselves to decide which choices are to be made. Darkness, which is itself a part of the physical plane, is surely one of these choices.

Fact: All civilizations reach a pivotal point in their development, during which individual choice becomes the determining factor in the further advancement of the society. These choices, which often seem irrelevant or inconsequential to the mechanisms, have a far-reaching impact on the particular life experiment in which they are involved. While the implantation of spiritual entities at this pivotal time can make a difference in the outcome, the implantation factor itself does not ensure success. The deep-seated instincts of the mechanisms often override the knowledge and training given to the entities in the spiritual plane. Fear is the primary motivation in the failure of many experiments. Often, when the developing society reaches a point of expansion, when their technology reaches a level of expertise allowing them to advance from their place of birth, this innate fear of the unknown, which can be traced to the mechanisms' primitive hunter/gatherer mentality, becomes an impassible barrier and the emerging civilization contracts upon itself. Only by expanding the boundaries of both knowledge and habitat, can a developing technological society meet the demands of its own internal growth. If expansion does not occur, implosion will be the result.

The Laws of the physical plane are exacting in their simplicity.

twenty

Arnie Watts slept until noon, resting, building up his energy reserves for the rigors that lay ahead. It was almost time—time to leave this chocolate stinkhole—time to plan and stalk—time to enjoy the true pleasures of the hunt. It was, he knew, his finest hour, and he relished the thrill of anticipation. Planning the hunt was the thing he did best. His talent, his forte. It was the time when he felt most alive.

He made a cup of coffee on the cabin's hot plate and traced his escape route on a map spread out on the night-stand. He would take 39 up to the interstate, then head east on 78. Somewhere along the way, most likely in Allentown, he would find a safe house, and there he would settle in for the duration, however long that might be. That was part of the thrill. There was no way to tell how long the game might go on. Sometimes it was hours. Other times it was days. Occasionally a week or more. The thought of it sent a shiver up his spine. Soon. Soon . . . the voice seemed to whisper in his head.

He folded the map and put it in his duffel bag. Then he showered and packed his clothes. The Nine, locked and loaded, went into the bottom of his kit bag with his tooth-brush and razor. Ready and waiting, hopefully not to be used. Guns were always a last resort, Watts knew, a sign of impending disaster and poor planning. He did a walk-through of the cabin, making sure all traces of Arnie Watts were leaving with him. His suitcase and equipment bag already loaded into the van, including the handcuffs and leg bracelets he'd salvaged from the New York adventure. Those tucked safely away, ready for use.

Soon. Very soon, he thought, standing outside in the parking lot of the boardinghouse, breathing in the crisp chill of the November afternoon. The sun sharp and bright, leaves dancing along the ground, as if looking for a place to hibernate for the long winter ahead. Arnie Watts thought that after the holidays, he might spend the winter in Florida. Maybe Jacksonville, where the bars and honkey tonks offered an endless stream of sordid action. You could buy most anything in Jacksonville, he knew. But buying was not the same as taking. Not the same at all.

He walked over to the main house, to turn in his cabin key and settle accounts with Old Lady Dish. It was time to move, to cover his tracks before the actual hunt. It would be a tough, but exciting couple of days, and Arnie Watts was smiling, anticipating the challenge. He knocked on the door and John Hammond answered, hardly surprised that he was moving on. And why should he be, Watts thought, since they had been spying on him out the kitchen window the last couple of days?

"I'll get Mrs. Dish," he said, hurrying away into the interior of the boardinghouse, as if fleeing the cold air. Actually, John Hammond didn't care to be around this Mr. Reynolds, who gave him the chills ever since that afternoon in the front parlor. Not that he would ever admit it to Mrs. Dish.

"So, you're leaving us, Mr. Reynolds?" Mrs. Dish asked the obvious, taking the key and forty dollars, scrawling out a handwritten receipt.

"Yes, ma'am." Arnie Watts flashed her his best salesman's grin. "Finished my business here, on my way home to Philly."

"Well, that's good," Mrs. Dish said, sounding almost too glad to see him go.

There was definitely something odd about the way she looked at him, Watts thought. As if she was trying to stare at him out of the corner of her eye, without attracting his attention. He didn't like it, and was glad to climb in the van and leave the Last Stop behind. She was a creepy old lady, he thought. Old people gave him the willies, old ladies in particular. As if being close to dying gave them some kind of second sight. Yes, he was glad to be moving again. Glad to be back in action. Watts swung up Route 422, pulling into the diner for a last meal with Anna Burrows and the diner crew.

"Tuna on rye and a cup of your best coffee," Arnie Watts said, sliding onto a counter stool, winking at Mary Jo, smiling at Anna. "I'd like to thank you folks for keeping me fed these last few days. You made it a real pleasure to be in your town."

"You're heading out?" Anna asked, hustling sandwiches to the lunchtime crowd.

"On my way home as soon as I finish lunch," Arnie said, blowing on his coffee mug. "Just wanted to stop in and say so long."

"Well, it's been a pleasure having you around." Anna stopped hustling and stood for a second in front of the counter. In her world, he knew, it was a high compliment when a waitress stopped being busy just to say good-bye to someone who would, in all probability, never tip her again. "I want to thank you again for the ride home last night," she said.

Arnie shook his head. "It was nothing."

"Well, it was, too, and I appreciate it," Anna said.

"Think you'll be coming back this way?" Mary Jo asked, pouring water into the coffee brewer. The lunch crowd was noisy and drinking coffee by the gallon to ward off the day's chill. Mary Jo, slightly overweight and slightly past middle age, had a reputation for rowdiness among the truck drivers, Watts knew, and was constantly bantering with her regulars. The reputation, he thought, was mostly talk and bravado, as reputations usually were.

"You never know." Arnie shrugged. "But if I do, you'll be the first one I'll look up."

Laughter and smiles all around. Arnie finishing his tuna

sandwich, saying good-bye and leaving a generous tip in his wake. Cranking the van out of the parking lot, his departure duly and officially noted, Watts drove down to the stoplight and took a right on Route 39, driving past the Burrows house on Holland Drive. The street quiet, the house at the end of the drive, empty. The father, David, working his shift at the candy plant. The girl, Betsy, was in school. Arnie Watts headed up Route 39 and turned east, driving for an hour until he came to a little town called Shartlesville. There he pulled into a Red Roof Inn, got a room for the night, and waited until dark.

Soon, the voice whispered in his head, but not tonight. Watts lay on the bed, drinking a beer while a grudge band played their tasteless video on MTV. Patience, that was the key. Give them a day or two to forget him. Then . . . then the hunt would begin in earnest.

The afternoon faded and darkness slipped like a glove over the world. Arnie Watts emerged from his room and shook himself like a large cat. He went into town and bought a foot-long sandwich, which he ate while he drove back along Route 22. It was eight o'clock, two hours before Anna Burrows got off work. He turned left on 39 and cruised past Holland Drive a couple of times. Few cars, even fewer people. The Burrows house alive now with lights and movement in the windows. He drove past two, three, four times, finally parking for a few minutes in the shadows, a quarter of a mile or so down the road. Checking his watch. Waiting. For something. A sign, movement of some kind. He didn't know what it would be, only that the prey was inside. Waiting for him. At nine o'clock the door to the house opened in a flood of light and a figure emerged, walking down the long drive-way, along the side of the road. The figure turned into a house down the street. It was the girlfriend, Watts knew, his eyes following her as she walked. Carrying books against her chest, her head down against the cold wind. His heart hammering, he waited until she was safely inside, then he drove off, back down 22 to Shartlesville and the Red Roof Inn. It was almost time, he knew. Almost time. And the thought of it filled him and caused his brain to hum better than any drug. Oh yes, it was almost time, the voice whispered.

Arnie Watts left the motel at Shartlesville at noon the next day. He had spent the night checking his equipment, making sure the cuffs and leg bracelets were in good working order, going through his prehunt routine—visualizing how the hunt would go, how the prey would react, how he himself would react in any of the various scenarios he imagined. Visualization was an important part of the planning process, he knew. It was essential to work things out in advance, to prepare contingency plans for the inevitable variations of the hunt. The variations were part of the thrill, part of the game that made the adrenaline dance in his body. Part of the incredible rush of the hunt. Arnie Watts, who had done all the drugs there were to do at one time or another, knew with certainty that this was the best high of all. The hunt, it was beginning, and the thought of it made his brain sing with electricity.

He drove across to Reading, just for something to do, to kill the afternoon. He strolled through the shops, treated himself to lunch at a nice restaurant. The day was warm for November, the sun bright, glinting off Christmas decorations the merchants had put up weeks ago, in an attempt to separate the herd from their money. As usual, it was a ploy that seemed to be working to perfection. Shoppers crowded together along the main street of Reading, cars filled the parking lots of the suburban malls. The people hurrying, for some reason, even though Christmas was still weeks away.

Arnie Watts had now made the firm decision to spend the holidays somewhere in the Northeast. After all, what was Christmas without snow? Just another day. He stopped in front of a display in a department store window. The Baby Jesus was lying in a manger, moving its mechanical arms, as if trying to escape the store window, Arnie thought, smiling, nodding to the others watching the display with him. The herd, going about their routines, unknowing, unsuspecting. Any of them could become prey, he knew, surveying the crowd. He could pick and choose, taking anyone he desired. He stepped back, away from the window, his eyes moving, like a lion watching a herd of gazelle pass by. Yes, any of them, given the right circumstances and the proper planning. The thought filled him with dark joy, as he strolled away the afternoon, imagining prospective victims. At one store, where the cashier seemed to be staring at him, he bought a doll, just in case he had company for Christmas. Like the Baby Jesus, the doll moved its arms and cried in an unreal, mechanical voice. But carrying the package, Arnie knew, helped categorize him as a shopper. It made him legit. Just one of the herd, going about his business, wandering around the corridors of a nearby mall like a rat making its way through a maze. In the glass ceiling tiles of the mall he saw the sky pass from bright blue to foggy gray. Yes, it was almost time. Taking his package, Arnie Watts retreated to the van and tried to calm himself.

As the evening gathered, he caught Route 422 outside Reading and drove west, following a winding country road filled with farms and deer-crossing signs, dogs and cats roaming the early twilight. Past small Pennsylvania towns where the people were ending their day with food and television. He glanced in their windows as he passed. People moving like ghosts behind the bright glass. Faceless shadows whose names he would never know. Through Myerstown, Annville, and Palmyra. They could all be the same places, almost anywhere in America. The same ghosts passing by the same windows. A few of them, he imagined, might be lucky and get laid tonight, even though it was only Wednesday and almost everybody who got any, got it on weekends. Friday and Saturday were the get-it-on nights in America, Arnie knew. A weekend orgy, regularly attended by the various members of the herd, even though hardly anyone ever talked about it. Bing, bang, boom, but only after *Saturday Night Live* was over. Pitiful, really, when you thought about it—people living their whole lives for a little Saturday-night action.

Arnie's mind was racing now, feeling the turn of the van's wheels beneath him. Stars blinking in the darkness between towns. The moon, a tiny slit of a winking eye, watching as he passed. Passing through Hershey, rolling down his window to take in the familiar smell, just for kicks, to excite his senses. Senses that were sharp and probing. Like radar, like laser-guided bombs. Like the radio or microwaves that pass through everyone, all the time, every minute of every day, every second that people were alive. Bombarded by these waves, from the instant we're born, until the instant we die, he thought. Is it any wonder that people are all sick and crazy acting? What kind of environment is that to live in? Arnie's mind, alive and burning. The hunt. Now. Here. This minute, this second—Jesus, feel the energy! A fucking smoking dick-rising engine-roaring motherfucking rush! Rush Rush RUSH!!

"The dishes are done," Betsy called into the living room. "I'm going to call Carol Ann."

"Just make sure you two get your homework done!"

Déjà vu vu vu. Did they really have the same conversation night after night? she wondered. Part of her said it couldn't be—that she would never fall into that sort of repetitive behavior. Like sitting down to watch the news at six-thirty every single night of your life. God, but her father was the most predictable person on the face of the earth. Welcome to the gene pool, she thought, realizing that they did indeed have the same exact conversation almost every night, and that she did call Carol Ann, who came over to her house to "study" nearly every school night. Talk about predictable. The phone was in her hand, and for a second Betsy thought that maybe they should change the routine. Maybe she would go over to Carol Ann's tonight, or maybe they would just talk on the phone. For some reason she didn't quite understand, Betsy thought there might be some hidden purpose to changing their school-night pattern. The truth was, they had been doing the same old thing for the last year, she realized, except when it was snowing or really cold. And even then they talked on the phone for most of the evening. Carol Ann was probably sitting by the phone in her house this very minute, waiting for it to ring. Maybe she wouldn't call tonight, Betsy thought. Maybe she would just go to bed early. There was something strange . . . something she couldn't quite put her finger on. It was a feeling. Like the way she felt before going to the dentist. Fear? Was she afraid? Of what? Fear was stupid, she thought, shrugging the feeling. But this pattern, this predictability would have to be discussed. Before long she and Carol Ann would be sitting around watching the news with her father. The tones pulsed on the speed dial.

"Hi, I finally got the dishes done," Betsy said. "You want to come over? OK, see you in a couple minutes. Hey, did you get your math done yet?"

The click of the phone. Betsy, sitting in the kitchen, feeling spooked for some unexplained reason. It was seven o'clock. The news was over. Her father came into the kitchen, going to the fridge to get a beer.

"You all right?" he asked.

"I'm fine," Betsy answered. "Carol Ann's coming over for a while."

"So what else is new?" he asked, kidding her.

Betsy gave him a much practiced roll of her eyes. She went into the living room and turned the front light on for Carol Ann. What was this, anyway? she wondered. This spooky feeling. She felt creepy all over, like it was Halloween and they were living next to a graveyard. Looking out the window she saw a familiar figure coming up the driveway, clutching books against her chest. Betsy Burrows smiled and shook her head. She could be so stupid sometimes, she thought.

At eight o'clock Arnie Watts was driving slowly up Route 39, cruising the area, watching the lights in the houses. He passed the Burrows house, once, twice, turning up the music to help crank his already pumping adrenaline high. His chest hammering, the night shadows wrapping him and the van in a tight, protective shield. He turned off the dash lights, further shrouding himself in the inviting dark. It was, he thought, a lot like orbiting the Earth in a space capsule, alone in the dark, watching the rest of the planet pass below. As if in response, Elton John's "Rocket Man" played on the radio. Perfect, he thought. Absolutely fucking perfect. The game already unfolding in his mind. The hunt planned to an inch of perfection. And it was happening now. Right this second. The pieces falling into place, just like he knew they would.

"And I'll be hiiiggghhh as a kite by then. . . ."

Did you have a good sleep, Yvonne?

Yes yes yes!

"Did you see Robert checking you out at lunch?" Carol Ann asked, her eyes bright and mischievous. They were sitting together on the bed in Betsy's room, school books and papers spread out on the covers. "I think he's got the hots for you. You should wear your red sweater tomorrow. You know, the one that—"

"I know which one," Betsy said, slapping at Carol Ann's arm. Honestly, the girl could be outrageous sometimes. "Robert's nice, but he's just a friend. I think you should go out with him."

"Me?" Carol Ann said, sounding shocked. "No way am I coming between you two."

"I hate algebra," Betsy said, changing the subject. "What did you get for number six?"

"X equals ten," Carol Ann said, looking over at Betsy's homework. "It's easy, really. You just have to remember to subtract from both sides of the equation. Right here, see? Did you get your history paper done?"

"Almost, I'll have to finish it over the weekend. My mom said she'd drive us to the mall Saturday."

"Great! I bet Robert and Jamie'll be there." Carol Ann winked. "Maybe we can go to the movies. . . . Hey, I've got to get going," she said, clipping her papers into her notebook. "The old parental units will have a fit if I'm late."

Carol Ann slipped on her coat, her gloves sticking out of the zip-up pockets of her ski jacket. Together they walked downstairs, and Betsy turned on the porch light. That odd, creepy feeling returning, like a black cat crossing her path in one of those Stephen King books, she thought.

"You want me to walk you to the end of the driveway?"

she asked Carol Ann. Her father, watching the 76ers game from his favorite TV chair, glanced up at them.

"Why?" Carol Ann asked.

"No reason," Betsy said, shaking her head, angry at herself for being weird.

"I'll see you at the bus stop in the morning," Carol Ann said. " 'Night, Mr. Burrows."

"Good night," he called, channel-surfing through the commercials.

Betsy, standing at the window, watched her friend walk down the driveway, then she went into the kitchen for a glass of milk. It was nine-fifteen, by the kitchen clock. Her mother would be home soon, Betsy thought. She went upstairs to see if she could figure out for herself why the answer to question number six was ten. No matter what they said, algebra was stupid.

She was reading the new Deborah Savage book an hour later when the phone rang downstairs. Her mother's car again, she thought. They really should trade that old clunker. Then her father called up to her:

"Betsy, did Carol Ann come back over? Is she upstairs with you?"

Panic, cold and deep, driving into her stomach. Like a volleyball spiked right into her midsection. She was up, running down the stairs, stumbling on the last step before she even knew she was out of the room. . . .

Flashlights probing the driveway like long sticks of light. Betsy beside her father. Carol Ann's father at the other end of the drive. He was holding something, Betsy saw, as he walked closer to them. A blue glove. Carol Ann's glove.

"Where is she?" Carol Ann's father asked, a strange, flat look in his eyes. "She's not with you folks?"

A car pulled into the driveway. The old Chevy clunker rolling up to the front door. Anna Burrows stepped out, looking at the two men and her daughter.

"What . . . ?" she asked, and Betsy ran to her, tears hot against her flushed cheeks.

"Carol Ann . . ." Betsy said, her voice cracking. Fear,

raw and sickening, pushing its way up into her throat like a stone.

"Should we call the police?" David asked.

Carol Ann's father stood in the driveway, holding the blue glove, looking confused. His mouth open, but no sounds coming out.

Heading east on Route 78, Arnie Watts slipped neatly into traffic, following the road signs toward Trenton, New Jersey. He had been to Trenton once before and found it to be a good, no-questions-asked sort of town. Trenton had a little of the Wild West attitude, which Arnie Watts understood and appreciated. It was the kind of attitude that made life interesting.

In the back of the van the girl was progressing through the first stages of the game. She kicked and pulled at her restraints, tried to rub the duct tape off her mouth. The cuffs and leg bracelets held her tightly to the single bench seat bolted down through the rear frame of the van. She could kick and pull all night long, Arnie knew, because that seat was going no place, and neither was she. Watts, however, was afraid she might hurt herself. Damaged goods were not cool. He took his eyes off the road for a second and glanced back through the sliding panel, which he kept open a crack to let some heat into the back compartment and also so the girl could hear the radio. She was stretched out across the seat, her arms and legs shackled to either end of the seat's metal brackets. She was wearing her jacket, jeans, and sneakers. Her eyes glared back at him, nostrils flaring over the duct tape across her mouth. Her eyes were wide, rolling white with fear and anger. Still, he thought he saw a glint of defiance in the girl's brown eyes. Defiance was good, up to a point. It was, in Arnie's mind, a sign of strength. Which was also good, up to a point.

"You might as well calm down," Arnie said quietly but firmly. "I'm not going to hurt you, and we've got a long drive ahead."

He turned his attention back to the road, tractor-trailer trucks roaming the night with him. Like the song said:

Bands of Gypsies rolling down the highway. In a few hours the girl would get hungry, and then he could give her some Big D to quiet her down. Sooner, if it came to that, but Arnie didn't like to force-feed pills. He'd gotten a nasty bite one time, fucking around like that. Besides, it did nothing to build up that feeling of trust. He turned up the radio, and eventually the girl stopped struggling, slowly learning the rules. Arnie Watts smiled. The hunt had gone well. The game was proceeding according to plan.

On a world deep in the heart of the Milky Way Galaxy, thousands of light-years from the Planet Earth, the heat of the day was fading. The herd moved out from the shade of the vine trees, onto the wide, grassy plain to graze. The leader of the Hooved Ones, a bull in his second decade of years, tested the wind cautiously. The breeze was swirling up from the river, as it often did in this season, bringing up a conflicting maze of smells. He stretched his thick neck and shook his head, heavy with its rack of pointed horns. He blew to clear his scent passages in an attempt to define the conflicting smells. To the east, the short-prongs were busy in the sea of tall grass, grazing and marking their territory. The ponderous water beasts were covering themselves with mud at the river's edge. Nesting birds, small rodents, and the dogs who preyed upon them roamed within his field of vision. He heard bark eaters feeding in the trees along the river. There was the faint, yet unmistakable odor of large cats drifting on the breeze. But they were across the water, he thought, and so could be ignored. The wind shifted and his nose was filled with the heavy musk of his own herd. He shook his head and blew again, nervous, as he always was in this season when the females were heavy and slow, filled with the extra weight of the unborn summer calves. His eyes, ears, and nose, however, picked up nothing out of the ordinary, so he bent his head with the others to feed.

The sun was bright in the cloudless, yellow sky, reflecting in sheets of dancing light off the calm, wide waters of the river. It was a day like most others in his life, in the life of the herd. Filled with light and warmth and the sweet taste of grass. With the playful lunges of the adolescents, as they fought mock battles among themselves, or practiced the rituals of mating. Carefully establishing the lines of dominance that gave order to their lives, and prepared them for their place in the herd, either as protectors or producers of the generations that would follow. The bull had seen a dozen generations brought forth. Had seen the herd multiply and break off into separate bands, colonizing all the world between the Great Waters. When he thought about all these generations, as he stood guard at night while the herd slept in the shelter of the vine trees, he was filled with pride at the role he had played. Protecting and serving the Hooved Ones was his duty in life, as it had been his father's before him, and all the males of his lineage, for all the time that could be remembered.

As they grazed, his mate came to stand beside him, rubbing her shoulder against his. She, who seemed always to know his thoughts, understood his nervousness in this Season of the Calf, and so left her place at the head of the females to offer him a part of her strength. He turned and stroked her back with his pointed horns, returning her sign of affection. They had been together throughout all of their years, chosen from among the others of their brood, to lead and to serve. He thanked the Grass God each day for her presence in his life. It was a thing he treasured above all else. . . .

The wind shifted again and his nostrils flared, his head jerking up. His mate stiffened beside him. A scent, thin as morning fog, trailed in the air. Then, as the wind turned, the scent became suddenly thicker. A sour smell, of carrion and blood. It was, he knew in the instant before the herd began to run, the smell of death.

The herd, twisting as one creature with one mind, ran first toward the shelter of the vine trees. But the wind, shifting and turning with them, caused confusion in the ranks, and the herd turned away from the scent, which seemed suddenly to be coming from the vine trees. Panic took them and swept them back toward the riverbank. And

even as the bull knew it to be a mistake, he was powerless to stop the herd's flight.

   In the low hills above the river the grass swayed and the
sun glinted off the smooth skin of large beasts, low to the
ground, waiting in ambush for the herd as it stampeded
toward the river. . . .

   And he bellowed, loud and long, in an effort to stop their
flight. Even as the Scaled Ones rose from their hiding
places in the grass, their mouths open, filled with grinning
rows of sharp teeth. Their scent overpowering now—a
wall of putrid death, which struck the herd like icy stones
falling from the sky. He bellowed again, in fear and anger
and frustration. And saw through the dust and crush of
bodies that the herd had turned in the face of the Scaled
Ones. The younger members of the herd, those who had
foolishly led the stampede, screeched in terror as the
claws of the Scaled Ones brushed their hind quarters, even
as they leaped and ran back in the direction of the bull's
booming call. . . .

   The herd, bunched together on the grassy plain, breath
coming in heated, panting, fear-filled gasps. The herd circling one another, even as the Scaled Ones rose on their
back legs and started forward toward them. The bull saw
quickly that the Scaled Ones had been denied their kill.
That all of his charges had avoided death, at least for the
moment, and were now waiting, panting and breathless,
as the Scaled Ones advanced across the hilltop. The bull
rushed forward to place himself between the pack of rep-
tiles and the herd on which they hoped to prey. The other
horned males followed him and together they formed a
wall of sharp antlers and pawing hooves. Bellowing, daring the Scaled Ones to attack. And the Scaled Ones
seemed to accept the challenge, fanning out, moving
slowly toward the bunched-up herd, their heavy bodies
lumbering, long claws digging the ground in deep furrows.
Terrifying in their silent advance, long snouts filled with
sharp, glaring teeth. Their eyes, the bull saw, were flat and
dead, their minds filled only with killing.

   And the fear that welled up inside him was replaced by

the sense of duty to those behind him as he prepared to fight and die, if necessary, to protect the herd.

Then, from the depths of the herd, came a muted cry of pain. Soft, yet sharp in its intensity. His mate was suddenly beside him. Despite the rage of the battle that was upon him, he stepped back and turned to her. And saw, to his horror, that her front leg was dangling uselessly, held above the ground—white bone protruding through her shin, piercing pelt and flesh. He knew instantly that the moment of her death was upon her . . . upon him . . . upon them all. He watched, hopeless and helpless, as she hobbled forward past the wall of sharp antlers and hooves, her head held high, even as the Scaled Ones fell upon her, ripping and rendering her flesh. Her sacrifice, her duty to the herd, complete and final. The bull watched, filled with horror and loss, as the Scaled Ones dragged her body back down the hill, across the bloodstained grass.

Night slipped down upon them and the herd retreated to the sanctuary of the vine trees, where they milled about and fell into an uneasy sleep. The bull, as was his duty, stood guard over them. He looked out across the darkened plain, testing the night air. Even within the confines of the herd, he knew himself to be alone. For all the rest of his days it was left to him to ponder the questions of duty, service, and sacrifice. And years later, when he himself slipped beneath the waters of the river as it surged in the spring flood, his final thought was that he charged into the pack of Scaled Ones on that long ago day and died with his mate.

 ## REFLECTIONS ON THE RELATIONSHIP OF ENTITIES IN THE PHYSICAL PLANE

In the spiritual world each entity's relationship to one another, and their relationship to the universe as a whole, is well known to them. These common and simple truths, how-

ever, become much more complex and confusing once the
entity enters the physical plane. This is particularly true in
life experiments in which the evolution of the mechanisms
themselves has not reached an advanced stage of development. In most instances where the mechanisms retain their
primitive physical, emotional, and mental states, the implanted entities have access only to instinctual and learned
knowledge possessed by the mechanisms and their current
society. The loss of this knowledge, which is so basic to
existence on the spiritual plane, often causes disruptions in
these relationships in the physical world. These disruptions,
which are a continuing cause of anxiety to many entities,
are in fact simply part of the learning experience in the
physical plane. Indeed, the disruptions themselves are a
necessary component in the context and scope of the experiment. The entities' lack of knowledge about their relationships to one another forces them to more deeply explore
such issues as emotional involvement, motivation, and the
dynamics of the various relationships themselves. Loss of
knowledge forces the implanted entities to rediscover past
relationships, and through experimental contact with other
entities, to develop new relationships with entities to which
they have not yet been exposed. Thus, the learning experiences are both varied and expansive. While these experiences may not always be of a pleasant nature, they
nonetheless serve to enhance the entity's learning process.

Of course, in more advanced life experiments in which
the entities have, over time, interacted with all the other
entities in the field of that specific experiment, the learning
process changes. Usually by this time, the mechanisms
themselves have evolved to a state more conducive to the
learning process. That is, the implanted entities have access
to a wider variety of instinctual and learned knowledge, and
so are able to direct both their learning and relationships to
a more advanced level. This level, which is admittedly rare
given the volatile nature of the life experiments themselves,
offers the opportunity for truly expanded learning. The love-
hate relationships so common to the early states of the experiment have usually been resolved, and the entities are

therefore able to use their allotted life cycles more productively. While this is generally the case only in experiments which have been fortunate enough to reach an advanced state, observations in this particular life experiment have yielded unusual and unexpected results.

While it is true that the experiment itself is admittedly flawed—an unavoidable conclusion given the dark nature of certain mechanisms and the increasing cycle of violence—a most unusual occurrence has been observed. It would seem that despite the primitive state of evolution in the mechanisms, certain entities have become aware, on some level, of the relationships between themselves and other entities. Clearly this occurrence is far from a universal experience, as is the case in more advanced life experiments, yet observation has confirmed that it is indeed taking place. This is, of course, not to be confused with the proliferation of religions and cults which claim to offer their members knowledge and salvation, usually through the revelations of various "enlightened" leaders. Rather, this phenomenon appears to be taking place on an instinctual level which would normally be beyond the realization of entities inhabiting primitive mechanisms. Also, it is taking a variety of forms. Most typically, it is a function of past physical and emotional relationships. Certain entities, despite the limitations of their mechanisms, now seem able to identify a few of those entities with which they have had strong physical or emotional ties during previous life experiences. The entities, lacking the facilities to confirm these relationships, are in many cases confused by this seemingly abstract knowledge. But the interesting aspect of this phenomenon is that they seem to be able to accept and even incorporate this knowledge into their learning experience.

Even more unusual, in a few documented instances, entities have actually used this instinctual knowledge, which most of them are not even aware of on a conscious level, to intercede in upcoming events along the time line. Interviews with entities recently returned to the spiritual plane have shown that in several cases, the entity placed itself in harm's way, actually terminating its life cycle so that another entity with which it has had past relationships in the physical plane, might continue its own learning experience.

Conclusion: The importance of this recognition factor cannot be overstated. This development, taking place in the absence of evolutionary factors, clearly shows an unexpected growth pattern within the entities themselves. The fact that it is taking place at this early stage of the experiment, and under less than desirable circumstances, is most extraordinary.

Question: Are the supposed flaws in the experiment a contributory factor in this phenomenon? Do the entities themselves somehow sense that for the experiment to continue, they must make strides forward, without the aid of time-induced evolutionary factors?

twenty-one

"**A**nd in Hershey, Pennsylvania, residents joined with state and local authorities in a massive search for a missing thirteen-year-old girl. Carol Ann Huxley was reported missing late Wednesday, after she failed to return home following a visit to a friend's house in this suburban Pennsylvania community. . . ."

The cable news networks picked up the story long before it made the papers. It was early Friday morning, and no progress had been reported. Dennison York had spent the night at Jenny's, as he often did these days. In fact, the three of them—York, Jenny, and the Dane—had been sitting in the office Thursday afternoon, staring at one another and at the stale files on their desks. York, making an executive decision, declared Friday to be an unscheduled holiday, and even the Dane had seemed relieved. The truth was, work had become oppressive, York thought, as he'd locked the door, leaving for a long weekend with Jenny. How much longer before he was forced to close the office for good, he wondered? It was an event that loomed ever closer on the horizon, he feared. And then what? Jenny took his arm before he was able to come up with a suitable answer, reminding him of his promises for the weekend. But then that night the Pennsylvania story broke, and they had been watching the reports closely.

"In a written statement to the press, the Huxley family

thanked all those searching for their missing daughter and issued an impassioned plea for her return. Hundreds of searchers turned out to comb the woods surrounding the rural area as authorities widened the search perimeters. Informed sources within the Pennsylvania State Police have confirmed that they fear the girl has been abducted.''

"They're not going to find her, are they?" Jenny asked, curled up on the couch beside York, an afghan wrapped around her legs and feet, both to keep the November chill away and to act as a security blanket, Jenny readily admitted.

"Doubtful," York admitted. "And if they do, it won't be around there. But that's one good thing about mass media coverage. It gets the word out in a hurry. Maybe somebody'll spot her."

"Does that really happen?" Jenny asked.

"Hardly ever," York said, watching as the girl's school picture was flashed on the screen, along with a toll-free number, which he knew would attract an endless series of crank calls. It was, he also knew, a sign of the authorities' desperation.

"You know, I didn't notice it before, but that picture looks a lot like the Stafford girl," Jenny commented in an almost offhanded manner. She was immediately sorry she had brought it up.

"It sure as hell does," York said, leaning forward, as if he could snatch the photograph off the screen. He was reaching for the phone before Jenny could say anything, as if it would do any good, she thought.

"Who are you calling?" she asked, but she could already hear the Dane's loud, gruff voice through the receiver.

"You've reached 555-2861, leave a message," the Dane's machine said.

"York here," Dennison said. "It's Friday, seven A.M. I'm going down to Pennsylvania to have a look at that Hershey abduction. You can catch me at the office in an hour."

Jenny was looking at him, he saw, as if he was some wayward child she had no hope of controlling.

"Do you think it's really necessary?" she asked.

"Won't know until I'm there," he said, leaning over to kiss her quickly on the cheek. "The Stafford file . . ."

"It's on my desk." Jenny sighed, drawing the afghan up over her hips.

"Sorry . . ." he said, in a futile attempt to apologize. "It might be important."

"I hope so," Jenny said, reaching up for a more appropriate good-bye kiss. "Good luck."

"Thanks," York said, heading to the bathroom to collect his toothbrush and shaving kit. Gena came out of her room to get ready for school, yawning and blurry-eyed, a photocopy of her mother in the morning. "How you doing, kid?" he asked.

"Fine," Gena mumbled, going over to the couch to steal some of her mother's blanket. "What's going on?"

"Not much," Jenny said, putting her arms around her daughter.

York stopped by his own place for a change of clothes and a road map. At the office in Manhattan he picked up the Stafford file and drank a cup of coffee, waiting on the chance that the Dane might call in. But the big man either hadn't gotten the message yet or wasn't about to spend his long weekend roaming the wilds of Pennsylvania. Not that York blamed him; it was probably another false trail. But the photo on the tube did look a lot like Yvonne Stafford, and there was a proven tendency for abductors to pick similar types, when the opportunity presented itself. Besides, he had a feeling about this one. It might just be the guy. But then, he had had the feeling before. York opened the file and looked for maybe the hundredth time at the picture he had gotten from Delores Sanchos in Port Arthur, Texas.

"I'm going to get you, you bastard," he whispered for the hundredth time.

In fact, the Dane did hear the phone ring. He heard the machine click on, heard York's voice over the speaker. He was, however, preoccupied at the moment. On his way out of the office on Thursday, he unexpectedly bumped into the woman he had seen earlier in the day. She was still wearing her long leather coat and sunglasses. Something about her smile seemed to hypnotize him, and now he found himself caught in the spiderlike grasp of her arms and legs. He moved against her, lost in the soft, deep confines of her body. When he struggled briefly to answer York's call, she held him tightly.

"No," she whispered. "Not yet."

And it was hours later before the Dane looked again at the red light blinking on the machine.

Did you have a nice sleep, Yvonne?

Eyes rolling in terror at the moment of realization. The thought of it made Arnie Watts's stomach grumble in anticipation. He popped a beer and waited. It wasn't usually this long a wait, but this particular hunt had been complicated by the fact that he didn't have a home base to operate from. It was a glitch in the planning that he realized, but hadn't properly considered. He'd driven first to Allentown, Pennsylvania, but had experienced, uncharacteristically, an intense attack of paranoia. So he'd driven on into Jersey, across to Trenton. But that city had changed since his last visit. Too many cops in Trenton, he thought, and no motels that looked right. The game required a certain privacy. He'd felt eyes on him in Trenton, like that old woman in Hershey. He'd stopped near a couple places, but it just hadn't felt right. The old sixth sense ringing like an unanswered telephone. So he kept the girl locked down in the back of the van and drove across the lower end of New York State, until they finally landed in Connecticut.

That was one of the primary rules, of course: Put distance between your crimes. Every mile, indeed every state Watts drove through, cut the odds of getting caught considerably. And outside of New Haven, on Route 95, he'd found the perfect place. A summer resort, with the staff levels cut down to the bare minimum for the slow off-season. Private bungalows, with TV and fireplaces, and with the price cut to the bone to attract anyone who might be traveling the New England corridor after the leaf-peeking season. The clerk at the Burgundy Inn was happy to rent him a place for a weekly rate, especially after he said he'd get his own towels and didn't require any maid service.

Yes, and the girl had been hungry after driving for eighteen hours. But now Arnie was wondering if he had put too much Demerol in her burger. She'd been passed out for hours now. Which was more than enough time to do the duffel bag trick and get her inside. More than enough time to make her comfortable on the wide, double bed. Arnie had even burned a couple logs in the hearth to make things nice. Now he was waiting, watching.

—Did you have a nice sleep?

The girl was stretched out on the bed, her hands and legs shackled. It was a good thing that he had the long leg bracelets for her, because she was so short, dwarfed by the long bed. He'd taken her clothes off, of course, to make her even more comfortable, and had covered her with a blanket to keep the chill off. A nice touch, he thought, which would help put her at ease. Trust was important and he hoped to build that into their relationship right from the beginning. They could really have a fine time here together, if she could learn to trust him. They might, Arnie hoped, even become friends. Do some traveling together, perhaps. Spend Christmas with each other in some little New England town. He'd have to get wrapping paper for the doll he'd bought back in Reading. Yes, she'd like that, he thought. If only she would wake up. . . . He wanted to touch her, to jiggle her shoulder, or squeeze her hand. But that was not part of the game. No, she had to wake up on her own. To turn and look at him. So he could ask her:

—Did you have a nice sleep, Carol Ann?

The girl's picture had been all over the news reports. Arnie even bought a paper with her name on the front page. He hoped to show it to her later, after they became friends. And they would become friends, he thought. Arnie Watts had a good feeling about this one. She had been quiet during most of the drive, and was grateful when he'd bought them Cokes at a rest stop outside of Poughkeepsie. She hadn't liked it, however, when he stopped by the side of the road so she could go to the bathroom. Yes, he'd stood right next to her, but it was only out of necessity.

"If I don't, you'll only run away and I'd have to catch you," Arnie said reasonably. "And if you ran, well . . . I'd be mad. Believe me, I don't want to get mad."

The girl, all but frozen in her fear of him, had only nodded and gone about her business, discreetly turning her back to him. Her fear was good, really, Arnie thought. Fear was something that could be overcome, given time. And now they had all the time in the world.

Outside the curtained window, the wind blew through the early evening darkness. It had started to rain an hour or so ago. The Weather Channel warned that the roads might ice up later, so it was nice to be inside, out of the elements. With a fire going and pizza on the counter, beers and soda tucked into the tiny refrigerator. It was quiet and peaceful. The best kind of night to get acquainted . . . only the girl was still sleeping, her breath quick and shallow. Almost as if she didn't want to wake up.

"Carol Ann," Arnie whispered, kneeling down beside the bed. "Carol Ann . . ."

She groaned once, rolling her head on the pillow. Arnie leaned closer. It was almost here—that magical moment, that energized second when her eyes would flutter open . . . her arm pulled against the restraints. Her body twisted, almost convulsing. Too much Demerol, Arnie thought, quickly pushing the thought aside. This was not a time to be thinking. The moment was almost upon them. The instant when the bond was formed which would allow them to be together until the ends of time. She groaned again, softly, her muscles contracting, her body stiffening, as though she might be coming out of her sleep. They were yards from the nearest bungalow, which was empty anyway, so he hadn't bothered with a gag. He would have to be quick, he knew, ready to cover her mouth if she screamed. But maybe she wouldn't. Maybe this would be the perfect one. The one who understood the true nature of the hunt. The one who would understand that he didn't really want to hurt her. That, like all the other members of the human race, he wanted only one thing . . . companionship. To be needed and loved. Not to be alone in this wasteland of life. To have someone to hold when the wind blew and rain splattered the night like dark drops of blood. . . .

She groaned, and it looked as if her eyes were fluttering open. The moment, it was upon them, Arnie thought. The fire casting long shadows against the wall. The wind and the rain, and this perfect, perfect girl. So young. So beautiful. So unblemished . . . yes! Her eyes danced open for an instant, blinking at the unfamiliar surroundings. Her face turned toward his. Staring, her mouth dropping. The electric fear, like lightning behind her eyes. The instant, the moment of realization . . .

"Did you have a nice sleep, Carol Ann?" he asked, his voice soft and reassuring.

Her eyes . . . for a split second they seemed to fill with tears. Her mouth open, but no sounds leaping forth to shatter the moment. Then her eyes seemed to roll back in their sockets. Her mouth slammed shut, teeth grinding. Her body jerked against the restraints. For a moment Arnie thought her reaction was one of intense terror, as sometimes happened. He was prepared to deal with that reaction, but not when her body stiffened and then relaxed, as she floated back into the arms of the sleep-inducing drug. Too much fucking Demerol, Arnie thought bitterly. The moment of realization, the bonding between them had not come. Not yet. Angry, he stared at her sleeping form for a few minutes, then went over to the refrigerator to get another beer. There was nothing to worry about, he thought, staring at the fire. After all, they had all the time in the world.

Route 76 snaked its way out of the wormlike mass of roads that surrounded Philadelphia. It was Friday afternoon and with the rain most of Philly's commuters were still safely locked away in their offices, for which York was thankful. He seemed to be making good time, although he wasn't certain he had taken the most direct route. The truth was, he didn't drive all that much anymore. Ronnie Bates had done most of the wheel work, then the Dane or Jenny. York was used to sitting in the passenger seat, where he could think. Face it, he thought, you're just not used to paying attention to where you're going.

A semi came up out of the rain and he blinked as it roared past, throwing a blinding wave of road spray onto the windshield of the Toyota. It took the wipers two swipes to gain control of the water, and by the time they did, York had drifted halfway into the outside lane. He cursed and yanked the car back. Asshole, he thought, wondering if he meant the trucker or himself. He felt as though he was driving like some senior citizen puttering down the highway on one of their last trips to Florida. He promised himself he'd take the wheel more often. He remembered a quote from a long forgotten book: You measure your age by the things you stop doing, because once you give something up, you never start again. Who said that? he wondered. He couldn't remember, and that made him even more angry with himself. He would have to be sharp to catch this perp, whoever the hell he was, and Dennison York was forced to admit that he didn't feel sharp. Not in the least. He felt tired, even though he'd only been on the road a few hours. He felt the first twinges of a headache and wasn't exactly sure how many miles until the turnoff for 322. A quick read of the map in his office had indicated that 322 would bring him close to Hershey. Now he wished he'd taken the time to draw the route on the damn map, like he knew he should have.

Actually, he wasn't even sure what he would do once he got to Hershey. Last year he could have been certain of getting first-class treatment, no matter which crime scene he showed up at, almost anywhere in America. But a year had changed things considerably. With his name out of the news, and his reputation tarnished by the Stafford case, York was well aware he didn't get the recognition or the cooperation once accorded "America's Number One Hired Gun," as the media had once been so pleased to call him. The bastards, he thought, glancing again at his map. They had been quick enough to turn on him. Running their cheap, smuggled hospital clips of poor Yvonne Stafford and harping on the missing member of her "so-called rescue team." Blood-sucking leeches . . .

And there it was, the cutoff for 322. And he had missed it!

"Goddamn it!" York yelled, slapping the steering wheel in frustration.

She moved again, finally, and Arnie Watts gave a sigh of relief. He had spent the last hours checking the girl's breathing, worrying over her pale, ghostlike skin. Too much Demerol. Too heavy a fucking dose, he thought, pacing back and forth in front of the burnt-out logs in the fireplace. He should've been more careful, he knew. The girl hadn't eaten in a long time. He should've taken that into consideration. Poor planning and even poorer execution, and now the whole fucking plan was in jeopardy. The moment, certainly, was spoiled beyond repair. She was too doped up now to realize what had happened. He was scared, even, to touch her, for fear she might go into some kind of shock.

But at least she was moving again, her small fists opening and closing, her head turning on the pillow. What to do? Arnie wondered. He racked his brain for an answer. It was possible, he knew, that she might actually die on him. That would be the ultimate fuck-up. To go to all this trouble for nothing.

Jesus, but she didn't look too fucking good, Arnie thought, leaning over the bed, looking at the girl's pasty skin. He lifted an eyelid and saw that her eyes had rolled back in her sockets. Not good. Not good at all. What to do? Her body was twitching now, like a guy Watts had seen once in a Detroit alley. Bang drunk and cracked to the max, the guy had puked, rolled over, and croaked, all in the space of about two minutes. Now Arnie was deathly afraid the girl was heading for the same sort of convulsions. Panicking, he filled the bathtub with cold water. Unlocking the cuffs and leg bracelets, he carried the girl into the bathroom and plunged her into the water. Her thin, white body jerked and thrashed. He had to hold her down as she flailed, arms and legs jerking and splashing. Finally she stopped and her head rolled back, the eyes opening.

Opening . . . yes! This was the moment, the instant of realization. She would turn to him now, her eyes wide. . . .

"Did you have a nice sleep, Carol Ann?" he asked, quietly.

Her eyes stared at him. Wide and open. But she didn't seem to hear him.

"Did you have a nice sleep, Carol Ann?" he asked again, waiting for her response.

Her eyes wide and open, yet dull and glazed. She was floating in the water. Paralyzed, it seemed. Staring at him.

"Did you have a nice sleep, Carol Ann?" he asked, louder, more urgent.

It was several moments before he realized that she did not hear him. Would never hear him. That he had been cheated of his prize. He stood for a long time, staring at the girl floating in the bathtub, cold and useless. And maybe . . . just maybe, she would've been the perfect one. All the risk, all the planning . . . It had been for nothing. Arnie Watts felt like crying. But then, oddly, there was this sound. Coming, it seemed, from someplace far away. He tilted his head, trying to hear. The sound, he realized, was coming from somewhere in back of his brain. In that dark, secret place where the voices came to him. And the sound was laughter. Dark and hideous, echoing up from the black well behind his mind. Laughter, insane and maddening. Arnie Watts shivered, as if he himself were lying there in the cold, dead water. . . .

Through a haze that seemed to have settled over his brain, he watched as his hands reached out, grabbing the girl. He saw himself shake the body, hard, as if something inside him was furious now at being cheated. He shook her, water splashing, his vision becoming clouded with dark waves of anger. Water droplets leaping out of her hair like swarms of wet flies. He would not . . . he would not be cheated! He shook her again, the girl's head rolling on her shoulders like a broken toy. Suddenly, in his mind's eye, the head stopped rolling. It seemed to stiffen on her neck, like a deflated balloon filled once again with air. Arnie Watts leaned against the cold edge of the tub, holding the body by its shoulders, blinking in disbelief. He felt detached, as though he were watching himself in a movie.

Then, incredibly, the girl's eyes fluttered, she coughed, but strangely made no sound. Arnie shook his head, staring at the girl's face. It was happening, but it was not happening. He knew this in one part of his mind—in that place where the mind recognizes the nightmare, but is so deeply involved in the context of the dream, that the brain is powerless to stop it.

—I'm dreaming, Arnie Watts wanted to say, but couldn't.

Maybe, the thought came from the dark place behind his brain, even as the haze drifted like a black cloud across his mind.

—I'm going crazy, he wanted to say, but couldn't.

Maybe, the black fog whispered.

And he shook the girl again, unable to help himself, caught up in the reality of the dream. The girl's head seemed to snap up, and this time her eyes opened, staring at him with a blank, dead look.

"Did you have a nice sleep, Carol Ann?" he heard himself whisper. His voice echoing in his ears like soft thunder.

The girl's body was cold and lifeless. It moved against him in jerking, dead motions, as if it did not care what was being done to it. Which was fortunate.

In the shadowy, gray realm between the spiritual and physical worlds, the Soul Catchers gathered, performing their assigned task. They collected the entity that had recently left the shell of its damaged mechanism. This entity, the Soul Catchers discovered, was in a profound state of shock and did not at first respond to their soft whispers. Starlight flickered around them, like tinsel on a Yule tree. The intense energy of the nearby sun struck them gently, causing their forms to shift and flow. The entity moved with them, floating like a seahorse in a warm current. Gradually the entity began to respond. There was a moment of panic, sharp and intense, as the entity caught a fleeting glimpse of its damaged mechanism. The Soul Catchers, however, were most proficient at their work. They turned the entity's attention away from events that no longer had any part in its life. They soothed the troubled spirit, brushing away the sparks of fear that danced like fireflies within the entity's soft, yielding form. They whispered reassuring thoughts and led the entity gently away from the physical world, passing into the bright tunnel, leading into the spiritual plane.

Starlight rushed by them now in long, bright lines, like meteors crashing into rarefied air. The solar wind brushed them, fresh and invigorating, as it blew through star systems, and through whole galaxies. In the instant it took to cross between the spiritual and physical planes, Time flashed pictures of the creation of the universe, from beginning to end, across the cloudlike walls of the bridge. In the instant it took to cross the gray realm into the spiritual plane, the entity was calmed, knowing that it was once again going home.

In the spiritual plane those whose task it was to remember the events taking place in the physical world duly recorded the circumstances surrounding the demise of the entity's mechanism. It was recorded that in this particular moment of time, there was no more despicable act taking place anywhere in all the universe. This was duly noted and remembered.

twenty-two

It was late afternoon when Dennison York finally made it to Hershey. The rain had turned to a damp drizzle, the sky dark, even though it was still an hour or so before sunset. He stopped at a roadside diner outside town and asked directions to the search command center.

"Head straight into Hershey. They're set up in the Kmart parking lot," Mary Jo said, pouring him a cup of coffee. "You can't miss it."

"Thanks," York said, surveying the few afternoon customers. Truckers mostly, a couple locals, and two county sheriff's deputies sitting off by themselves in a corner.

"You a cop?" Mary Jo asked, smiling. She asked simply because she had seen more than her fair share of them lately, and this particular customer did not quite fit the mold.

"Not exactly," York answered. "Private Investigator from New York. Just passing through and thought I'd see if they were making any progress."

"None I've heard," Mary Jo said, shaking her head. "Hard to believe that little girl could just vanish."

"It surely is," York agreed. "You think those fellows would mind if I asked them a couple questions about how things were going?"

"Joe and Earl?" Mary Jo laughed. "You can bet those two don't know any more than I do! Probably even less.

But come on over, I'll introduce you. What'd you say your name was?''

The waitress, York quickly discovered, was correct in her assumption. Joe and Earl either didn't know, or couldn't say, how the investigation was going. If, in fact, there was anything for them to know. Facts, York gathered, were few and far between.

"They haven't found her yet, that's certain," Earl said, sipping his coffee, pulling apart a sticky bun. He was a heavyset man, in his middle thirties, York guessed. A terrible insurance risk, but a friendly sort, once York presented his official identification. "All they got is her glove, and her daddy found that alongside the road by their house. Damnedest thing, like she walked right off the face of the Earth.''

"But it's not for lack of trying." His partner sat up and stared at York, as if feeling the need to defend his community. "There's been two hundred people combing the woods for her these last couple days. Most of 'em volunteers, too.''

York nodded sympathetically. A lost child fueled something basic in the human psyche, he knew. People who never knew the family would turn out in droves to help with the search, and they would stay with it until the police all but dragged them out of the woods. It was a common pattern, although in most cases the effort was usually futile. A fact that York did not mention.

"Who would I talk to over there?" he asked. "I've got a case a year or so old that looks a lot like the one you've got.''

"Well, we're on our way back there right now," Earl said, checking his watch. "I suppose you could follow us back and talk to Sheriff Hill.''

Sheriff Robert Hill did not seem pleased to have another outsider in town, asking questions he couldn't answer, and wouldn't even if he could. York understood why. There was a separate tent set up to corral the press. The local newspeople were there, of course, and York saw a CNN truck, as well as a couple other network rigs. Hill, undoubtedly, was being hounded to within an inch of reelection. The missing girl had the sort of all-American good looks that made the story a hot one at the moment, but one that would fade to the back pages in a few days, if no progress was made.

"They'll have a press briefing around five," Hill said, waving his hand toward the press tent. "You'll get everything we've got, which isn't too damn much."

The sheriff turned away to attend to other more pressing matters, and York, seeing nothing better to do, wandered over to the press tent. For the most part, it looked like a cattle call at some obscure movie location. People milling around, drinking coffee, talking quietly to colleagues; waiting impatiently, nervously, for something to happen. There were gloves, hats, tape recorders, and laptop computers cluttering up the few open spaces. The computers lying open and ready, like some strange, new kind of mousetrap. Ready to crunch down on any information the PR people in charge were about to release. With the owners, York noted, only a step or two away from their machines, as if anyone would steal them with an army of cops within shouting distance. There was a kerosene heater set up in the middle of the tent, and York made his way over to it. Warming himself seemed to be the most productive thing he could do at the moment, although the small portable burner was rapidly becoming overmatched by the encroaching chill. Many of the press corp, he saw, were wandering over to the Kmart, where he suspected business was booming. And no doubt with the stock boys in back changing prices as fast as they could, York thought cynically.

"You're Dennison York, aren't you?" a voice said behind him, and York turned into the well-practiced salesman's smile and chiseled good looks that branded the man as a television reporter. The man put his hand out, and York, who didn't like pressured introductions, was forced to respond.

"Jesse Campbell," the man said, pausing to give York time to recognize him, which he didn't. "From the Entertainment News Network," Campbell added.

York nodded, making the comment that the two words didn't seem to go together. Surprisingly, Campbell laughed it away, as though he was thoroughly used to such reactions.

"Read a piece about you in *People* magazine last year," Campbell said. "Sure trashed the hell out of you when that Stafford case went sour."

"Yes, they did," York admitted. A couple of the other press people had their noses in the air, pointed at him and Campbell. Wondering, York knew, if there was anything new they could use to fill their evening time slots.

"Say, did you ever find that asshole you were hunting?" Campbell asked. "Got one of your boys, as I recall. They ever find the body?"

York shook his head, answering all the questions at once. "No."

"Did the family hire you? Is that what you're doing here?" Campbell asked, his voice dropping suddenly to a whisper. He seemed intensely disappointed when York shook his head. Still, the man kept probing, with all the subtlety of a runaway train. York, feeling suddenly trapped, began looking for an avenue of escape.

"What is it, then?" Campbell asked, more to himself than York. A light suddenly went on in the man's eyes, and York cringed. "You think the cases might be related?"

"No, nothing like that," York lied badly, pulling away. He worked his way out of the press tent, heading for the relative safety of the Kmart. He was dismayed to discover that Campbell was following him. "You're going to miss your press conference," York said, hurrying now.

"Won't miss much," Campbell replied, lengthening his stride until he was alongside York. "Even if they knew something, they're not about to leak it to the whole world. Listen, Mr. York, maybe we can help each other. I can introduce you to the family. . . ."

It was morning and she came awake slowly. Blinking, yawning, watching the light come in through the curtains. She awoke, for a moment, without fear. Yvonne Stafford didn't realize it at first, this missing element. Like forgetting your jacket at a friend's house, or leaving your purse under the seat in the movie theater. For a moment you don't realize the item is missing, even if it's something bad in your life. Maybe, she thought . . . maybe the counselors and the doctors and her mother were right. Maybe time did heal all things. Maybe, just maybe, it would be all right. . . .

Then: panic! Cold and sharp, like icicles plunged into the back of her neck. The encompassing, shivering terror. Something, someone, was watching her! She could feel it. Eyes on her body. Staring. She pulled the covers up to her chin, suppressing the urge to scream. The first rule of the damned:

Never, ever attract attention to yourself.

Her bedroom door was open, she realized. Just a crack. And someone was watching her. She was certain of it. The old memories flooding back. The mind-numbing terror. It jerked her awake, filling her eyes with an animal-like fear. She listened. There were no sounds. The house was quiet, as though empty and deserted. Except for her . . . and whoever was watching her.

"Who's there?" she asked, summoning her courage, afraid of the answer. Had HE come back? Had HE somehow found out where she lived? Was everyone murdered in their beds . . . leaving her alone, with HIM? "Who's there?" she asked again, louder.

"It's just me," the voice came back, the door creaking open. The voice high and hesitant. Her brother, James, stood in the doorway. Watching her.

"What do you want?" she demanded, angry at the intrusion, at the fear that returned so suddenly. Like a snake appearing magically at her feet, curling around her ankles.

"I was just wondering . . ." James said, sounding sorry now that she had discovered him.

"Wondering what?" she asked, her voice more harsh than she really meant it. James was just standing there in his pajamas, a strange look on his little-boy features.

"I hear you sometimes," he said hesitantly. "You know, crying. I was wondering if you were OK."

And her eyes filled suddenly, unexpectedly, with tears.

James, looking frightened at this quick turn of events. Embarrassed and frightened, both at the same time. He looked at her again, then turned to leave.

"Wait," Yvonne said, swallowing her tears. "Come here," she said, patting the bed. James, used to following his older sister's orders, padded barefoot into the room and sat on the edge of the bed, hardly knowing what to expect. Yvonne reached over and hugged him. Even though it startled him, he did not try to pull away.

"Maybe," his sister whispered into his ear. "I'm sure trying to be OK."

This was not exactly the answer he was looking for, but it was close enough. He hugged his sister back, pretending he understood.

Arnie Watts hadn't been able to sleep a wink. Which was hardly surprising, he thought, with a body floating in the tub. Bodies, they were truly a fucking curse. He had been awake all night, twisting and turning, trying to come up with a viable plan to dispose of the damn thing, but his brain just didn't seem to be working right. And, he had to admit, it wasn't just the body. It was what had happened. Something that had never happened before . . . He kept remembering the laughter, dark and foreboding, leaking out of his brain like sewage bubbling up from an underground septic tank. Laughter that was not his . . . actions that were not his . . . and that thought sent shivers of terror through him all night, as he lay staring at the shadows fluttering over the dark ceiling. It rattled him, he admitted. Interfered with his thought process. And he was usually so damn sharp during a hunt. Able to anticipate and deal quickly with any unusual problems. But this hunt . . . it had not gone according to plan. At least not Arnie Watts's plan. The body . . . he kept seeing it come alive in his hands. Even though he knew better. Knew that it was just a body, nothing more. Something he had to get rid of when the hunt was over. And it was over, that was for sure. Usually he had a lot more time to deal with this eventuality. Usually he had a plan in place. But not this time.

As the night shadows were replaced by the far less frightening ghosts of daylight, Arnie Watts was struck with the unavoidable conclusion that he had made a huge mistake, perhaps bigger than he imagined. And he was deeply afraid that if he couldn't pull himself together and think clearly, he was bound to make another. Mistakes with bodies, he knew, usually proved fatal. And fuckups tend to run in cycles, with each compounding the previous one.

He shook himself and got up, turning on the TV, hoping for some clarity. He found none, but at least the television was noise, providing much needed company. For some reason he couldn't quite fathom, Arnie Watts didn't care to be alone with himself. He went into the bathroom to pee, carefully avoiding looking in the tub. He stood at the sink and splashed water on his face. Looking in the mirror, he cursed—the fucking eye was twitching, and he hated that. Hated it! He looked like hell, he was forced to admit. Like a man who'd had no sleep. Like a man who had huge problems, and no plan to deal with them. Out of the corner of his twitching eye, in the reflection of the mirror over the sink, he couldn't help but see the bathtub, and the girl's body, white and bloating. Cold and useless. He shivered, remembering how it felt, touching his own body. No, he admitted, things had not gone according to plan. Not at all.

Samuel Huxley and his wife, Karen, were still in the heavy stages of denial, York discovered, almost upon entering their modest, tidy house on Holland Drive. They were an odd-looking couple, York thought as Jesse Campbell from the ENN made the introductions. After which, he sat back on the couch and hoped for a story to develop right before his eyes. Samuel Huxley looked old enough to be the abducted girl's grandfather. While his wife, a tiny, youthful-looking woman, hardly looked old enough to have a thirteen-year-old daughter. . . .

But then look at Jenny, he said to himself, the thought of her flashing across his mind like a warm wind. It was strange, how some people reminded you of warmth, while others left you feeling cold. York found himself preoccupied with these thoughts while Mr. Huxley related the story of his daughter's "disappearance," all of which was familiar territory to York and anyone with a passing acquaintance with the television news. But it was important, York knew, to let people tell their stories in their own way, which was often more revealing than the actual story itself. Samuel Huxley, for instance, kept referring to the "disappearance" and the many leads the police were following. None of which had sounded promising to York, but he listened, nodding appropriately. Mrs. Huxley, however, remained silent and withdrawn. Only at the end of the story did she say anything.

"The 800 number is providing a lot of leads," she said hopefully.

"That's right!" Samuel Huxley said, patting his wife's shoulder encouragingly. "There's been a number of sightings. Some of them real close by. They'll find her, we're sure of it. God will bring our daughter home to us!"

"I sincerely hope so," York said, trying not to inflect too much into his voice. He had the Stafford file with him, spread out on the coffee table in front of the couch. He opened it, thumbing through the reports and photographs. "I know it's difficult, but I'd like to ask if you've seen any strangers around," York said as delicately as possible. "Perhaps this man?"

He laid the picture of Arnie Watts, grainy from the cutting and blowup, on the coffee table. Jesse Campbell, he noticed, leaned forward with the Huxleys.

"No." Samuel Huxley picked up the photo and handed it to his wife, both of them shaking their heads. "Never seen him before, that I can recall. Who is he?"

"I'm not sure," York admitted. "You said your daughter was visiting a friend at the time of her disappearance. Do they live close by?"

"Oh, my God, that's Mr. Reynolds!" Anna Burrows said, staring at the picture, then at her husband, David, who nodded in agreement. Fear caused her voice to rise above its normal level. "He was right here . . . right in our house! He came every day to the diner. . . ."

Jesse Campbell beat York to the phone, barely. York cringed, knowing the headlines were already in the making.

The problem, basically, was one of disposal. It was not unlike the few barrels of toxic waste that trash collectors find themselves saddled with every once in a while. The solution to that problem, of course, was to dump the barrels under a pile of garbage in the nearest landfill. The difference was that human bodies were a lot easier to trace than a few barrels of toxic waste. Also, Arnie Watts knew, the human body tends to attract incriminating evidence—fibers, hairs, fingerprints, bite marks, and the like. He suspected that barrels of toxic waste did much the same thing, and therein lay the real difference between the two disposal problems: Most of the time cops will go to extraordinary lengths when bodies are involved. But no one ever called out the National Guard search teams over a few barrels of poison, no matter where it happened to be dumped.

As the day progressed, Arnie Watts found himself staring at the closed bathroom door with increasing frequency. He'd tapped the motel ice machine for as many cubes as he could carry and dumped it all into the bathtub with the girl's body. He'd also tied the body's arms and legs, in an effort to keep the package as neat as possible. Time was a problem, obviously. The other problem was water, just like that long ago time in New York. The only open water in the vicinity was ocean, specifically the Long Island Sound. And as Arnie was well aware, you can't dump a body in the ocean without a boat. There was, it seemed, no good solution to the problem. At least none he could think of. In truth, his brain wasn't nearly as sharp as it should have been. As if he were drunk, Arnie thought. His mind out of focus, unable to think clearly. And then there was this other odd feeling. An empty, lonely feeling. Like that time in the sixth grade, when all his so-called friends had locked him in the school basement and left him there for the whole day, sitting against the cold cement blocks, alone and crying. Aban-

doned, the thought came to him. You've been abandoned
again. And the thought struck him as odd. He was, after all,
alone.

"Jenny? It's Dennison." York held his hand over his other
ear, trying to block out the sound of traffic rolling down
Route 422. A truck roared by, rattling the fillings in his back
teeth. Even on Saturday afternoon the heavy eighteen-
wheelers banged by, only a few feet from the pay phone
York was using a mile or so from the Hershey command
center. He missed the cell phone, missed it dearly. But, unfortunately, there just wasn't enough money to keep the
damned thing. Modern miracles, he knew, were expensive.

"I'm fine," he answered her question, the first one always
asked. Everyone, he decided, expects bad news when the
phone rings. "Listen, I've got a positive ID on our perp
down here. That's right. The family next door to the victim
recognized the Port Arthur picture. Only problem is, the
press got hold of it. It'll probably be on the evening news.
I know, but it might work to our advantage. Did you hear
from the Dane? No, he didn't mention any weekend plans
to me. If he calls, ask him to stick near the phone. The
perp's long gone, of course, but I'm going to stay down
here to see if I can pick up any leads. I might need him
later. Right, I'll call you when I hear anything. Yeah, me,
too. Talk to you soon."

York replaced the receiver and rubbed his eyes. He was
tired, but felt somehow that there was something else here.
Something he needed, another piece of the puzzle. Anna
Burrows said the guy came to the diner every day for a
week. That meant he stayed someplace nearby, although the
waitress had no idea where. Maybe he slept in his van, York
considered. The van's description was now in the hands of
the police, without the plate number, however. Anna hadn't
noticed it; neither had anyone else at the diner. And VW
vans were common enough not to attract attention. But
maybe the cops would turn up a trucker who'd spotted it.
There were surely enough truckers around in this part of
Pennsylvania. And the FBI had now been called in. Their

people were thorough, if somewhat arrogant, York knew. He thought briefly about trying a hypnotist to jog Anna Burrows's memory, but decided it probably wouldn't hurt to canvass the motels first. He jangled the empty chain under the pay phone, then headed back to the diner to see if he could find a local phone book.

Mrs. Dish and John Hammond were sitting in the front room, watching the evening news, eating supper on TV trays that had been bought when both of them were in their forties. Her husband, Murphy, in fact, presented the trays as a Christmas gift in the hope that his wife might allow him to watch the third quarter of the four o'clock Sunday game, something he hadn't remembered seeing in years. The plan worked only on special occasions, however, as Mrs. Dish insisted on eating supper at the dinner table, with each family member properly washed and in their respective seats. A practice she refused to relinquish, even though her family these days consisted of Mr. Hammond, the ever-absent Nomad, and an occasional passing motorist. But this was unquestionably one of those special occasions. The entire town had been turned upside down by the events of the last few days. Everyone in Hershey, in fact, was seeing more news than they ordinarily did in a month. So Mrs. Dish cut her chicken on a rickety old tray, the legs of which were held in place by cracked slips of brittle plastic.

"Do you know the family?" John Hammond asked. Mrs. Dish shook her head, irritated that the old man repeated the question every couple of days, and at the fact that she was being forced to watch car commercials during dinner.

"Wish I was ten years younger," John said. "I'd be out there in the woods helping those fellows look for her."

He said this with such conviction that Mrs. Dish believed him, even though she knew Hammond scowled behind her back when asked to go out to the woodpile to bring in logs for the fireplace. He was, she knew, a man who took his retirement seriously.

The cascade of commercials was ending and the news coming back on when the doorbell rang. John Hammond looked up at Mrs. Dish, who was busy with a mouthful of chicken, then at his own empty plate. The ringing had now turned to knocking.

"I'll get it." Hammond sighed, pushing the tray away, lifting himself to his feet—as if he would soon require one of those push-up chairs, Mrs. Dish thought. The man obviously needed more exercise, she said to herself, already planning more trips to the woodpile for Mr. Hammond.

He left the room as the newscaster came back on, shuffling papers and looking up expectantly into the camera. She was young and much too thin, in Mrs. Dish's opinion, but something in her eyes commanded attention.

"We have a breaking development in the Hershey abduction story," the woman said, sounding excited and almost glad to be part of this whole, tragic affair. "Police have just released a photograph of a man they say may be involved in the kidnapping. . . ."

And Mrs. Dish found herself staring right into the eyes of Mr. Reynolds of Cabin #3. Her fork clattered onto her plate, sliding off to fall soundlessly on the shag rug.

"Marjorie, there's a man at the door who wants to talk to you!" John Hammond yelled. Mrs. Dish, however, didn't hear him.

"That son of a bitch," Mrs. Dish whispered, even though she hadn't used words like that in decades.

"I knew we should have called the police," she said, pulling newspapers out of the tied-up stack by the kitchen pantry. "I said it, and by God we should have done it!"

She glared at John Hammond, who stood by the stove with Dennison York. Hammond, who hadn't seen the picture on the television, looked both confused and guilty.

"You couldn't have known," York said, trying to play down his excitement. Mary Jo, the waitress at the diner, had told him about the Last Stop Motel. He, in fact, had passed it on his way into town, but it seemed like one of the many closed-down lodging places one saw in small towns which had been passed over by the interstates.

"Oh, yes, I could!" Mrs. Dish insisted, pulling out a copy

of the *Conway Examiner,* opening the pages to a sketch of Arnie Watts, restaurant bandit. "Right there!" Mrs. Dish said, her eyes blazing as she pointed to the picture. "That's him . . . the rotten bastard!"

York nodded, realizing he was looking at the same article Jenny had seen. And he was struck, suddenly, by the interlocking web of fate that seemed somehow to so profoundly affect the lives of human beings. He experienced a moment of clarity so intense, he grabbed the corner of the table to keep himself from staggering. He realized that happenstance and luck play no part in the human experience. That the wheel of life turns in carefully prescribed motions. That all things happen for reasons that may be beyond the understanding of mortal beings, but they happen, nonetheless, for specific reasons. And in that moment, even though he would never know it, Dennison York had a brief, fleeting glimpse into the mind of God.

"I have a receipt, someplace. . . ." Mrs. Dish was saying as she searched through a stack of bills on the kitchen counter. "Here!" she said, waving a slip of paper at York.

He took it and saw that the old woman had scratched down the license plate of Arnie Watts's VW van.

On a street corner in New Haven, Connecticut, the wheel of life was turning, inexorable and unstoppable.

Late Saturday afternoon, the wind crisp off the salt water of the Sound, whisking away the exhaust fumes from the cars of a multitude of Christmas shoppers. Arnie Watts drove carefully down the main drag. Downtown New Haven, he saw, had done all it could to entice the nearby residents with lights and displays. So cheerful and filled with the spirit of the holidays, the shoppers hardly gave a second thought to the fact that the toys and clothes they were purchasing with high-interest credit cards would be half price after the first of the year.

It was a thing, Watts remembered, that upset his father to no end. And even while the old man ranted and raved, his mother would smile—covering her fear, he learned—and say that it was Christmas and he could bring the shirt back when the sales started, if he really wanted to. The old man always did, Arnie thought, a smile tugging at his lips, even as memories of the family, with the ratty Christmas trees and the few gifts piled up underneath, reminded him of all that went on in the house under the cover of darkness. The violence, the terror . . . He shook his head, knowing now that his mother was trying to pretend those things didn't happen, pretending they were a real family. Pretending that a monster didn't sleep beside her. That the monster didn't visit her son and daughter in their bedrooms, drunk and stinking in the darkness, swaying and mean. But still, the old man returned his Christmas shirt every year, the first week in January. In some ways, Arnie thought grudgingly, the old man had been smart.

He drove the van through the crowded streets, the girl's body in the duffel bag, strapped to the rear seat. Arnie stopped at the Golden Arches, had a Big Mac, and studied the Dumpster in back of the restaurant as he ate. Maybe he'd come back after they closed and drop the Army bag in with their garbage. It might just get picked up and hauled to a landfill someplace. It might, he considered. But then, it might not. Some bum, poking around, looking for leftover hamburgers, might find it and zip it open. Imagine the look on the wino's face, he thought, grinning. That fucker would swear off the bottle for good. But then the Law would surely get involved. And Arnie Watts knew he hadn't been too careful lately. He sure as shit couldn't afford another screw-up. Dumpsters were no good, he decided, crumbling up the food wrapper, throwing it on the floor of the van. Something better would come up, he thought, pulling the van around the drive-in window, back into the afternoon traffic. It always did.

Lesia Stafford took her daughter's hand as they left the complex where Yvonne's doctor had her office. The hand holding was not the sort that took place between a parent and a small child, but was rather a means of contact and support both offered to the other. It had been weeks, months actually, since they had begun their weekly visits to the New

Haven therapist, and Lesia prayed every night that the
woman would help the healing process. The healing had
begun, Lesia thought sometimes as she saw glimpses of the
person her daughter used to be—like when Yvonne seemed
to care what it was they were having for dinner, or smiled
coming home from school. True, Yvonne's grades were not
what they once were, and she seemed reluctant to expand
her group of friends beyond a few casual acquaintances. But
all of that would come in time, the doctor said. Lesia certainly hoped so, but in her heart wondered how much more
time would pass before what was left of her daughter's
childhood vanished altogether.

"Hey, would you like to do some shopping?" Lesia
asked, smiling, nodding at the rows of lights strung over the
street, shining like stars on a clear, moonless night.

"I guess so," Yvonne said, sounding unenthused. Her
daughter was always this way after a session, Lesia knew.
As if it was a difficult task to return to the real world. Which
it probably was, Lesia thought, squeezing Yvonne's hand.

"I saw a toy store on Main Street," Lesia said, trying to
sound upbeat. "Maybe they have that thing your brother
wants. What was it?"

"Power Rangers," Yvonne replied, walking in step with
her mother, but dropping her hand to let Lesia know she
realized the ploy that was being used on her. Still, she had
to admit that trick worked to some extent. Thinking about
upcoming holidays did boost her spirits.

"Aren't the lights pretty?" Lesia asked. "I wish it would
snow. Just a little. I love snow on Christmas."

There wasn't any need to reply, Yvonne knew. Her
mother was talking in that nervous way adults do sometimes, as though the sound of their voices comforted them
somehow. The two stopped and looked at some of the window displays. Christmas trees and bright, winking lights.
Santa Claus figures that smiled and moved their heads and
arms. Elves and the wide-eyed, plastic faces of mannequin
children looking at presents and angels and the Baby Jesus
surrounded by pretend animals as he lay in his manger. . . .

In the reflection of a window, in which tiny wooden reindeer stood on a floor of white cotton, Yvonne Stafford saw a van pull up to a stoplight. Something caught her eye and she turned. A scream rose up in her chest and was muffled by a wave of fear that suddenly gripped her throat. The van, parked at the light for a heartbeat, passed on into traffic. But the terror . . . the terror shook her, turning her legs to water. She felt herself slipping to the ground, clutching at her mother's arm. The terror . . . it couldn't be! It just couldn't be, she told herself. But it was! It was HIM! Even as she held on to her mother's arm, she felt herself slipping . . . slipping away into a darkness that was frightening beyond words, but a darkness with which she was all too familiar.

"Yvonne . . . Yvonne?" she heard her mother say, the words echoing and fading in Yvonne's mind as she watched the van disappear into the bright holiday lights. "Yvonne . . ."

The terror crushing her. HIM! It was HIM! The image of HIM returned like some dreadful, haunting spirit buried in the graveyard of her mind.

"What is it?" her mother asked, her voice frantic, yet oddly distant.

Yvonne Stafford felt her feet sliding away from her, as the wheel of life turned beneath them all.

"I don't know, she wouldn't say a word!" Yvonne heard her mother say from downstairs. Lesia's voice on the verge of hysteria. Her father, speaking softly, yet firmly, trying to understand. He couldn't, of course, Yvonne knew. No one could understand. HE was out there! Maybe driving down their street this very moment! The ride home had been a blur, a hazy memory which she barely recalled. Checking time after time to be sure the car doors were locked. Watching each vehicle pass them. The terrible fear that HE would be at the wheel of every car, truck, and van on the highway. And when their own car had finally been parked in the imaginary safety of their garage . . .

"She just ran upstairs when we got home!" Lesia was saying, tears now choking her voice. "She refused to go back to the doctor's. I don't know what happened. . . ."

"I'll go up and talk to her," she heard her father say. His footsteps heavy on the stairs. The soft rapping on her door. "Yvonne? It's me, honey. Can I come in?"

Silence, like the black mirrored waters of a lake, late, late at night. James Stafford pushed the door open. It was dark inside, the gray, fading afternoon light beating like soft moth wings against the drawn curtains.

"Yvonne?" he said, whispering, stepping into the room. His daughter, he saw, was sitting on her bed. The covering quilt pulled protectively around her. "Yvonne, what's wrong?"

He walked carefully toward the bed and sat down next to his daughter. She was staring straight ahead, her jaw tight. She was shivering, and so he put his arms around her. Yvonne, however, did not respond. She seemed intent on staring at the open door of her room.

"Yvonne, I can't help you if you don't tell me what's wrong," he said, filled suddenly with a sinking, helpless feeling that he might actually not be able to do as he promised, even if she confided in him.

"Do we have a gun?" Yvonne asked, her voice flat, emotionless. The question stunned him and James Stafford found that he could only stare at his daughter, his helplessness and fear mounting.

"We have to get a gun," she said, staring at the door, tears leaking out of the corners of her eyes.

"Yvonne . . ." he said, pulling her closer. As the covers fell away from her, he was chilled to discover that she was clutching a long kitchen knife in both her hands, holding the weapon tightly against her chest.

"We have to get a gun," she repeated, and Stafford's own eyes filled with tears as he saw the dull, flickering light of madness flash across his daughter's face.

"Why?" he asked softly. "Why do we have to get a gun?"

"Because I saw HIM," Yvonne said, turning to him, melting into his arms. "I saw HIM!"

He held her for what seemed to be forever as she shook and cried against his chest.

• • •

James Stafford came down the stairs, carrying the kitchen knife. His wife and son were sitting in the living room, holding each other as if the family had just received devastating news about a close relative. Seeing them, he held the knife behind his back.

"She's asleep," he said reassuringly. "Maybe you should call the doctor."

Lesia nodded and moved to the phone. Later, as the night settled around the house like a fog, Stafford considered what his daughter had said. Yvonne was sleeping upstairs. The doctor had prescribed a tranquilizer. Lesia had taken one of the pills herself and was curled up on the couch. James Junior had been assured that everything was all right, even though the little boy had accepted the news with doubt. Just as Stafford himself now had doubts. The doctor said that Yvonne was suffering what was undoubtedly a temporary relapse. That someone she had seen reminded her of her attacker. It was common, the doctor said. James Stafford, pacing the kitchen, looking out the window at the cars passing by, found he could not be entirely sure of that assumption. His daughter, he knew, had an inner strength that almost defied words. The fact of her survival testified to that. Stafford dug through his wallet and pulled out a card he had not looked at for a long time. Even though it was late, he picked up the kitchen phone and left a message on the answering machine at Dennison York's office. The man had said, after all, that Stafford could call him anytime, day or night. York, he thought, seemed to be a man of his word. Hanging up the phone, Stafford went into the living room and sat in a chair facing the front door, listening as the sounds of the night passed over the world.

In a galaxy in the Comma Cluster, in a network of stars known for their spectacular suicidal tendencies, a shielded vessel held orbit at the far edge of the destruction field.

The yellow flower of the sun exploded before him, the high bands of its radiation shooting outward, even as the star mass itself began to collapse. Eventually, calculations showed, the collapse would form a black hole, down into which all matter, including light, would be pulled.

Pulled to where? he wondered, watching the secondary explosions as the star's planets were swept away in the holocaust. He watched them, popping like grapes thrown into a fire. There were, thankfully, no higher forms of life populating these planets in this particular epoch, and so he was not forced to endure a dying race's last, futile calls for help. As an empathic being, it was a thing he always dreaded. And in this millennium, when the number of exploding stars seemed to be slightly above the statistical norm, he had seen more than a few such situations. Especially, since in this millennium, it had been decreed that the time and energies of his race were to be used in the study of the phenomena of exploding stars and the creation of black holes.

It was, he knew from implanted memories, the third such study undertaken by his race in this field. The previous two having been implemented in past ages, eons before this recent study had been decreed. And he was pleased to be a part of this present series of experiments, as the subject of black holes had interested him since the moment of his awareness. Of course, his mechanism had been programmed specifically to take part in this study, he knew, so that he would find joy and satisfaction in his work. The knowledge of this manipulation was buried deeply enough so as not to cause him concern or anxiety at the fact of his programming, but was included in the basic makeup of his mechanism, as it was in the primary function level of all such mechanisms generated by his species.

He watched the explosion for a while longer, a year or two by galactic time, directing instruments aboard the vessel, which gathered information across a wide variety of the spectrum field. When he deemed the time to be right, he launched a probe into the heart of the collapsing explosion. The probe, which he himself had helped design, would hopefully shed some light on the question of where, exactly, matter went when it was pulled into the depths of the black hole event.

He smiled to himself, considering the joke about "shedding light" on the mysteries of a black hole. It was a joke which he shared with his labmates when the probe was being engineered. Ndy, the woman who later became his wife, seemed particularly amused whenever the joke was repeated. She had been younger then, a student like himself. In the years before he left to observe the present event, now unfolding in such spectacular fashion before him, they became formally mated and had generated three mechanisms before his departure into the vast light-years separating his home world from the now collapsing star. He kept her picture, and those of their young ones, in his sleeping quarters below the command desk. Of course, while he himself had not even reached middle age, he was well aware that twelve thousand years, more or less, had passed on the home world. And that before he returned, twice that amount of time would be recorded into his race's history. Even now, the mechanism Ndy had inhabited was long since turned to dust, as well as those of their young ones and the thousand or so generations his children had produced. Still, while he and Ndy had never been formally mated before, they had taken the vow of continuance and so would be reunited again, if not in this life, then the next. He looked forward to that time—to discovering the mechanism she inhabited, to know once again the joy of her entity.

The probe had now disappeared into the event horizon. He double-checked the data-retrieval bands and saw that they were functioning, even now beaming information back toward the laboratories he had left so long ago. He then began the process of preparing his vessel for the deep-space run to the home world. He took a moment to sight the sun that had given birth to his race, a dim, barely seen point of light, blinking in the vast, star-studded depths of the galaxy. And he smiled, thinking of home and the girl who awaited him. He looked forward to loving her again; after, of course, he passed the ocean of space and time between them.

He made his way down into the sleeping chamber, knowing that the probe's information would be waiting for him when he returned to the home world. He knew, also, that in the time that passed, new studies would be decreed. New adventures planned, and he looked forward to taking part in them, after the mechanism he now inhabited ceased to function and he was reborn into a new life. Just as he had, time upon time before. His race, which had been a part of the universe for millions of years, had long since understood the deeper mysteries of time and rebirth. God had surely smiled upon them, he thought.

He sat for a moment on the edge of his sleeping cylinder, contemplating these mysteries, as he knew he was programmed to do. Finally, when he was at peace with himself, he initiated the computer sequence that would activate the engines of his vessel and flood the interior of the ship with the preserving cold of space. He swung himself into the sleeping cylinder and pulled the airtight cover down. Lying on his bed, he took the picture of Ndy and his young ones, looking into their faces, which smiled at him from across twelve thousand years of time.

"I'm coming home to you," he whispered as the gasses hissed in the sleeping chamber, covering him like a gentle mist. And he fell into a long dream of the universe, in which music played in soaring, endless couplets, like the sound of stringed instruments, light-years long, vibrating in the solar winds. And in his dream he danced among the stars, as the engines of his ship, drawing their energy from atoms in the almost-vacuum of space, propelled him home, at a speed just below that of light.

REFLECTIONS ON THE TIME CONSTRAINTS OF THE LIFE EXPERIMENT

In any life experiment there are uncertainties. Given the complex nature of this type of experiment, there are always factors involved which remain unpredictable and beyond the control of those responsible for implementing the experiment. Discovery, after all, is the only rationale for any endeavor of this sort. The volatile nature of the physical world, and of the mechanisms themselves, presents a series of variables which can have either a positive or negative impact on the outcome of any experiment. One factor which has a decided effect on the chances of an experiment's success can, however, be predicted with a certain degree of accuracy. That factor being, of course, time.

Once planetary formation takes place around a prospective life-bearing star, and differentiation occurs, it then becomes a relatively simple matter to construct a time line around which an experiment may be implemented. The emergence of dominant beings who are likely candidates for spiritual implantation occurs at specific points in the development of the star and its planets. As has been previously noted, however, the window of opportunity is quite limited, given the delicate balance of planetary evolution and the sun's fluctuations as it progresses through its own life cycle. Thus, it becomes necessary to implant the spiritual entities into the primitive mechanisms at the earliest opportunity. It is at this point that the operational constraints of the experiment fall upon the entities themselves. While the time frame needed to construct a viable technological society varies in each life experiment, it does fall between a definable statistical range. It is during this limited period, a moment really on the cosmic scale, that the entities must develop the technological and social skills necessary to impact both planetary evolution and their own development. Failure in either of these categories will result in a discontinuance of the experiment caused by the mechanisms' inability to survive climactic and organic changes in the planet's environment.

The dichotomy here is that many of the planetary changes are caused by the mechanisms themselves as they strive toward a technological-based society. It would seem, therefore, that a viable argument against the development of a technological civilization might be constructed. This argument, however, fails to consider the finite nature of the physical plane. As previously noted, life experiments are fueled by vast but limited energy reserves, and so do, in fact, end. Therefore, the choices made by the mechanisms regarding both resources and social structure quickly become the defining factor in the experiment. Individual choice becomes critical particularly in the areas of knowledge accumulation and learning experience. Given the time constraints and the complexities involved in building a technological society, it becomes imperative for the entities, in each succeeding generation, to extract the necessary knowledge from the resources of the physical plane. Aberrations, of course, are unavoidable, and are sometimes seen by the mechanisms to be inconsequential, as would be the case if life experiments were infinite. But when the energy reserves become depleted within a specific life experiment, that experiment terminates without regard to the subjects.

The infinite, however, can be achieved. The delicate balance of planetary and solar conditions which gave birth to the mechanisms do not necessarily have to be the cause of their demise when these conditions change, as evolution dictates they must. The goal of the experiment is to create advanced, implanted mechanisms who are able to survive planetary change, and even the death of their sun, by moving out among the stars where true knowledge awaits them.

Observation: The tenacity required to achieve this ultimate goal is, admittedly, beyond the statistical range of probability. Still, recent developments in this particular life experiment, specifically the recognition factor achieved by certain entities, even within the primitive structure of their mechanisms, hints at the possibility of success.

twenty-three

As she did every day the office was closed and Dennison York was out of town, Jenny rang in to see if there were any messages. It was now early Sunday morning, and she was on the couch with a mug of coffee, flipping through the news channels to see if there were any developments in the Pennsylvania abduction. And, she admitted to herself, to see if the United States government had bombed anyone during the night. The answer seemed to be negative on both counts, as there was no mention of either subject in the headlines. The phone was ringing in the office and she listened to the recording, pushing the retrieval code at the end. She almost fell off the couch when James Stafford's voice came on, telling York he suspected his daughter might have seen "the creep who attacked her" as the man drove through a streetlight in New Haven, Connecticut.

"The doctor is sure it was just somebody who looked like the guy," Stafford's voice went on to explain, coming over the phone in strained, obviously concerned tones. "But Yvonne . . . well, she seems pretty sure. Anyway, she's really shook up. I thought you should know. Give me a call when you get a chance. . . ."

The line buzzed and beeped as the tape rewound. Jenny put the receiver down and stared at the phone for several seconds, hoping it would ring, hoping Dennison would call so she could relay the message. It didn't, of course, and she had no idea where he was staying in Hershey. Indeed, if he was still there. Stafford's message seemed almost unbelievable, but Jenny knew all too well that York had traipsed halfway across the country chasing down slimmer leads.

Do you believe in fate? she remembered asking him, only a few days ago. My God, she thought, what if it was true? She punched in the Dane's number and his machine came on.

"It's Jenny," she said, noticing her voice was shaking, as well as her hands. She believed the girl, Jenny realized suddenly, although she couldn't have said why. "Give me a call at home as soon as you can. It's important, I think. . . ."

The woman left early in the morning, and the Dane decided it was just as well. They both enjoyed each other, there was no question about that. But he thought she knew, as he did, that what passed between them was a momentary thing. One of the pleasant diversions life offers every once in a while. Besides, the Dane thought, it beat the hell out of tramping around the countryside with York, even though he did feel a twinge of guilt about not calling his boss back. But the experience, he decided, had been well worth a little guilt. He had not had a woman like that in . . . well, he had never had a woman like that, he decided. Not even Inga. In fact, he suggested they see each other again before he left for home, but somehow he doubted it would happen. She smiled at him, buttoning her long leather coat, then, with a wink and a wave, she closed the door behind her.

Off to church, she said, laughing. Sure you don't want to come along?

The Dane shook his head. He was going to visit his own gods—those of strength and iron. He waited until she was truly gone, her scent and soft cries fading from the apartment. Then he went out into the cold, damp morning air, caught a cab to Gold's, and banged weights until his muscles cried out in protest and sweat danced along the contours of his body like steaming dew.

After, he stepped again into the quiet New York streets,

picked up the ridiculously thick *Times,* and had breakfast
downtown before heading home. Jenny was on his machine
and she sounded upset. He flicked through the pages of the
Times as he called her house. He was a little taken aback to
hear her answer before the first ring had completed its cycle.

"It's me," the Dane said, cradling the receiver, flipping
through the paper. He stopped, sensing Jenny's tension
through the phone lines. "What's up?" he asked, feeling
strangely tense himself, hoping that nothing had happened
to York. Damn it, he should've gone with his boss, he
thought. Since when did a roll in the sheets take precedent
over one's responsibilities? He had the sudden image of
Dennison York in a hospital bed . . . or worse. He had become a poor soldier, the Dane thought. And for that, he
knew, there was no excuse.

"Is the boss OK?" he asked when Jenny took a second
to respond to his first question.

"Yes, yes, he's fine," Jenny said, as if she was suddenly
able to read the Dane's mind. Actually the call, while an-
ticipated, had startled her, and she spilled coffee on her robe
when the phone rang. "At least he was when I talked to
him yesterday. He's in Pennsylvania, looking into that kidnapping. . . ."

"I know," the Dane said, somewhat relieved now that
his most dire thoughts had not proved true. "I missed him
at the office," the Dane lied—a small lie, but one he knew
Jenny caught immediately. "He's always running off, chasing shadows," the Dane said, hating the fact that he was
making excuses.

"Not this time," Jenny said. "He had someone ID the
Texas picture. They're pretty sure our guy's involved."

"Where's Dennison now?" the Dane asked, angry at
himself. He should've known. York was like one of those
pit bulls they were always talking about on the news. He
grabbed on and never let go until he got the desired results.
"I can be there this afternoon."

"I think he's still in Hershey, but I'm not sure, exactly,"
Jenny said, trying to collect her thoughts. Everything about
this morning felt strange, as if she was moving under the

influence of something beyond her control. "He called yesterday and wanted you to stick close in case he needed you. But there was this message on the office phone this morning. . . ."

By noon the Dane had rented a car and was on his way to New Haven. Both he and Jenny agreed that would be York's next destination, once he got wind of the possible sighting. The Dane would go there, visit the Stafford family, and begin the legwork. Jenny would coordinate, once York called in, as he was sure to do. She would call the Staffords and let them know members of the team were on their way. The Dane, pushing the speed limit on Interstate 95, felt that this time they might actually be close, although in truth he could give no basis for his feeling.

Beneath him, the wheel of life turned and turned.

Arnie Watts twisted on the damp sheets of the bed in his rented room. Once again, he had not been able to sleep for most of the night. Strange, troubled thoughts seemed to plague him. He kept seeing shadows twisting in the darkness near the bed. Nameless, faceless shadows that dissipated like colorless smoke whenever he jumped up to turn on the light. Finally, in desperation, he left the light on and covered his head with the pillow. But still sleep evaded him, until just before dawn, when he fell into the coiled arms of a hideous nightmare. A nightmare in which he seemed to be almost awake, yet strangely distant. . . .

His confusion swirled about him like a mist. The mist seemed to enter his lungs as he struggled to breathe. Slipped into his mouth as he suddenly found himself gasping. The mist—like a drug, further confusing his senses, his mind.

—What have you done? the voice asked, rising up from black depths of the dream. The voice, heavy with accusations.

—What have I done? Arnie whispered, the question sliding across his brain, darkness obscuring both question and answer.

The black wave roaring into his head. Like a thunder-cloud filled with sudden, blinding bursts of sheet lightning. The nightmare, leaping, exploding upon him—a dark flower opening behind his mind. As violent and sudden as death. And each time the lightning flashed, the question repeated:

—What have you done? The voice heavy in the middle, yet carrying the crinkled sound of laughter around its edges. And that voice, distant and dark, sounded to Arnie Watts like the cracking of thin, brittle bones.

What had he done? Arnie Watts asked himself, struggling to remember. But the mist, swirling in his head, black as a shroud, seemed now to have engulfed the whole of his mind. It covered his eyes, filling his ears with numbed silence, until he could not even hear the sound of his own heart beating. Filling his lungs until breathing seemed to be a distant, half-remembered memory. Something that belonged entirely to another life. And at the edge of the blackness that was now the whole of his existence, lightning flashed on the horizon in ever-increasing frequency. Shadows moved, floating in the darkness. Coming closer, becoming clearer with each blast of the distant lightning. Fear shook him and he wanted to scream, but the black mist filled his mouth like dark, swirling, drowning water. The shadows became clearer, and he heard the terrible sound of echoing laughter rising up in the mist. Lightning flashing, consuming his brain with sharp, stabbing blasts. The shadows swiftly changing shape with each burst of light. The world of darkness and shadow, rolling around him in a haze of gray and black

and he found himself sitting unnoticed around a roaring fire watching as armor-clad beastlike warriors laughed and drank frothy liquids from the bladders of their victims cracking bones with fanged teeth and sucking out the marrow as flutes were carved from the bones of the dead and a steady pounding rhythm was kept by slaves striking the open-mouth skulls of the vanquished and he heard himself

scream soundlessly as the attention of those around the
fire turned suddenly to him

lightning flashed and he was surrounded by the pale
shapes of rotting corpses and they moved shuffling across
the endless dark plane and from their mouths came a
moan low and deep and he thought for a moment it was a
song and knew in an instant of intense clarity it was a
prayer and the realization filled him with unspeakable horror as he heard his own voice join their ghostly chorus and
he was with them shuffling through the darkness their
mournful cries rising up to be swallowed by the night and
the dead shuffling toward a gray dawn that never grew
closer and the dead crying wailing praying for the end of
time the dead alone and alone and alone

lightning flashed again and again and beasts with nee-
dle teeth and razor claws rose up from the darkness snapping and growling ripping his flesh from his bones and no
screaming no pleading no crying no begging would make
it stop and the lightning flashed again and again and again

Until he was lying in his own stink and vomit, twisting
on the bed. Gasping, his breath coming in long, hot waves.
His eyes burning, his flesh crawling, as though worms
wilted beneath his skin, struggling to free themselves. And
he rolled off the bed, crawling to the bathroom to clean
himself of the filth . . . only to find the girl's body, bloated
and forgotten, floating in the dark water of the tub. NO NO
NO! his brain yelled. She was in the back of the van, locked
away, out of sight, out of mind. But he saw her anyway,
floating. Her eyes open, staring at him. And he wanted to
scream, but could only choke and gasp.
—What have you done? the voice asked. The laughter
booming in his head, ripping his skull, echoing off the inside
of his eardrums, fraying each nerve, each cell of his body.
—Don't ever die, the voice warned him, laughing, low and
dark. . . . Don't ever die. . . .
Arnie Watts, curling into a ball on the cold tile floor,

shivered with a terror that gripped his heart like ice and blurred his eyes. Arnie Watts, understanding well the frailty of human flesh, knew that he would die. That the day and the hour, even the means of his death did not matter. He knew it was inevitable and unavoidable. That no place on earth could hide him from it. And Arnie Watts, who had given death over and over and over, lay on the cold tile floor and wept. Wept, like the damned.

Mrs. Dish cooked bacon and eggs every Sunday morning, despite the fact that she suspected such heavy fare had done in her late husband. Still, Sunday didn't seem the same without the smell of bacon filling the kitchen. The smell of fresh coffee and frying meat drew Mr. Hammond and the overnighter, Mr. York, down from their respective rooms.

Dennison York, who had been persuaded to spend the night, smiled at her as she poured him a cup of her dark coffee. And, she noted with satisfaction, he did not seem ill-disposed to eat his share, dipping a corner of toast into the runny yolk of her fried eggs and chopped onions. She even accepted his credit card for payment on the room, even though she didn't entirely trust the use of plastic money, which her husband Murf had always said was a curse that would eventually bring down the economy.

York chewed on the next-to-last piece of bacon and listened as John Hammond talked about the virtues of capital punishment as the definitive means of dealing with anyone who would abduct a little girl. Mrs. Dish seemed to agree in principal. York, who had himself been judge, jury, and executioner, barely acknowledged the discussion. Ending another human being's life, he knew, was not a thing to be taken lightly. And it was a discussion usually engaged in by those who had no experience in the matter.

"They should televise the executions," Hammond was saying. "Let the criminals see what they're gonna get!"

"Maybe," York conceded, wondering in the back of his mind if this was typical conversation around the Sunday breakfast table.

"Please, Mr. Hammond." Mrs. Dish grimaced, signaling

to York that this sort of morbid talk was not the norm.

Hammond took the last piece of bacon, scowling at the admonition.

York spent the night at the Last Stop Boardinghouse, as it had been late when he finished combing through Cabin #3, in which the perp had stayed. The search had turned up nothing useful, although York suspected the FBI would be able to pull fingerprints, which would match the van and the apartment back in New York, and most likely the restaurant in Myrtle Beach. All of which would do nothing to actually catch the man. York had given the license plate number to the command center, as well as the location of the perp during his stay in Hershey. The police would be at the Last Stop this morning, he knew, to do an in-depth runthrough with Mrs. Dish and John Hammond. Turning over all the stones, finding only worms and beetles underneath.

"Do you mind if I use your phone to call my office?" York asked. Mrs. Dish curled her eyebrows at the request. "I'll be using my calling card," he said, and then she nodded, smiling, sort of, York thought.

Sunday traffic was heavier than he would have suspected. The wheels of commerce, York realized, do not take many days off. Trucks rolled by him on 95 as he passed through the tip of New Jersey and pushed on toward New Haven. The Dane was a couple of hours ahead of him, York figured. He hoped they would meet up at the Stafford house, although if the Dane got wind of the perp, York knew the big man was not likely to stop just because he happened to be alone on the front lines. Nor would York expect him to. This was a game of inches, where lost minutes could mean a blown opportunity. Did Yvonne Stafford really see the perp driving by? It was possible, he knew, however unlikely it might seem to someone who worked strictly with the laws of probability. But those laws, he knew, also, were often suspended when it came to the inner workings of human relationships. Experience taught him that there were connecting lines, external forces at work within the lives of people. He knew with absolute certainty that it was entirely possible for fate—or whatever name one wished to apply to the force that laughed in the face of probability—to arrange a course of events that would bring the perp and his victim into close proximity to each other. Wasn't that the very thing which caused him to track down leads all over the country, hoping for a chance encounter with the man who had killed Ronnie Bates? Hoping that fate might somehow intervene? Yes, and then what? he asked himself. There was no ready answer to that question, he knew. There were only miles to be driven. And then perhaps some answers. York pushed the speedometer up a couple of notches, trying to force his mind to the immediate task at hand.

At home in New York, Jenny was attempting to do the same. York had called in several hours earlier. He received Stafford's message, and the news that the Dane was already en route, with barely contained excitement. He gave her the license plate and the description of the perp's green-and-white VW van.

"That's assuming, of course, he hasn't switched vehicles or plates," York said, forgetting Mrs. Dish's ban on cigarettes, lighting up a Dunhill with matches off her kitchen stove. Something about inhaling cigarette smoke helped him to think, although he tried unsuccessfully to hide the ree-mergence of his habit from Jenny.

"The Dane said he'd call in from the Staffords'," Jenny said. "I'll relay the descriptions to him. You're having a cigarette, aren't you?"

"Yes," he admitted, his mind sensing the worthlessness of a lie. "I promise I'll quit when this is over."

"You'd better!" Jenny said, realizing she was nagging him long distance, and in the middle of an investigation, to boot. Tough shit, she thought, knowing that she wanted him around for as many years as possible. "Anything else I can do here?" she asked, making an effort to soften her tone, at least for the moment. Her job, after all, was one of support. There would be plenty of time to nag him later. At least she hoped there would be. The strange feeling she had about the day and the unfolding events would not leave her.

"Yes, there is," York said, ignoring Mrs. Dish's glaring look at his cigarette. "It's a long shot, but I want you to call the directory service in New Haven and get a listing of all the hotels and motels in the area. Talk to the phone company supervisor and use our hunting license number. But get that listing, if you can. Call the front desks of those places and see if you can trace the plate or the vehicle description. He stayed at a boardinghouse in Hershey. Maybe we can get a fix on him in New Haven."

"I'll do my best," Jenny said.

"I know you will," York said, smiling, as if there had ever been any doubt about that.

"I love you," she said suddenly, sensing he was about to hang up. "Please, be careful."

"Me, too," York replied. "And you can bet I'll be careful."

The phone line went dead and Jenny replaced the receiver, filled again with an odd sense of dread. Something for which she had no basis, but that fact did not make the feeling any less real. Before starting a task that would undoubtedly add unprecedented dollars to her phone bill, money that the business might or might not have in the coffers to repay her, Jenny knocked on the door of her daughter's bedroom. Both to rouse Gena from a sleep that threatened to stretch into the afternoon, and to have someone to hold, if only for a moment or two.

"Jeez, mom," Gena complained, finding herself suddenly awakened by a smothering hug from her mother. "Is something wrong?"

"No," Jenny whispered, losing herself in her daughter's warmth, wondering if she was telling both Gena and herself the truth.

Yvonne Stafford had no illusions of warmth. At least not in her heart. Each time she swallowed, the taste of fear was there on the back of her tongue. It tasted like a penny she had gulped down once, on a dare from members of the P.S. 364 Bomb Squad. Those girls, their faces and laughter once so close to her, were now only distant memories. Memories of a past life. A life in which there had been no fear, no unnamed terror. In this new life the terror was much too real. The memories sharp and painful. In this life, at this moment in time, she refused even to leave the sanctuary of her room. Preferring the imagined safety of her bed to the realities which waited for her in the outside world. She had seen HIM, even if no one else wanted to believe her. She knew now a simple, yet startling truth: Reality is not based on what other people think. Instead, it is based entirely on what you yourself know to be true. And HE was out there, no matter how much anyone else wanted to pretend otherwise.

The Dane pulled up to the Stafford house around two in the afternoon. It was, he thought, a neighborhood straight out of the American dream. Rows of houses set along quiet, tree-lined lanes. People jogging on the sidewalks or walking their dogs in the crisp, clean afternoon air. Kids playing in the thin layer of snow that dusted the lawns here in suburbia. No graffiti on the walls, no garbage blowing down the streets or piled up in empty lots. He thought that this was a vision of what America could be, and what it should be. A land so rich that there was no need for any of its people to live in squalor, to grub for food in garbage cans, to live without heat or education or any of the bare necessities of existence. Yet, he knew well the realities and the strange dichotomy of life in this country. He saw it, walked by the lower end of the scale every day. And here at the upper end of the scale, it hardly seemed as though the people here lived in the same world as those wandering the streets of New York. It was a thing so bizarre and confusing to the Dane that he could only stop and stare. Just as the people were staring at him as they passed. Him, a stranger in their warm, protected sanctuary. He could not fault them, really, for being protective about their privileged life here. It was, after all, exactly what the founders had envisioned at the very beginning. But something, somehow, had gone terribly wrong. He could feel it, even as he stood in the middle of affluence. And the people here felt it, too, he knew. That was why they stared at him out of the corners of their eyes as they went about their business. A Viking raider in their presence. Had he come to visit, or to plunder? he heard them wondering.

James Stafford opened the door and greeted him. The Dane had met Stafford only a couple of times back in New York, but the man seemed to remember him. Seemed glad, actually, that he was here. Yes, the mercenaries have arrived, the Dane imagined Stafford thinking. Perhaps now everything would be all right.

The Dane realized quickly the illusion of safety and security that prevailed on the streets outside was just that—an illusion, carefully constructed and preserved by the inhabitants of suburbia, who knew in their hearts the true state of the world. Who could not, especially if you watched the TV news every night from behind locked doors, with electronic security systems set to inform you if outsiders encroached on your domain? This, he knew, was not at all the way the founders imagined their dream would unfold. He longed for home, for Sweden, even if he and Inga could only find their own imagined safety in each other's arms. . . .

The Dane drew short breaths, trying not to curl his nose as he stood in the front hallway. The Stafford house was filled with the ripe smell of fear. An odor like sour meat, which languished even in the warm greeting of Stafford's formal handshake and the unsteady smile of his wife.

"Is Mr. York with you?" Lesia asked, leading him into the living room.

"I believe he's on his way," the Dane said, smiling reassuringly. "Is your daughter here?"

"She's upstairs," Stafford said. "She's . . . she's not feeling well."

The Dane nodded, watching as a young boy stood in the doorway between the living room and the kitchen, staring at him.

"I . . . we believe Yvonne saw the man," Stafford said, nodding toward his wife. "I didn't know what to do. . . ."

The Dane nodded again, surveying the premises with a practiced eye. There was little or no security. The perp could walk right in, if that was his intention.

"Did this man see your daughter?" the Dane asked, realizing he was being abrupt. But it was, he felt, a question that needed to be asked.

"No . . ." Lesia Stafford answered quickly, glancing out the window, as if this were the first time the question had occurred to her. In her husband's eyes, however, the Dane saw that this possibility had been strongly considered. "No, I'm quite sure he didn't," Lesia said again. "If it was that man at all. The doctor said it was highly unlikely."

"Maybe you should tell me everything you recall about the incident," the Dane suggested, making a point to walk over and lock the door. "Any detail that you can remember . . ."

Lesia related the story, and then the Dane asked to speak with Yvonne. He was beginning to think that it might be, as the girl's doctor indicated, a case of mistaken identity. It had happened so quickly, Yvonne seeing the man's reflection in a store window. Although, he admitted, there was no real way to be sure. Even if it was the perp, odds were he hadn't seen the girl and so was not actively stalking her. That, although he had not spoken of it, even to Jenny, had been his greatest fear. That the man had come back to clean up unfinished business. Yvonne was, after all, one of the few people in the world who could actually point to him and say: Yes, that's him!

"She wanted to know if we had a gun," Stafford whispered to the Dane as they climbed the stairs. "I don't, but . . ."

Hearing that, the Dane smiled to himself. The girl obviously had a strong sense of self-preservation and an equally strong will. The Dane admired those qualities.

When he saw Yvonne Stafford, however, the Dane's heart crumbled. Her fear was like a living thing. He felt it, even standing in the doorway of the bedroom. He was, the Dane quickly realized, deeply afraid for her.

"Yvonne, honey, this is Mr. Ekendland," James Stafford said softly. "He's here to help. . . . It's so dark in here," Stafford said, more to himself than to his daughter or the Dane. He moved across the room to open the curtains and blinds, as if he was suddenly embarrassed to find his daughter living in a cave. The Dane stayed by the door, not wanting to frighten the girl any more than she already was. Light swept into the bedroom in rolling clouds, raising specks of dust in its passing. The girl glanced at her father, then back at the huge figure blocking the doorway.

"Hello," the Dane said, trying to smile, cutting off the greeting before he asked how she was feeling. It would have been an incredibly stupid question, he thought.

Yvonne blinked for a moment, adjusting to the bright, invading light. Then, as if suddenly remembering her manners, she smiled weakly at the Dane, who found himself without words as he watched the girl swallow her fear, brushing back a strand of hair from her face.

"Hello," she returned his greeting, sitting up straighter on the bed, pulling the blanket around her.

The Dane sensed the strength in her, that she was able to push her fear aside and greet him. The light seemed to rejuvenate the girl. She blinked, her eyes catching the sunlight, her resolve showing in the sharp set of her chin. The Dane, who prided himself on his own strength, nodded back. There was no doubt in his mind that this young girl was a warrior in the classic sense of the word, despite her present circumstances. He wondered at the depth of the terror she had experienced, that it would bring her so close to the breaking point. Even the strongest person has limits, he knew. Yvonne Stafford seemed to have found hers. But even as she reached the extent of her endurance, she had fought back, refusing to have her spirit broken. The Dane felt that he wanted very much to protect her, and to avenge her, if possible.

"Sorry to disturb you," the Dane said, knowing there was no need to question the girl. Whether or not she had actually seen the perp was irrelevant. Clearly, she believed she had. "I just wanted you to know I was here."

"Thank you," Yvonne said, her smile deeper this time, as if she were suddenly waking up from a terrible nightmare. Her father came and sat down on the bed with her, taking her hand.

"I'll just go downstairs and use the phone, if that's all right," the Dane said, turning from the room. Stafford nodded, but then the Dane stopped and looked back at the girl. "You don't have to sit in the dark," he said, feeling as though this was something Yvonne needed to hear. "It's going to be OK."

Yvonne Stafford smiled again, as if she was making herself believe the blond giant's words. The Dane nodded, his footsteps heavy on the stairs.

"He has a gun, doesn't he?" Yvonne asked as the footsteps faded.

Stafford sighed and squeezed his daughter's hand.

Arnie Watts was also hearing footsteps. And he, too, had a gun. The Nine was loaded, the safety off, even though each time he heard the footsteps and peered through the heavy curtains of the motel room, there was no one outside. The parking lot was empty for the most part, except for his van and a couple of other cars. A few people walked down by the main office on occasion, but no one, it seemed, was making the long trek up to the hilltop bungalows. In some part of his mind, still twisted and confused by the nightmare and the dark voice laughing at him in odd, blinking moments, Watts knew this was the way things had been for the last several days. Even when the girl had been alive, strapped to the bed. Even when she had been floating in the tub. Was she still there? He turned quickly, rushing across the room to check. No, thank God, he thought, shaking from the memory of the dream. The horror of which touched him still, even as the day emerged, casting aside the shadows of the night. But the night, Arnie knew, was only hiding. It would come again, and when it did Watts had no idea what he would do. One thing was certain, he sure as hell was not going to sleep. Maybe not ever again.

He paced the room, pulling a beer from the tiny fridge tucked under the writing table. Come on, get yourself together, he thought, feeling the twitch working overtime in his eye. No matter how bad, it was just a fucking nightmare, he told himself, peering out of the corner of the curtain.

Footsteps, fucking footsteps. And nobody there. He wanted to turn the television on, crank up MTV as loud as it would go. But then he wouldn't be able to hear the footsteps. . . .

What he really wanted to do was leave. Run, someplace, anyplace. But where do you go to outrun a nightmare? Where do you go to escape death? And it was not just the nightmare or the insane fear it had planted in him, like a bad acid trip a break-in buddy had once out in Phoenix. Fucker went completely nuts, Arnie remembered. Saw snakes on the walls and bugs crawling up his legs. Nervously Arnie glanced around at the walls. No snakes, thank God. Not yet anyway, the thought slipped like an eel into his brain. Jesus, Jesus, he was fucking losing it! Watts banged the beer bottle down on the nightstand, licking his fingers as it frothed over. No, it wasn't just the nightmare or the fear that seemed to paralyze his brain. There was something else. Something missing. He had no plan, Watts realized, and seemed unable to formulate one. He wanted to run. But to where? He wanted desperately to get rid of the body in back of the van. But was unable to come up with any ideas on how to do it. It was, he thought, as if he was abandoned, cut adrift to fend for himself. The voice, which had been a part of him for so long, seemed to have vanished. No voice, no plans in his head. Only horrifying memories of flashing lightning bursts and dark, hideous laughter. He was abandoned, he knew suddenly, and left for dead.

Don't ever die, he remembered the voice telling him. Don't ever die. . . .

The thought chilled him and he shivered, peering out the window, the Nine never leaving his shaking hand.

The entity had been observing the lines of continuance on a planet in the Gamma Cluster for an extended period of time. The stars themselves made a full rotation in the sky, before the entity stirred and blinked. That is, it changed its particle charge from positive to negative. And in so doing adjusted its habitat in the spiritual plane, taking the form of a particular male being, a mechanism in which it had known many pleasurable life experiences. As it blinked, the entity created a pastoral scene from the life experiment it had been observing, and sat for a time beside the calm waters of a pale blue lake. Using only the visual and audio spectrums of the mechanism, the entity watched waves lap against the shore, listened to the wind blowing through the thick needles of the conifer trees. Smoke rose in long columns from fishing villages dotting the lake. Small boats floated along the far shore, although the entity had not chosen to complete the scene, and so the boats and villages were empty. At the edge of the created vision the muted gray shadows of the spiritual plane encroached, even though it was well within the entity's power to make the scene as complete and lifelike as it chose. The entity could, if it pleased, populate this vision with whatever beings it wished to conjure, and could, if it so desired, call upon other entities in the spiritual plane to join with it, and together they would create a learning experience that might last for hours, or for eons. Such was the power of all entities in the spiritual plane, to create their own realities.

But the entity, for the moment at least, wanted only peaceful solitude. Within the male body, he stretched the muscles of the mechanism, feeling the power that lay waiting beneath the leathered exterior of the skin. At this present time in the life experiment of this species' world, the mechanisms were still in the latter stages of the struggle for dominance. The outcome was assured, and so entities had been implanted. But it was a primitive world in which the lessons learned were primarily those of physical strength and power. When the entity had been involved in that world, of course, it had gloried in those lessons, learning them to their fullest extent. Wrapped within the frame of this particular mechanism, the entity had made war under the most violent and savage conditions. It rode great, snarling beasts into the very heart of the enemy, winning fame and glory for itself and its tribe. Remembering this glory, the entity reached up and scarred the mechanism's chest with long, raking claws, smelling and tasting its own blood, as all the great warriors of that world did to celebrate their victories. Yes, the entity thought, licking the blood from its fingers, that had been a grand adventure.

But now in the spiritual plane, it was left to the entity to ponder these lessons. As was the task, and often the burden, of all entities returning to the spiritual plane. Scenes like this, the entity knew—small islands of projected reality—were even now taking place all across the infinite realm of the spiritual plane. But reflection was often a tiresome thing.

The entity blinked again, restructuring its charge.

And was born once more into the physical world, into the life experiment with which it was involved. The entity melded this time with the mechanism of a new-born female, who would grow to live a life of simplicity in the wide, empty grasslands of the Northern Provinces. In this place, where she was one of several hands of children, the female tended flocks, carried water and dung for the cooking fires, until a dozen of the planet's years passed. Then, for reasons that remained a puzzle to her lineage for generations, the female stood in front of a charging horse as raiders swept down upon her clan's encampment. . . .

And the Soul Catchers collected the entity, which had just been released from its damaged mechanism, soothing the fireflies of fear dancing like sparks in its shifting form, leading the entity back into the realms of the spiritual plane.

When the entity recovered from its latest excursion into the physical world, it returned to observing the lines of continuance within the context of the life experiment. Perspective, it was all a matter of perspective, the entity decided.

twenty-four

Jenny harassed the New England arm of the phone company until finally a supervisor approved her request. An operator read off a long list of motels from the New Haven area, and then Jenny began calling. Hours later a desk clerk at a place called the Burgundy Inn, looked out the glass windows of his hot-house enclosure, and told her the van she was describing seemed to be sitting outside one of the hillside bungalows.

"Would you like me to ring the room?" he asked, uncomfortable at the oddity of her request.

"No!" Jenny said, slamming the phone down.

"Are you OK?" Gena asked from the kitchen, where the refrigerator door looked to be permanently open.

"No!" Jenny said, her hands shaking, wondering if York had left any of his cigarettes in the bedroom. She was pawing through the drawers a few minutes later when the phone rang. The Dane was on the other end, asking why her line had been busy for the last hour.

York was following directions he'd written down almost a year ago, so it took him awhile to find the Stafford house. He pulled up and parked at the curb, wondering if any of the cars were the Dane's rental. He wondered also if Jenny had had any luck. . . .

James Stafford was coming out the front door, walking

quickly down the concrete path to the sidewalk, before York was able to close the car door.

"Mr. Ekendland was here," Stafford said, speaking so fast the words seemed to run into one another.

"The Dane?" York asked, not used to hearing the name. Stafford nodded, handing York a note.

"He left about forty-five minutes ago." Stafford sounded as if he had just run a four-minute mile. "He said to give you this."

York unfolded the note. The Dane's handwriting was scrawled, but the words leaped out at him:

Possible ID on the van, the note said. At the Burgundy Inn on Ocean Drive, off 95. On my way there to check it out.

"Where's Ocean Drive?" York asked, already getting into the car.

"You go back on 95 and get off at Exit 10. It's the first left," Stafford replied. "Do you want me to come with you?"

But York was already slamming the car into gear, pulling away without another word.

It would be night soon, Arnie Watts knew. And he was afraid. It was a fear that was as great as it was intangible. What was he afraid of, anyway? he asked himself. A dream? He kicked at the bed, angry at himself. You're afraid of a fucking dream?

—Don't ever die, the thought came, and the fear shook him, haunting and deep. Stopping him in midstride, as he paced the room.

Footsteps? He heard them outside. Heels clicking on tarmac. He rushed to the window, clutching the Nine, parting the curtains with the barrel of the gun. His eyes blinking at the sunlight, the sun low now, sweeping the buildings, reflecting in the distance off the glass windows of the desk clerk's office. The footsteps fading into a soft echo, as they did each time he looked out at the compound. No one there, just the empty lot. His van tucked away, parked in the shadows of the bare, leafless locust trees. The van, with its Pennsylvania plates and the girl's body locked in the back. He should change the plates, he knew. Maybe just ditch the van altogether. Toss the body in the woods and park the van on some side street. Hop a bus and go, go, go—somewhere, anywhere, away from here.

That wasn't much of a plan, Arnie knew, shaking his head. Shit, it wasn't hardly any plan at all. Besides, something told him it was dangerous out there. No, better to hole up here in the room, he thought. At least until it got dark. Then, by God, he would run! Go someplace, anyplace, away from here. He promised himself that when night came, he would act. Just hop in the van and get the fuck out. Patience, that was the key. A plan would come to him. It always did.

"Got to keep yourself calm," he whispered. "Don't lose your nerve now."

Arnie Watts, however, knew he was lying. Knew that his nerve had long since fled. He went to the fridge and popped himself another beer. He sat down on the edge of the bed and drew deep, staggered breaths. Calm . . . calm, he told himself.

—Don't ever die, the thought came again, creeping into his brain like smoke from a fire that was burning in his heart.

Footsteps? He got up from the bed and peered out the window.

The Dane pulled the rental car up into the shadows near the main office of the Burgundy Inn. He parked close to the building to keep himself and the vehicle out of sight, away from the back rooms and the cabins perched on the small hill above the office complex. He checked his weapon, working the slide on the .45. It was a semiautomatic and his favorite weapon for close quarter work. The .45 was a large piece and not many men could use it efficiently, but it fit the Dane's hand like a warm coffee mug, and he was as comfortable with it as most people were with their car keys. He released the safety and dropped the firing hammer carefully on the chamber round. He got out of the car and closed the door softly, slipping his gun hand into the pocket of his coat. It was important not to alarm anyone before the moment of attack.

The desk clerk was watching him from the interior of the office, no doubt hoping he was not about to be robbed, the Dane thought. He smiled and nodded at the man, before pulling the door open. More alarm control. Motel desk clerks, he knew, were a jumpy bunch these days. With his free hand, the Dane flashed his hunting license in the clerk's direction.

"There's a warrant out on one of your guests," the Dane said, and of course the alarm bells began ringing in the clerk's eyes. "I'm here to pick him up."

"I knew it!" the clerk said, glancing over his shoulder at the VW van parked in the upper terrace of the inn's lot. "There was something strange about that guy!"

The desk clerk of the Burgundy Inn was a plump, balding man, around forty, the Dane guessed. Although his weight, which he carried badly, added years to his actual age. Probably a man who went home every night, wondering how it was he had ended up as a motel desk clerk. The Dane followed the man's eyes and saw the van that Jenny had described.

"That's his vehicle," the Dane said, feeling the surge of adrenaline that always came at this moment in the hunt. It was a sensation he had not felt for a long time, one which caused all the carefully honed muscles in his body to tense. It was a feeling the Dane prized above all others. "Anyone else in the cabin with him?"

"Registered as a single occupant, signed in as Paul Reynolds," the clerk whispered, filled suddenly with a terrible feeling of apprehension. "Cabin 553, up on the hill, four doors down from where the van's parked. I don't think there's anybody with him. I've been trying to keep an eye out. . . ."

The Dane nodded, feeling the man's surge of fear.

"Anyone in the adjoining cabins?" the Dane asked, surveying the grounds. His appreciation of the adrenaline rush was gone now as he prepared himself for the task at hand. Those who thought too much about what they were feeling, he knew, did not last long in the mercenary business.

"No," the clerk said, checking his log briefly, even though he was certain of the response. This did not seem like the time to make a frivolous mistake. "Should I call the police?"

The Dane shook his head. "Just give me a master key to the cabin and keep everyone out of the way." This one is mine, he didn't say, his blue eyes turning into small slits. This one is for the Stafford girl and Ronnie Bates, he thought, already at the office door, planning his movements around the far edges of the Inn's property.

The Dane moved carefully, but swiftly, like a stalking cat, keeping to the shadows, keeping himself below the line of vision of anyone who might be watching from the cabin window. If, indeed, the perp was still there. Whoever he was, the Dane knew the man had an almost uncanny sixth sense. He knew also that he would have to be very cautious in his approach, as there was the very real possibility the perp still had his kidnapping victim with him. The field of fire would have to be surveyed with particular scrutiny, if the situation came to that point of finality. Which, in his heart, the Dane hoped it would.

York followed Stafford's directions and got back on 95, following the parade of exit signs, which seemed to pass with excruciating slowness. Exasperated, he pushed the accelerator to the floor, the lines in the road passing in a confused blur. He wished again he had the cell phone to call Jenny, to tell her he was all right. She would be worried, he knew.

It seemed stupid to be watching television, Jenny thought. She called the Stafford house and knew that York had been there, briefly. And that he had gone off after the Dane. Like a man possessed, James Stafford told her. On the TV screen one of the teams had done something that caused Gena to yell and clap her hands. Since when did Gena know anything about football? she wondered.

"What?" Gena turned to her, and Jenny realized she had

asked the question out loud. "The Giants scored!" Gena said. "That's Mr. D.'s favorite team, you know."

"Mr. D.?" Jenny asked, knowing who her daughter was referring to, but hardly believing the nickname.

"Mother . . ." Gena said, staring, almost in disbelief. "The man who spends the weekends here?"

"Yes, I know," Jenny said, reaching out, pulling her daughter to her. There was a brief moment of hesitation, then capitulation, as Gena hugged her mother back.

"Are you all right?" Gena asked.

Jenny shook her head. From somewhere deep inside, tears glazed her eyes. It seemed stupid to be watching television, when the whole world was at risk.

Footsteps? Arnie Watts glared out the window. The sunlight all but blinded him for a moment. No one there, of course. There was never anyone there. While he waited for the cover of darkness to escape, Arnie drifted back to sit on the bed, drinking his beer, clutching the Nine, trying to come up with a plan.

The Dane came out of a small stand of trees that had been left standing purely for aesthetic value when the ground here had been bulldozed to accommodate the buildings of the Burgundy Inn. The trees ran along the high slope of ground where the Inn's cabins sat, perched above the rest of the compound. Below, the pool, safely out of reach from the trees's leaves during the summer and fall months, was drained and covered. Beyond the pool, rows of rooms, with a couple of cars scattered among them. There was no one within range of any stray shots that might be fired. The Dane took all of this in, as he moved between the first two cabins. The perp's van was parked off on the far side of the upper lot, well away from the fifth cabin, which was the target objective. The Dane circled around back, coming out of the trees again at the rear of the perp's crib. No back entrance, he saw, with some displeasure. Just a small bathroom window, set high in the cabin's rear wall. So, it would have to be a frontal assault, not that it mattered to the Dane, who had played this game dozens of times. Surprise was the key, he knew. A quick burst of energy through the door, and the target would probably be too startled to react. He might try to run, the Dane considered, but as there was only one way out, that meant the perp would have to go through him. The Dane smiled to himself, relishing that possibility.

He drew a breath and crept along the side of the cabin, keeping close to the cedar shingles. Close, yet being careful not to scrape the wall. No noise, no warning. A quick burst through the door. He stopped for a moment, flush against the corner of the cabin. The door would be the problem, as the perp undoubtedly kept it locked. The Dane held the clerk's desk key in one hand, his gun in the other, and stepped toward the door, keeping himself flat against the front wall. . . .

Footsteps? Watts shook his head. It was all in his mind, he knew. But then from somewhere down below, he heard a car pull up and the door slam. As though somebody was in a hellova hurry. He got up from the bed and pulled a corner of the curtain away from the window. . . .

Just as he slipped the key into the lock and prepared to shoulder his way through the dead bolt, the Dane heard a vehicle pull up near the front office. It made no difference at this point, as he was already committed to the assault. The Dane snapped the key in the lock and pounded the door with his shoulder, nearly taking it off the hinges. The dead-bolt chain held for an instant, then flew off the jam, the door crashing against the wall of the cabin. Just as the door hit the wall, the Dane heard another sound. He thought for a brief moment it might have been the wall itself breaking. His momentum carried him into the cabin and as he tried to catch his balance, the Dane realized he was staggering. He felt a blow that struck his ribs, as if someone had hit him with a baseball bat. He crashed against the wall with the door, a thundering roar in his ears. And time seemed to go into slow motion for the Dane. Like the first moments of a car crash, when the world seems to move frame by frame, instant by instant. He twisted and saw a figure by the dark curtains of the window. A silhouette, outlined by the bright light now streaming through the broken frame of the door. A figure surrounded by the hazy smoke of small-arms fire. And the Dane realized he had been shot. That the figure was even now focusing the barrel of a weapon on him. But everything was moving slowly, the scene unfolding before his eyes, frame by frame. The Dane, falling, raised his own gun and squeezed off two quick rounds. The figure lurched, he saw with satisfaction. Then light flashed again in front of his eyes and he was thrown down onto the floor, as if a huge hand had reached out of the sky and crushed him to the ground. . . .

Below the terraced slope where the cabins looked down on the Inn's main compound, Dennison York heard the shots. He saw the open door of the cabin above him, smoke drifting from the entranceway like morning fog. The desk clerk came to the front door of the office, panic written across his face in pale, sweeping lines. York saw the man was about to run toward the road, fleeing the sound of gunfire.

"Get back inside!" York shouted, already running up toward the cabin. "Call the police and an ambulance!"

York ran up the steps leading to the upper parking lot, drawing his own gun, trying to keep low. He zigzagged across the open tarmac, expecting any moment to hear shots ringing out in his direction. At least he hoped he would hear them. You never heard the one that gets you, he knew, until it was much too late. He crouched for a moment by the perp's van.

"Dane!" he shouted, keeping his eyes on the entranceway. "Vir! Are you hit?"

No answer, only the long, deep silence that oftentimes follows violence. As if the whole world is somehow holding its breath, stunned by the sharp sound of gunfire. A sound, York often thought, which was never meant to be heard upon the earth. But it was, every day.

York made his way to the front of the van and sprinted to the cabin next to the one with the open door. He crept across the front, dropped down, and crawled along the flag-stone walk, keeping himself below the curtained window, tight against the wall, until he was at the broken doorway. From inside, the silence of the aftermath was like a dark, soundless scream. Straightening himself, drawing a deep breath, York dove inside, searching the room with the barrel of his gun. . . .

Arnie Watts hardly knew what happened. First footsteps, although there was never anyone there. Then a car door slamming. Then the door to the room crashed open and he'd fired. Then more shots and he was thrown against the far wall, slipping down into a sitting position, trying to catch his breath, which seemed an almost impossible task. He and this big blond fucker, staring at each other across the splash of sunlight pouring through the door. The blond guy, watching him with flat, glazed eyes, as a pool of dark blood spread out from under his big frame. Like ink, Arnie Watts thought, looking down, seeing the same dark splotches around his own legs. Outside, someone was shouting. . . .

The Dane was quite surprised to discover he could not move. Not a finger, not a muscle. It was, he thought, as if all the electricity had suddenly been discharged from his body. He was aware of a figure slumped against the wall on the other side of the room, although he couldn't seem to remember how the figure, or he himself, had gotten into these strange positions. Not that it mattered. The Dane was aware that none of this mattered anymore. That he was, in fact, dying. It was not so bad, he thought, waiting. Realizing suddenly that his body was no longer breathing and that a strange silence seemed to have settled over him. His heart had stopped beating, he realized. It was a sound that had been with him since the first moment of his life. A sound you don't even know is there . . . until it's gone. Gone . . . I'm going, he thought. And his last recollection, before he drifted away from his body, was that he had stayed in Swe-den with Inga, and they had raised fine Viking warriors to-gether. . . .

• • •

Sliding across the floor of the room, York saw first the body of the Dane, lying in a widening pool of blood. Then he glimpsed another body in the shadows, propped up against the wall of the cabin. No one else. No one else . . .

The man against the wall moaned and York was on his feet instantly, kicking away the man's gun, which lay near the dark, curtained window. Not that there seemed much chance of the asshole getting to it. The perp looked to be hit pretty hard, although at first glance York thought it probably wasn't fatal. The Dane, unfortunately, had not been that lucky. York backed quickly toward the door and saw the Dane was already dead. York swallowed the pain and the anger. There would be time later to mourn.

"Where's the girl?" he shouted at the perp.

It took Arnie Watts a moment to realize the man was talking to him. Where did this guy come from? Watts found himself wondering. Couldn't this fucker tell he was shot? Then the man was right on top of him, shoving a gun into his face. Snarling, spitting, like some kind of mad dog.

"Where's the girl, you fucking scum?!" York yelled, trying to control himself and not pull the trigger on this dirtbag.

"I'm shot," Arnie Watts whispered, his voice seeming to echo in his ears.

—Don't ever die, the thought came to him.

And the memory of it terrorized him even more than being shot. Far, far more . . .

"I need a doctor," Watts pleaded, watching in horror as shadows seemed to obscure the outer edges of his vision.

"Tell me where the girl is, and I'll get you a doctor," York promised, softening his tone.

"She's . . . she's locked up in the back of the van," Arnie Watts heard himself say. "But . . ."

York was already on his feet, searching around the room for the van's keys. He found them on the nightstand and rushed out to the van, fumbling with the rear lock.

"Carol Ann?" he called. "Carol Ann Huxley! Can you hear me?"

The door finally opened and York peered into the back

of the van, blinking, trying to adjust his eyes. There was no one . . . only a canvas army bag. York leaped into the van, and ripped open the zipper, hoping. . . .

"Sweet Jesus Christ!" he cried, gagging, staggering out of the van, falling on the hard, frozen ground, his gun slipping away. Pulling himself to his feet, he retrieved the weapon and ran back inside the cabin, almost slipping again on the Dane's blood, which was spreading across the floor in a wet stain.

"You rotten, fucking bastard!" York said, his voice as cold and hard as the ground outside.

"She's dead. I tried to tell you!" Arnie Watts said, as if this were some sort of acceptable answer.

—What have you done?

The memory of the voice's accusations flashed across his brain.

"It wasn't me," Arnie Watts said. "It was the voices . . . they made me do it. Honest to God, I never wanted to! The voices, they told me everything. . . ."

York stared at the man, overcome with anger and horror. This man, this monster, who preyed upon children, who murdered Ronnie Bates and now the Dane. This beast in the guise of a human being was now telling him that voices made him do it? This heinous creature, who had destroyed countless lives—both victims and families—was even now planning his insanity defense?

"I need help, mister," Arnie Watts said, clutching at the blood running out of his legs. "I've been shot. I need help, bad. . . ."

Yes, you do, York thought, staring at the man, seeing the faces of his victims. York's hand twitched at his side, the gun brushing his thigh. And he almost did it. Almost brought his weapon up. Don't do it, the rational part of his mind told him. Remember the last time? Remember what it did to you? And he saw again, as he did so often in his dreams, the bodies of the two young bangers who had killed his son, splattered against the porch steps on that long-ago day in LA.

"Fuck it," he said, slipping the gun into the pocket of his coat.

"I need help," Arnie Watts pleaded again. "You know I need help."

Don't ever die, the memory whispered again in Watts's head. I won't, he whispered to himself. Not now, not today . . . From outside, the sound of approaching sirens split the air, like the crying of carrion birds. And even though the game had ended badly, Arnie Watts knew he was not going to die. Not now, not today.

"Fuck it," York said again, slipping on his gloves.

He stepped over the dark smear spreading out from the Dane's body and picked up the .45, which had fallen from his friend's hand. Watts saw the movement and panic gripped him again, raking his chest like sharp claws.

"I need help!" Arnie Watts thought he yelled, but really it was only a soft, croaking sound, his voice smothered by fear.

—Don't ever die. . . .

You need help, all right, York thought. And the gun leaped in his hand, the sound of it deafening in such close quarters. The bullet slammed into Arnie Watts's body, and the look on the man's face as he died, York thought, was one of stark, naked terror.

York put the weapon down by the Dane's outstretched arm, took off his gloves and went outside to sit on the front stoop to wait for the authorities.

He drew deep, cleansing breaths. Knowing that this was another scene that would be played over and over again in his dreams.

"Fuck it," he whispered, knowing he would do the same thing, over and over again, until there was no need to do it anymore.

The entity that was once Arnie Watts did not want to leave the cocoon of its damaged mechanism, even though the mechanism had ceased to function and could no longer process sensory data from the outside world. Blind and deaf, the shell of the mechanism was cooling rapidly.

Without the anchor of an electrical charge, the entity was no longer able to hold its position, and so slipped out of the mechanism.

In the gray realm between worlds, the Soul Catchers gathered, drifting on the solar winds, sliding across the radiation bands separating the spiritual and physical planes. Like wisps of fog they manifested themselves before the entities that were even now separating from the physical world. One entity reached for their projected hand and was collected, soothed, and escorted to the bridge between worlds. The other entity, through which streaks of darkness ran like some putrefying disease, was filled with terror at the fact of its mechanism's death. Bolts of fear-generated energy snapped within its shifting form. The entity shrieked in soundless horror, the scream freezing like water vapor in its mouth, as the Soul Catchers approached.

The Soul Catchers, however, were most proficient at their work. In the end, it made no difference to them whether an entity willingly crossed into the spiritual realm, nor were they interested in the reasons behind this entity's abnormal behavior. They, being neither judge nor jury, offering neither condemnation nor redemption, simply went about their task of collecting the recently freed entity.

The entity that was once Arnie Watts felt itself in the grip of paralyzing fear. As it slipped from its mechanism, shadows—dark and foreboding—seemed to materialize out of the confusing swirl of color and vibration that was now the physical world. The entity was helpless as the shadows engulfed it. . . . In an instant they were in a tunnel, the dark walls of which were filled with grim, accusing faces. The faces of children. Faces that seemed to invoke distant, disturbing memories. Memories that the entity tried to hide from itself and from the encroaching shadows. But clarity, it soon discovered, is both the gift and the curse of the spiritual realm. Memories from its past life rushed in upon the entity, like dark, swirling, drowning water.

Memories that brought neither sorrow nor remorse, but only a maddening, penetrating fear.

—Don't ever die, a voice whispered, reaching out from the depths of time and space. And it seemed that all the darkness of the universe collapsed in upon the entity in an avalanche of all-consuming black. Darkness, thick and total. Darkness in which there was no space or time, no movement, no sound, only emptiness. Is this Death? the entity asked, the thought lost in the dark void. Then, with the suddenness of an explosion, lightning flashed.

The entity found itself in a small cage, cloaked in the flesh and fur of a tiny animal. Sunlight assaulted its eyes and it blinked . . . scurrying, trying to find a way out of the cage. From above, came a loud humming sound, like that of a large insect dropping out of the sky. The entity, wrapped in its blanket of flesh and fur, froze in panic at the sound. A memory, fleeting and almost forgotten, caused its heart to leap about in its chest, producing a fear that approached madness. From above, a shadow passed, and then the small mechanism was struck by a large, heavy object, which attached itself to the animal's back. The entity screamed, a high-pitched, squealing sound of terror, as the insect's arms unfolded and wrapped themselves around the entity in an ever-tightening grip. It screamed again as the fly's feeding tube pierced the mechanism's flesh. The entity felt a terrible pain, deep within itself, as the damselfly began to extract the juices of its life. . . .

But there was no death. Not now, not ever, the entity soon realized. There were only long moments of suffering, followed by even longer periods of fear. Lightning flashed.

The entity, now in the form of its former mechanism, Arnie Watts, surrounded by others of its kind, moved, shuffling, across the endless dark plane of the damned. From their mouths came a moan, low and deep. The song, which was a prayer. His own voice, mingling with the ghostly chorus, as together they shuffled through the darkness.

Their mournful cries, rising up to be swallowed by the night. The dead, shuffling toward a gray dawn that never grew closer. The dead, crying, wailing, praying for the end of time. The dead, alone and alone and alone . . .

lightning flashed